DEADLY LINKS

PAUL MURPHY

TO LISA:
THANKS FOR BEING A WONDERFUL FRIEND,
GREAT PROMOTER, AND THE INSPIRATION FOR
THE MOST MEANINGLESS CHARACTER IN
THE NOVEL!

Black Rose Writing

www.blackrosewriting.com

ISBN: 978-1-61296-221-4

PUBLISHED BY BLACK ROSE WRITING

www.blackrosewriting.com

Printed in the United States of America

Deadly Links is printed in Constantia

To the memory of Bellringers

and Murphys who have passed on.

Acknowledgements

Deadly Links could not have been written without the help of others.

Special thanks to my editors, Mike Murphy and Nancy Kilpatrick, who whipped the book into shape.

Heartfelt thanks to Sandy Trunzer, David Reid, Danny Toner, and Rita Vetere for their support, input, and expertise. Their significant contributions are scattered throughout the chapters of *Deadly Links*.

Many thanks also to Denise Rago, Phil Sexton, and Brian Henry, each of whom helped push me to the finish line.

And thank you again to Nancy Kilpatrick, who taught me how to write a novel. Any evidence to the contrary found within these pages is entirely the fault of her humble student.

DEADLY LINKS

PART I — IN THE DEEP ROUGH

"Of all the hazards, fear is the worst."

—Sam Snead

CHAPTER 1

Growls broke the predawn quiet. Michael Flanigan sat at his kitchen table, massaging his temples. He took a gulp from a tumbler of orange juice, splashing some next to an old coffee stain on his Toronto Maple Leafs T-shirt. He checked his watch. It was just past five a.m.

Danny was here.

A staleness hung in the room. On the counter, an uncapped tequila bottle stood next to a line of Molson Canadian empties, like a king presiding over the pawns of a drunk's chessboard. A Pizza Hut box sat on top of the fridge. He cursed himself for the hangover, his first in months.

Tequila. Did I black out?

He seldom heard a peep from his border collies when they were out for their morning constitutional, until they clawed at the back door to come inside. He gave it a minute, hoping they would settle down before the coffee finished brewing.

Michael looked out the bay window. A fat, hazy moon peered in, the morning still cloaked in darkness. He squinted at the layer of fog blanketing the grounds at the rear of his country home. He could see nothing beyond the reflection in the glass that stared back at him. Nothing but the fog. The outdoor light hadn't worked for weeks. He had little motivation for household chores since Emily...

He reached behind, flicked off the kitchen light, and took another look. Still nothing.

The dogs barked, persistent and agitated.

Damn it.

He'd have to go out.

He got a flashlight from a kitchen drawer and pushed the button three, four times. Dead. He found another in the adjoining laundry room and clicked it once, bouncing a light beam off the wall. He slipped into his sneakers and stepped out the back door onto the low cedar deck.

The warm mid-June morning hit him as he exited the air-conditioned house. The fog was thicker than he'd thought, now that it surrounded him. He inhaled deeply, the heavy, humid air still a welcome contrast to the weary aura lingering indoors.

He stepped onto the grass, the morning dew seeping through his porous old shoes. The dogs didn't let up. He pointed the flashlight toward the back of his property, in the direction of the staccato howls. Training the light on the ground in front of him, he navigated the balls and toys that littered his path to the fence. He made a mental note to avoid the swing set that he couldn't see.

Heavy fog often made him think of a scene from the movie *An American Werewolf in London*, the one where Griffin Dunne's character ambles along the murky Yorkshire moors, just before the four-legged antagonist rips out much of what had attached his shoulders to his head.

Painting the rear perimeter with the flashlight, he detected movement thirty yards away, near the chain-link fence that stood between his property and the eighth fairway at Foster Glen.

"Paulie," he called. "Silvio." He lowered the flashlight to his side. "C'mon, guys."

The dogs ignored him.

As Michael got to within a few feet of the fence, a crash from behind startled him. He slipped on the wet grass, slamming his ass onto the ground. The flashlight clattered off the fence. The dogs snarled. He identified the noise as an upended garbage bin. The dogs paid no attention to the sound of scurrying raccoons.

What the hell is out here?

Now on all fours, he made a futile grope for the flashlight, which had shut off when it hit the fence. The pleas from the dogs surged to a crescendo.

The middle finger of his flailing left hand penetrated the link fence and *squished* into something pressed against the opposite side.

He snatched back his hand, scraping it against the metal fence. As he tried to suck the pain from a knuckle, he slid backward on top of the flashlight. Michael jerked it out from under him and aimed it at the fence.

It was his turn to yelp.

CHAPTER 2

Michael peered into the dining room mirror like he was looking at someone else. Grey speckled his bedraggled black hair, and his face displayed a neglected stubble. He felt beaten down, older than his forty-four years.

He'd always felt a sense of safety and serenity in Burlington, just thirty-five minutes west of the metropolis of Toronto. His view of the world was changing.

At least his oversize, tree-lined lot kept curious neighbours at an ignorable distance. He had just retreated from the chaos brewing at the front of the house, where TV and radio crews were setting up and police cars clogged the road.

Rejoining his visitors, he slumped into the same kitchen chair from which the dogs had roused him two hours earlier. Paulie and Sylvio lay at his feet. The sun had risen and the fog had cleared. He watched a mix of uniformed and plainclothes police personnel hover by a thicket of trees just beyond the back fence, where a strand of yellow tape surrounded their investigation. A man in a tan suit operated a video camera, as if making a home movie whose star was about to be carried off set on a gurney.

A stocky man in wire-rimmed glasses, a fedora, and an elbow-patched sport jacket stood just outside the kitchen, speaking softly into a cell phone. The man had introduced himself as Detective Leo Speagle of the Halton County Regional Police Department. Michael thought Speagle resembled a slightly younger version of Lou Piniella, the Chicago Cubs manager.

A light-skinned black detective, about Michael's age, sat at the end of the small table with his back to the window, arms folded across his chest, staring at Michael. At least six and a half feet tall, Detective John Alberts had not said a word since sliding his card in front of Michael minutes before. His biceps bulged from under his light grey suit.

Speagle snapped his phone shut and joined them at the table. He made some notes in a small brown notebook that was dwarfed further by the cop's meaty hands. It brought to mind Michael's wannabe writer friend, Danny Higgins, who carried around a notebook to jot down ideas that came to him, for whatever story he had on the go.

When did Danny leave?

Speagle set his hat on the table and said, "Mr. Flanigan, tell us anything you remember around the time you made your discovery this morning."

"I already told those cops," said Michael, jerking his thumb in the direction of the crime scene crew out back. He squeezed his hands together in his lap to stop them from shaking.

Speagle hunched over the tabletop. "We'll be out of here before you know it."

Michael got up, poured a cup of coffee, and sipped it until a cylinder or two ignited. He sat down, with Paulie and Sylvio still at his feet, and told the detectives about the dogs summoning him into the predawn fog. He didn't mention passing out on the couch after pounding back beer and tequila.

At first, he told them, he thought he had stuck his finger in a pile of mud. "And then," he said, quavering, "and then I flashed the light back at the fence. And I saw his face, pressed against the fence. It looked all muddy, bloody, I guess. I must have stuck my finger in his eye... or where it should have been."

He looked back and forth at the two detectives. "His eye was... gone, wasn't it?"

"What else, Mr. Flanigan?" asked Speagle.

"There was so much blood," said Michael. "And his other eye..."

"Take your time, Mr. Flanigan," said Speagle. "You've had a tough morning."

Michael ran his palms over his face, then closed his eyes and replayed the scene.

"His other eye was open," he said, "staring at me. I ran the flashlight down his body. He was naked. Something in his mouth, something bulging... white." Michael opened his eyes. "Hey, it could have been a golf ball."

"Did you recognize him?" asked Alberts, finally joining the conversation.

"I don't think I ever saw him before. But considering the shape he was in... who knows?"

"Anyone else in the house with you?" asked Speagle, looking around.

"I live alone." Michael reached under the table to pet the top of Paulie's head. "Just me and the dogs."

Speagle glanced out to the backyard. "I noticed the toys and swing set."

"Emily liked to keep the toys here for when friends or family visited, for their kids. Clint, my sixteen-year-old, lives with his mother, my first wife Denise, in Kingston. My stepdaughter Sophie hasn't lived at home for a while now."

"Emily's your second wife?" asked Speagle.

Michael nodded.

"You divorce her, too?"

"She died," said Michael, thinking Speagle should already know that.

"Our condolences," said Speagle while writing in his notebook.

"What did you do then?" asked Alberts.

"It occurred to me that whoever did it might still be out there. I got my ass back in the house and phoned 911. I put the dogs in the basement. I just got them settled down a few minutes before you walked in."

"You must have got some blood on you," said Alberts.

Michael raised his hands; turned them. "I washed it off as soon as I could. The cops outside checked me over."

"Have any company last night?"

"Danny Higgins, an old friend." Michael filled them in on his day, from going out for dinner with Danny, to coming back to his house to relax, have a few drinks, and watch the U.S. Open. He didn't remember who was winning the golf tournament, how much he had to drink, or what time Danny went home. He crashed on the couch and slept until the dogs woke him.

Speagle continued to take notes.

"You don't remember much?" said Alberts.

"I guess we did have more than a couple of drinks."

"Was your friend driving?"

"*I* had a few drinks," Michael said.

"Do you do that often, have quite a bit to drink?"

"No. What has that got to do with anything?"

"If you can't remember..."

"What, do you think I had something to do with this?"

"Did you?"

"Oh, come on."

"Relax, Mr. Flanigan," said Speagle.

John Alberts leaned in, palms flat on the table. Sensing the big cop liked to intimidate, Michael held his gaze. He resented being treated like a criminal in his own home.

Alberts sat back in his chair. "Just answer a few more questions," he said, and after a glimpse at the empty beer bottles on the counter, added, "and you can go back to whatever it was you had planned for today."

Michael sighed. "What did you say your name was, Sergeant?"

"Alberts. Detective Alberts."

Paulie snarled. Sylvio followed his lead. Alberts flinched.

Michael smiled. He reached down to pet the dogs and said, "Good boys." After walking them to the basement door, he returned to his chair in the kitchen.

"Well, *Detective*, I've been through enough lately that I'm not going to be intimidated by your act." Michael looked away and shook his head, then turned back to Alberts. "Go ahead and ask your damn questions... whatever it takes get you the hell out of my house."

"What have you been through lately?" asked Speagle.

The two cops glanced at each other, then turned their attention back to Michael. He sensed they knew more than they were letting on.

Speagle tapped his pen in the air in front of Michael. "Michael Flanigan," he said. "You're that guy, from the golf thing. Up north. You're Tommy Flanigan's boy."

Michael said nothing.

"You guys stood to make a lot of dough, didn't ya? And then you inherited some more," said Speagle. "Quite a bit more."

"I invested a little in the development."

Speagle fidgeted in his chair before continuing in a softer, grave tone. "And then, your wife…"

"And then my wife," said Michael.

"Where do you work?" asked Alberts.

"Until recently, I taught at T. J. Walsh."

"You aren't working?" asked Alberts.

"Look, it was dark and foggy. I didn't see or hear anyone else out there this morning, or last night." He stood up and pushed in his chair. "Now, if there's nothing else."

The two cops looked at each other and nodded.

Speagle tucked his notebook inside his jacket pocket and put on his fedora. "We'll call you if we need anything else," he said.

Before the detectives got to the kitchen doorway, Alberts stopped and turned back. "Aren't you at all curious about the identity of the dead man behind your house?"

"He was naked. I figured he wouldn't have had any ID." Why was he defending himself?

Speagle retrieved the notebook from his pocket. He opened it and held it down by his waist, peering through the bottom of bifocals.

"Vincent Fronda, age thirty-five." Speagle read it like a roll call for the dead. "He was a photographer," he said, and looked up at Michael before adding, "Belonged to some local club."

"Never met him," said Michael, hoping his expression didn't betray him.

"What did your late wife do for a living, Mr. Flanigan?" asked Alberts.

"My wife?" Her life had been well-documented in the media. "She worked at the art centre downtown. She worked in the gift store, taught some photography classes. Whatever needed doing, as far as I could tell."

Speagle made a note.

The three men stood in silence for a few seconds, the detectives staring at Michael as if hoping he'd say more. When he did not, Speagle said, "Would you mind writing down the address and phone number of your friend Higgins? We'll need to speak with him. Just a formality."

Michael took the pen and notebook from Speagle. A single word in capital letters was underlined at the top of the page: PHOTOGRAPHY. Michael hesitated, without looking up, and wrote down Danny's address and cell phone number.

Alberts said, "We'd appreciate it if you stuck around, in case we need to reach you."

"Where would I go?" asked Michael. "You know, technically this didn't happen on my property. It was on the golf course. Are you asking my neighbours to stick around in case you need them?"

"Don't go too far," said Alberts. He and Speagle turned and left.

Michael felt a little woozy. He belched, and tasted the tequila again. He grabbed a bottle of water and sat back down.

He hadn't lied to the detectives. He had never met the dead man. But he thought his late wife may have.

CHAPTER 3

Standing under the shower, Michael wondered how long the police tape would remain, branding his property a murder scene. He would bet money that Vincent Fronda—*Vinnie?*—was a guy in Emily's photography club. He attached nothing good to the name, but couldn't remember why.

He stepped out of the shower and shook out two Advil from the bottle on his dresser. Sitting on the edge of the bed, he tried in vain to recall anything between cocktails with Danny and waking up on the couch.

He fell back on the bed and closed his eyes.

The phone woke Michael a couple of hours later. Disoriented at first, the events of the early morning soon came back to him. After a half-dozen rings, his voice mail picked up the call.

He felt rather refreshed, all things considered. He usually recovered quickly, perhaps his curse.

The ringing started again.

"Anything you want to tell me?" said Danny Higgins when Michael answered the phone.

"Higgy. Shit, man, I was gonna call you."

Alberts and Speagle had put Danny through a similar drill, and his friend verified for them that he had left Michael asleep on the couch just after eleven.

"Hopefully they figure he was killed before then," said Michael, pulling at the drapes for another peek at the yellow police tape. "You shoulda seen him, man. Fucking butchered."

"Un-fucking-believable. It coulda happened while we were sitting there watching the tube."

"Tequila. Didn't know I had any in the house. Must have been collecting dust at the back of the cabinet." Michael shivered. The last time he had tequila was at a student pub in Kingston, when Danny was at Queen's University. It was the last stop on a night of bar-hopping. He was barely twenty. Four hours of that night never came back to him, like a black hole in his memory. He vowed then never to touch the stuff again.

"I don't remember anything about the U.S. Open," said Michael.

"Not surprised, dude. You had recorded it, but you passed out before the first round ended."

"It's not coming to me."

"Coupla no-names were on top. Tiger has a bad wheel, his knee I think. A few more guys were a stroke back. Appleby, and Rocco Mediate, and maybe a couple other guys. They all should be outta the picture before they make the turn today. What's it matter anyway?"

"It doesn't," Michael said softly. He cursed himself again for getting so plastered.

Michael noticed a wiry man taking a large camera from a van that had "Metro TV" printed on the side. "Aw shit."

"What now?" asked Danny.

"TV guy from Toronto. Reminds me of last year."

"With Emily," said Danny. "So who was the guy who bought it?"

"Vincent Fronda. You know the name?"

"Isn't he the jerk Emily was all upset about that night at Pepperwood?"

"You're right. He was the guy. She did know him. Emily was pissed. She called him Vinnie, right?"

The memory resurfaced. Danny had taken a one-day writing workshop at the arts centre the previous summer, and afterward met up downtown with Michael and Emily for dinner. Emily was in a rage, to the point of tears, over the nasty behaviour of the now-dead photographer from her photo club.

"And when I asked her about it," said Michael, "Em just said

17

Fronda wasn't worth ruining our dinner over. She smiled, did a one-eighty, and changed the conversation."

"The dirtbag spread a rumour about her," said Danny. "He said Em slept with the owner to get her work into some gallery that wouldn't give Fronda the time of day."

"Why didn't she... why didn't *you* tell me about it?" Any sympathy Michael had for the slaughtered man disappeared.

"She swore me to secrecy, afraid of what you might do to the scumbag... may he rest in peace. For the record, she'd never met the owner."

Michael remembered Emily's tears, but hadn't pursued the story behind them. He had been preoccupied with his own battles at school.

"The cops can't be thinking that you killed that prick because he gossiped about your wife, and then you left him behind your house for all to see?"

"I dunno. They saw all the booze. I don't know what I think." It did sound like a preposterous notion, but Michael knew the local cops were not happy with him after the aggravation he had caused them in the fall.

"They didn't arrest you, so just forget about it," said Danny. "It's time for a boys' night. I'll try to get something going in the next few days."

If only he could.

Michael ignored the doorbell. He dressed, took another Advil, then quickly crammed as many T-shirts, shorts, and underwear as he could into a small travel bag. Descending the winding staircase to the foyer, he barely discerned the blurred movements of a visitor, or visitors, through the frosted windows that framed his front door. The doorbell rang again. He looked through the peephole. A man with a camera stood on his porch next to a woman with a microphone, a puffed-up blond he recognized as a talking head from Metro TV.

He locked up, front and back, checked his key chain, and stepped through the door leading from the side vestibule into the garage. He got the dogs into the back of the Range Rover, opened the garage door with the remote, and flew out onto the driveway. He felt his tension abating for the first time that day.

Minutes after dropping the dogs at the kennel, Michael jumped onto the ramp for Highway 407.

Kevin and Tracy Wynne had called three times in the past week to extend an open invitation to their cottage up in Muskoka, the region of pristine lakes and majestic forests dubbed "God's Country" by its residents. They were taking off for a few weeks and he'd have the place to himself. Michael wavered on the invite and hadn't returned their last message. The Wynnes planned to put the cottage on the market, and had offered Michael a family discount, a consideration he no longer needed. "We may just have a surprise for you if you come up in the next week," Tracy had said in their most recent conversation, after grabbing the phone from her husband. With Emily's sister that could mean just about anything, big or small.

The slaughter at the Foster Glen Golf and Country Club would no doubt garner front-page attention. He bristled, thinking of the article that appeared in a local rag when Emily died. He shook the memory, avoiding a descent into the lurking emotional shithole.

He punched the FM buttons until Sarah Harmer sang to him about "Oleander". He grinned. Before meeting Emily, this easy listening station would not have been an option on his car radio dial.

Early in their relationship, he had changed the station while a passenger in Emily's car. His future wife immediately changed it back. "My car, my music," she said, before singing along, and quite badly, with the closing chorus of whatever song it was.

A week later, while cruising down the highway on their first weekend away together, Emily discovered that Michael had preset a couple of soft rock stations for her in his old Jeep. She was soon accompanying another Sarah—Sarah McLachlan—to "Fumbling Towards Ecstasy". Later that night, he sat at the foot of their bed in the cozy little inn she'd picked out for the "special night for us". "This is for Sarah," she whispered in his ear while unzipping his jeans. "And I ain't fumblin'."

Michael swallowed hard. Their marriage hadn't been perfect, but she was a hell of a woman, who had deserved better from him.

The news came on the radio as he took the northbound exit for Highway 400. "*The home of Burlington multimillionaire Michael Flanigan was the scene of a grisly homicide earlier today,*" began the lead story, erroneously naming his property as the murder site. He turned it off.

He called Danny to tell him he'd be at the cottage indefinitely, and to not gather the boys for a night out just yet.

He blinked hard, in an attempt to stop Vinnie Fronda from giving him the one-eyed stare.

An hour later, he merged onto Highway 11 just north of Barrie and cranked the volume on Don Henley's "Heart of the Matter".

He wondered what Tommy would think, hearing his son referred to as "Burlington multimillionaire Michael Flanigan".

As he drove through Orillia, Michael spotted Weber's ahead on the right, with the ever-present lineup snaking across the parking lot of cottage country's landmark burger joint. Still forty minutes from the cottage, his growling stomach reminded him that he hadn't eaten since last night's pizza.

He parked and joined the lineup. The doors to Weber's were open to accommodate the overflow, and the aroma of burgers sizzling on the grill stirred his hunger.

A well-worn ball cap stood out from the crowd, about a half-dozen people ahead of him. When its owner turned to the side, the "B" on the front of the cap confirmed his identity: Dave Douthwright, the Good Samaritan of Lake Muskoka. Michael wondered if he'd ever seen the Wynnes' lakefront neighbour without his Boston Red Sox hat. Emily always had time for Dave, and Michael used to tease his wife that Dave had a crush on her.

A chiselled and tanned blond man ahead of Michael in line

turned and asked, "Is it always like this?" Michael nodded, and they chatted as the queue inched ahead. The man had perfect white teeth set off against his sun-bronzed skin and blue eyes, but Michael managed not to resent him, as the Adonis was as friendly as he was handsome.

The stranger raised an open bag of sunflower seeds. "Something to tide you over?"

Michael declined and glanced over the shoulder of Adonis toward the sound of a creaking door, and grimaced at the sight of the portly man exiting the men's room. Michael shifted sideways, using Adonis for cover, hoping the man wouldn't notice him.

Michael turned away from the approaching footsteps, waiting for them to pass.

"Flanigan?"

Michael turned to the ever-present pout and angry eyes of Bobby George.

"You two know each other," said Adonis. They were together, and from what Michael knew of Bobby's post-divorce lifestyle, they really were *together*.

Emily's ex-husband was a bloated lump. Michael had not seen him in three years, since Bobby first moved back to Burlington from Calgary. He was at least fifty pounds heavier, but an extra chin and puffy lids could not mask his nasty countenance.

Adonis introduced himself as Frank Toner while offering his hand. Michael now wished he'd jumped the queue and joined Dave Douthwright in line.

Michael's BlackBerry buzzed. He had an incoming email from Danny.

Stepping off to the side, he put the phone to his ear and said to no one, "Uh huh, uh huh... Okay, I'll be there as soon as I can." He extricated himself and was soon back on Highway 11, unfed, mildly ashamed of the lame fake phone call, and put off by his encounter with Bobby George.

CHAPTER 4

Michael pulled into a roughed-out parking spot and walked down the sloped gravel driveway. A silver Hyundai Elantra he didn't recognize sat outside the cottage. As he went to knock on the screen door, he heard Eric Clapton's voice spilling from the master bedroom overhead, a room where he and Emily had spent many nights. The music muffled a brief exchange that was followed by laughter. He looked back at the Hyundai, and still nothing clicked.

So much for his getaway. The Wynnes may have tired of waiting for a response from him and extended the invitation elsewhere.

Not prepared to hightail it back to the city, he decided to sweat out the hangover that was trying to reclaim him. He went back to his car to throw on some jogging gear. He could check back on the mystery visitors later.

The ground was damp and the blackflies thick. He was glad he had the foresight to pack the bug spray. Michael followed a dirt path that wound behind the cottages that sprinkled the bay. The generous size of the lots maximized both privacy and property values. He and Emily had hoped to own such a place someday, if they could ever afford it. And when they finally had the means to buy every cottage on the bay, she died before they could act on their dream.

The path often afforded Michael a view of Mrs. Sutton, the voluptuous free spirit next door, who rarely covered her ample gifts while lounging on her dock in the corner of the bay. He thought back to a day two summers ago when Emily, an infrequent runner, joined him for a jog along the path. The topless temptress had her wares on full display, causing Emily to crack, "No wonder you're so horny when you come back from a jog."

He approached a stretch that wound behind the cottage of the immodest neighbour, a section of the path bordered by a twelve-foot drop on the property side of the walkway.

"*GRRRRR!*"

Michael lost his footing as he turned toward a snarling German shepherd. He stumbled over the path's inside perimeter and skidded down the near ninety-degree incline. He reached for and missed a half-ring section of a gigantic root jutting from the embankment. A shelf that protruded about halfway to the ground failed to slow his descent.

He hit the level earth hard, landing face first in the mud. He slowly turned onto his side. Eyes closed, he did a quick mental inventory to gauge the damage to his aching body.

Confident that nothing was broken, he wiped his face and opened his eyes. He slowly lifted his head. Five feet away, a pair of sandalled, tanned feet turned into long, shapely legs. He hung his back head down for a moment to compose himself, and slowly uncoiled to a standing position.

He recognized her immediately, even though he had only ever seen her from a distance. Mrs. Sutton's ginger locks fell over a sheer, bulging camisole, with black bikini bottoms completing the outfit. Observing her from next door, he had pegged her as being in her early thirties. Up close, he thought her face looked a few years older and her body younger by about the same.

Aware he'd admired the view for a couple of beats too long, he looked up to an amused, crooked smile.

"You okay?" she asked.

"Considering."

"Anything I can do for you?" Affected sexuality oozed from her breathless tone.

Her cottage stood fifty yards behind her. Before he could answer, a man with thinning grey hair appeared at the door.

"Everything okay, dear?" the man hollered.

"Just chatting with a neighbour, sweetie," she replied, not

taking her eyes off Michael.

"That's Harold," she said, extending her hand. "I'm Tina."

He wiped his hand on his shirt. "Michael," he said, taking her hand.

"You sure you're alright now?" she said. "Harold's a doctor."

That didn't surprise him. Harold looked like he'd been getting the seniors' discount for years. He'd need a life of affluence to land the creature standing before Michael dripping sex from every pore.

"It was nice meeting you, Tina," he said, "but I should get going."

"Likewise, Mike," she said, and licked at the corner of her mouth. "Some other time then."

Michael turned and walked away. He had noticed an enormous rock on Mrs. Sutton's finger. While he had vowed never to cross that line again, Tina the Tease awoke something dormant in him. He knew in his heart that Emily would want him to get on with his life, in all ways. They had even discussed it. On the drive home from her Aunt Maria's funeral years before, where her Uncle Stephen had fallen apart, Emily had warned Michael through her own tears, "Don't spend months crying over me if I go first, or I'll come back and haunt your sorry ass."

Michael was back at the cottage within a minute. The Hyundai was gone. Relieved to have escaped his fall with minor cuts and bruises, he brushed himself off and walked around to the rear.

Lawn chairs were folded against the back railing of the elevated deck. He took in the view of the bay. Dense underbrush covered every inch of the ground below except for three evergreens that Kevin had planted several years back. Kevin had promised Tracy the previous summer that he would trim back the tangle. Michael empathized with his brother-in-law, the fellow procrastinator. Why drive hours to relax for the weekend, just to a waste the better part of a Saturday hacking your way through a miniature forest that looked just fine the way it was?

He walked across the deck to the large family room window. He cupped his hands around his eyes and pressed his nose to the glass.

The place is empty.

He returned to the opposite side of the building and grabbed his travel bag from the car. He stood for a moment by the cottage door, and listened.

It's empty.

He pulled his keys from the bag and went inside.

A bare shoe mat in the small foyer gave way to the family room that hogged most of the main floor. The room was cluttered with lumpy old furniture of clashing colours. The beds were made in the two rooms off to the left.

Michael walked over to the knee-to-ceiling window he'd peered through from the deck just a minute before. He scanned the shoreline eighty feet away and saw the Wynnes' motorboat moored next to Kevin's catamaran, but no sign of life.

I'm alone.

He set down his bag just outside one of the bedrooms.

"Hello, Michael."

Michael jumped, spun around, and gasped.

She wore a damp, one-piece navy swimsuit, her dirty-blond hair hanging wet over bare shoulders. Shivering, she cupped her elbows with her palms, hugging herself.

He moved toward her, opening his arms, and his heart raced. She fell into his arms, and sobbed into his shirt. He held her tight, kissing the top of her head and then her cheek.

"I missed you, sweetheart," he said.

"Me, too," she said, sniffling. "I never meant to—"

He pulled her face to him to stifle an apology that wasn't necessary. "Okay, that's enough," he whispered in her ear. "Let's cut ourselves some slack."

After some hesitation, she nodded into his shoulder. He felt her body sag, her tension ease. He stepped back, and as she turned her left side to him to blow her nose, he smiled at her

25

angelic profile, with its unblemished cheek, jaw and neck lines.

"My God, I never realized until this moment how much you look like your mother," he said. "You're so beautiful."

Smack.

"How could you, Michael?"

The blow was not hard, but he felt the emotion behind it. Michael brought his hand to his cheek. "What was that—"

"Don't, Michael," she said, pushing past him. "Just... don't." She fell into a swivel chair by the window and turned away from him.

"Sophie, what the hell—"

"You cheated on my mother."

"Oh," said Michael. He sat in a worn brown chair near his stepdaughter. For the first time, he noticed two piercings on her upper right ear and a tattoo of a fierce-looking animal on the shoulder below. The symbolism of her contrasting profiles was not lost on him.

"It seems like a long time ago," said Michael.

"It just happened for me."

"You just learned about it?"

"Does it matter?"

"It was just the one time, and without a doubt the stupidest thing I've ever done."

"Ya think?"

"We were in a bad patch. Things weren't—"

"Stop," she said, thrusting out a palm.

"Look, your mom and I were back on track, getting counselling, doing better. Doing okay, as a matter of fact."

She rolled her eyes, a gesture he had witnessed almost daily when a younger Sophie resisted the presence of her new stepfather.

He wondered if part of her anger was directed inward for missing her mother's funeral, and for their awful fight the last time they had been together.

He found two beers in the fridge and set them on the old pine coffee table. He opened his and took a swig.

"What's the tattoo?" asked Michael.

"A badger," replied Sophie.

"Still the old soul, I see," he said. "Listening to an album Clapton made before I started shaving."

She swung the chair to face him and twisted the cap of her beer. "Been playing in the sandbox, Pig-Pen?"

"I went for a little run when I got here," he said.

"Looks like you went for a crawl."

He smiled. "Had a wee accident."

"I didn't pick it out," she said.

"The tattoo?"

"The music."

"Right."

"He's older," she said, and gave him a look he'd seen countless times when she wanted to light him up, get a reaction.

He wouldn't give her that satisfaction, but did wonder about her older man, and Sophie just learning about his affair, and what it all meant. He sipped his beer and looked out the window. She turned and shared the view.

Michael's mind wandered back to that day. He had got out of his car to a shouting match between his wife and stepdaughter, coming from inside the house. He couldn't make out what they were saying until he opened the front door to find Sophie standing in the doorway, raging at her mother, who sat on the stairs with her head in her hands.

"Who are you to judge?" Sophie had shrieked through tears. "You're no better than me. You're no better than anybody."

Always protective of Sophie, Emily told Michael the next day that the matter had been settled and made him promise to never speak of it again.

—

Michael wondered what the past eight months had been like for Sophie, and what could have come between her and her mother. Emily had talked openly with her about drugs, sex—about everything. Michael often teased them about their propensity to engage in matter-of-fact discussions on the most intimate of subjects. "Do you gals ever talk about the weather?" he would ask.

Emily would not judge Sophie for a misstep in her life, nor would one surprise her, given his stepdaughter's independent and contrary nature.

He leaned forward in his chair. "When your mother died, I felt like I... lost both of you."

Sophie stared out the window.

Michael slid his chair closer and asked, "Where have you been, Soph?"

She drank some beer, burped, and set the bottle on the table.

"Fuck you, Michael." She leapt out of the chair and ran upstairs. A door slammed. She stomped down less than a minute later, grabbed Michael's keys from the table inside the door, and ran out of the cottage.

Sophie walked in a little after seven thirty, carrying a bag of groceries and a six-pack of Sam Adams.

"You okay?" asked Michael, showered and back in the same chair he'd occupied before her abrupt exit.

She allowed a smile and said, "I was 'til you showed up."

"I do have that effect on women," he said.

"Mom said things went south for you guys when she found out she couldn't have any more kids," said Sophie, true to form, a ton of bricks from left field.

Michael ignored the comment.

"Hey, I forgot to tell you I saw your dad at Weber's on the way up," he said.

A flash of surprise soon vanished from her face, replaced by a pout and a shrug.

Sophie's kinky hair partially hid her face, her mother's face. Not really a pretty girl—really not a girl any longer—but with a look, and look in her eye, that had that *something*, a face just off the mainstream of pretty faces.

"Go easy on the cooties," she said, nodding at his headgear.

He tipped the brim of the Blue Jays cap he had found hanging on the doorknob of a bedroom closet. "Yours?"

"Check out the Matt Stairs autograph on the back."

He took it off and found the scrawl of the Jays' Canadian-born slugger. "I thought I had my Leafs cap in the car," he said. "Must have left it at the house."

"I prefer the thinking man's game, as you used to call it," said Sophie. She snatched the baseball cap from him and put it on. "I'm gonna make dinner."

"I suppose you're the surprise Tracy was hinting around about," said Michael, reaching for the salad.

"I didn't know you were coming up," said Sophie.

"Someone special?"

She sipped her wine, frowned.

"I take it that was his Hyundai," he said.

"It's a rental," she said and cut into her steak. "When were you going to tell me about the asshole you found behind the house this morning?"

He stopped his wine glass halfway to his mouth. "You heard?"

"On the car radio."

"Asshole?"

"Fronda, the guy Mom told us about."

"Right."

"Did the cops make the connection, that he knew Mom?"

"They knew they were both into photography."

"They don't think you had anything to do with it?"

"I can't imagine."

She nodded, satisfied.

"Where's the Beetle?" asked Michael.

"I got a drive up here."

Michael lit a candle. "Where have you been, Sophie?"

"After Mom died, looking back I think I avoided anything that reminded me of her. It wasn't a conscious thing, but…" She reached back to flick the switch on the wall behind her, killing the overhead light. "I couldn't stop thinking about her," she said. "I felt so… hollow. You were going through your own hell, and frankly I just didn't feel strong enough to be around you. So I just took off. I guess I felt that I could just grieve on my own, get it over with, and I would come out the other end, good as new. Crazy, eh?"

"Not so crazy." He turned and looked out over the water. The skies had cleared. The lake was calm. Moonlight bounced off a mammoth slab of rock next to a tiny island that guarded the entrance to the bay.

She'd tell him where she had been when she was good and ready, if that day ever came.

"I did read the papers… about Mom," said Sophie. "People can be such jerks."

Michael took a healthy hit of his wine. The news media reported that Michael had inherited millions not long before Emily died, adding that he and Emily had been in counselling when Michael received the inheritance from his father. She died soon after, under horrible and mysterious circumstances. Let the reader connect the dots.

"To add to the tragedy," he said, "one of the people in the group on the escarpment that day, a woman named Amodeo, had a fatal heart attack shortly afterward."

"I didn't hear *that*," said Sophie.

"They found her a couple of days later in her home, wearing the same clothes she had on when she went on the outing with your mom. She'd had a pacemaker for years, was due to get it replaced they said."

"Holy crap." Sophie looked off toward the lake, then back at him. "So what does that have to do with Mom?"

"Probably nothing."

Michael didn't mention that Pickett's Farm, where Emily had met her end, is next door to the property of Michael's old schoolmate, J.P. Northcott, whose alibi that night had an odour that still lingered for Michael.

Sophie emptied the rest of the bottle of Shiraz into her glass. "I was supposed to be there that day," she said. She had a drink. "I was supposed to be at Pickett's Farm, helping her out with the photography class, but we had our fight, and then I... Oh, Michael, maybe I..."

The tears flowed.

The conversation had lightened by the time they cleared the table and loaded up the outdoor composting unit. They sang along to seventies music playing on a cottage country radio station. Sophie knew the words to most of it, from the Eagles to Cat Stevens.

Just after ten o'clock, late for cottage life, they said their goodnights. Sophie stopped at the foot of the stairs.

"I want to go there," she said, "to Pickett's Farm."

CHAPTER 5

Michael woke with the reading light on and a crossword puzzle on his chest. The clock on the night table read 2:22 a.m. The chances of getting back to his wine-induced sleep were slim. Rather than lie there until the sun came up, he packed his bag and left a note. Traffic would be light, and he could be home before dawn.

Let her invite her older man back. Sophie was twenty-two, after all. And who was he to object—the "fake parent" as she used to call him, more often than not with affection.

He vacillated on the drive home. Life would be so much easier if he gave in to the fact it might have been an accident. The notion of shedding the weight of his thirst for justice—revenge? —had its appeal.

Two and a half hours after leaving the cottage, Michael held up the chain to the overhead light as he jangled through the multitude of keys in search of the one to his front door. The keys slipped from his hand. As he bent to pick them up, he rested his hand on the door.

It pushed open.

He knew he had locked up before leaving the house. He ran through the short list of people who might have a key: Sophie, Clint... Kevin and Tracy? He made a mental note to get his security alarm fixed.

Aware of his pounding heart, he unzipped the end compartment in his travel bag. He shuffled through the contents until he found the Swiss Army knife that he'd carried for years. He had yet to open a beer or carve up an apple with it.

What the hell am I going to do with this?

He pulled out the switchblade and stepped inside, feeling kind of silly as he followed the tiny weapon into the house. He slid the back of his hand up the panel of switches just inside the door, flicking on a foyer light. He set down the bag and stuffed the keys in his pocket, leaving the door open.

He crept forward.

His head jerked toward a sound from the adjacent sitting room to his left.

A silhouette moved in the shadows.

"Who the hell are you?" asked Michael.

A blow from behind sent him face down onto the ceramic tiles. His attacker pounced on him as footsteps approached from the front. He took a feeble, blind swing behind him with the knife. A hand grabbed his arm and bent it back until the knife bounced off the tiles. He struggled, felt a stabbing pain, and counted at least three hands holding back his arms. He tried to pull free, took another thump to the head, and faded to black.

"Why are you taking me in?" asked Michael from the back of the unmarked police car. "I'm the one who was attacked."

"We need to drop by the hospital to make sure you're okay," said Speagle into the rear-view mirror. "Oakville-Trafalgar is on the way to the station. It'll be quicker than driving all the way downtown to the Joseph Brant emerg."

Michael massaged his wrists, which had been tied, like his ankles, with nylon rope.

"How did they get in?" he asked. "I didn't see any sign of a break-in."

"Doesn't take much," said Speagle. "I see you have a security alarm system."

"I haven't been turning it on. It started going off on its own recently, for no reason."

"You might wanna get that fixed."

His head throbbed, and he was tempted to make one of those

promises to God—"If I never have to see Speagle and Alberts again..." The struggle to remember what had happened to him seemed all too familiar.

"What about my home? They turned the place upside down."

"We're minding it, and Higgins is there to make sure we don't steal anything," said Speagle. "You're lucky your buddy goes out for his morning coffee."

He was right about that. Danny thought Michael was dead when, curious to see his car in the driveway and not in Muskoka, he found a conscious but dazed Michael lying on his kitchen floor.

Alberts had said nothing at Michael's house, nor a word since they got into the car.

They cut across north Burlington and headed east along Highway 5 toward neighbouring Oakville. They passed an accident scene, busy with emergency vehicles and mangled automobiles, including a rusty old Honda hatchback on which the Jaws of Life were being applied. Speagle slowed down, Alberts identified himself, and they were allowed through the blocked-off road. Michael hoped they beat any victims still breathing to the emergency room.

He shook his head, dismayed by his callous indifference to the tragedy. He wondered if he'd recently become a self-centred prick, or was just now tuning in to his shortcomings. Some poor bastard gets accordioned inside his Civic, with his face propelled through the windshield and a stick shift jammed up his ass, while his wife sits home staring at the clock. And Michael Flanigan worries that it may inconvenience him.

"You sure you have no idea what the intruders might've been looking for?" asked Speagle.

"No freaking idea," said Michael, not wishing to share any thoughts he might have on the subject.

"And you didn't get a look at these guys?" asked Speagle.

"I told you, I can't remember anything. Someone knocked me out when I walked in the door. I have no idea who it could have been or what they were looking for."

"You should relax until the docs can take a look at you," said Speagle.

The emergency ward at Oakville-Trafalgar was packed, even without the pending additions from the roadside carnage.

The detectives were flipping through magazines when Michael exited the examination room less than an hour later. A long-limbed doctor, who looked like he could still be playing varsity basketball, informed him that no obvious signs of a concussion had been detected, but he needed monitoring.

The waiting room crowd now spilled into the hallways, including a pair of screaming teenagers being wheeled on gurneys to the front of the line.

Speagle spoke briefly to the doctor, presumably to get confirmation that Michael was adequately marinated and fit to be grilled.

The detectives handed Michael off to a slim, female uniformed officer at the Halton Regional Police headquarters, a modern complex resting on a few acres of prime Oakville real estate. The officer led Michael from the airy foyer through a long hallway. They turned a corner and the policewoman deposited Michael in a small room with a table and four folding chairs.

He had been to the station a few times of his own volition, but had never managed to get past the front desk. He wondered what kind of groundwork those visits had laid for the treatment he would receive today.

Alberts entered the room carrying a brown paper bag. Speagle trailed, not looking up as he peered into an open manila folder. The officer closed the door behind them. Michael wondered if the petite woman in uniform would park herself outside, ready to burst in to save her fellow officers if Michael overpowered the fire hydrant Speagle and the behemoth Alberts.

Alberts set the bag on the table, pushing it partway toward Michael.

"Michael Liam Flanigan," said Speagle. He looked up at Michael, grinning, and closed the folder. "What part of Sweden is your family from?"

Michael sat stone-faced.

"Still feeling okay?" asked Speagle.

"Considering," said Michael, glancing at the bag.

"They found another body this morning," said Alberts, who let it sit there for a few intensifying heartbeats, before adding, "on the golf course... your golf course. In a sand trap on the ninth hole, just one hole past where they found Vincent Fronda."

"Holy shit. That's horrible. But why ask me about it?"

"The deceased is one Jacqueline Kimberly Zetterfeldt."

Michael's lungs emptied. He flushed, dropped his head.

"You knew her?" asked Speagle.

"Sh-she... her husband was my principal at T.J. Walsh." Michael looked up at Speagle. "I knew her, a little."

"How little?" asked Alberts.

"I saw her at the odd school function. She seemed nice." Michael turned to Speagle. "How did she... what happened?"

"Ever see her on the golf course?" asked Alberts.

"No."

"Ever golf with her husband?"

"No."

The detectives sat silent, unblinking.

Michael sat back in his chair. *How could they know?*

"She suffered plenty," said Speagle.

Oh God. Michael dropped his shoulders and shut his eyes for a moment.

He looked up at Speagle. "Was she..."

"She wasn't raped," said Speagle.

"You aren't teaching any longer, are you?" asked Alberts.

"No. No I'm not," said Michael.

"Why'd you leave?" asked Speagle.

"I didn't need the job anymore."

Alberts said, "The money from your father."

Michael nodded. *Prick.*

"Mr. Zetterfeldt have anything to do with it, you quitting school?" asked Speagle.

"Why do I think you already know the answer to that?" asked Michael. He told them his story. He taught for fourteen years at T. J. Walsh Public School in midtown Burlington, and coached the girls basketball team. He had loved his first twelve years on the job, teaching physical education and geography to seventh and eighth graders. But things changed with the arrival of the new principal. Graham Zetterfeldt, a controlling and unbending administrator, instituted ill-conceived rules and hare-brained teaching assignments that bewildered teachers and students alike.

"He made me teach math, of all things."

"You can't do math?" asked Alberts.

"Funny."

"I loved my job, felt I made a difference, helped the kids. This joker comes along, imposing his authority just because he could, upsetting the staff. We battle constantly. Morale goes into the shitter. At least two colleagues I know of, who were damn fine teachers, took early retirement because of him."

My God. Jacquie's dead.

"The last straw for me came when he nixed a golf program I had put together for the kids at the school," said Michael. "The kids already got wind of it, were excited about it—a lot of these kids' families aren't well off, and they would likely never pick up a club otherwise—and then Zetterfeldt killed it because he decided it was a *bad fit.* I threatened to go to the school board, but we both knew whose side they would take.

"I'm telling you, if you'd said it was him that they found murdered, I woulda cracked open the champagne. He was ruining people's careers, which in some cases meant their lives.

But if you think I had anything to do with killing his wife..."

"You slugged him," said Speagle.

"I felt bad about that," said Michael.

"I'm sure you did," said Alberts, "Not like you to lose your temper."

"When I believe in something, I fight for it," said Michael. He sat back in his chair. "I admit that wasn't the right way to go about it."

"He didn't lay any charges," said Speagle.

"Some crap about him thinking it was in the best interest of the school to put it behind us."

"Sounds like a real jerk," said Alberts.

"He doesn't give a shit about that school."

"That sort of behaviour has a way of catching up with a fella, Mr. Flanigan," said Speagle. "Someday you'll be the one wakin' up with a crowd around ya."

The two cops were both smiling now. They were enjoying this.

"Hear about any problems between Zetterfeldt and his wife?" asked Speagle.

Could Zetterfeldt have killed his wife? "I don't see it," said Michael, answering a question they didn't ask. "When I did see her, Zetterfeldt treated his wife like his prized possession." Jacquie had shared her contempt for that role—during the little time they had spent together. "Besides, I don't think Zetterfeldt has the balls for it."

"Did you tell us you didn't know the man that was killed behind your house?" asked Alberts.

"That's right," said Michael.

"Mr. Flanigan, I mighta been born at night," said Speagle. "But it wasn't last night."

"I never met him."

"Did you know *of* Vincent Fronda?"

"My wife knew him through her work, her photography."

"And you didn't think that was worth mentioning?" asked

Alberts.

"I honestly didn't make the connection until after you left, really not until I confirmed it with Danny."

"Now why would Danny Higgins know that your wife knew this guy and you weren't sure?" asked Alberts.

Michael hesitated, then replied, "I forgot."

"Was Fronda a friend of your wife?" asked Speagle.

Feeling his fear on his greasy palms, Michael said, "From what I understand, he was quite rude to my wife, insulting even. Emily said it was nothing to worry about, just a mean little man who wouldn't play nice in the sandbox."

"Lots of bad things happening on golf courses," said Speagle.

"Are you a hockey fan, Flanigan?" asked Alberts.

"Excuse me?"

Alberts opened the paper bag, grabbed it by the bottom, and turned it upside down. He shook it as if anticipating a mishmash of contents to spill onto the table. Only one item fell out: a dark-blue baseball cap, with a Toronto Maple Leafs logo on the front.

Michael's mouth went dry. It was a hat like many others, but he'd bet it was his missing cap, and he could only imagine where they found it. He picked up the cap and looked inside. There it was, written in magic marker:

Mikey Flanigan

Emily had labelled the hat, the nickname implying a little boy prone to losing his things, before giving it to him for his fortieth birthday.

"I've been looking for this," he said.

"Uh huh," said Alberts.

"It was found near Mrs. Zetterfeldt's body," said Speagle, "in the next bunker."

Michael clenched his teeth to stop the tremor in his head.

"You can't possibly think that I—"

"Who should we be looking at, Mr. Flanigan?" asked Alberts.

"The mayor? Perhaps the old guy in his nineties from Mount Nemo who just gave two million to some charity?"

"What are you—"

"Well isn't that your style?" asked Alberts, the decibel level rising. He was now standing and glaring down at Michael. "To deflect blame in the direction of a leading citizen?"

Now Michael got it.

Northcott.

He had wondered when they would get to this. Michael stood up and kicked his chair back. "You don't scare me. I've done nothing."

"Please sit down," said Alberts. He picked up Michael's chair and motioned him into it. "Now."

They both sat down.

"How did Mr. Zetterfeldt respond when you threatened to go to the school board?" asked Speagle.

Michael's eyes danced around the room, searching for the memory of that moment in the teacher's lounge, when he'd challenged Zetterfeldt in front of a handful of colleagues in ringside seats. "He said something like I'd better think twice about that, if I didn't want to get burned. Something like that."

"How did you respond to that?"

Michael squinted at Speagle, addled by another shift in gears. Speagle must have questioned the other teachers. "I think I said... I'd like to burn his f'ing house down, something stupid like that."

Alberts smiled. Speagle nodded.

"Don't tell me," said Michael. "His house?"

"To the ground," said Speagle.

Michael sank in his chair, feeling like he'd just four-putted and had the putter shoved up his ass. "I'd like to call my lawyer now," he said.

"We thought you might," said Alberts.

CHAPTER 6

"Why am I in here?" yelled Michael. "I'm not under arrest!" If he'd had a tin cup, he would have rattled it against the bars.

The fear that grew in Michael when bullied by the detectives escalated as he entered the holding area in the bowels of the Halton County police station.

About two dozen men occupied the stark cell. A quick scan of his new roommates, and air heavy enough to put the average gym locker to shame, suggested few tax cheaters or investment fraud artists in the mix. Some ignored him, others stared. He tried to avoid eye contact.

"Got a smoke?"

Michael recoiled from the slithery voice coming from behind him. He turned, then took a step back.

A greasy man, with glazed-over eyes and canary-coloured teeth, grinned and fondled his crotch. Thick and with a few inches on Michael, the man smelled like a three-day bender and wore about a week's worth of dark stubble.

"I don't smoke, sorry," said Michael.

"What's your name, boy?"

"Uh... Mike."

"You can call me Cuz, Mike."

"Cuz?"

"Cuz."

Images of a prison movie staple caused Michael's worst fears to bubble to the surface. But this guy was more *Deliverance* than *The Shawshank Redemption*, Michael thought, with a definite cousin-cornholing quality.

The guard was nowhere in sight, but Michael planned to call for him if his immediate future grew any bleaker. He glanced around the man's large form, searching for a sympathetic petty criminal or wife abuser. The cellmates he could see had turned away. Michael did the same.

A clammy paw squeezed Michael's forearm just below the elbow. Breath like a swamp fell hot on Michael's cheek.

Cuz murmured in his ear, "Well then, what else have you got for me?"

Fuck it, thought Michael. He wiped spittle from his face. He lowered his hand, now a fist. *If I get the first one in...*

He took a deep breath, clenched his jaw.

He swung around hard and fast.

Cuz caught Michael's fist before it reached his jaw. He twisted Michael's arm and pushed him to his knees.

"That's quite a haymaker, boy," said Cuz, "and now I gotcha wheres I wanchya." He showed Michael his teeth again, those that he still had. The agitated anticipation in the black eyes leering down at Michael disclosed his aggressor's intentions.

Cuz spat in Michael's face, and not the thin and watery variety. The discoloured mass hung on Michael's eyelid. Michael tried to yell for the guard, but the hand around his throat reduced his plea to a pathetic gurgle.

Cuz reached for his zipper... then squealed, releasing Michael from his grasp. Michael fell back onto the cell floor, gasping for air.

A curly-haired man, more Goliath-like than Michael's mugger, had Cuz's testicles in one hand and a clump of his filthy hair in the other. The man bounced Cuz off the wall. The fallen predator lay curled in the corner, holding his privates and whimpering.

The man turned to Michael.

"You alright, Michael?" he asked.

Michael wiped his eye with his sleeve and looked up at the man. "Do I—"

The man grabbed Michael's hand and pulled him to his feet.

Holy shit. "Artie?" said Michael. "Artie Smitters. Hey man, I can't thank you enough."

Footsteps approached from the end of the hallway.

Artie Smitters nodded and walked away.

Two smiling cops looked through the bars, assessing the scene. Michael assumed no investigation of his assault would ensue.

Rita Manale sat next to Michael in the interrogation room, upright and knees together, wearing a puffy white blouse buttoned to the neck and a plain, knee-length skirt. She removed a pressed handkerchief from her petite handbag, unfolded it, and dabbed at the corner of her mouth.

Her schoolmarm persona didn't mask her appeal, nor did it stop Alberts from showing teeth that he'd hidden from Michael since he met him.

"I understand one of the men in the holding area grabbed you?" asked Speagle. "You okay?"

Michael glared at Speagle. The detective asked often about his well-being, but Michael doubted that he gave a shit.

Rita threw her hanky on the table. "Leo, what the hell was my client doing in that fucking cell? And where was the goddam cop on guard, off playing with his pecker?"

Alberts dropped both his pen and jaw. Speagle chuckled, like he'd just heard an old joke but still liked the punch line.

Rita crossed her legs and slung an arm over the back of her chair. "We can deal with your questionable judgment regarding the treatment of my client later," she said, her rasp suggesting a habit of at least a pack a day. "Right now I want to clear up any confusion about Mr. Flanigan's connection to the bodies that have been piling up around town.

"And don't come at me with that stupid ball cap. Do you think my client would kill someone and then leave behind an article of his own clothing... with his name on it? As for some off-the-cuff remarks he may have made to Mr. Zetterfeldt, there was a room full of teachers present in the teachers' lounge when my client made those remarks. He made sure there were plenty of witnesses whenever he said *anything* to Mr. Zetterfeldt, given how little he trusted the man. Do you really think he'd put a sign on his forehead that says, 'Come and get me, I'm a killer.'?"

"Your client admitted that he has no alibi from approximately ten o'clock last night, when he said good night to his stepdaughter, until Danny Higgins found him on his kitchen floor just after seven this morning," said Speagle. "According to Detective Goldberg's report, both the murder and the fire occurred sometime between midnight and two a.m."

"Leo Goldberg?" asked Rita.

"Are most of the detectives in this place named Leo?" asked Michael.

"Just four," replied Speagle, deadpan.

"I was at the cottage until at least two thirty," said Michael, turning to his lawyer. "I already told them that. I came home and got slugged."

"And you can't remember a thing during the previous night's murders," said Alberts.

"You think I knocked myself out?"

"Relax, Mr. Flanigan," said Speagle. "We know the blow wasn't self-inflicted."

Michael pieced it together. "And here I thought you were asking the doctor if I was okay."

"Call off your dogs, Leo," said Rita. "His alibi is on her way."

In the front seat of Rita's car, Sophie rested her head against the window of the passenger door. Michael leaned forward from the back seat and put his hand on her shoulder.

He soft-pedalled the details of the latest murder, the break-in at the house, and the questioning by the police. He assured his stepdaughter that the visit to the police station had been a mere formality.

Rita strutted through the parking lot like she owned it, tossed her bag beside Michael on the back seat, and took the keys from Michael.

"All done," she said, and drove out of the lot.

"Thanks for saving my ass back there, Rita," said Michael. "In more ways than one."

"Thank your stepdaughter for riding in from Muskoka on her white horse."

"Don't I know it," he said. "How'd you get down here, Soph?"

"Thank God you got up a couple of times for a pee," said Sophie, skirting the question. "I know you were still at the cottage until at least one thirty."

"Michael, if they thought you were guilty you'd still be talking to Speagle and his sidekick," Rita said. "You were totally co-operative, offered your DNA and anything else they wanted. Leo Speagle's been doing this a while. I sense he's pretty damn sure you're innocent and doesn't want to waste any more time on you.

"You didn't jump at the chance to point the finger at Zetterfeldt for his wife's murder. You're covered for both the homicides and the fire, where no one was hurt, by the way. Zetterfeldt was allegedly out looking for his wife, who didn't show for a seven o'clock dinner reservation and was seen earlier in the night at a local cougar bar. But it might not be totally over. They could look at your phone records, your email."

Cougar bar?

Michael pictured Jacquie Zetterfeldt humping some kid half her age. "Won't they need my permission to do that?" he asked.

"Just a judge's."

"Let 'em look."

"Speagle plays the good cop, but don't drop your guard. I've known him for years. I'd bet that he was the one that had you tossed in the cell."

"Sounds like a swell guy. I could have been raped, if not killed."

Sophie turned and made a face.

"Your imagination's getting the better of you," said Rita. "I know it wasn't fun back there. But this is Oakville, Ontario, not Buttfuck, Mississippi." Rita turned to Sophie and said, "If you'll pardon the expression, my dear."

"Hey," said Sophie, waving her hand. "I hear Buttfuck is a lot like Oakville, but without the malls."

Rita laughed.

"I wasn't imagining the horny hillbilly," said Michael.

"They have cameras on that holding cell," said Rita. "Someone was watching you the entire time. At least they should have been."

Cameras. Michael hadn't thought of that.

"Besides," Rita said. "I understand another client of mine was looking out for you today?"

"Artie Smitters?" asked Michael.

"The one and the same."

"Artie went to my high school, Notre Dame, when I first moved to Burlington."

"What was he like back then?" asked Rita.

"He seemed to intimidate people, without really trying to," said Michael. "I never saw him raise a hand to anyone. I hadn't seen him again until maybe three year ago. He approached me at Foster Glen, remembered me from school, and asked if I'd put a good word in for a job he was after in the pro shop. He ended up getting the job, was very grateful. He seemed to be doing okay."

"He's not there anymore?" asked Sophie.

"Huh. I don't know," said Michael. "After my wrist started acting up again, I stopped playing altogether for most of last summer. I forgot about Artie. Never really thought about him again until I saw him today."

"He's an electrician now," said Rita. "He replaced all of the old knob and tube wiring in my house."

"What's he in for?" asked Michael.

"For being chivalrous. We'll leave it at that," said Rita. "He won't be in there much longer."

"Thanks to you," said Michael.

"He's a good man. He brought his little girl to the house once. Cute kid, about ten or eleven I'd say. You can tell she's got Daddy wrapped around her finger."

"Artie's married?"

"Not anymore. I get the feeling the mother has the kid most of the time. He's quite an amazing guy. When he finished the job at my house, he noticed my new stereo system, still in parts and all over the floor. I'd been struggling with the damn thing for two nights."

"He put it together for you?" asked Sophie.

"In about twenty minutes," said Rita. "Never looked at the manual once."

Michael's thoughts turned to Jacquie. He slumped back in his seat and said, "Speagle said she suffered, and quite a bit."

Rita glanced at him through the rear-view mirror. "The detectives aren't sharing much about what happened to Mrs. Zetterfeldt."

As they approached Michael's house, Rita said, "Looks like you still have company." She pulled over to the side of the road.

Police cars queued up behind Danny's pickup along the side of Michael's long driveway.

"Aw shit," said Michael. "Can we just keep going?"

"Not a little curious to see if they found anything?" asked Rita.

"I just want to get some sleep. Danny can keep guarding the fort for now." He figured the police were just dusting for fingerprints, and wouldn't know if anything was missing anyway.

"Say no more," said Rita.

Michael crashed for a few hours on Rita's couch before she dropped off Sophie and him at home. Once the police left, Michael listened to Danny curse the cops for ten minutes, then thanked him and sent him home.

Danny had addressed the ransacking as best he could,

returning furniture to its place and moving any portable damaged items to the back of the laundry room. That inventory included family portraits from his office wall, assorted broken dishes, and Emily's banged up iPod. He was able to start up the latter, which went to the middle of a song by Feist, a tune that came with a guarantee to trigger Emily's "Goofy Dance".

The top middle drawer of the desk in Michael's office had been pried open. A knife from Emily's best silverware was found on the floor. The drawer was empty, but he thought that's how he'd left it, and had locked it out of habit.

He closed and locked his office door, and removed a floorboard from behind the desk. He reached up behind the wall panel and pushed a button that set in motion an upgrade he had done to his home soon after he moved in.

The panel slid open to one side, revealing a shallow compartment containing the "family treasures". A couple of short love letters to Emily, that Michael had penned after she died, sat atop a box of fake jewelry, which nudged against a sandwich bag of old coins. The loose change was authentic, but not worth enough over face value to deserve such a safe and secure home.

He removed the items and pulled out the rear partition, exposing the safe for which he had designed the miniature lair. While there were no signs of entry, he entered the combination. Satisfied that the contents had been untouched, he closed things up and checked the rest of the house.

He remained steadfast with his decision, when questioned by Speagle, to offer no guesses on the motives of the burglars. Only Sophie and Rita knew of his little vault in the wall, and he planned to keep it that way.

They were after something else. But what in God's name was it?

That evening, Michael found Sophie on the back deck. The police tape was long gone from the murder site just a stone's throw away on the Foster Glen fairway. The Murphy brothers, Gary and Shaun, both set up over shots within feet from where

Vincent Fronda met his fate. Michael knew that the next shots from the twin postal workers might not get included on their final scorecards, a practice for which they'd become so renowned that trimming strokes off one's score was referred to at the club as "Murphin' it".

"I liked hanging out with Rita," said Sophie.

"She's always been there for me," said Michael. "I knew her for years before I met your mother."

"Nothing ever happened between the two of you?"

"We make good friends."

"Did you know she'd like to be a psychologist someday?"

"Would she now?"

"Have you talked to your brother lately?" asked Sophie.

"Your Uncle Eamonn?" asked Michael. "Not for a while." Not since his younger sibling had threatened Michael the previous summer.

"*Uncle* Eamonn. Sounds kind of funny."

"Isn't that what you've always called him?"

"When I was a kid. It sounds kind of weird at twenty-two. I guess I don't think of him as an uncle."

"More like a brother, maybe?" asked Michael, thinking this was another sign of Sophie wanting to be treated like an adult. An older man will do that to a girl.

"More like a friend, I think. I hope he's doing okay. It'd be nice to see him."

"There was a time when you wanted nothing much to do with him, and rightly so I suppose." He recalled her horror at fifteen to learn that his kid brother took drugs, before she had cultivated her try-anything-once approach to life.

"I was a little naïve," she said. "Mom said you and Eamonn had a big scrap last year, and you hadn't been speaking. How's that going?"

"I'm working on it."

"Why does money so often come between family?"

He shrugged.

"Michael?"

"Yes, Sophie."

"What's going on, all these people dying?"

"I don't know, Soph, but I`d sure as hell like to find out."

Michael leaned back and closed his eyes. He felt himself recharging, replenishing. A swelling fury boiled in him, some directed at the cops who verbally battered him and tossed him to the lions, the bulk of it a missile of wrath ready for a strike at an unknown enemy. It burned in him, but he would control it, use it. A swath of unanswered questions nagged at him, and people were fucking with his life, but he found a new resolve. He was ready for the fight—for his reputation, for the truth, and maybe for his life.

PART II — MAKING THE TURN

"I never learned anything from a match that I won."

—Bobby Jones

CHAPTER 7

Michael had been relaxing at the kitchen table that terrible day in October of 2007, the Saturday of the Thanksgiving weekend. He had just returned from a golf vacation in Prince Edward Island, feeling good as he leafed through an album of old vacation photos, the windows open to let in a soft breeze and the scent of the warm autumn day—when the knock came to the door.

He opened the door to a platinum blond policewoman of about twenty-five, standing on his stoop, cap in hand. A solemn-faced policeman stood behind her, partway down the drive.

The cop at the door appeared nervous, softly shifting her weight from one foot to the other.

"Sir, are you Michael Flanigan?" she asked, stilted, uncomfortable.

Michael nodded.

"Was Emily Baggio your wife?"

Time slowed to an excruciating pace.

The cop in the rear, just over Blondie's shoulder and within earshot, winced. Michael began to put two and two together, and reached for the door jamb for support.

"What do you mean *was*?" asked Michael.

A neighbour's dog barked. Across the road, Bonnie Bertram from two doors down pulled a wagon carrying toddler Matthew.

Horrified recognition at what she had just uttered washed over the policewoman's face. She brought her hand to her forehead, and bit her bottom lip. Sweat forming on her upper lip revealed a faint moustache.

From behind, a cheer went up on the golf course, a shout of chip-in level decibels.

"Oh, I-I'm sorry. I meant—"

"What happened to Emily?" asked Michael.

"I'm sorry, sir. There's been an accident," she said, her lips quivering. "Your wife is dead."

Part of him died with Emily that day. The fire had already died from their marriage, but what an inferno it had once been. True and compromising, she gave her all to their union. They may have been little more than friends at the end, but a better one he never had. She made him better, and he didn't really get that until after she was gone.

And there he'd sat three days ago, at that same kitchen table, as strangers with badges interrogated him about the horrible death of a man he had never met. He sensed a journey of discovery ahead, where he would learn the secrets behind the horrors, and break through the darkness that had blanketed his life since his father died.

On Monday morning, two days after the break-in, Sophie hopped in her mother's MINI Cooper, still sitting in the space out front where Emily always parked it. She headed for the north country and her mystery man.

Michael called the Wynnes to put the wheels in motion for purchasing their prime piece of lakefront property in God's Country. They quickly agreed on a price, and all that was left was the paperwork.

He went upstairs and moved from room to room, still unable to determine if anything had been stolen, other than the eighty or ninety bucks he had left on his dresser.

What the hell were they looking for?

The murder of Jacqueline Zetterfeldt made not just the front page of the Burlington Post, but the Toronto Star as well. Detective Leo Speagle had not provided the media with any gruesome details about the murder, but did say that no evidence had yet been uncovered to link this killing to the one behind the Flanigan house less than twenty-four hours before. While the bodies piling up on his home course had become a national story, Michael's name had so far been mercifully absent from the latest lead. The media had clearly not tied the murders to the break-in at Michael's. Nor should they, he thought.

He went back downstairs, flopped into a family room chair, and closed his eyes. Emily... Fronda... Jacquie Zetterfeldt. The only person within a couple of degrees of separation of each of the deceased was Michael Flanigan.

His gut told him all events were connected.

Was it all somehow tied to Emily?

He decided to go hit a bucket of balls, hoping some time on the range would clear his head. He had the golf bug again. His wrist felt better than it had since his surgery the previous year. He called Danny, who was busy writing, making "real progress on my story". Michael told him he'd be at Foster Glen at three o'clock if he changed his mind.

Michael pulled a letter out of a folder on his desk, addressed to his father, Thomas I. Flanigan, on the letterhead of the "Northern Preservation Society".

"I" stood for "Ignatius", *the fiery one,* and Michael's father certainly was that the day the letter arrived at his downtown office. Michael had hoped to take him to his favourite restaurant for his seventy-fourth birthday, but old Tommy said he was too pissed off to eat.

"At least the fuckers had the balls to sign this one," Tommy had said that day, making reference to a threatening note he'd received from "another band of gutless tree-huggers". The hate mail began before Tommy had even won the deal on the land up north, and then ramped up after he sealed it.

The letter, from Society president Joyce Hogarth, proclaimed Tommy a greedy, self-serving capitalist, willing to sacrifice acres of the most beautiful wilderness in Muskoka, "solely to line your own pockets". The correspondence infuriated his father and pre-empted their lunch, and precipitated a series of angry phone calls, threatening letters, and legal bills.

Michael had to assume that he had inherited his father's enemies. Still, it required quite a leap to consider that Emily may have died because his old man pissed off some well-intentioned conservationists.

He read the letter twice. The fanaticism he had perceived when first reading it that day in his father's office just wasn't there. Had he been under the spell of his father again, snowed under by his emotion?

Michael yanked a sand wedge from his bag and commenced his warm-up routine. As he twisted his torso from side to side, he noticed Foster Glen teaching pro Randy Goodman setting up in the instruction zone, twenty yards away. Eyes glued to his student, Randy ignored Michael, who couldn't blame him. She was stunning.

His pupil seemed captivated by the words of golfing wisdom pouring out of Goodman, who shared tips on alignment and club speed with an enthusiasm Michael had never witnessed in him.

As if she could feel Michael's eyes on her, she turned and, peeking through a mass of black locks, caught his stare. She smiled, with a playful look that said "Caught ya".

Goodman looked over and said, "Hi, Mike." His tone said, "Not now."

Michael turned and spilled out some range balls from his bucket, nudging one to a grassy patch. He skulled the ball, causing it to touch down after a low, unimpressive flight. He looked to his left. Goodman's student attempted to suppress a laugh.

I should take her home and show her my trophies.

Michael hit the next ball clean, followed suit with the next, and then another. He exchanged the wedge for a nine-iron, and then worked his way down the bag. His wrist co-operated. He felt his swing coming back.

With each exchange of clubs, he stole a glance at Goodman's class of one. Each look in her direction lingered a little longer. She now seemed oblivious to his presence as she followed Goodman's directives to get on the balls of her feet and keep her head down.

When class had concluded, she remained on the range to practice what she had learned.

She talked to herself as she set up to take a swing, repeating the mantras Goodman had just instilled in her: "head still", "club back slowly". She was elegant when frozen in time, but clunky in motion. Her swing needed work, plenty of work.

Two teens walked by, bantering about a playoff in the U.S. Open. Michael had been so preoccupied he missed the Sunday round. He slid the five-wood in his bag, went back to his car and deposited his clubs in the trunk. He changed out of his golf shoes and walked toward the clubhouse, and noticed the golf student was down to her last couple of balls. She sliced her driver badly, just as he stepped up behind her.

"Did Randy teach you that?" he asked.

"I picked that up on my own," she said, in a muted British accent. "I was watching you earlier. What time does your lesson begin?"

He laughed. "I just wanted to tell you that I won't be needing my balls anymore."

She looked at him, wide-eyed. "I beg your pardon."

He repeated what he'd said, to himself, dropped his chin to his chest, and snorted.

"My bucket," he said, lifting his head and pointing to his overturned container of range balls.

"Very kind of you to offer, but I have to get going."

He examined her long fingers, wrapped around the club. She had no ring, or tan line from one.

"Michael. Michael Flanigan," he said, extending his hand.

After a brief hesitation, she shook his hand. "Jessie," she said.

"Nice to meet you. Jessie."

"I really should be going."

He watched her walk away, all the way to her car. She didn't look back.

—

Michael spotted Goodman sitting alone in the clubhouse at a table off to the side, drinking coffee and chipping away at some paperwork. Most heads in the half-full room were tilted up toward the big TV in the corner, where Tiger Woods filled the screen in his familiar final round attire of red jersey and black trousers.

"How's biz?" asked Michael.

"Seems it's raining every damn weekend," said Goodman. "How's the wrist, Mike?"

"So far, so good. How's the game, Randy?"

"Humbling."

"It never ends."

"A beautiful layout, Torrey Pines," said Goodman of the renowned San Diego course as he turned his attention back to the TV.

"Tiger and Rocco in a playoff. Whoda thunk?" said Michael.

"It's Mediate by one, coming up eighteen. Tiger screwed up his knee. He's really hurting. Been grimacing through the first seventeen holes."

"My God. Rocco might do it."

"You think?"

"Nah."

They settled back and watched Tiger reach the green in two shots, sink a challenging two-putt to force a sudden-death playoff, and defeat Mediate on the first extra hole, limping all the way. Tiger being Tiger, the 2008 U.S. Open champion.

"What else is new?" moaned an elderly man at the next table, as he slapped down a twenty in front of the man next to him.

"Was that a new member you were giving the lesson to?" asked Michael, keeping his eyes on the TV.

Goodman nodded. "She may never break a hundred, but she can play with me anytime."

"What's her story?"

"Just joined. Jessie Hargreaves. She's a personal trainer and life coach, whatever the hell that is."

"She got any more lessons booked?"

"There are golf stalking laws, Mike."

"Just curious."

"Uh huh. Well, your curiosity might be satisfied if you came by here Saturday morning at around ten o'clock. Just don't mention I told you."

"Don't think I can make it," he said. Michael planned to stay in Kingston until Saturday morning. He thought it just as well, as it would look a little more than coincidental if he reappeared at her next lesson.

"Glad to see you're back in the game, Mike."

Michael smiled.

Maybe I am.

CHAPTER 8

Working the mingling crowd just off the podium, the well-put-together man whispered in the councilman's ear, got a slap on the back from the local hockey legend, and shook the sea of hands presented to him, including the mayor's.

"It's just about time to get started," said the mayor to about a hundred citizens gathered on the lawn outside the one-story building.

A woman emerged from the audience, pushed her way to the podium, and lunged at the man in the expensive-looking suit and perfectly coifed hair. She hugged him, crying. "You're a great man," she said.

After handlers eased the woman aside, the man said, "Let me say that I do this as much for myself as for the community—"

"We love you," yelled a second woman from the middle of the crowd, her hands resting on the back of an elderly man's wheelchair.

"—as we all know that there is nothing more rewarding than serving one's fellow man."

The mayor pulled back the covering from the sign in front of the new-looking building, revealing "Northcott Hospice" in block letters.

"This makes a nice bookend to your wing at the hospital, J.P.," said His Honour.

James Paul Northcott III took a step back, wiped a tear, and in a trembling voice said, "You'll have to excuse me," before exiting to thunderous applause.

Why can't people see through this phony creep? It was a question Michael had asked himself for years. He turned away from the proceedings and lowered the car window. He spat onto the road and drove away.

—

It was a muggy evening, more like late July, less than five days since he stuck his finger into Vinnie Fronda's eye socket. While death had become his constant companion, Michael continued to feel better, ready to move on.

Driving past Foster Glen, he peeked at the driving range, just in case Jessie Hargreaves had decided to get in a little extra work on her short game. She had not.

He took in the countryside as he drove: the smell of the evergreens; the relaxed gait of the odd pedestrian ambling along the stony shoulder; the expansive properties; the feel of being away from it all, although just minutes from the city.

Michael decided to leave the dogs another two or three days, while he pondered a visit to Kingston to see his aunt. Paulie and Silvio loved the kennel, their version of a vacation retreat.

He thought of Emily showing a mild interest in learning to golf. She had even taken a couple of lessons from Randy Goodman the previous summer, but Michael didn't encourage her much, suspecting she wasn't really into it. Or perhaps he preferred to keep golf for himself, where he could be with the guys, in a world of his own.

"The funeral home... Northcott?" asked Danny as he rolled down the passenger side window. "You're bringing that up again, after all this time?"

Michael said nothing.

"For chrissakes, Mike," said Danny. "A couple of months ago the guy was named Burlington's citizen of the freakin' year for 2007. And okay, maybe he was also asshole of the year, but c'mon."

They drove in silence to Appleby Line, where Michael turned right and headed toward the city. "Don't you ever just know something cuz you just *feel* it?" he asked.

"Yeah, I just knew the Patriots were gonna beat the Giants in the Super Bowl," said Danny. "I felt that big-time, in my pocketbook."

They stopped at a light less than a block from their destination. A perky twenty-something with purple hair bounced across the street in front of them. She flashed a coy smile at Michael on the way by.

Danny stuck his head out the window and said, "Wanna shoot some pool, darlin'?" The young woman picked up her pace.

Michael shook his head. "Sometimes I think you've just woken up from a teenage coma."

"How about you, Mike?" asked Danny as they walked across the lot.

"How about me what?"

"What, how about me what? How about are you ready to maybe ask a nice lady out for a bit o' sushi or something?"

Michael frowned, gave him a look.

"The hang-dog look doesn't become you, Mike," said Danny. "Keep your chin up and your pecker will soon follow."

"I did see this woman today, at the driving range of all places," said Michael. "A British gal."

"Alright then. Did you talk to this lovely limey?"

"I kind of embarrassed myself in front of her. Then she left."

"Oh," said Danny. "The usual."

Exiting the still-bright evening into relative darkness, they were welcomed by a concerto of colliding billiard balls that rang through the bar. Most of the tables in the cavernous room were already occupied, busy for a Tuesday. It had to be a league night.. A waitress walked by with a tray of draft beer, followed by a teenage boy weighed down with two baskets of chicken wings and a large pizza. The Tragically Hip's "The Kids Don't Get It" blared from the sound system.

The familiarity comforted him: the old-style hall, with an

ambience derived from a real lack of any; the staff in jeans and T-shirts, no cheerleader-type waitresses in matching uniforms. For a moment he had an odd sensation of being in a time warp, as if this crowd remained from the last boys' night out many months before, awaiting his return, unaware of the demons he'd faced in the interim.

Eddie Kan stood by the table in the far corner, chalking a cue, while checking out a game between a pair of young women two tables over.

"Where's Nirenberg?" asked Michael as he approached the table.

"Opera tickets," said Eddie. "Got 'em from a customer."

"The cultured mechanic."

Michael and Danny selected cues from the rack and ordered beer from a waitress patrolling the corner tables. Bouncy and short, she wore black jeans, a plain olive T-shirt, and ten extra pounds. She hung an extra long smile on Michael and dragged her eyes over him, up, down and sideways.

"What bubbly enthusiasm," said Eddie as she walked away.

"Like farts in my bathwater," said Danny.

"I didn't take you as a bath guy," said Eddie.

Danny pulled out his notebook and scribbled something in it.

"You putting that in your book?" asked Eddie. "Will I get a credit?"

Danny just smiled.

"I thought your friend Da Silva was going to grace us with his presence some night," said Eddie.

"Next time," said Michael. He had left two messages for Fern, but neither was returned.

"Three for pool sucks," said Danny.

Michael laid his cue on the table and said, "Why don't we sit down and grab a bite?"

They found a table near the front and got another round. Danny pulled out a Pro-Line betting ticket, and turned his attention to a baseball game on the TV behind the bar.

"Why do you bet on baseball?" said Eddie. "It's too hard to pick."

"How do you like Obama's chances?" asked Michael.

"He should be the guy," said Eddie. "It sure would say a lot about how far the U.S. has come if they voted a man of colour in."

"People become racists because they don't really know anyone like the people they've decided they hate," said Danny. "They don't know anyone of that race or religion or whatever, and they're fucking *afraid of them*."

"I wasn't really speaking of racism, per se."

"I think you were."

"What about misogynists?" asked Eddie. "Don't they know any women?"

Danny burped and said, "They know too many."

"They let you drink, Michael?" asked Eddie.

"It was mainly the pills," said Michael. "The odd beer won't kill me."

"I'm surprised you're even here tonight, with all that's happened."

"This is just what I needed," said Michael, who updated his friends on the interrogation at the police station and the incident in the jail cell.

"What the fuck," said Danny. "You didn't tell me about making a new friend at the cop shop. Did you get his address at the trailer park?"

"Holy crap, Mike," said Eddie. "If it wasn't for bad luck."

"All this crap has pissed me off just enough to wake me up and get me going again," said Michael.

"The golf corpse," said Danny. "You know her?"

"The what?" asked Michael.

Eddie frowned at Danny and then said to Michael, "Did you know her? The Zetterberg woman?"

"It's Zetter*feldt*," said Danny. "She didn't play for the fucking Red Wings."

Eddie snapped his fingers. "Of course. Zetterfeldt was your principal, right? Any chance he did it, then set fire to his house to throw them off his trail?"

"Maybe she was fucking around on him and he found out about it," said Danny.

Michael cringed. "We should hit the links soon," he said, steering them from the subject.

"I'll have to get back to you," said Eddie. "I just got a big file and may have to act on it quickly." All discussions related to Eddie's work seemed to involve a "file".

"Michael, I hear your uncle's taken over at the helm of your dad's company," said Eddie. "I haven't been up to Muskoka, or even talked to any of those guys, since I helped broker the deal for *Oliver's Landing*."

"Helped?" asked Michael. "My father said you and your little consulting firm made it all happen. I gotta admit I loved seeing the land for the golf resort swept out from under J.P. Northcott."

"I know what you're saying," said Eddie. "I also heard a rumour that Northcott was buying Foster Glen."

Michael's jaw dropped. "Pardon me, Kan Man?"

"I heard a coupla guys in suits talking about it, the last time I was at the club," said Eddie.

"Mike's on a Northcott jag again," said Danny.

"Emily?" asked Eddie. "I remember how you... *were* back then, Michael."

Michael shrugged, drank some beer.

"You were pretty medicated at the time," said Eddie.

"Well now my head is clear," said Michael. "And like our old hockey coach used to say, I have to keep my feet moving. Northcott was home that night, virtually next door, with no alibi. And Dad, with me along for the ride, won the bid for the land that Northcott had pegged for the golf resort community of his dreams. And then the old man turns around and develops a plan for a golf resort himself."

"*Oliver's Landing*? You think he could kill your wife because he lost a business deal?" asked Eddie. "You're talking about a guy who has created hundreds of jobs in this town, given a fortune to charity. I'm sure he's lost his share of deals over the years. Should they be looking for a trail of bodies?"

"Eddie, I'm not convinced *someone* didn't help her down that cliff," Michael.

"Based on what?"

"I've known Northcott had evil in him since he killed my dog when we were eleven, just because it chased him home and embarrassed him in front of the neighbours. They never proved it, but Buckley was perfectly healthy and died two days after he chased the little coward home."

"Oh, yeah. He snuffed Buck," said Danny. "At least I remember Mike and I were both sure of it at the time."

"You guys know his story," said Michael. "The girl he assaulted when he was fifteen. It was just after Mom died. Then the kid he was suspected of poisoning, after he caught Northcott cheating in a junior golf tournament."

"Ducky McDonough," said Danny.

"Paul McDonough," said Michael. "He was in the hospital for over a week."

"I know what you're saying, but I've heard all of this before," said Eddie. "You said they never proved he was involved with any of that. Didn't Northcott beat you in some tournaments, when you were kids? And did he not steal a girlfriend of yours, back in the day?"

"What's that got to do with anything?" asked Michael, who still shuddered at the memory of Northcott walking down Johnson Street in Kingston, his arm around Cathy Wall, as Michael watched in horror from the front chair in McQuade's Barbershop. "Listen, I've heard stories from credible sources about him firing people for the most petty of reasons, long-term employees with families to feed."

"Forgive me, Michael," said Eddie, "but I always wondered if, when you were so hostile with the police after Emily died, if you weren't a little angry at yourself. And frustrated, for not being there, for not saving her."

Michael stiffened, opened his mouth to respond, but said nothing. Michael admired Eddie's honesty and direct manner, but he could be a little too damn smart at times.

"We're all gonna die anyway," said Danny out of nowhere.

"Who are you... Woody Allen?" asked Eddie.

Michael eyed Danny. Always an unmade bed, his recent weight gain gave him the look of a lumberjack that had gone to seed.

"There's one more point I want to make," said Eddie.

Michael sighed.

"It's actually a question," said Eddie.

"So ask it," said Michael.

"Let's say J.P. Northcott has never been born, and you have no history with him bouncing around in your head. Would you still think, based on the facts as you know them, that your wife's death was anything but an accident?"

Michael quickly replayed the picture of Emily's death as he envisioned it in his head. "I've been suffocating from these... these *layers* of death surrounding me, closing in on me. It's scaring me more than just a little. I need to do something to fight through it, so I can breathe, get past it."

"Yeah, I know what you're saying," said Eddie. "But you didn't answer my question."

"The cops will be throwing all their resources at the recent deaths," said Michael, "and that's fine by me, considering how close to home they hit. But I doubt they'll have any motivation to dust off Emily's case. I need to find out, both for her and for me. I'm trying to be..." He lowered his head. "I wanna be... better."

"You're going to look into her death, on your own?" asked Eddie.

"Gonna buy a piece and a trench coat?" asked Danny.

"For starters," said Michael. "I'm going back to the scene of the crime."

CHAPTER 9

"I guess it was a working farm at one time," said Rita as they pulled up in front of the country estate early on Wednesday morning. Pickett's Farm looked like anything but.

"I don't remember much about this place," said Michael.

"You've been?" asked Sophie.

"Not long after your mom... was here," said Michael. "I had started drinking quite a bit, plus I'd already gotten to taking painkillers for my wrist. Too many." He undid his seat-belt and turned to his stepdaughter. "I eventually ended up in rehab, Soph."

"Holy crap, Michael. I had no idea."

"How long had Emily known the Picketts?" asked Rita.

"She met Agnes Pickett at some fundraiser a few months before she died," said Michael. "They hit it off and Mrs. Pickett gave Emily full access to her property for doing her photography. Mrs. Pickett's husband wasn't around anymore, and Emily would spend time with her."

Agnes Pickett stood on the porch wearing a yellow dress with a floral pattern and one of those old lady hats with a big brim, which she wore tilted off to the side. Michael thought she looked like a proper southern belle from *Gone with the Wind*, with Pickett's Farm filling in for Tara.

A red MG convertible at the corner of the house roared to life and sped down the drive, Mrs. Pickett waving after it.

The elderly woman stepped gingerly down the porch and gave Michael a warm, extended hug. It felt like a gesture of condolence, all these months later. She directed them to the pathway up to the escarpment.

"What do you recall about the morning Sophie's mom died?" asked Michael.

"It was foggy. Oh my, yes. Very foggy. Thick as pea soup," said Mrs. Pickett, wagging her finger. "I thought Emily's group would like to see the fall colours. I asked Emily if she'd rather wait until it cleared, or do it another time."

Foggy, like the morning he found Vincent Fronda.

"I let them take the ATVs," said Mrs. Pickett. "Most of them said they wanted the exercise. But it is a bit of a hike. Some were older. There was the poor woman with the bad heart. I don't mind telling you I don't make that walk anymore."

"What did Emily say when you suggested they could wait for the fog to clear?" asked Michael.

"She said the fog made it all the better."

"Mom loved to shoot foggy mornings," said Sophie. "I imagine it was a low-lying fog."

"Now that you mention it, dear," said Mrs. Pickett. "The fog was hugging the ground that day."

"How would you know that, Soph?" Michael asked.

"I paid attention when Mom talked about her photography. She spoke so passionately about it. How could I not?"

Meaning how could I not?

As they walked past the corner of the house, Michael noticed the barn at the rear was elevated, with entry ramps on opposite sides. A garage was carved into the base of the barn, and the ATVs were in plain view.

"May I take one of the vehicles?" asked Michael.

"You surely may," said Mrs. Pickett. "My grandson loves riding in those things."

"Did my mom walk or ride that afternoon?" asked Sophie.

"She was on foot when I left them."

"Then I'll walk," said Sophie.

"Me, too," said Rita.

"Agnes, was that your grandson who drove out of here just after we arrived?" asked Michael. "I love those little MGs."

"Oh, no," she said, and laughed. "That wouldn't be Arthur's style. That was young Jimmy from next door. He comes by to help me out with some of the chores."

"Jimmy?" he asked.

"Yes, Jimmy Northcott. A lovely boy."

Little Jimmy Northcott.

Sitting behind the wheel of the ATV, Michael examined the lay of the land ahead.

A path, easily wide enough for the vehicle, wound through the trees on the incline leading to the ridge of the escarpment. Michael reached the end of the path and waited for the women. He pictured Emily on that foggy morning, escorting her crew of camera-lugging students up the hill.

Rita and Sophie arrived fifteen minutes later.

"Are you going to tell me what's on the clipboard, counsellor?" Michael asked Rita.

"The police report."

"The police report?" asked Michael.

"Much of this is only so much surface information," she said, scanning the report. "I'm not sure what it will tell us. There's a witness list and statements, plus a police officer's notes."

"They weren't very forthcoming when *I* demanded to see their reports," Michael said, reaching out to take the clipboard.

"I guess it depends who makes the request," Rita said with a wry smile. "And there's a time to demand and a time to ask."

"My instincts were good when I asked you to join us," he said, as he flipped through the three-page summary.

Rita extended her hand, and he handed the clipboard back.

"The Bruce Trail runs the length of the escarpment from the Niagara Peninsula to Tobermory on the Bruce Peninsula," said Rita. "The Trail nudges some of these properties. I'm guessing the Picketts didn't want hordes of hikers and bikers enticed by an unmarked path branching off into their land, so they ended it here.

"There were seven people besides Emily in the group that day," she said.

Michael nodded. He had yet to hear anything that he didn't

already know.

Rita continued.

"Two members of the group, Teresa Amodeo and Mickey McIvor, were flagged as requiring special attention. Teresa Amodeo had a heart condition. We know what happened to her. Mr. McIvor... recent knee replacements. The ages of the group ranged from twenty-eight to seventy-two.

"They set out from the bottom of the hill at approximately 5:45 a.m., in keeping with their plan to reach the top of the hill well before sun-up. On October 6, sunrise was at 7:22. Even though only two people were listed as requiring special care, two ATVs were used by the group." Rita paused. "Makes sense. The weather had been a little unpredictable. It had rained the night before, was quite foggy in the morning when they got here, and it rained again later that day."

"Or they just jumped at the chance to use an ATV," said Sophie. "They are kinda fun. Dave Douthwright has one up at his cottage."

Michael looked off in the direction of the Northcott estate to the northeast. The small forest and rocky hills would have made it difficult to span the terrain from where he stood.

"This must be where they left the vehicles before finishing the trip on foot," said Rita.

Michael parked the ATV and hopped off. He felt the ghost of his wife standing beside him. The scent of pine trees soothed him. It had been Emily's favourite smell.

"The best time to shoot is during the sweet light of the early morning, the twilight just before sunrise, or just after sunset," said Sophie, who slathered on bug spray that she pulled from her backpack before offering some to the others. "At twilight, the light is indirect and soft. Harsh shadows are eliminated. *That* is when they would have wanted to start their cameras clicking."

"I thought twilight happened at the end of the day," said Michael. He enjoyed hearing Sophie talk the language of photography that her mother had passed on to her.

"Twilight is either from sunset to dusk or dawn to sunrise," said Sophie. "Mom called it the 'magic hour'. If sunrise was at 7:22 that day, twilight would have likely been a half hour or so earlier."

"I guess the acorn doesn't fall very far," said Rita.

"You couldn't give me a better compliment, Rita, but I wasn't in Mom's league as a photographer."

"Your mom wasn't formally trained, was she?"

"Mostly self-taught, but she did take the odd course, to stay current with things."

"She went on a course somewhere last spring," said Michael.

Sophie jerked her head around and snapped, "Savannah. She went to Savannah, Georgia." She marched on ahead.

In a few minutes they cleared the trees and the ground levelled out. The edge of the escarpment sat further away than he remembered, a good five-minute walk from the trees.

As they neared the edge of the cliff, Rita stopped and said, "The group stopped about fifty yards from the edge, right around where we're standing, give or take... there's a shed off to the left." She pointed in that direction to a small building. "The others in the group said that Emily had told them not to go off on their own until the fog cleared, and repeatedly reminded them not to get too near the edge of the escarpment."

"But she did," said Michael.

"As they stood here," said Rita, who then read verbatim from the clipboard. "'Ms. Baggio reached into her pocket, shined her flashlight on a piece of paper she had pulled out, and asked the others to stay put while she checked on something'. The group members had conflicting stories on which direction she headed in, as they had trouble getting their bearings in the fog. The majority seemed to think she walked off in the general direction of the escarpment edge. Based on the timing we're working with here, I imagine that would have been about six thirty, or a few minutes after."

Rita dropped the clipboard to her side. "That was the last time anyone saw her."

Michael breathed deeply. Sophie seemed okay, and rested her chin in her hand, digesting the information, deciding what to make of it.

"Why would Mom walk to the edge by herself in the fog?" asked Sophie of no one in particular.

"Maybe she went ahead to determine where they should set up," said Michael.

"I don't see why," said Sophie. "Mom came up here a couple of times, preparing things. She would have just devoured the place."

Michael nodded. Her logic was sound. "What about the note or whatever it was she had in her pocket?" asked Michael. "The police said they never found it."

"She was one to make lists," said Sophie. "She may have just reviewed what she wanted to cover that day."

Michael chewed on that for a minute. He'd considered the possibility of a to-do list before—that was one habit of Emily's that he did remember, did notice—and hadn't given it much consideration. But it seemed to resonate more coming from Sophie, who so far had impressed him with her insight.

"Why would the bunch of them be unsure of the direction she went in, even in the fog?" asked Sophie. "She would have been using her flashlight, no matter how well she knew the surroundings."

"They were distracted," said Rita, "Soon after Emily left the group, Teresa Amodeo began feeling ill, dizzy. She fell. The group was afraid she may have broken something. It says that Mrs. Amodeo cried, moaned, repeated the words 'Help me' three or four times. They formed a circle around her... Jenine Huntley, a veterinarian, knelt down to examine her. At that point, Mrs. Amodeo calmed down, got up and pronounced herself okay, saying it happens all the time... she apologized to everyone, seemed embarrassed... asked if someone would please take her home. Jenine Huntley walked her to an ATV and took her home. That was around seven o'clock."

"I still find it hard to believe that someone didn't hear

something," said Michael.

"A couple of people in the group thought they heard something rustling, maybe falling. They thought it was an animal. They determined later that—"

"It was Mom. She was falling," said Sophie. She turned to Rita. "She didn't scream?"

"Her injuries suggested—"

"She hit her head as soon as she went over," said Michael.

"Your mom likely lost consciousness soon after she began her fall, from striking the escarpment wall," said Rita.

Sophie dropped her head and closed her eyes. "Teresa Amodeo had a heart attack, right?" she asked.

"Didn't find her for a couple of days," said Michael.

"Didn't someone check on her the next day?" asked Sophie.

"From what I understand, everyone involved assumed someone else would be looking in on her," said Michael. "The Huntley woman left on vacation the next day, and Mrs. Amodeo had no family here. The police assumed she was out or away when they swung by her house."

"You can bet Mom would have been looking in on her the next morning."

Rita flipped to the last page of the report. "They found Emily at 9:21 a.m. on Saturday, October 6, at the bottom of this cliff. It was estimated that her point of departure would have been close to this shed, if not directly opposite.

"It does say here that they questioned Mr. J.P. Northcott, the neighbour on the north side of Mrs. Pickett. Mr. Northcott was home alone that night. His family was up at their island on Georgian Bay."

"Home alone," said Michael.

They reached the small building, a nondescript storage shed about half the size of a one-car garage. A door on the left side faced inward from the lip of the cliff, and a dirty window in the middle on the same side provided a fuzzy view of the shed's contents.

The door was locked. Michael pulled the keys for the ATV from his pocket, and stuck the extra key on the chain into the lock. It opened, and they went inside.

The shed was bare, with three empty rows of built-in shelves on the wall to their right.

"It stinks in here," said Sophie.

The wood floor was covered in twigs, dirt, assorted garbage, and what looked like animal excrement.

"The shed was locked the night of the accident," said Rita. "Nothing suspicious was found inside."

Michael stepped out of the shed and Sophie soon followed. He walked around to the other side and stopped, not really struck by the imposing view of the escarpment until that moment. The rim of the cliff was less than twenty yards from the shed.

The vista beyond froze him, not so much because of its beauty, which was undeniable. He leaned back against the shed and turned his head away.

He closed his eyes, a fragment of his last visit sifting back into his memory. He had crumpled to the ground and wept that day, crushed from thinking what Emily's last moments must have been like, bouncing off the unforgiving rock face. Dying alone, with no one who could help her, without him there to help her, to save her.

He opened his eyes. Sophie stood ten yards from the edge, her camera raised. "Sophie?"

"I'm taking some photographs," she said. "The ones Mom never got to take."

Outside her home, Rita leaned into the open window on the passenger side of the car. "Michael, look at the police report, think about things now that we've paid our visit, and then let's talk about where your head's at with this thing."

"And you're hoping I will conclude?"

"To live your life. Enjoy it. It seems you haven't for so long."

"I plan to, Rita."

"You're buying that cottage?"

"Closing the deal soon."

"Well go enjoy it. Take the kids. Swim. Go fishing. Or just sit on the damn dock for a few weeks."

"I will. Soon."

"Michael, I wanted to help you get some closure, not to start some cockeyed investigation. Make a few calls if you think it might tell you something about Emily's passing, but stop living inside your goddam head. That's what Emily would want."

CHAPTER 10

"How'd you hook up with Veronica Donovan after all these years?" asked Michael, glad to get his mind off his trip to Pickett's Farm. The bright midday sun suggested a good day for the drive to his hometown, and a better one for hitting the golf course.

"I found Ronnie on Facebook," replied Danny, as Michael got on the 407. The toll highway ran north of Toronto and would allow him to bypass the metropolis on the way to Kingston, which sat three hours to the east on Lake Ontario.

"Isn't that mainly for kids?"

"Anybody can use it. I got on to do some research on social networking for this story idea I had, and thought I'd have some fun looking around to see who was there. Ronnie's been divorced for a while... set herself up online using her maiden name, so she was easy to find. Her daughter got her into it."

"How old's the daughter?"

"Fourteen going on twenty-five, according to Ronnie. Anyway, we chatted for a while, and then you mentioned going to Kingston, so I gave her a call, and here I am on the road to find out."

"Maybe you'll be finding out what it's like to be a stepdad," said Michael.

"Let's see about getting laid first."

"Right. Priorities. What's Ronnie like?"

"Nice tits as I recall."

"Sounds like you're preparing to unload the charm on her with both barrels," said Michael.

"She sounds nice. Same old Ronnie."

The conversation wound down and they listened to music on the radio. Michael turned up the volume on a Led Zeppelin tune as he exited the 407. He drove south through the town of

Pickering toward Highway 401.

"How is that book coming along, Danny Boy?" he asked.

"It's coming," said Danny. He turned to Michael and nodded. "It really is coming along."

"Good to hear."

"I was thinking about Allyson the other day," said Danny.

Michael turned down the music.

"You sure don't see it coming," said Danny.

Michael turned off the radio. If Danny Higgins was about to allow a rare peek inside, Michael would not miss any of it for a Jimmy Page guitar riff.

"We were so hot for each other for the first couple of years, so freakin' happy to be together. What happens?"

"Life, I guess. Maybe the surprises run out."

"You and Emily seemed to keep it together for a long time. What was your secret?"

"Blind luck as much as anything, I suppose. Not too long ago I would have told you having an honest and open relationship, keeping the communication lines open, all of that, but... I don't know. I'm not sure I did such a great job with any of that."

"You been watching Oprah?"

"You asked."

"They only want you to be honest to a point," said Danny. "My ex, for example. About six months before she hauled her ass out the door, Allyson comes into our family room while I'm watching a game. I mute the TV, giving her my full attention. She said she'd just watched a documentary upstairs... on sex. I think, great, maybe I'll be havin' a little sumpin-sumpin."

"Aren't you street?"

"So Ally asks me if I think of other women when we're having sex. So I say, 'What the hell else am I gonna think about?'"

Michael had to laugh. "Maybe you should share that anecdote with Ronnie over dinner," he said, "while you're staring at her cleavage."

"I might save it for the second date."

"I don't think I got so much as a blow job off her after that," said Danny, who simmered for a few seconds. "Who am I kidding? I didn't have to be married for long to figure out that a blow job is a sex act performed by single women."

"Lovely sentiment."

"You know, Ronnie Donovan was never too inhibited," said Danny. "Let's hope she's maintained her attitude... and her boobs."

"A boob man all the way."

"I am that."

"And honest."

"To a point."

"To a point."

Michael had a quick nap after they checked into the Sheraton Four Points Hotel in downtown Kingston, a block from Lake Ontario. He changed and walked toward the lake. He turned the corner on Ontario Street and found his aunt, Lucie Donzelle, waiting on the street in front of Woodenheads.

He hugged his late mother's sister and, as he opened the door to the restaurant, saw Danny zip by in a red Ford Focus rental, no doubt in a hurry to see how well Ronnie Donovan had aged.

His aunt enjoyed the "Parisian flavour" of her name, using the French spelling of her first name to sync with the surname she got from her late husband.

A mix of university students, families, and couples, young and old, produced a pleasant hum inside. The aromas drifting down from the open kitchen on the upper level teased Michael's mounting hunger.

They settled into a corner table by the window. Their waitress touched Michael's arm three times while reviewing the specials, and smiled back over her shoulder as she walked away from their table. She was about Sophie's age, which Michael's aunt was quick to point out.

Michael reassured her that he was doing well, had got past the shock of finding the murdered man—not mentioning the assault in his home—and had begun to move forward. He gave her a rundown of what Sophie and Clint had been up to, as best he could, and responded in the negative when she asked if he'd "met any nice girls". Lucie had loved Emily, but she wanted her nephew to get on with his life.

"Did you drive down here just to see me?" asked Lucie.

"You did sound like you needed to see me in the flesh before you'd believe I was okay."

"Well it's the newspapers, you know."

"So don't read 'em."

"Don't be smart, you. Do you remember phoning me several months ago, not too long after you lost your Emily? It sounded like you'd had quite a bit to drink." Lucie raised her eyebrows and added, "And it was a Monday."

The look on his face must have answered her question.

"I didn't think so," she said. "I don't remember a lot these days, but I won't soon forget that call. You were going on about how you thought Emily's death was no accident, and the police didn't care. Nobody cared. Then you mentioned that horrible boy, J.P. Northcott... how you smelled a rat and would like to kill the so-and-so." Lucie gave a disapproving shake of her head. "I was worried about you. I called the next day to ask if you were okay. I left you a message, but I never did hear back from you."

Michael loved that Lucie shared his loathing of J.P. Northcott. She and Michael's uncle had lived down the street from Michael at the time his cherished mutt had died. When his parents and the rest of the adult world didn't believe his suspicions about Northcott having a hand in Buckley's death, she had taken him aside and said, "Don't you worry. He'll get his someday."

"I'm sorry, Lucie," said Michael. "I wasn't much good to myself or anyone else after I lost Em."

She waved her hand, dismissing any need to apologize.

"I just withdrew," he said. "I was drinking more than I normally would, trying to kill the pain I guess."

"Was?" she asked.

"Definitely past tense. I never really had an addictive personality, and I finally recognized alcohol for the depressant it was. Rather than comfort me in my mourning, it exacerbated the process."

"Pretty fancy talk. I hope you mean it. What about this J.P. business?" she asked. "Do you really think he may have had a hand in Emily's death?"

"You never cared for him."

"Him or his filthy old man. Big Jim gave me a drive home from the hospital one day—we were both working over at Kingston General at the time—and he tried to force himself on me in my own driveway. Thank God Momma taught me how to use my knees."

"Holy sh... I never knew any of this."

"Not the kind of thing you share with your fair-haired teenage nephew."

"Now I know where J.P. gets it," said Michael. "I was just talking to the guys about the girl he assaulted."

"Behind St. Mary's School. Natalie... what's her?... *Jenkins.* Anyways, I wasn't about to take any crap from his father. The next time I saw him he was walking down University Avenue with his wife. You remember Mrs. Northcott? I actually liked her. So anyways, I walk up to him on University Avenue and slap the high and mighty look off his face, and I tell him if he ever lays a finger on me again I'll rip his nuts off."

"You didn't," said Michael. "In front of his wife?"

"She wasn't for long after that. She stuck with him when he lost his job and had to move the family to Burlington to work in the factory. But she was back here before long."

"You are my hero."

"Don't worry. J.P. will get his someday," said Lucie, echoing what she had said over thirty years ago when Buckley died. "A leopard can't change its spots, and this skunk can't lose his stink."

Lucie insisted Michael spend the night. His resistance proved futile, as he knew it would, having no memory of ever winning an argument with his mother's younger sibling.

He hugged her outside her door just after eight the next morning, and promised again to stay in touch.

"Maybe you and I can play some golf the next time you're down," she said.

He had forgotten that his aunt had taken up golf.

"I was planning to," he said. "Let's pick a date and do it."

"Bullfeathers you were. But I'd love to."

Michael took a deep breath and rang the doorbell at his ex-wife's on Barrie Street, directly across from City Park and half a block from Lake Ontario, in a beautiful old section of town. Denise and Clint lived in the rental property, owned by her parents. He reminded himself again that at least Clint had a good life in Kingston.

"Hi, Dad," said Clint, who opened the screen door and greeted Michael with a welcoming smile and a self-conscious hug. The two of them often took a while to reconnect and, awkward or not, the embrace thawed some of Michael's tension.

Denise stood in her familiar pose, arms folded and leaning against the wall, shredding him with her eyes.

"How's it going, Denise?" he asked, hoping Clint's mother would at least try to put on a friendly front for their son. "How's the job going?" His ex had never shown much gratitude for the contacts he'd used in his hometown to get her the admin job at the university.

"Hello, Michael," she said, and turned to walk away. Without turning back, she said, "Not too late tonight, Clint."

He looked at Clint, who just shrugged, resigned to the

dynamics of his divorced parents' relationship.

He expected some improvement in her disposition after a recent increase in her monthly support payments. Maybe things would change when she figured out just how much her lifestyle could be enhanced if she played ball.

Clint threw his clubs in the trunk. They drove down Barrie Street and turned onto King for the scenic drive along the lake to the golf course.

"I'm looking forward to playing The Hill," said Michael. "You getting lots of use from your membership?"

"Yeah, Dad. Thanks again," said Clint.

"Everything okay with Mom?"

"I'm working on her. We'll get that pickle out of her butt someday."

Michael wondered how many children of divorce ran the emotional gamut that Clint had; feeling responsible when their parents split up, then hoping for years that they would get back together, and eventually taking it upon themselves to bring civility to the broken union.

Clint grew silent.

"You sure everything is okay, buddy?" asked Michael.

"Things are okay," said Clint, half under his breath.

"But?"

"Mom's been hanging around this guy."

"Oh yeah?"

"Reid Davidson." Clint spat out the name, like he didn't like the taste.

"Where'd she meet this guy?"

"Night school. Mom's trying to become a yoga teacher."

Michael did think Denise looked more fit when he looked beyond her scowl that morning. "What do you think of Mr. Davidson?" he asked.

A shrug, Clint's response to many things these days.

"Do you like him or not?" asked Michael.

"Not really."

"You know it's normal for Mom to want some company."

"I don't trust him."

"Has he lied to you? Is he nice to your mom?"

"He acts like we're great pals, and we aren't. Plus..." Clint's voice tailed off.

"C'mon, buddy. No need to be shy with your old dad."

"Well... when Mom kinda says things about you that maybe aren't so nice, he kinda like agrees with her, and then he'll turn to me, all understanding like, and say things like, 'I'm sure I'd have issues if I went through everything he has.'"

Michael immediately despised Reid Davidson.

Less than fifteen minutes later, they pulled into The Hill.

"Why would they put the nickname right on the sign?" asked Clint as they turned in to the course entrance. "I've never seen that."

Michael glanced over at the large sign to the right of the entrance, installed since his previous visit. The oversized gold lettering read, "Awahilidihi Golf and Country Club ('The Hill')".

"I think so people won't sit at the front gate trying to pronounce the name of the place they're visiting," said Michael. "Before they added 'The Hill', cars were always backed up at the entrance, blocking traffic while trying to say the proper name of the course... causing all kinds of accidents. It was crazy."

Clint looked over. Michael grinned.

"Very funny, Dad," said Clint.

"I thought so."

"But really... do you think it's a hilly course?"

"Not especially."

"Then why would I call it 'The Hill'?"

"From the name I guess."

"But it's not even pronounced *hill* in the name. It's pronounced *heel*."

"All good points, pal. Why don't you call it by its proper name from now on... *Awahilidihi*?"

Clint paused and said, "The Hill. Works for me."

They spotted Danny talking to a man who was slipping on golf shoes while sitting on the open back of a blue Honda CRV. Michael thought he recognized the other man, but Clint confirmed it when he said, "Holy shit, Dad."

Lanny Paulson, a local rock musician starting to get a lot of attention on the national scene, waved to Clint as he inched toward him, like he was an old friend. Danny introduced them, and said Paulson would round off their foursome. Michael knew some of his music, and liked it. He'd seen him play a few years back in a small club with his old band, *Eggs for Gnudi*.

"Remember, he's no different than the rest of us," said Michael. "Just relax and be yourself. Look, he even drives an SUV."

"And he's got two kids, Brendan and Jared," said Clint. "His wife is Terri-Lee."

Michael pulled Danny aside. "Lanny Paulson?"

"He's a friend of my cousin, and not a bad golfer."

"Nice, Higgy. You knew Clint was a big fan."

"Don't start with me," said Danny. He walked over to join the conversation with Clint and Paulson.

They spent about fifteen minutes on the driving range. Michael admired his son's lean, muscular frame, and the noticeable improvement in his swing. Clint glanced over to see if Dad was watching when he made a particularly good swing.

Paulson looked as comfortable with a golf club in his hands as he did with his guitar. Danny told Michael that the rocker was almost a scratch golfer.

"Scratch? You said he *wasn't bad*," said Michael.

"That isn't bad."

Michael's wrist felt as strong as it had for a long time, and he looked forward to playing more often.

Clint put his bag on the back of one of the carts, and Paulson immediately placed his clubs next to Clint's. Clint looked at his dad and beamed. He'd be riding with the celebrity musician.

Danny asked Michael if he wanted to play for five dollars a hole, and added that he'd want a stroke per hole. Michael declined, feeling Danny had little chance of coming out ahead, even with the stroke advantage.

"Maybe not with Clint around," said Michael.

Michael recognized a barrel-chested man standing in the next group behind the tee, towering over the others in his foursome. "Hig, who is that big guy playing behind us?"

"That's Jackson Corey. You would have seen him a hundred times on TV when you were a kid."

"The hockey player? Who did he play for again?"

"Everybody."

"Oh yeah. He got around, didn't he? A real tough mother, as I recall," said Michael. "But that would have been decades ago."

"He's almost sixty. Can you believe it? And avid. Golfs in the shittiest of weather, all year if they'd let him. He was coming off eighteen when I was here a couple of months ago, and it was really fucking coming down I'll tell ya."

Clint barely acknowledged Michael during their round, the laughter between Paulson and Clint often piercing the midday humidity.

"Don't worry, Mikey boy," said Danny. "No dad has a chance next to a rock star."

Michael had anticipated being a fairly young dad when Clint reached his current age, and imagined this phase of their life would include many golf games, ball games, chats about life. But the divorce got in the way, and Clint had a busy life of his own. There were just too many miles and not enough hours between them.

When he did find himself standing beside Clint on the edge of the thirteenth fairway, Michael blew it.

Michael's pitching wedge slammed into a tree on the follow-through of his chunked approach shot. His ball bounced short of the green, and he rammed the wedge into the tree again. He tossed the club into the woods.

"You're not good enough to get that mad," said Clint.

"Pardon me?"

"That's what you said to me when I was a kid and took a tantrum after a lousy shot, and broke my club."

Tantrum? Shit.

"Remember what you made me do when I tossed my club in the garbage?" asked Clint.

Michael did. He retrieved his mangled wedge and placed it in his bag. "That will serve as a reminder to me, young man."

Clint laughed. Michael cursed himself.

"You'll be beating me before you know it," said Michael, as they walked off the eighteenth green.

"I know I will," said Clint.

Michael flipped his keys to Danny, and walked over to chat with someone he saw outside the pro shop. Danny and Paulson drove the carts to the parking lot to drop off their clubs.

Michael approached the slight, greying man, who didn't recognize Michael at first.

"Barney, it's Michael Flanigan," he said, extending his hand.

The little man returned a smile of recognition and a handshake.

"How's my favourite lefty?" asked Michael, shaking the hand of his former Little League baseball coach, Barney Farrell. Barney's name had come up over a glass of wine the night before in Lucie's apartment. She delivered Avon products to one of his neighbours and would invariably run into Barney when making a delivery.

They chatted for a few minutes. Michael learned that Barney had played a few rounds with Lucie at Awahilidihi, and that Barney lived in the lakeside condo across the road from the club, down the hall from Lucie's Avon customer. He said The Ports was pricey but worth the money, had spacious units, with all the amenities and, if you were on the south side facing the water, a great view. When Barney mentioned that neighbours down the hall from him were anxious to sell their place, Michael thought the notion of a second home near Clint had its appeal.

Barney offered to talk to the owners. The wife had some health problems, and they were moving to Arizona. Short on time but not on money, Barney thought the couple might be willing to sell for a fair offer, without putting it on the market.

"Talk to Mom about maybe spending more time in Burlington?" asked Michael, as he drove his son home.

"You know Mom," said Clint.

"Sorry about losing it on thirteen today, buddy," said Michael.

"You've had a lot of stuff going on."

"Stuff?"

"You were... sick. Then they found the guy behind your house."

Great. "Where'd ya hear all this, Clinton?" asked Michael.

"Mom... the newspaper."

"Reading the paper regular now?"

"Mom shows it to me."

I bet she does.

"You look like you had a good night," said Michael as he approached Danny, who was slumped, eyes closed, in a chair in the hotel lobby.

Danny opened one eye and grinned. Enough said.

They had a quick bite in the hotel restaurant and hit the road. Michael learned that Ronnie was "trying to break up" with her boyfriend—"Whatever the fuck that means," said Danny— and that Danny had promised not to mention their night of passion to anyone until she straightened out her personal situation. "Who the fuck am I gonna tell?" asked Danny.

Michael popped into Barney Farrell's condo. Mr. and Mrs.

Lavallee, the couple heading to Arizona, were not at home, but if their place was half as nice as Barney's, Michael was interested.

Danny was asleep when Michael returned to the car. After he got onto the 401 heading west, Michael left a message for Jenine Huntley, the veterinarian from the Pickett's Farm excursion, and put the Rover on cruise control.

Michael's Uncle Don called as they drove through Belleville, not yet an hour out of Kingston.

"Are those activists up in Muskoka driving you nuts now that you're in charge?" asked Michael, talking over Danny, who snored next to him.

"I curse your old man every day," said Don Flanigan, Tommy's younger brother.

"I'm sure you're keeping the investors happy. I can't wait to play *Oliver's Landing.*"

"Mikey, I know you heard the rumours that your club might change hands," said his uncle. "We'd been taking a look at it ourselves."

"Foster Glen?"

"It's been sold."

"Has our family expanded its golf interests?" At that moment Michael wondered why he hadn't pursued it himself. God knew he could afford it now.

"Someone else bought the course."

"Someone else who?" Michael then braced himself, having just remembered the rumour Eddie had shared at the Boston Manor.

"J.P. Northcott."

CHAPTER 11

After dropping Danny at home, Michael picked up the dogs from the kennel and took them for a long walk.

Northcott owns Foster Glen.

Michael couldn't shake the nauseating sense of being violated.

He returned home, had a shower, and went downstairs to his office.

He perused the copy of the police report that Rita gave him, but soon felt it was just busy work, not sensing much substance in his scribbled additions in the margins. Rita had done a thorough job of sharing the salient points during their morning at Pickett's Farm. His first-hand read revealed no new details of merit. But it did trigger a desire to speak to some of the people who were on the scene.

Michael flipped to what was listed on the report as the "Witness List", essentially the names of those on the escarpment with Emily that day.

Teresa Amodeo, x-ray technician (retired), 55
Kristian Rodriguez, sales rep, 33
Markie Forster, musician, 28
Verena Dark, piano teacher, 32
Jenine Huntley, veterinarian, 42
Mickey McIvor, postal worker (retired), 72
Harold Strawberry, casino manager, 62

An appendix to the report had the contact information for the group.

Teresa Amodeo's age jolted him, having assumed she was older than fifty-five. He wondered how many good years he had left.

He didn't know what to make of the fact that Northcott's son was a regular visitor to the property where Emily had died. He'd heard the young man they called Little Jimmy had his problems, but wasn't a bad kid. A few years older than Sophie, Jimmy had been just a year ahead of her at high school. Sophie described him the way most did, as a good kid, just a little slow. But having a son like Little Jimmy would not be good for the ego of a proud man like J.P. Northcott.

After going through the report for a second time, he decided to shut it down for the day. The crime, if one had been committed, was cold. The urgency to nail a guilty party in Emily's death had diminished. He felt he had the luxury of making the search more of a marathon than a sprint.

He just didn't know what to make of it all. He didn't know anything, really.

He went to Foster Glen, to enjoy his home course while he could. He got in a quick eighteen with three new members who all worked at a small software company. They talked about new releases and stock options and vested shares. He mostly kept to himself and shot a 74. His game was coming around.

Michael left the club and caught the next train into Toronto from Burlington Station. Let someone else drive today, he thought. His improving game aside, the round of golf hadn't relaxed him. An image of Northcott hovered behind every green. He needed to unwind, to clear out the noise in his head.

Jenine Huntley returned his call as he travelled east from downtown Toronto on the Queen Street streetcar.

"Did you know Emily well?" asked Michael.

"Just from the arts centre," she said. "I was there taking a Photoshop course that your wife was giving. She was a wonderful teacher, so passionate about her photography."

"She was that."

"Oh, and I ran into Emily with her friend... Ruth somebody, at the library one day. Just chatted for a minute."

"Ruth?"

"A volunteer, I think."

"Did you see Ruth at the arts centre, maybe at the Photoshop thing?"

"Just that one time at the library."

"You didn't see where Emily went when she left the group that day?"

"You could barely see at all up there. Emily read something she had taken from her pocket, and she wandered off seconds later. And then with Mrs. Amodeo... I told all of this to the police."

"I understand you tended to Mrs. Amodeo."

"She seemed like a nice lady, had a charming Italian accent. Why are you asking about this now?"

"I just feel like I need to know everything I can about what happened that night. You understand," said Michael.

"I feel bad that I didn't see it coming, with Mrs. Amodeo I mean, her dying so soon afterward. But it didn't seem like she was in that much trouble. She came around very quickly, waved it off like something that happened all the time. I'm afraid I never got a real good look at her. It was still dark, the fog so thick, and she had that scarf wrapped around her head and neck. I heard someone say she was sensitive about some scars, from an accident she was in years ago."

Michael thanked her for her time and was about to hang up.

"There was one little thing," said the vet. "I don't know if it really means anything."

"What was that?" asked Michael.

"Mrs. Amodeo pulled away from me when I touched her, when I tried to take her pulse. In fact, a moment later she said she was fine, just like that."

"So what? He owns the golf course you play on," said Michael's ex-cop friend Fern Da Silva, from his seat on the street-side patio of Quigley's Pub in Toronto's Beaches neighbourhood.

"So what? It's been my oasis for more than ten years," said Michael. "And now *he* owns it?" He should have expected little sympathy from his pal, never one himself to let such things infringe on his peace of mind.

"Your *oasis*," said Fern. "It's not like he's going to be following you around the course. Would you be able to pick the previous owner out of a crowd?"

"I know he won't be. I won't be playing there anymore."

"Don't be such a pussy, Michael. If he even gives a shit about you, getting back at you over some deal he lost, whatever. You'd be playing right into his hand, letting him take this away from you."

Michael stared into his beer.

"You came all the way into the city to talk about this shit?" asked Fern. "You gonna visit your stepdaughter while you're down here?" asked Fern. "She lives down the street, no?"

"I couldn't get hold of her, and I'm bound by a no pop-in rule. I just wanted to get away for the day."

"Just as well. Who wants to walk in on their twenty-some-year-old daughter?"

Michael went to the men's room. He returned to find Fern smiling through his goatee at a young waitress. Fern rested his elbow on the railing, giving the waitress a close-up view of his bicep while running his hand through his bushy brown hair. From experience, Michael knew that she could be telling him that she just learned how to count to ten, and Fern would hang on every word that came out of her mouth.

"Shannon, bring my friend Michael here another Guinness," said Fern, and both men watched her slink across the patio until she disappeared inside the bar.

"How is that cushy corporate security gig anyway?" asked Michael.

"I've just moved on to something else."

"What kind of trouble are you getting into now?"

"I hooked up with this private investigation firm downtown," said Fern. "More cabbage than the corporate job, and *that* money made my cop salary look like chump change."

"Got a dingy old office with bad lighting, like those private dicks in the movies? Do you carry a gun?"

"This job is more brains than bullets. I haven't taken the safety off my revolver."

Michael mentioned his plans to look a little harder at Emily's fall from the Niagara Escarpment, and his suspicion of a connection to the other murders.

Fern snickered. "You wanna do a little investigating yourself? Maybe you should come and work for us."

"Why don't you come and work for me?" asked Michael.

"The police called it an accident."

"They were incompetent, and they didn't care."

Fern slammed his palm on the table. "No... they... weren't. I know a lot of cops out your way. They have good reps, get the job done." The serenity remained in his voice, contrasting those eyes of Fern's that said not to fuck with him or his mood could suddenly change for the worse.

"You wouldn't know it, the way they acted with me," said Michael.

"Did you want them to lie down and see how much shit you could pile on them? You took a swing at one of them, a police officer for chrissakes. You should be in jail. He felt sorry for you. The way *they* acted? Christ."

"It seemed like the left hand didn't know what the right one was doing, which was probably chokin' the chicken."

"Any regional outfit has issues communicating with the city cops. Bureaucracy and all that shit."

Shannon set down Michael's Guinness.

"Emily was a great lady, but shit happens," said Fern. "You go on a jag. Three months, four months, the pills, the booze. You in *the facility*. What is it you said again? The cops are lazy doughnut-eating frauds, couldn't care less if your wife was murdered."

Michael cringed as he recalled barging through the doors of the police headquarters, unshaven and likely hungover, the same police station in which he'd been interrogated by Speagle and Alberts. He had demanded an update on the investigation of his wife's death, implying not enough was being done to find her killer, insulting the collective ability and integrity of Halton's finest.

"Oh yeah, man," said Fern. "I still have my sources on The Job. You call them Barney Fife, Keystone Cops, shit like that. Then you toss Northcott's name out there as a suspected murderer."

"Okay, so I—"

"And now Michael the schoolteacher, with more money than sense, is going to solve everything and make up for all the times he wasn't the greatest husband in the world." Fern took a drink and added, "Well join the fucking club."

Michael had long drink of beer, trying to ease the sting of Fern's assessment.

"How am I doing?" asked Fern.

Michael didn't recognize the woman in the orange ball cap and sunglasses until she was a few feet from her husband, who had his back to her. Karin Da Silva threw a manila envelope in front of Fern and said, "Will you grow up and sign the goddam papers?"

She ignored Michael and stormed off in the direction she came from. Fern called out, "Got a pen?" and raised an open hand over his head. She walked back and handed him a pen. He slid out the papers, signed them, returned them to the envelope, and waved it over his head, not once turning to look at her. She grabbed the envelope and walked away.

Michael had picked out the word "Divorce" in the heading of the document.

"Holy shit, Fern. I had no idea. And here I am—"

"Forget it, man. It's all for the best."

They drank in silence for a few minutes.

Michael thought Karin had likely just had enough. Emily

once asked Michael after a night out with the Da Silvas if Fern had "an eye for the ladies", calling him "too charming for his own good". Emily probably saw this coming, as she tended to see things in people, both good and bad, that others did not.

"I have some unanswered questions," said Michael, sensing a meekness in his own voice. "If nothing comes of it, I plan to move on, satisfied I've done what I could."

"Northcott looked at you in a funny way at the funeral. Is that it?"

"The wake."

"Whatever. Northcott *looked* at you. You can't believe Emily would just fall. Yadda fuckin' yadda." Fern sat back in his chair and shook his head. "Mike, that is the kind of chaff cops have to cut through to get to the important stuff, the stuff that might actually tell them something."

"I think I'll just head out," said Michael, rising from the table. The second beer under a hot sun had been a mistake.

"Suit yourself," said Fern, who sipped his drink and turned away to wink at a pair of thirty-something women in "Beaches Jazz Festival" T-shirts strolling by on Queen Street.

After spending more than two hours at his desk, Michael had managed to contact all members from the Pickett's Farm outing but one. He had learned nothing new.

On his third attempt with the final name on the list, he reached Mickey McIvor, the retired septuagenarian with the knee replacements.

"Mr. McIvor, may I ask you about your trip to Pickett's Farm with my wife?" asked Michael.

"Weren't no farm," said McIvor.

"I'd have to agree. Do you recall anything unusual about the morning my wife died?"

"Well, her dyin' was kinda unusual."

Michael winced.

"She did waste a lotta words telling us not to get too close to the edge of the cliff, like we were a buncha damn fools," said McIvor, "and then down she went."

"Anything specific that maybe didn't seem quite right to you?" asked Michael.

"Not right how?"

This wasn't going to be easy.

"Did anyone behave in a way that seemed odd to you?"

"The whole damned thing seemed odd to me."

Michael wasn't going to get much more from old Mickey. He took one last shot. He summarized Jenine Huntley's version of what had happened, thinking he might tweak something in McIvor's memory.

"Now wait a second," said McIvor, just as Michael had given up on him. "You mentioned your wife takin' a look at a piece of paper before goin' off on her own."

"Yes?"

"That's right. She did. And she was annoyed."

"Excuse me?"

"She looked at the paper, read some kind of note it looked like. Got this pissed off look, shoved it back in her pocket, thought about it for a second, and then off she went."

CHAPTER 12

Michael awoke to the sound of his doorbell. A matronly but cheerful volunteer from the local women's shelter was there to pick up the clothes that Sophie had apparently offered to donate.

He found four cardboard boxes marked "SHELTER" stacked in the corner of a seldom used sitting room. After a random check, he recognized much of the clothing as Emily's. He pulled out a ratty brown sweater she wore almost exclusively in the downstairs rec room, when either the winter chill or the summer air conditioning had taken root. He smelled her and wilted. These moments still snuck up on him, hammering home once again that she was gone and not coming back. He wanted to scream at the old clothes and tell his wife that he was sorry he wasn't there when she needed him.

A few articles were set aside on a nearby table. Michael assumed that Sophie had second thoughts while loading up the boxes, and decided she didn't want to part with these items. They included a smart maroon suede blazer and a tattered pale-blue ski jacket that had kept Emily warm longer than Michael had.

He put the sweater on the table and helped the volunteer put the boxes in the back of a van.

Back inside, he picked up the blazer, but could only smell dry cleaning.

He found a five-dollar bill in the pocket of the ski jacket and smiled, recalling Emily's delight whenever she unearthed such a treasure.

He reached into the other pocket and found a hole in the lining. A bulge in the bottom of the jacket buckled in his grasp. Reaching back into the pocket and into the lining below, he squeezed the corner of the object and pulled it out through the lining hole.

A small blue notebook.

Emily had jotted three brief notations on the first page:

> visit farm house
> decision about The Golfer soon?
> confirm visit to farm

He leafed through the other pages. All were blank.

The Golfer? At times Michael's late wife had called *him* "The Golfer". What decision did she have to make, and was it about him?

And why would she make a note to confirm a visit to the farm *after* the note to remind her to visit it?

He told himself this was only so much doodling.

The doorbell rang again.

Danny started the playback of the recording, after telling Michael he would not believe what he was about to hear. It turned out he'd been correct.

"Let's get these off." A woman's voice through the crackling *interference.*

Shuffling, clanging, banging.

"They're clearing off the desk," said Danny.

"That's it. Suck it," said a man's voice. The voices were breathless, barely audible... grunts... moans... sex talk.

"Better than porn, don't you think?" said Danny.

"And why are we listening to it?" asked Michael.

The static grew louder, muffling the raunchy exchange.

"Oooh yeah... oh yeah. Grind it, baby. Fuck yeah, grind it."

"Grind it? There's too much static," said Eddie. "Did she say 'Grind it'?"

"Grind-fucking-it," said Danny.

Michael turned to Eddie. "You were in on this?"

Eddie shrugged, showing some red through his dark cheeks.

"*Grind* it. I got married too young."

"Didn't we all?" asked Danny.

The audio went to nothing but static for almost a minute, and then came back clearer than before. The main event had ended. Books were dropped onto a desk with a thud, a chair slid across a hardwood floor. A moment later a door opened and closed.

"So much for pillow talk," said Eddie.

Michael shook his head. "Should I know these people, and if I do, why am I listening to them bumpin' uglies?"

"Are you kidding me?" asked Danny. "That's your old pal Northcott, banging his girlfriend... some whore, whatever."

"I won't even ask where you got this stuff," said Michael, examining the recording equipment labelled "MegaEar". He set the device down and said, "Play it back again."

Danny obliged. The voices were still not recognizable to Michael.

"A buddy with the property management company told me he looked after the building where Northcott had his so-called office," said Danny. "I guess it looks more like Hef's grotto. A big couch, a bar. I thought it might be nice to get something on him for you, maybe talking about some shady deal or another. Who knew we'd get this?"

"And that's why you think that's Northcott?" asked Michael.

"It's his office," said Danny.

Michael's brow furrowed. "*His* office?"

"The one downtown, on Locust. You showed me it one time. And my buddy has seen Northcott coming and going."

Michael chuckled.

"What?" asked Danny.

"Gentlemen, I believe you have saved for posterity a sexual encounter between an unidentified yet eager young lady and Councilman Wayne Wojciechowkski."

Danny and Eddie lost their smiles and looked at each other in obvious disbelief.

"Who?" asked Danny.

"Wojciechowkski," said Michael.

"*Wo-juh-CHOW-ski?*"

"Close enough."

"Could you spell that if you had to?"

"Not likely."

"Whack Job Wojciechowkski?" asked Eddie. "The party animal who's always in the paper?"

"The one and the same," replied Michael.

Danny slid down in his chair. "He uses Northcott's office for shagging?"

"No," said Michael. "Based on this little sample of homemade porn, it seems that he uses his own office for that. It's his office. He took it over last year, after Northcott moved out."

"How do you know?" asked Eddie.

"I stopped in there when I went looking for Northcott, right after Emily died. Whack Job answered the door himself, said he just moved in."

"Oh well, we had some fun," said Danny.

"Are you kidding me?" yelped Eddie. "We spent a night sitting in a car so we could record a couple of strangers having sex. Who knows what laws we broke?"

"Whack Job," said Danny, sniggering. "*The Grinder.*"

Michael walked through a sunlit atrium on the main floor of the Halton County Arts Centre in downtown Burlington. He went past an overhead sign that read "Administration" and turned down a narrow hallway. He knocked on a door with a shingle reading "Ferguson Boone – Director", then complied with a sonorous invitation to go in.

The cramped room got an injection of warmth from the array of photographs that covered the wall opposite the doorway. The man behind the desk introduced himself as Director Boone.

If Ferguson Boone's office fell short of expectations, the man himself did not. Michael noticed a stark contrast between the man and his surroundings, thinking he dressed more like a Fortune 500 executive than the caretaker of a gathering spot for the local artsy-fartsy. But while his James Earl Jones intonation impressed even more in person than it had over the phone—no syllable uttered by Mr. Boone went unattended—Michael found it amusing to hear the rich baritone emanating from the wiry director.

Michael thanked Boone for agreeing to meet with him on short notice. He restated his interest in the planned expansion of the centre, which he had mentioned to Boone on the phone. He asked the director if fifty thousand dollars would make a tangible dent in their fundraising goal.

"Mr. Flanigan, that is an extraordinarily munificent gesture."

He had Boone's attention.

"My wife and I had discussed how we should share our good fortune with others," said Michael. "Helping out the local arts community was near the top of her list."

Mr. Boone nodded and smiled, as if he knew that to be true. "Please have a seat," he said, opening a palm toward the chair opposite him.

"Is it art centre or *arts* centre with an *s*?" asked Michael, who then took a seat.

Boone smiled and said, "Technically I suppose it's the latter, but it would seem that conventional discourse with regard to day-to-day dialogue is the singular reference. The two are indiscernible in normal speech, but I tend to favour the proper elocution."

"Well said," said Michael, who found nothing conventional about the director's elocution.

"Happy to clarify," said Boone.

Is that what you did?

"Emily and I didn't talk much about the work she did here," said Michael. "But I got the sense she was sort of a jack-of-all-trades."

Boone nodded. "She worked in the gift shop, helped us plan

events, did fundraising. She taught photography courses, as you know, and even filled the role of docent."

"What role?"

"She gave tours of the centre. She knew the background on virtually all of the pieces on display here. While Emily's passion was photography, she truly appreciated any masterful work of art."

A young woman in blue jeans and plain black T-shirt walked in without knocking. She set down a tray containing two takeout coffee cups with fixings on the side.

"Thank you, Lisa," said Boone, who watched her exit before continuing. Lisa filled her jeans well.

"What can you tell me about Vincent Fronda?" asked Michael when he had Boone's attention again. "I found his body behind my house about a week ago. You probably heard about it."

"It's been a topic of discussion at the centre," said Boone. "With all due respect to the deceased, Mr. Fronda was a less-than-exemplary member of our photography club, and also of the centre. I did not care for the man, but he paid his dues like everyone else, so..."

"What had Emily been working on?"

Boone took off his glasses and looked out his window at the centre parking lot, as if something out there would jog his memory.

"Not atypically, Emily had a few things on the go," said Boone. "I'd been in Europe for a few weeks, and had returned just days before she passed. She was wrapping up some last minute details on a forthcoming exhibition."

"An exhibition?"

"The Mentoring Project for New Painters. We ran it from late October through early December. It is an exhibition of new works, a project meant to be a significant transformative learning experience for..."

Michael's mind roamed as Boone droned art-speak. Had Emily mentioned the exhibition to him? What details had she been wrapping up?

"... the primary focus," continued Boone, "being on ideas and concepts for each artist. Some technical studio-oriented skills are incorporated as they relate to each artist's own concepts."

Boone took a breath and Michael jumped at the chance to end the sales pitch for an event that ended months before. "Emily's job was mainly to organize this exhibition?" he asked.

"She performed the majority of the preparatory functions," said Boone. "A volunteer... Ruth... Ruth... *Eisentraut* assisted her with any needed research for such projects."

"Did Emily work with her a lot?" asked Michael, assuming she was the same Ruth that Jenine Huntley had mentioned.

"They did. They were quite a contrasting duo."

"Contrasting how?"

"Ruth was shy, withdrawn. Plain, drab clothes, a bad haircut. Wouldn't look me in the eye when I'd see her. The poor woman was devastated by your wife's passing. Ruth didn't seem to mingle much with the other volunteers. She was usually glued to Emily's hip.

"Do you know if they spent time together away from work?"

"They shared a booth at the annual Arts & Crafts Show up in Milton in late September, an extracurricular activity unrelated to their work here at the centre."

"Milton," said Michael to himself. He had returned home late from the golf course the Sunday before Emily died, aware that she'd worked a show of some sort. But he'd forgotten the location, and didn't recall asking her about it.

"I recall Emily telling me afterward that it was not a very productive weekend," said Boone. "There's no predicting how sales will be at those things."

"What kind of research would they do for their projects?" asked Michael.

"Primarily wading through archives, either at the library or here at the centre, searching for potential candidates that fit the theme of an upcoming event. And of course there's that Internet," said Boone, doing a typing motion with sinewy black fingers as he said it.

"Would much research have been done for the Mentoring exhibition?"

"That particular event would have required minimal effort in that regard, given the theme. But..." He paused. "Huh."

"What?"

"When I returned from the Continent, a colleague mentioned in passing that Emily had spent time off-site that week carrying out some research. I didn't give it much thought at the time, but now I must admit that I don't know what research she would have had yet to do."

"Could it not have been for a future event?" asked Michael, who'd been away that week on a golfing excursion to the east coast. "Em was always trying to stay one step ahead."

"But the October exhibition for the Mentoring Project was to have been her last project. She handed in her notice the day I returned from my trip. Surely you knew."

The expression on Michael's face surely told Boone that he surely did not know why his wife had quit the job she loved.

"When did you last speak to Emily?" asked Michael.

"She phoned me the day before she died, asked if I could meet with her the following afternoon."

"Did she say what she wanted to talk to you about?"

"Not a hint. Emily did seem rather... agitated. She said she'd rather speak to me in person, but... we didn't get the chance."

Michael hadn't observed any signs of agitation in his wife. Could it have been related to her spat with Sophie? Emily said it blew over quickly, but was emphatic that he never mention it again.

"Did the exhibition go off well?" asked Michael.

"Eventually it was quite well received. But the exhibition was delayed a week because of the fire. We had to push back the kickoff to later in the month."

"The fire?" *Jacquie's house. Lotsa fires happening.*

Boone waved his hand. "We experienced a conflagration one evening while I was away. No one was hurt, but two works on loan from Bronte Creek Provincial Park were ruined. It was Emily who persuaded them to allow us to hang their paintings here, suggesting it would be good cross-marketing, get more people to visit the park. They charge twelve bucks to get in, you know."

Michael, amused to see Boone drop his airy guard, supposed arts centre directors were not well compensated.

"Were either Emily or Ruth working the night of the fire?" he asked.

"They helped extinguish it," said Boone. "They prevented the damage from spreading. We had closed for the evening, but neither had gone home yet. Thank God they were unscathed."

"When exactly was the fire?"

"September twenty-sixth. I got a call from my assistant during a one-day stopover in Brussels."

Michael had Boone clarify the sequence of events leading up to Emily's death.

The fire occurred a few days before Emily and Ruth had worked the Arts & Crafts Show in Milton. Emily had spent the week after the show finishing the prep work for the art exhibition and doing research for an unknown project. She died the following Saturday, on Thanksgiving weekend.

"Mr. Boone, you said Ruth was devastated by my wife's death."

"On the morning of the accident, I came upon Ruth in the rear gallery, holding a picture of Emily and her daughter."

"Sophie," said Michael.

"We had just received the horrible news," said Boone. "I asked Ruth if there was anything I could do, and then the tears started. She looked so pitiable sitting there, dark lines under her eyes, sobbing, inconsolable. She eventually ran out of the room, and never returned."

"Could I have that picture, the one Ruth was holding?"

"We forwarded all of Emily's personal items to you, Mr.

Flanigan. I assume Ruth must have taken the photograph with her... as a keepsake."

Michael stood up and went to the array of photos on the side wall. Boone appeared in most of them: the mayor with his arm around Ferguson Boone; Boone between two thirtyish blonds, an arm around each of them; and so on.

"Is Ruth in any of these pictures?" asked Michael.

Boone got up and stood next to Michael. "I don't think so," he said. He scanned the wall. "No, she's not in any of these."

Michael spotted Emily in a group picture. "When was this taken?" he asked, pointing his finger at the photograph.

"That is a staff photograph, taken last summer." said Boone.

"Was Ruth not working here then?"

"Yes, but she's not in this picture."

"Do you know why?"

Boone shook his head and said, "Frankly, I hadn't noticed that she was missing from the photo."

Shy, withdrawn, plain, thought Michael. She wouldn't have been missed by anyone, except by Emily.

Michael saw a familiar face in a snapshot from another black-tie event. The man is standing at a round table of eight or nine people, holding up a long-stemmed glass. Boone is sitting at the table, looking up at the man, smiling—smiling at J.P. Northcott.

"You know J.P. Northcott," said Michael, nodding toward the photograph.

Boone turned to the wall behind him, and smiled. "Another generous benefactor."

"Do you have an address or a phone number for Ruth?"

"She hadn't been here long. She said she was staying with friends until she found a place, and would provide details in due course. That day never came."

"You never spoke to her again?"

"After she left, I tried to reach her using a cell phone number she'd given us, but it was dead. Something tells me she moved away... back to Germany, perhaps?"

Michael stood up and thanked Boone for his time. He stopped at the door and turned to Boone. "Where would there be artwork in Bronte Creek Park?" he asked.

"Why, in the Spruce Lane Farmhouse."

As Michael descended toward the sound of the television in his basement, he recognized the voice of ex-Toronto Blue Jay Jesse Barfield telling the viewing audience that a wrist injury had messed up Vernon Wells's swing. Michael could empathize with the Toronto slugger.

Michael entered the rec room. The most avid Blue Jay fan he knew was stretched out on the couch, munching on potato chips and sucking back a Coke.

Clint insisted that it was not the presence of his mother's new boyfriend that led to his decision to visit Burlington. He added that, "Mom and the asshole were talking about going on a trip to Europe anyway." He wanted to hang out with his dad, to have some "quality time". *Yeah, sure.*

Both Michael's son and stepdaughter could work him, and he minded little. Elated to get an extended visit with his son, he also found guilty pleasure at being the parent of preference, if only temporarily.

They chatted for a few minutes before Clint turned his full attention to the baseball game.

Michael sat in the chair next to the couch. He leaned back onto the headrest and closed his eyes.

Visit farm house. Confirm visit to farm.

The farm was Pickett's Farm, and the farm *house* sat in Bronte Creek Provincial Park. The mystery had been solved.

But the other entry in Emily's notebook, on the pending decision about "The Golfer", intrigued Michael much more.

CHAPTER 13

Michael's chest tightened when he turned into the entrance at Foster Glen. He hadn't crossed paths with Northcott in several months.

His anxiety eased somewhat at seeing Danny chipping onto the practice green. Northcott was nowhere in sight.

His morning muffin and coffee kicked in, and he had a small window of time before he had to deal with it. The mild colitis that had plagued him on and off for years crept up on him in recent days. Stressful times would awaken the sleeping monster, often at the least opportune moment. He felt for those deeper into the throes of the disease, as his infrequent bouts brought on abdominal pain and desperate flights to the nearest restroom.

He ducked down the back stairs of the clubhouse, past a string of offices to a private bathroom well off the beaten path.

He settled in and leafed through a months-old Golf Digest, and tried to ignore the burning below. He stopped at an interview with Jack Nicholson, of all people, who said to his interviewer, "Well, I ain't king of the links, but it's never too late to improve." *Right on, Jack.*

Michael heard voices from the next room, which he thought was Randy Goodman's office, based on his knowledge of the layout. The dialogue seemed aggressive, between a man and woman.

The man grunted, several times. Was he eavesdropping on another office quickie, this time live versus Memorex? A picture of Randy Goodman mounting Jessie Hargreaves over his desk flashed in his head, which he shook to dislodge the visual.

The woman squealed... pleasure? She cried out again, and Michael had a feeling she could be in trouble. No, not his boy Randy.

"Fuck you," said the woman. The man grunted.

Does she need help?

Michael finished his business, opened the door, and stopped, listened.

Nothing.

He exited the bathroom. He crept toward the closed office, looked around, and put his ear to the door. Still nothing. He knocked on the door and opened it.

He stepped inside and stopped in his tracks. A wild-eyed woman sat sideways in a charcoal leather loveseat in the corner of the small office, her legs swung over one end.

She wore a golf glove on her left hand and a navy visor over a wild mop of hair, auburn he'd call it, and nothing else, nothing but a lascivious grin. Blood trickled from the corner of her mouth, which she ignored as it ran down her chin onto an impressive breast.

She was alone.

She giggled, kind of a mad chortle.

She didn't move, making no attempt to cover herself with the clothes scattered across on the floor.

He caught himself staring.

"You like my titties, do you?" she said. Blood seeped into her mouth as she said it, and she spat it on the floor.

"Are you okay?" he asked, sensing he'd just heard some consensual rough play while in the john.

She cupped her breasts and held them up, though they didn't need much help, and pointed them at him.

"Would you like to suck on them?" she said, hanging an open-mouthed, glassy glare on him.

"Miss, you're bleeding quite ba—"

"Wanna fuck 'em?" she said, and squeezed her breasts together.

"You should get that looked at, miss," was all he said. He darted from the office, to rabid laughter from the other side of the door.

He had walked into one man's fantasy, a no-strings romp with an oversexed and voluptuous stranger, and had taken a pass.

It wasn't just the blood. She seemed... *disturbed*.

He looked around the crowded clubhouse when he reached the main floor, and felt like he was re-entering reality after a brief visit to some kinky alternate dimension.

He laughed a nervous laugh and said, "What a kooky club."

Michael joined his friends on the driving range. Danny stepped back to greet Michael while Eddie hit.

"Looks like Mr. GQ is off his game a bit today," whispered Danny.

"No kidding," said Michael. Eddie was unshaven, had his shirttail half tucked in, and his hand shook as he reached for another ball.

"Where's our fourth, Tiger?" said Michael, using the nickname Danny had placed on Eddie years before because of the racial mix he shared with Tiger Woods. "There's no symphony in the afternoon, is there?"

"Nirenberg? Had to work," said Eddie.

"It's his shop."

"He's backed up."

As Eddie teed up another ball, Danny said, "His eyes are bloodshot, too. He's been on a bender."

Michael tried to recall when he'd seen Eddie Kan have more than two or three beers.

"And you know Asians can't drink," said Danny.

"Pardon me?" said Michael.

"Everyone knows that."

As he rotated through his clubs, Michael couldn't get the encounter in the downstairs office out of his head. He wondered how often Randy Goodman had availed himself of the hot little nympho's services—and if his old friend was responsible for her bloody mouth. She seemed happy enough. He would assume it was an accident for the time being, the collateral damage resulting from a pre-lesson warm-up with a willing student.

"Either of you guys seen the pro today?" Michael asked as he checked his alignment over the ball.

Danny stepped back from his ball. "Goodman? I asked for him at the pro shop," said Danny. "The little broad behind the counter said he was sick or something, didn't make it in today."

"Are you sure about that?"

"Am I sure about what? That she said that, or are you asking did I search the grounds to make sure she wasn't lying to me, that Goodman wasn't hiding behind some bush trying to get out of working today?"

Michael sighed and hit another ball, slicing it badly. He teed up another, and stopped in the middle of his backswing when he heard a familiar voice coming from behind.

A curious mix of golfers occupied the three end spots on the driving range: Burlington Mayor Benny Franoz, Detective John Alberts, and J.P. Northcott.

The politician and the cop hit balls while Northcott dressed down a gaunt, pasty man with an orange hairpiece on the next tee block.

Alberts and Northcott?

"I don't know if I can do this," said Michael.

"Do what?" said Danny.

"Come out here and play on this guy's course, like nothing happened."

"I know what you're saying, Michael," said Eddie, "but they say you should keep your friends close and your enemies closer."

"And you tell me I watch *The Sopranos* too much," said Michael.

"That's from *The Art of War*," said Eddie, "spoken by a Chinese general and military strategist whose name escapes me at the moment."

"I'd like to take that iron out of Northcott's hand and shove it down his throat," said Michael.

"That would help a lot," said Danny.

"He's right," said Eddie. "Chill. Be civil with the guy. If you think he's guilty of any wrongdoing, why would you let on that you suspect him?"

"You're gonna get your chance sooner than you thought," said Danny.

Michael turned to see J.P. Northcott walking toward him.

"Hi, fellas," said Northcott, like they were old friends. "I am so glad to see that you could join us today." He shook hands with each of them, saving Michael for last.

Northcott extended his hand. Michael hesitated, but then took it, for Emily.

"I'm happy to have you as a member at my golf club, Michael," said Northcott. "And truly grateful that your pop's company so graciously offered to sponsor a hole at our little tourney. No better cause than the women's shelter."

Michael stood stone-faced, trying to hide his contempt at this phony fuck. He wondered at that moment how many women Northcott had abused since cutting his teeth behind St. Mary's School as a teenager. He forced a smile.

"Someone break the club rules?" asked Michael, eyeing the chastised man with the bad rug.

"Not the time or place to be making an inappropriate political comment to our mayor." Northcott shook his head and looked over at the man, as if he were a misbehaving child. "But I fear I may have been a little hard on the fellow."

"Looks like a good day for a game," said Danny.

"It's actually supposed to rain," said Northcott, "but what are you gonna do?"

Michael looked up at the clear blue sky, and then back at Northcott. "I guess weather is like people. You never know what darkness lurks behind the sunny façade."

Danny snickered. Eddie grimaced.

"Well, have a good game, Flanigan," said Northcott, his smile intact. "And let me know if there's anything I can do for you and your friends, today or anytime. Hey, maybe we can have a game sometime."

The balls on this guy. "I'm sure we'll be seeing each other," said Michael.

Northcott turned and walked away.

"Your civility act needs a bit of work," said Eddie.

"I still have to look in the mirror," said Michael. "*Have a game sometime.* Northcott has no respect for the game."

"What the hell does that mean, anyway?" asked Danny.

"It means he has no respect for himself," said Eddie.

They went off as a threesome. Eddie and Michael got on a cart and Danny drove solo on another. The marshal, a bright new hire named Rahim whom Michael felt was employed beneath his capabilities, led them to the fourteenth tee. The "shotgun start" would allow each group to tee off at the same time from a different hole. They passed the tenth hole, where Northcott's group waited to tee off.

Michael could not get over seeing Alberts with Northcott. He thought back to the interrogation at the police station, and the detective's admonishment of Michael regarding his accusations toward Alberts's "leading citizen" golf buddy.

Northcott and Mayor Franoz both waved, displaying teeth much too white to have been maintained naturally after four plus decades. Michael thought Northcott showed signs of Botoxed eyes as well. Alberts tipped his cap to Michael, even flashed a smile. Michael did not return it, more from shock than surliness. *Now he's my buddy.*

A curvy woman, her hair tucked under her golf cap, stretched on the tee block, her back to the passing foursome.

As they drove alongside the fairway on number ten en route to fourteen, Michael looked back to the tee block. The female in the Northcott group didn't wait for the sound of the starting horn and teed off early, revealing a hitch in her swing reminiscent of

PGA veteran Jim Furyk. Her ball cut the fairway in two and received a generous bounce. She had the hitch working for her, too.

After they each parred the fourteenth hole—Danny commented that *he* might start hitting the booze after Eddie dropped a twenty-foot putt—the skies burst. They took refuge under nearby trees.

A man displaying a chiselled form through a drenched Foster Glen golf shirt pulled up a few feet beside him. Michael assumed he was a course marshal.

"Gentlemen, we've been notified that there's lightning in the area," he said. "You should hear the horn soon. We're asking that all golfers leave the course."

The man, with much of his head wrapped with the hood on his rain jacket, looked familiar to Michael.

"Do we know each other?" asked Michael.

A look of recognition set in on the man. He stuck out his hand. "It's Michael, right? Michael Flanigan?" Michael shook his hand and nodded. "Frank Toner," said the man, flashing a bright smile through the rain. "We met at Weber's, up in cottage country."

Bobby George's friend. Emily used to observe that some people would show off wide, toothy smiles, but "their eyes aren't smiling". Michael hadn't noticed it outside the Muskoka burger joint, but Frank Toner had one of those smiles.

Michael and Danny found an empty table, while Eddie hit the clubhouse bar.

"Did you hear what happened to Artie Smitters with his job here at the club?" asked Michael. "When I came back from my wrist injury, it didn't hit me that he wasn't around anymore."

"Why would you notice?" asked Danny. "It didn't affect you."

"What is that supposed to—"

The sound of breaking glass from the other side of the room interrupted them. A waitress, embarrassed and apologetic, had dropped a tray of drinks. A second woman put her hand on the woman's shoulder and said something, then crouched to the floor to help the young server gather the larger pieces of glass.

Michael's pulse accelerated. The second woman was Jessie Hargreaves, golf student, her hair wet and golf shirt clinging.

"Hig, that's her... from the driving range," said Michael.

"*Her?* Why the hell are you still sitting here?"

"Playing tournaments already?" asked Michael when he reached Jessie's table.

She turned to face him. "Why, Mr. Flanigan. How nice to see you."

She remembered my name.

"I see you also got caught in the rain, Jessie," said Michael, thinking she looked wetter and better up close.

"Yes, and just as I was beginning to dry off a bit, I had to make a dash out to my car. So here I sit, still dripping."

He liked the sound of that, wasn't sure why.

"My friends here from Royal LePage Real Estate had a last minute no-show and asked me to join them," she said. "Randy was sick and my lesson got cancelled, so I said, 'Why not?'"

She introduced Michael to the realtor on her right, who soon rejoined another conversation.

Michael said, "Jessie, I was wondering... I know you don't really know me, but, I was wondering..."

"I would love to go out with you, Michael," she said, and threw the sweetest smile at him he'd ever seen.

When Michael returned to his table with her card in his hand and an ear-to-ear grin, it soon became apparent that his friends had witnessed his exchange with Jessie Hargreaves.

"Well?" asked Eddie.

Michael smiled and flashed her business card.

Danny hooted, and Eddie offered a high-five. Michael put his head in his hand, and turned enough to peek through his fingers at Jessie's table, praying that her attention was elsewhere.

She sat where he'd left her, trying to muffle her laughter with the palm of her hand, just like she had that day on the driving range.

Eddie finished his beer and went for another round.

"A little hair of the dog, Tiger?" asked Danny when Eddie returned.

Eddie had a sip of his beer. "Come again?"

"You didn't seem quite yourself when you got here today," said Michael.

"I had a late night," said Eddie.

"Since when do you have late nights?" asked Danny.

Eddie put down his beer. "I know what you're saying. Yesterday I lost two of my biggest clients. The same day. Huge clients."

"What happened?" asked Michael.

"That's just it. I don't know. One sent me an email, for God's sake, not giving me any reason for leaving. The other left me a phone message, sounded... weird. Also no reason."

"So you went out and got wasted?" asked Danny.

"I opened some wine with dinner. I didn't have much to drink, but it doesn't take much with me."

Danny shot a grin at Michael.

"Eddie, you're a great consultant, for chrissakes," said Michael. "You've built up a good business. You always seem to be getting new clients... new *files*."

"It just seems too coincidental," said Eddie. "I knew both of these guys pretty well, the decision makers. We got along. I've done good work for them, never a problem, and they've acknowledged that many times over. And they know each other."

"What do you think is going on?" asked Danny.

"Someone told these guys something about me," said Eddie,

before emptying his glass. "Gotta hit the can."

Northcott and his playing partners were being seated at a table by the window marked "Reserved". Michael knew Northcott would eat this up, the grand entrance to join the filthy masses of the little empire he now ruled. But that wasn't what held Michael's attention as he sat open-mouthed, staring at a woman whose chair was being pushed in by Northcott.

The woman with the Furyk-like swing took off her golf cap, and dark reddish curls fell down her back. As she shifted sideways to slide into the chair, Michael thought, *I know those legs.* The last time he saw them, saw her, she was one floor down, bleeding from the mouth and offering him a tit-fuck. She showed no sign of injury, and looked stunning from a distance.

Was it Northcott who was with her in the basement? Did he hit her? Did she like it?

"Lottie Denison is her name," said Danny. "I don't think she's a friend of Mrs. Northcott."

Northcott delivered a tray of beer to the table of the guy in the toupee from the driving range, and patted the man on the back.

Michael grunted. "What do you make of that?"

"Maybe he's trying to be better," said Eddie, as Northcott headed their way.

"Sorry we couldn't scare up a nicer day for this, boys," said Northcott, leaning with one hand on the back of Eddie's chair and the other on Danny's. "We're still gonna feed you, and there's some nice door prizes to be had," said Northcott.

"Thanks but we have to get going," said Michael.

"But there's prizes," said Danny.

Michael glared at him.

"Mr. Higgins, I understand you're working on a novel," said Northcott. "Very commendable indeed."

"How did you know that?" asked Danny.

"You know William Diehl was in his fifties when he had his first novel published," said Northcott. "I know some people in the publishing business. Let me know if you'd like me to put in a good word for you when you're ready to get your masterpiece out there."

"Sure," said Danny, beaming. "Thanks, J.P."

"My pleasure, Dan. And I hope to see you boys out for the Foster Glen Classic next week. We should have a good field this year."

Northcott glanced at Michael, slapped Danny on the back, and went back to his table.

"Hey, he was trying to be nice," said Danny as he sat on his rear bumper, pulling off a golf shoe. The rain had let up, but the course was in no shape for the tourney to continue.

"Wake up," said Michael.

"He just bought the mouthy dude with the scary hairpiece a round of drinks."

"Where will you be taking your date for dinner?" asked Eddie, obviously changing the subject to lighten things up. "A client's brother just opened a Japanese place in Oakville." He pulled a card out of his wallet and handed it to Michael.

"Is it like a sports bar?" asked Michael, inspecting the card.

"No, but he's a huge sports fan. The food is great, and the atmosphere is good for a first date. Low lights, relaxed."

"Okay," said Michael, looking at the card. "Chico's Maki it is."

CHAPTER 14

"Sure I remember that name," said Sophie. "Ruth worked with Mom at the arts centre. And she was with her at that Milton show where Mom sold all the prints."

"How much did she sell?"

"I don't know. A coupla grand worth."

"Did you know Ruth?" asked Michael, wondering why Boone thought Emily got shut out in Milton.

"I wasn't at the arts centre that often."

Danny had said the same thing when Michael asked him the question.

"Mom mainly saw her at the centre, I think," said Sophie. "I remember her telling me a little about her, how shy she was, but that she was really smart and, you know... nice. You know Mom, always looking after the strays."

"I understand Ruth was really shaken up when your mom died. They found her crying, holding a picture of you and your mom."

"Must be the one Mom kept at her desk."

"Ruth wouldn't be into something like that class your mom took to Pickett's Farm?"

Sophie shrugged. "There would have been no reason for her to go."

"Soph, did you know your mom had quit her job down at the arts centre?"

"She did?"

Michael phoned Ferguson Boone.

"Why didn't you think Emily did well up in Milton?" asked Michael.

"From her reticence," said the arts centre director.

"Sorry?"

"When I inquired about the show, she just said, 'Don't ask'. So I didn't."

Michael parked his car in front of Jessie's bungalow on Hurd Avenue in downtown Burlington a few minutes before noon. Her home was simply yet impeccably landscaped, with two colourful rock gardens sitting kitty-corner on a plush green lawn. A deep blue Mercedes convertible sat in the driveway. He reckoned personal trainers must do alright.

Jessie greeted him in a simple red summer dress, which she made elegant. She wore little makeup, a natural beauty if ever he saw one. She fidgeted nervously as she gathered her bag and sunglasses, and he liked that, too.

Michael was glad that he'd decided on a lakeside restaurant within walking distance of Jessie's home. The stroll to the lake was free and easy, comfortable. He could try the Japanese place Eddie suggested another time—with any luck, in the same company.

They got a table for two at Spencer's, on the railing of a patio overlooking Lake Ontario. A warm breeze played with Jessie's ebony locks. She pulled gently at the corner of her eyebrow, a nervous habit that Michael found cute.

They both ordered Caesar salads. The waitress brought a large bottle of Evian and poured them each a glass.

"So what brought you to Burlington, Jessie?" asked Michael.

"Just look around, Michael. It's a lovely city, with a gorgeous little downtown. Safe, clean, great restaurants like this one."

Safe. He used to think so.

"Are you from here?" she asked.

"We moved here when I was in high school for my father's work. He was a real estate developer. Made a killing."

Jessie took a sip of water and said, "I did some checking up on you, Mr. Flanigan."

"Did you now?"

"Informally. You know, asking around the golf club, a bit of googling."

"I guess you couldn't have learned anything too bad."

"Hmm, let's see," she said. "Nice chap. Likes to party a bit. Was a dedicated, well-liked schoolteacher." She dropped her eyes to the table, then raised them back to him. "I also learned that you lost your wife last year."

He nodded.

"I'm sorry, Michael. I didn't make the connection at first. I do remember reading about it. A horrible fall, wasn't it?"

"It was."

She reached over and placed her hand on his. She said it again. "I'm sorry."

Jessie slid her hand back to join the one in her lap. "Did you meet your wife on the golf course?"

"This is a first for me."

Jessie smiled.

"I met Emily and her daughter Sophie in the park one day," said Michael. "They had a booth set up at an art show. When Emily was quite young, she had gotten herself pregnant with Sophie, who is now my stepdaughter. Em married her boyfriend, Bobby George, three weeks before her nineteenth birthday," said Michael. "A 'shotgun wedding' she called it, and then would always say, 'and I shoulda shot him with it.'"

Jessie laughed. "I like her already."

"Emily left him when she was twenty-four, the final straw being his announcement *on her birthday* that he preferred the company of men. I met her less than a year after her divorce, and married her six months later."

"Is the ex around?"

"In a manner of speaking. Sophie's twenty-two... she doesn't see him much."

"They have issues."

"She blows hot and cold. She's figured out his act now that she's older, but..."

"But he's still her father."

Michael nodded. "Sophie and I have had our moments, too, but things are pretty good with us. She comes and goes as she pleases... between our home here and her apartment in Toronto."

"The best of both worlds."

The waitress slipped their salads in front of them.

"Oh yes," said Jessie. "There is one other good thing I learned about you."

"What's that?"

"You've got lots of money," she said, with no trace of a smile.

Michael waited for the punch line. None came. "I beg your pardon?" he said.

Her eyes opened wide and she laughed into her palm, spraying part of a mouthful of water between her fingertips.

"That must have sounded dreadful," she said. "What I meant to say was I am happy to know you have money, because it means you would likely have no inclination to go after mine. Forgive me, but a girl can't be too careful."

"You have money?"

"I don't need to work."

"Does this mean you're paying for lunch?"

"Sorry, fella. You asked me. But I promise to treat next time."

"But you do work. Randy tells me you're a personal trainer," said Michael, the reference to "next time" not lost on him.

"And life coach."

"You enjoy whipping people into shape?"

She smiled. "After I *whip them into shape,* I like to think that, after they've attained their physical goals, they can move on, spend more time looking into their own eyes and less time checking out their bods. They can see who they really are, become the people they want to be... find their own peace."

"Have you found this... *peace*?"

"A work in progress," she said. "But I think I'm in a good

place."

Their waitress brought him a coffee, a green tea for her. They sat back and watched the sailboats glide across the lake.

"So tell me about this partying," she said, and at that they set off on a two-hour conversation of discovery.

Michael liked what he unearthed, someone kind and intelligent, with a self-deprecating sense of humour. He felt like he was coming back to life on that restaurant patio. Jessie didn't *act* beautiful or well-to-do or smarter-than-you, but still had an appealing quiet confidence, a comfort in her own skin. Above all else, he wanted her desperately, each throaty laugh elevating the hot sensation running from his chest to his groin.

"*Who's* allergic to *poultry*?" asked Jessie.

Michael sat back and spread his arms wide. "Michael Flanigan, walking freak show. I've got a few allergies, the usual stuff, but that one reigns supreme. No KFC for me. I could be gone like *that*," he said, snapping his fingers. "Anaphylactic shock. Almost bought the farm once or twice."

"You are joking?"

"I try to travel with my EpiPen. One shot in the thigh, and I'm good to go."

"Have you got it with you now, this Epi-thing?"

"Um... no."

She smiled at him, let it hang there.

"How did you end up going to school in North Dakota?" she asked.

"I was a three-sport guy. Baseball, hockey, golf. Baseball got me into the school, but I thought I had my best chance at golf."

"Best chance at playing professionally?"

"That was my dream, but..."

"I noticed a scar on your wrist. Was that the culprit?"

Michael laughed. "I wish I could blame it on that, but I've only had this scar since early last year."

Michael told her about Clint. Jessie ran through a brief recap of a failed marriage that led her to the door of a women's shelter.

He told her his father had funded the local shelter. She knew of it, and had made plans to volunteer her time there.

"I suppose this is the moment where I could tell you of the tragic abuse I suffered, but that wouldn't be genuine, given all the poor women and children who have been through real hell," she said. "I got out before I really got hurt. No major scars to show for it, I'm quite happy to say. He wasn't the type to hunt me down, like so many of them are. The wanker moved on to some younger tart."

She did not elaborate further, other than to say he had more money than class. She was "chuffed to bits" with a divorce settlement that left her quite comfortable, as her abusive ex had to pay for his bad behaviour for the first time in his life.

Jessie returned from the ladies' room and didn't sit down.

"Are you going to walk me home, Mr. Flanigan," she said, "or shall I hail a taxicab?"

They walked back to Jessie's, three hours after they'd left. The day had grown warm, sweltering.

"Could I interest you in a glass of lemonade?" she asked, curling up her bottom lip as if to suggest "and whatever else we think of".

"I'd love to Jessie," he said. "But I really have to get going."

He couldn't tell if the look on her face was shock, hurt, or both.

He cupped his hands around her face, and kissed her, long and soft. She smelled good, tasted good. He pulled back and slid his hands down to her shoulders.

"I'll call you," he said. "Soon."

"You'd better."

Rita was still in purple silk pajamas when Michael arrived at her bungalow in Kilbride, a few miles north of Burlington. It was after three thirty in the afternoon. The country fresh smell that usually greeted him when he walked through her door was replaced by what his grandmother would have called "the stench of a beer parlour". Two dirty wine glasses and an empty six-pack of Dos Equis sat on her kitchen counter.

"This coulda been my place on many a Saturday morning," said Michael. "Hell, most mornings for a while there."

Rita dragged on her cigarette. "I'm seeing someone who likes a drink," she said, flicking an ash into an old brown glass ashtray with "LABATT'S BLUE" engraved on the side.

"By all means, smoke 'em if you got 'em."

"Don't push it," she said.

"Am I gonna meet this one?" he asked.

"You all of a sudden interested in my sex life?"

"I just had a date myself."

"Congratulations."

"Someone I met at the club."

"Something you wanna to tell me?"

"I just don't know how I feel about it."

"How you feel about *her*."

"She's smart, funny, kind. Very attractive. A British girl."

"Sounds awful. There a problem?"

He told her about rejecting Jessie's post-lunch invite.

"So what stopped you?"

"Maybe I'm having trouble moving on."

Rita shook her head. "The fish keep jumping in your net, but you won't fix the goddam hole in it." She then mumbled something to herself. He heard a "for fuck sake" in there somewhere.

"What's that mean?" he said.

She grabbed something off the counter. "Here's your tickets," she said, handing him an envelope with "BLUE JAYS" hand printed on the front.

"I just feel like it might be a little soon," he said.

"Michael, you told me yourself that you've started to figure out you really didn't know a lot of what was going on in the head of your so-called soul mate."

"Emily?"

Rita's bulging eyes said, "Who else would I be talking about?"

"Wow," he said softly.

"Get on with your life."

"I'm trying."

"Are you now? You're a good man, Michael. Lose the guilt. It's a wasted emotion."

"Guilt?"

"I'm not just talking about Emily. Think about it. When the father you could never please leaves you a fortune, not only can you not enjoy the money, you can't give it away fast enough. It's like you're trying to give it back."

"Pardon me?"

"That king's ransom you keep in your safe at home for anyone you feel needs it worse than you—which means about ninety-nine percent of the population. And you give it to them in cash, for chrissakes. What's that all about? How much did you give away this week?"

"Not a cent for weeks."

Rita got up and walked toward the front door. He followed and they stepped out onto the veranda.

"Thanks, I think," he said. Her stiff hug confused him.

"Why don't you pay another visit to Dr. Gordon? She really was helping you," she said. "It was tangible. I'd hate to see you spinning your wheels indefinitely. How long do you think your little crumpet is going to put up with you carrying around all this baggage?"

As he started to walk away, she called out to him.

"One more thing," she said, "for the next time you get the urge to drop by out of the blue to ask my permission to boink another... your latest fling. The therapist is out."

She slammed the door behind her.

–

Michael called Jessie, who said she "would love to go to a baseball match".

He then called Dr. Brenda Gordon, the psychiatrist he and Emily had gone to for counselling, and made an appointment.

Michael got out of his car in front of the exhibition building at Heritage Park in the nearby town of Milton. Ferguson Boone had given Michael the phone number for Mary Jo Kelsey, an event coordinator who had a professional relationship with Boone and the Halton County Arts Centre.

An elderly gentleman in overalls pointed out Mrs. Kelsey, who was sitting alone on the bottom step of a long stairway that led to the loft level above. With natural blond wood throughout, the building had a quaintly attractive and countrified appeal to it.

A few people were setting up tables in a sectioned-off portion of the main floor, and a couple more were doing the same upstairs. Michael guessed a wedding reception would soon be underway.

Mrs. Kelsey looked up from a binder in her lap as he approached. As earthy as the surroundings, the denim-clad woman looked to be in her late fifties.

Michael asked her about the Arts & Crafts Show the previous September.

"Oh sure," said Mrs. Kelsey. "I remember that pair. Like two peas in a pod on Friday and they weren't speakin' by Sunday, all o' that sandwiched around a pretty heated scrap on Saturday afternoon."

"Did you happen to hear what they were arguing about?" asked Michael.

"I didn't, but Iva Clifford from Lowville was set up right next to them, sellin' those knitted sweaters o' hers, hand over fist. Iva got herself an earful, the two of 'em fightin' and carryin' on over some *painting*. And the language," said Mrs. Kelsey. "All due respect."

Michael waved off any concern of offending, amused that Mrs. Kelsey's dropped virtually every "g", yet kept it while over enunciating "*pain-ting*".

"If you know Iva, she made out like she was so offended by all the profanity," she said. "But you could just tell she loved passin' on her account of the conversation, *word for word*, if you know what I mean. Your wife seemed a little agitated right from the get-go, you ask me."

Agitated. The same word Boone had used to describe Emily's state of mind.

"Do you know which painting they were arguing about?" asked Michael, wondering if the piece had a history that included passing through a provincial park and ending up in a fire.

"That's what was so weird about it all. I don't think either o' them were sellin' paintings that weekend. Iva just said that what's-er-name... Ruth. Ruth pointed her finger at your wife, and said, 'Who gives a damn? It's an effin painting.'"

CHAPTER 15

Hearing about the clash between Emily and Ruth Eisentraut both troubled and intrigued Michael. He sensed a path forming in front of him.

What effin painting?

His thoughts turned to Northcott. Before running into him at Foster Glen, Michael hadn't had any contact with Northcott since the previous fall. After Michael's drunken accusations and the subsequent warnings from the authorities to stay away from Northcott or risk legal action, he'd had good reason to steer clear of him. Didn't he? Was that just an excuse?

Was he afraid of confronting him?

He did have a way to get a clearer sense of whether J.P. Northcott had any involvement in Emily's death.

He could ask him.

The Flanigan home, which Clint called "The Ranch", looked like public housing compared to the acreage spanning beyond Michael's sightlines. Parked just down the road from the imposing entranceway to the Northcott estate, with the Burlington city limits visible in his rear-view mirror, Michael felt he was about to enter a place far away, if distance were measured in either wealth or moral fibre. If he looked behind him, he could see the entrance to Pickett's Farm just down the road.

The front gates to Northcott's spread were wide open, inviting him in. A little surprised at the lack of security, he drove through the gates and parked near the front of the house.

A Hummer sat at the end of the driveway. *Very Northcott*, Michael thought. *Compensating.*

Not a soul in sight, Michael got out of the car and climbed

the front steps. As he reached the top step, the quiet was broken. He turned toward the south side of the house, and saw two snarling Dobermans, in full flight and coming his way.

He bound down the steps, two at a time. Could he beat them to the car? The angry barks grew louder... closer.

He slipped on the bottom step and tumbled onto the crushed-gravel driveway.

The dogs closed in.

I'm fucked.

He ripped his keys from his pocket.

The drooling, four-legged savages were less than fifteen feet away.

He curled up with his arms over his face, wondering where they would get him first.

The dogs stopped just a few feet away, their growls softened.

He remained still. Seconds passed. They dropped to their haunches. Silent. Still.

Thank you, God.

A man in formal attire, not quite a tuxedo, stepped out from the side of the house. Jowly with a tuft of grey hair resting on a pink scalp, Michael guessed the man was in his early sixties. The man slipped what looked like some sort of remote control into his pocket. Michael rose to his feet, slowly.

"Are we okay here now?" asked Michael.

"Quite alright, sir," answered the man in a haughty British accent. He yanked the device from his pocket like an over-the-hill gunslinger and waved it in front of him. "This gadget controls Ginger and Mary Anne via their collars. All very high-tech, you see."

Michael had heard of shock collars but had never seen one, hadn't had the need. But these mutts were not Paulie and Silvio.

"What's with the dogs?" he asked, quietly, not yet convinced the dogs would remain docile. "It coulda been kids visiting, or a little old lady?"

"But you are neither," said the man. He dismissed the dogs,

and they retreated to the rear of the house. "Although you are looking a little worse for wear, sir," he added, and handed Michael a handkerchief.

Michael rubbed his badly scraped cheek and winced, then dabbed along the wound. No gravel had embedded in his flesh.

"Thanks for calling them off. Mister..."

"Charles, sir," said the man. "Whom shall I say is calling?"

"Michael Flanigan to see J.P. Northcott." He handed the hankie back to Charles. "He isn't expecting me."

"Mr. Northcott is in the lounge, with Mr. Toner." Charles spat out both men's names as if each syllable squirted a shot of vinegar into his mouth, reminding Michael of when Clint coughed up the sour-tasting handle of his mother's new boyfriend.

Michael followed Charles into the foyer. He'd played road apple games as a kid at smaller venues. He thought again that his own "ranch" seemed at least a couple of rungs down the food chain.

Charles led Michael to a cozy room with dark wood trim and black leather furniture. Frank Toner stood sentry at the doorway. Michael wondered where Bobby George fit into this picture. He had never been aware of any connection between Emily's ex and Northcott, but knew if one existed that nothing good could come of it.

In shorts and a damp T-shirt, Northcott looked like he'd just worked out. He sipped on a can of beer in front of a TV. David Feherty, Michael's favourite golf announcer, stood next to a driving range, interviewing someone Michael didn't recognize. Northcott chuckled at something Feherty said. He had yet to acknowledge Michael's presence. Even sweaty and casually attired, Northcott had an air about him, reminding Michael that such a man could ride salt-and-pepper good looks, well-crafted charm, and a cutthroat nature to this elevated station in life.

"Good to see you again, Michael," said Toner, teeth bared but his eyes saying, "What the fuck are you doing here?" The more he saw of Frank Toner, the less he liked.

Not turning from the TV, Northcott said, "Frank, why don't you leave Mr. Flanigan and I alone for a few minutes?"

Charles followed Toner out of the room, but not before rolling his eyes for Michael's benefit.

"Michael, have a seat," said Northcott, muting the TV. Michael took the chair opposite him. His host showed no sign of surprise or concern at the unexpected visit. While Michael felt tense and uncomfortable sitting across from him, Northcott seemed serene.

"Can I have Charles get you something cold?" asked Northcott.

Michael shrugged. "Why not?"

Northcott looked at his watch. "I think it's time for a cocktail. Let me get it," he said, before leaving the room.

Oh, the common man.

He returned in a few minutes with their drinks. Michael took a sip. Crown Royal and ginger, light on the latter.

"That's your drink, right... when you're having a real drink?" asked Northcott.

Michael nodded, then frowned. "How did—"

"I didn't get all this by not knowing about people," said Northcott, casually waving a hand.

Michael took another drink, the soothing effect filling his veins before he set down his glass.

"I see you got your boy Toner a job at Foster Glen," he said.

"I may have put in a good word for Frank a few weeks ago," said Northcott. "He's one of my top people, but I find I don't require his services on a regular basis."

"His services?"

Northcott just smiled and tapped on his cheekbone. "I see you met my girls. The dogs are quite diligent in protecting their home."

Michael ran a finger along the cheek that had met the driveway. "How is your other girl... Paula?" he asked.

Northcott set down his drink, and his smile disappeared.

"She's just fine," he said. "How's that little brother of yours, Flanigan... the one that's still with us?"

"He's doing well, thanks." Michael guessed that Northcott knew of Eamonn's drug problems. "Did you know we named the development up north after my other brother, Oliver... the one who's no longer with us?"

Northcott examined his fingernails, looked at his watch. "To what do I owe this pleasure, Michael?"

"It's no secret that you and I have never been friends."

Northcott shrugged and smiled, a let-bygones-be-bygones gesture.

"And I know I said some nasty things to you just after my wife died," said Michael.

"You were upset, and quite inebriated as I recall. It's understandable."

"I guess I should say that's quite understanding of you. Northcott, if you can manage to put our history aside—"

"Our history?" asked Northcott.

"Just hear me out, J.P., without getting upset or having your boy Frank toss me out."

Northcott smiled, looked amused, folded his hands. "Done."

Michael took a deep breath. He hated that Northcott didn't share his anxiety. Could his long-running, gnawing feud with the man sitting across from him be one-sided, his rival unaware that one existed?

Michael wiped sweat from his brow. He pulled a folded piece of paper from his pocket. Unfolding it, he said, "My father got a letter from this woman at the 'Northern Preservation Society', a group that gave my father a lot of grief about the golf resort development up north."

"May I see that?" asked Northcott, reaching over. Michael handed him the letter.

Northcott chuckled. "I got this one, too. They started when the land was still up for grabs." He handed the letter back to Michael.

"My father said he got even nastier mail from another radical outfit, but unsigned."

"God's Countrymen," said Northcott.

"Excuse me?" Michael had suspected Northcott of sending the more threatening notes. Hiding behind a false identity, sneaking in the dark, seemed as much Northcott as the tank parked outside.

"God's Countrymen. Just another band of fanatical losers with too much time on their hands," said Northcott. "Tommy told me he got the same crap from them. We eventually had a good yuk about it over a few scotches. I think Tom was sitting right where you are now when we discussed it."

"My father? Here?"

"You surprised to hear that your old man clinked the odd glass with the likes of me?" asked Northcott.

"He never mentioned it."

"We weren't thick as thieves, but we had a mutual respect."

Not a chance. "I guess I am surprised at the timing," said Michael. "If you were discussing the letters, you must have been in the middle of the fight for a pretty special chunk of real estate."

Northcott waved off Michael's comment. "That was just business, not personal."

Another remark that Michael had difficulty swallowing.

"Flanigan, I believe things happen for a reason. I'm having a blast with Foster Glen, have all kinds of plans for it, and it may not have happened if I'd gotten involved with... what did your old man call it?"

"*Oliver's Landing.*"

"Right, that's it," said Northcott, still not saying the name. "Is there anything else, Flanigan? My time's getting a little short."

"Something has bothered me since my wife's wake, and I thought I should finally just come out and ask you about it."

Northcott sighed. "So ask, Flanigan."

"When you visited the funeral home," said Michael, "you looked at me in a way that made me think you, I don't know, had a secret or something. Like you knew something, something that I didn't."

"I knew something? You're asking me this now?"

"I was officially ordered to stay away from you and your family."

"And yet here you are."

Michael sipped his drink. Northcott hadn't touched his since first wetting his lips.

"Knew something about what?" asked Northcott. Michael looked at him for several seconds, trying to delve into the abyss beyond the slimy façade, then took another drink. It was going to his head. He put the glass down, pushed it across the small end table.

"Do you know anything about my wife's death?" asked Michael.

"Just what I read in the papers."

"I always felt you knew more, thought maybe you had something to do with it."

Northcott's eyes turned to fire. Michael held his gaze, tried to read him.

"I had nothing to do with Emily's death. *Nothing.* As far as I know, the police ruled it an accident, and I know absolutely nothing that would suggest otherwise."

If Northcott was lying, he was good at it.

"I gotta tell you," said Michael, shaking his head, "I really thought you—"

"Flanigan, why would I want to harm your wife? And knocking her over a cliff? Violence is so... unimaginative."

"There was the real estate battle up north."

Northcott bristled. He got up and stepped toward Michael. "Just who the fuck do you... you come into *my* home... I have won and lost many huge business deals in the past, and no one ever got killed. And now you're saying I had some twinkie thrown over a cliff because your dumb mick old man—"

Michael sprang from his chair. Northcott sidestepped

Michael's fist as it flew by his chin. He grabbed Michael's arm and spun him around. Michael landed face-first on the ground for the second time in less than an hour.

Northcott pinned Michael to the hardwood, put his face close to his, and said, "Tommy was right about you."

The next voice Michael heard belonged to Frank Toner. "Anything I can help you with, Mr. Northcott?"

Something flicked off Michael's cheek. And again.

"Everything's under control here. Isn't that right, Flanigan?"

"I'm cool," said Michael.

Northcott let him up and stood back. Michael wiped a sunflower seed shell from his cheek. A few more shells spotted the surrounding area. Toner grinned with soulless blue eyes from a few feet away.

"Now is there anything else, Flanigan?" asked Northcott, waving Toner away. "Or may I see you to the door?"

Michael ignored him and headed for the foyer.

At the door, Northcott put his hand on Michael's shoulder, and said, "I apologize for my poor choice of words back there. I am sorry for your loss. Losing your wife and father so close together must be very difficult."

Michael just looked at him.

Northcott opened the door, and said, "I must tell you again, I had nothing to do with your wife's death, and have no knowledge of what happened that day, beyond what was reported in the media. Now, I must ask you to stop making these accusations, to me or to others. Are we clear on this?"

Michael stepped outside.

"And just one last friendly piece of advice, Michael, and I mean this sincerely. If you keep digging into other people's business, you may learn more than you bargained for."

Michael turned around to face Northcott. He recognized the expression, from the night at Dwyer's Funeral Home.

"I'm not afraid of you or your pretty boy goon," said Michael.

"Perhaps you should be," said Northcott.

Michael walked down the front steps to his car.

"Careful driving home, Flanigan. You've been drinking again." Michael heard the door close behind him.

He felt Northcott had exploited the fact that Tommy could not corroborate the implication that Michael's father had spoken ill of him to his worst enemy. He knew his father loved him, in his way, despite the fact he never accomplished what Tommy had hoped for—to be more like him.

A voice from behind him said, "Thanks for stopping by."

He turned to see Charles looking most un-butler-like, leaning against the side of the house, a cigarette hanging from the corner of his mouth.

"Good to meet you, Charles."

"Freddy Charles," he said, the airiness gone from his tone. "His royal highness didn't think 'Freddy' sounded quite posh enough, if you get my meaning."

"Same for the accent?"

"It's all about appearances with his nibs. I find myself staying in character sometimes even when the need's not there."

"Listen, Charles—"

"Freddy to my friends."

"I take it you don't like your boss, Freddy."

"Bleedin' wanker, he is," said Freddy out the corner of his mouth. He took a drag from his unfiltered smoke and spat out some tobacco. "Treats the mutts better than he does me."

Freddy had to be privy to at least some information that the world outside Northcott's domain was not. His purple, bloated snout gave Michael an idea.

"I appreciate you keeping the dogs off me earlier, Freddy," said Michael. "Any chance I could thank you by treating you to a pint or three some night?"

On the drive home, Michael thought about what Northcott had said.

You may learn more than you bargained for.

A strange van, rusted with multiple dents, was parked in front of his house. Michael then remembered asking Artie Smitters to come by sometime to look at the security system. Michael wondered if the vehicle could pass a road safety test. A tool box of a similar vintage sat inside his front door.

Michael followed the sounds of laughter coming from the basement.

Artie and Clint were parked on the sofa, sharing pop and chips while Bill Murray's *Caddyshack* character screamed at a gopher that was chewing up his golf course. Clint looked elfin beside his new friend.

"You guys sound like you're having fun," said Michael.

Artie turned, looking both surprised and guilty, and sprang to his feet. "Michael. Hi. I, uh... I hope you don't mind."

"Make yourself at home, Artie."

"I fixed the security alarm," said Artie, like a kid announcing that he'd finished his chores. "It won't be going off for no good reason no more."

"I want to show you something," said Clint as Artie's shitbox pulled away. He led his father around to the back of the house, to an immense tree stump just off the back corner of the guest house.

"What do you think?" asked Clint.

Clint had set up a target on the side of the stump for his stepsister, the avid archer, a passion she picked up from her father, Bobby George. Their shared loved of the sport helped maintain what remained of their tenuous bond. During a recent visit, Sophie told Clint how she had trouble finding time to hit the archery range.

"You're a good man, Clint," said Michael. "Whadya say we pick out a nice set for Soph to use whenever she's here? We might even become half-assed bowmen ourselves."

"Awesome, Dad. This is such a great place when we're all here."

CHAPTER 16

Michael finished leaving a voice message for Lucie as he pulled onto Jessie's street, advising his aunt that he planned to make a return trip to Kingston in the near future and would like to play a round of golf with her while in town.

He had a message into Barney Farrell as well. Michael had decided to make an offer on the three-bedroom condominium owned by the emigrating couple in Barney's building, and wanted Barney to put in a good word. Michael had never set foot in the place, but the sellers had forwarded him pictures. It was a beautiful home with an attractive price tag. He was anxious to get a deal done before the owners changed their minds.

Michael had altered his plans for the condo, and couldn't wait to see the look on Lucie's face when he presented his aunt with her new home. Although she often complained about her cramped apartment, he knew she might be a hard sell for such an extravagant gift. But he thought he could convince her to act as live-in caretaker in a place that he would use as a home base when in Kingston.

He parked in front of Jessie's house a few minutes before nine. Her front door was open a crack. He rapped on the stained-glass window and nudged the door just enough to see a box marked "GOODWILL" on a bench in the front hall.

"Hi there," called Jessie from inside. "It's on the bench inside the door."

"Only me," said Michael, and he pushed the door open. He walked along a hallway toward the back of the house, passing a combined dining room and sitting room. Both furniture and décor seemed tasteful and expensive, but what did he know?

He found Jessie in the kitchen, trying to reach something that seemed out of her grasp. She dropped from her toes to her heels and turned to face him.

"Hi there," she said again. "I thought you were coming by at ten."

He gently struck his forehead with his lower palm. "*Ten* o'clock. I can come back."

She wore an oversized pullover with a Toronto Blue Jays logo and, as far as he could tell, not much else. A shoulder and most of her long legs were on display, with untamed hair completing quite a picture.

"Don't be silly, Michael. I've already showered. What happened here?" she asked, running her hand slowly over his scraped cheek, barely touching it.

"It's nothing. Really. Long story short, I got chased by some nasty dogs, if you can believe it, and tripped and fell. I'm fine."

She looked at him for a moment, then nodded, as if satisfied that he was okay.

She turned back to reach for the top shelf, which was crammed with bowls and dishes, and in doing so exposed the top of her legs, and just a little something more.

He sensed a stirring. "What are we trying to reach here?" He moved a little closer. Her scent stoked the fire in him.

"Red bowl." She extended a little further. "On... *top*."

As he reached up to help, she maintained her position, and he felt himself press against the firm curve of her hip. For a moment he got lost in the smell of her, and pressed harder.

He came back to earth and stepped back.

She turned around, mouth agape and brow furrowed. A serious stare became a grin, her lower lip jutting sideways. She stepped closer, reached down...

"Jessie, I—"

... and gripped him through his shorts

"What have we got here?" she said, unblinking, not taking her eyes off him. "We do have an hour to kill."

He pulled her close and kissed her. She offered her tongue and scrambled for his belt buckle. He slid the pullover over her head, and treated himself to a view that dizzied him.

As he pulled his jeans down below his knees, Jessie scrunched up on the island counter behind her, wrapped her legs around him, and took him deep inside her. *It's been too long,* he thought, and the sheer pleasure of the moment conflicted with his efforts to savour it. Her moans and the hot tongue darting in his ear tipped the balance.

"Oohh... Michael darling."

"Oh God."

The sound of the doorbell... didn't register in his mind... until he was beyond the point of return.

Footsteps.

His BlackBerry fell from his jeans pocket and bounced off the kitchen tiles.

Jessie yelled, "Shit" and slid off him, and grabbed her shirt.

At the moment of her extrication, a fierce orgasm exploded from him, spraying the island.

"*Coming!*" she yelled. She punched her head through the neck of her shirt, and laughed to the verge of tears as she left the room.

Michael grabbed a dish cloth and a roll of paper towel. He quickly cleaned himself and then the island, while a muffled conversation carried on at the front door.

He froze. The voices he heard were not just those from Jessie's conversation. Another voice, distant, behind him.

He reached under the kitchen table and picked up his phone.

He read the display: "Aunt Lucie".

Don't tell me.

He brought the phone to his ear, listened—"Michael. *MYYY-CHAEL.*"—and deliberated whether to answer his aunt or hang up.

"Hi there, Auntie," he said, with as much nonchalance as he could muster.

"Michael dear, are you alright?" she asked.

"Um, yeah, I'm fine," he stammered.

"I... oh my. Were you..."

"How long have you been waiting for me to pick up the phone?"

"Just for the record, Michael, you called me. I'm guessing by accident, but anyway... how long? I'd say long enough." She let out a laugh, said, "Goodbye, dear," and hung up.

Jessie returned to the kitchen and Michael slipped the phone in his pocket.

"I'll forever wear a smile whilst chopping my vegetables on that island," she said.

He had to laugh. "I'm a little... out of practice," he said.

"Something tells me that won't be a problem moving forward," she said, taking his hand. "Let me show you the rest of the house."

They arrived at the Rogers Centre in downtown Toronto during the third inning of the Blue Jays game, the scoreboard showing Seattle ahead 4-1.

"I bet Ichiro's been busy," said Michael.

"Whatever you say, love," replied Jessie.

Before he could tell her to wait for a break in the action, Jessie started down the row to their seats. As they sidled down the row, Gregg Zaun went the other way with an outside fastball, lining a shot off the right-field fence.

"Fer chrissakes."

He turned to see a beer-bellied, unshaven man of about thirty in a Blue Jays jersey, juggling a plate of nachos and a king-size cup of beer, and shaking his head at Michael. A young lady sitting beside the man, apparently his date, lowered her head and covered her face with her hand.

"Care to have a freakin' seat?" asked the man.

"Sorry," said Michael, and they moved on.

Travis Snider homered for the Blue Jays on the next pitch. The man down the row and one back was on his feet and waving a

Blue Jays banner, Michael's etiquette breach forgotten.

"We probably should wait 'til the referee blows his whistle next time," said Jessie.

At the end of the next inning, Jessie said, "Those nachos look good." She slid her hand along Michael's thigh and said, "I seem to have worked up an appetite." She stood up and said she'd bring him a beer. He watched her glide along the row of seats and up the stairs.

When she still hadn't returned after the bottom of the fifth, Michael scanned the concession area at the back of their section. He picked Jessie out of the crowd, even from a distance, the vision that she was. She was crouched beside a teenage girl in a wheelchair, sharing a laugh and a box of fries. Jessie caught Michael's eye and pointed at him. She smiled and waved, as did the disabled girl.

He turned back to the game.

After the next inning, Jessie returned, carrying a tray of beer. She stopped to offer a pint to the beer belly and his gal. The man jumped to his feet and overdid his thank-you, cap doffed and handshake prolonged. This did not go unnoticed by his frowning female companion, who tugged at his sleeve, pulling him back to his seat.

"Nice touch," said Michael, taking his beer and putting his other arm around Jessie. "Maybe if things don't work out with us —"

"I gave him my number."

"I see you made another friend up top."

"She's called Tanya. Quite a special little girl. Funny, smart. It's a shame that many people don't realize that these kids with cerebral palsy have all of their faculties and are just like the rest of us, inside bodies that have let them down so miserably."

She could make me better, Michael thought.

After the game, Michael slipped into the men's room while Jessie hit the souvenir stand. While standing at the crowded urinals, a familiar voice from behind said, "C'mon, sonny. My teeth are floating." Michael finished up and turned to find a grinning Elliott Kennedy, a Toronto baseball columnist from Kingston and a fixture around the local ballpark when Michael was a kid.

Michael waited outside, and Kennedy came out a minute later.

"Hey, Coach," said Michael as they shook hands. "I read your Sunday column about the ex-Jays the other day. Nice piece on Leiter."

"How are you, Mike?" asked Kennedy in his gravel voice. Michael tended to only see him at Kennedy's annual backyard clambake, and had not spoken to him since Emily's funeral.

"Doin' okay, thanks."

"Will I see you at my barbecue? The first Sunday in August."

"It's on my calendar."

"Your boy still working on his changeup?"

"He seems to be leaning more toward golf."

"Sorry to hear that. How's your other kid, the stepdaughter?"

"Sophie? Okay, I guess." Michael thought Kennedy looked concerned.

"Look, Mike, I don't want to be telling stories outta school and all that..."

"But?"

"I saw Sophie at a game here a while back, and she was in pretty rough shape. Wasted, I mean. Coming out of the ladies. A couple of the kids who work here were holding her up. I kinda feel bad bringing it up. Probably just a youngster sowing some oats and getting a little carried away. But I thought, if it was my kid..."

"I appreciate you bringing it up, Elliott. She had a rough patch when she lost her mom." Michael then realized that the previous baseball season had ended for the Blue Jays before Emily died. "When did this happen?" he asked.

"Coupla weeks ago."

CHAPTER 17

Michael stepped off the practice tee block, slid the four-iron into his bag, and pulled out his hybrid.

Am I "The Golfer"?

Was she thinking of leaving me?

"Ferguson Boone," said the arts centre director, just as Michael was about to hang up. Michael heard a faint giggling in the background, and pictured Boone offering his lap to the comely young woman who had fetched them coffee during his first visit to the centre.

"Mr. Boone. Michael Flanigan. Just a quick question. You mentioned that my wife was involved with an event that included some work of local artists from Bronte Creek Park, from the Spruce Lane Farmhouse."

"I did."

"What can you tell me about the paintings, the ones that were damaged?"

"They weren't worth a lot, but they were on loan—and they were *art*—so Emily felt horrible as a result. Not that she had any culpability in their destruction."

"Were they good paintings?"

"There was a lovely piece by Suzanna Sanders, called *Birthright*."

"And the second?"

"The other painting was attributed to Elaine Cavendish, a somewhat eccentric painter from Halton Hills."

"Attributed to?"

"Yes. Miss Cavendish had not signed all of her work before she passed away many years ago. The assumption is that she deemed the works unfinished, or hadn't yet decided to show them to the world."

"This work wasn't signed?"

"No."

"Was it worth something?"

"It would have topped out at forty, maybe fifty thousand, even after she died."

"When paintings increase in value."

"As a rule."

"And it was hanging at Bronte Creek Park?"

"Her family's wishes."

"Was there an investigation on the insurance claim?"

"I understand the family's compensation was deemed both fair and legitimate."

"How did it become attributed to Elaine Cavendish?"

"Over the years, local art buffs, armed with the knowledge that Miss Cavendish had not signed all of her work, determined that the style of the painting was unambiguously Cavendish. Apparently this information surfaced during the insurance investigation."

"They do their homework with these things."

"They did with *The Golfer.*"

"So tell me more about the crack surveillance team," said Fern from the top step of the porch when Michael answered his door.

"The what?" asked Michael.

"Higgins and Kan. The recording of the politician puttin' it to one of his constituents."

"Right. Quite the pair."

"Would you go to jail for that idiot Higgins?"

"Is that why you're here?"

"Why are you so tight with that guy?"

"We've been over this. We go way back. He's always been there for me."

"Did you erase it?"

"I thought you didn't want to work for me."

"I am now."

Michael sat down on the step. "I'm going to pay you," he said. He realized it was Fern's first visit since he'd bought the house.

"I know you are," said Fern. "And I don't come cheap. You *are* loaded now, right?"

"I am that. Why the change of heart?"

"This isn't a game, Mike. You can't be associated with crap like this, morons playing with surveillance equipment like they're on Mission Fucking Impossible."

"That's why you're here? You want to protect me from myself?"

Fern hesitated. "Ah shit." He turned his head to spit. "Before I started down the path to a divorce, I didn't have to worry about the price of Leafs tickets. I shoulda hid my assets better."

"You'll be well compensated. And I had no idea what Hig and Eddie were up to."

Fern looked into Michael's eyes. Fern once said that he could tell if a perp was lying by "just looking inside". Michael must have passed the test, as his P.I. changed the subject.

"And the visit to Northcott wasn't smart," said Fern.

"Where did you hear about that?"

"Doesn't matter. This shit has to stop. *Now*. And destroy that little audio clip. It's illegal."

Michael nodded. "So now what?" he asked.

"I'm doing this as a licensed investigator, on my own, not on behalf of my firm. I'll need a retainer."

"Whatever you think is fair. We can work out the details later."

"My efforts will be controlled, limited. I have a source or two who might have access to information that's out of the reach of a citizen like yourself."

"Limited?"

"I'm not gonna be pounding the pavement, knocking on

doors. Just so you know what you're paying for. I'll reach out to a few targeted people."

"Targeted?"

"There is substantial risk here, for me and for others. That's what you're paying for, plus any information I provide."

"Got it." Michael assumed that Fern had sources that wouldn't be accessible to most people, and perhaps should not be available to Fern. But who was he kidding? That's exactly why he was hiring him.

"Give me all you have, who you've talked to, your little suspicions, whatever," said Fern. "I'll evaluate, work out a strategy... which may be to do nothing, in which case you can get on with your life.

"And under no circumstances are you to discuss this with anyone. No one, not your lawyer friend, not Higgins, no pillow talk. *No... one.*"

Michael looked away.

"You've already told someone," said Fern. "A girlfriend?"

"I kinda told the guys I was gonna check out Pickett's Farm."

"Did you go there?"

"With Sophie. And Rita."

"Well for... okay, not another word. Tell them you've decided it's a dead end, you had a change of heart, whatever it takes."

Easier said than done, Michael thought. "You'll be forced to get to know Burlington now. It's a great place."

Fern curled up his lip and nodded, à la De Niro in one of his gangster roles. Michael commented on the resemblance.

"I'm Portuguese," said Fern.

Michael stood at the whiteboard in his office, where he did his best to chronicle the events of his macabre life since he'd lost Emily.

He paced Fern through it, from just prior to Emily's death, mentioning all parties he'd talked to or about along the way, from

Speagle and Alberts and Jacquie Zetterfeldt to Ruth Eisentraut and Teresa Amodeo and Bobby George. And J.P. Northcott. He also spoke of *The Golfer,* the mysterious note that Emily took from her pocket at Pickett's Farm, and everything in between.

"Kind of a mess, huh?" asked Michael when he was finished.

"It's all good," replied Fern, seated at Michael's desk.

Fern grabbed a second notebook from his bag. "I checked out these characters, the bark-eaters who don't want the golf resort going up on the so-called heritage land up north."

"You already started working."

Fern read from his notes. "'The Northern Preservation Society and God's Countrymen.' I don't see any of these people as a threat. The Countrymen have a half-assed storefront office in Gravenhurst owned by one of their members, a retired school bus driver. There isn't a person in there under sixty, and they fall all over themselves trying to be polite."

"You went up there?"

"No way to get a feel over the phone for how much of a threat there might be."

"I thought you'd make some calls."

"You don't know what my retainer is."

Michael was impressed.

"I read through their literature," said Fern. "Talked to them for a while."

"And?"

"I think you could make everybody happy if the blueprint for *Oliver's Landing* was modified just a little bit."

"How little?"

"I understand the plan calls for a second eighteen holes."

"Yeah."

"Could you live with nine holes on the back course?"

"Turn an eighteen-hole layout into nine? That's a little bit?"

"The majority of the land that has these people losing sleep at night is where the back nine of that layout is going. If you can live without it..."

"It's not that easy, and it's not up to me. It's still land owned by the shareholders of *Oliver's Landing*. There are huge investors looking at the place, and seriously. Would these geriatrics put up the cash to buy the land back?"

"What do you think? The land would have to be donated. Would make for some great PR."

"The investors are more interested in making money."

"I'm just saying," said Fern, throwing up his hands. "They could get their names outta the newspapers, get rid of the protesters."

"What about the second group? The preservation society?"

"Joyce Hogarth. She's eighty-one, and has diabetes and bad arthritis."

"Yeah, she wrote the letter."

"It's just her."

Michael got more coffee and sat in the corner chair. He felt he had shared all he could remember, while still holding back his relationship with Jacquie Zetterfeldt. "I think that's most of it," he said, scanning the whiteboard.

"Tell me more about this painting," said Fern. "What's the story on *The Golfer*?"

Michael told Fern about the reminder that Emily had jotted in her notebook, the unsigned work attributed to Elaine Cavendish, and the eavesdropped conversation between Emily and Ruth Eisentraut at the Milton arts show.

"To me it seems Emily was more upset than Ruth over the fire at the arts centre," said Michael.

"The 'Who gives a crap?' comment," said Fern.

Michael nodded. "About 'the effin painting.'"

"As in *one* painting, and two had been destroyed in the fire," said Fern. "So do you figure this effin painting is *The Golfer*, based on your wife's notes?"

"I wondered if there may have been some sort of insurance

scam going on."

"With the friend Ruth?"

Michael shrugged.

"How much would it be worth, if it was a Cavendish?" asked Fern.

"Fifty thousand, on a good day."

"That's chicken feed for art, Mike. This old gal may have been well-known around here, but fifty thousand tells me we're not talking Paula Figueiroa Rego."

"Who?"

"She's a Portuguese artist. I did some grunt work for a colleague a while back who was investigating a potential art scam for a big insurance company."

"I'm impressed."

"Art theft may sound glamorous, makes for a good movie, but it rarely pays. A lot of people still try, mind you. It is a huge global business, but most pieces sell for ten per cent of their value, often less."

"Can the crooks usually find someone to buy it?"

"Maybe a quarter of pilfered art is never recovered. Panicky thieves burn the evidence, works are stashed away and forgotten or, when we're talking precious gems and metals, broken down into their component parts. Plus it's much harder to store stolen paintings than you'd think. Over time, swings in humidity and temperature can damage a painting, or even destroy it."

"This one got destroyed in a fire."

"Mike, this is so nickel-and-dime. No one is going to get killed over this painting, if that's where your head is going. Did your buddy at the arts centre say anything about an insurance investigation?"

"I don't know who got paid for what, but I get the sense it was put to bed without any hassle."

"Okay. What else you got?"

Michael hesitated, then asked, "Fern, is our communication considered confidential, given our new professional working relationship?"

"Am I obligated not to discuss this shit with anyone else?"

"More or less."

"I would never divulge anything we've discussed, no matter how seemingly insignificant, unless directed to do so by you and you only. "

Michael got a kick out of Fern's fluctuating vocabulary.

"Unless, of course, I'm directed to do so by the court," added Fern.

Michael chewed on that caveat for a few seconds. He didn't like the taste.

"Hypothetically, what if I knew someone in the middle of one of these events," asked Michael, "and my knowledge of them had absolutely nothing to do with anything, but revealing this fact might falsely raise some suspicions concerning my involvement with that event?"

"Events? Your knowledge of them?" asked Fern. He went to the whiteboard. "Hypothetically... did you do one of the ladies on the board here?"

Michael knew the look on his face answered Fern's question.

Fern put his finger close to the whiteboard, and slowly moved it over the female names on the board. He stopped at "J. Zetterfeldt", turned and looked at Michael with a self-satisfied smirk.

Michael fell back into the chair. "How did you..."

"I hear the late Mrs. Zetterfeldt was one fine-looking lady. Who else could it be, where it would also raise some suspicions about your involvement in all of this shit? Your lawyer friend? Maybe old lady Pickett? Not much of a process of elimination."

"It was just one of those things—"

"What, you're explaining your sins to me now? C'mon, Mike None of us is without our peccadilloes. Our little missteps help us fit a little easier into the next guy's shoes."

Michael realized his own crime-solving acumen paled next to Fern's experienced, analytical approach. His most glaring shortcoming, according to Fern, was a lack of objectivity. "You're too wrapped up in this," was how Fern put it. "My business is just that. Business. I can't make it personal, and I don't."

"Speaking of personal," said Michael, "this is a little off the beaten path…"

"Spill it. I have a date."

"Eddie's been losing customers, big customers, at a rate that's hard to fathom. His rep is the best. I talked to him earlier. He thinks someone is carrying out some kind of smear campaign."

"Maybe he's just paranoid, doesn't want to face the music."

"I don't think so."

"And you want me to look into it."

Michael nodded.

"Got any names to put to these customers that are bailing?"

"A couple."

"It's your dime."

"Good," said Michael. He looked back to the whiteboard. "So what have we got?"

Fern took the marker from Michael and added a heading in block letters at the top of the board:

WHO GAINS??

"I have to admit that after my little chat with Northcott, I have some doubts about him being involved with Emily's death," said Michael. "He may be a prick, but…"

"But?"

"But with all this other crazy shit… someone's jacking me up. As much as my gut tells me now that Northcott probably didn't kill my wife, it's also telling me these latest killings are connected to each other, and to Emily… to me."

"You're all over the place, Michael. We're focused on Emily, remember. If it takes us somewhere…"

Artie Smitters stuck his head in to ask if his daughter could visit him at the Flanigan residence. Michael assured him she could visit anytime. Artie thanked him and left.

"Visit him?" asked Fern. "You running a hotel now?"

Michael told Fern about his history with Artie.

"With everything that's happened, I feel better with him here," he said. "And he's a great handyman. I'm just starting to realize this is a big place to keep up."

"So you brought home someone you ran into in jail, to look after your kids?"

"He's a good guy. Rita vouched for him."

Fern rolled his eyes. He and Rita had met in court on occasion, including one memorable time where she caught him on a procedural technicality that resulted in an accused arsonist walking away a free man, making Fern look bad in the process. Fern's comment to Michael at the time was, "We clean the shit off the streets and she spreads it right back."

"A good guy who happened to find himself in jail with you," said Fern.

"Fernando, let's not forget that I was in jail, too. I hear Artie just threw some jerk out of a pub who was being extremely inappropriate with a waitress. The guy wasn't hurt. It was nothing."

"Well, if he was being inappropriate."

"Look, I trust the guy. I got him set up in the guest house out back."

"If someone really wants to get to you or the kids, there's not much Artie Smitters is going to be able to do about it."

"Thanks for the comforting thought."

"He seems a little slow."

"He's a little... deliberate, in his speech."

"Deliberate?"

"Hey, he fixed our alarm system like it was nothing."

"Like the Rainman countin' toothpicks."

"Can we drop it?"

"I'm just sayin'."

—

"Michael, your wife did beautiful work," said Jessie, admiring the array of Emily's photographs that lined Michael's main floor hallway. "I barely know what button to push, even with those new cameras that make it so easy. So many people don't realize what an art form photography is. They think, 'Well, I own a camera, so I could just take this picture myself'.

"I could never take a photo like, well... like that," she said, pointing to an eerie black-and-white shot of a solitary old man walking through a park. "Or that one," she said, moving on to a print of the Ontario countryside, where sunlight played with lush oranges, reds, and greens. They were two of Michael's favourites.

"Emily did have a passion," said Michael.

Jessie looked back and forth from the sombre black-and-white to the brilliant rural landscape. "I sense that Emily's art reflects a vast array of moods," she said. "Do you think that's the case, or am I reading too much into this?"

Michael had never tapped into the notion, but from what he'd learned since Emily's death, he found the observation insightful.

As they neared his office, he noticed the busy-looking whiteboard, put his arm around Jessie, and ushered her past.

Clint came by to ask Jessie if he could get her anything, the third time he'd done so in the half hour since she walked in the door.

Michael showed her the basement next, skipping the room that he once used as his office. He didn't want to interrupt Artie while he set up the security cameras.

The doorbell rang, and moments later Rita entered the kitchen behind Clint.

"Rita?" said Michael. "I was expecting Sophie."

"What a warm reception," said Rita, who smiled and

introduced herself to Jessie.

Michael learned that Sophie the no-show had invited Rita to dinner without advising the rest of the family, apparently not remembering their special meal plans with Jessie.

While Jessie and Rita got acquainted, Michael went outside to start the barbecue. He stepped back inside, chatted for a bit, and took a serving plate, piled with steaks next to a bowl of orange bell peppers and yellow zucchini, out to the deck. As he sprinkled the herbs from Provence that Sophie brought back from France the previous year, he pictured his stepdaughter, shit-faced and being helped out of a ballpark ladies' room.

He popped his head back into the kitchen. Jessie had found ingredients for a Caesar salad, and tutored Clint on its preparation. "Now *this* will impress the ladies," she said.

Jessie engaged Rita in a spectrum of conversation, from their favourite movies to the Canadian presence in Afghanistan.

Michael joined Rita on the deck while she had an after-dinner smoke.

"I hear your laddish pal Da Silva was here earlier," she said.

"You won't let it go with him, will you? I'm surprised he finally made the trek out here."

"I know he's your friend, Michael."

"But?"

"I've seen him in action. And I don't mean when he's sitting on a bar stool charming some buxom beer-slinger who was still watching Sesame Street when he was walking the beat in Toronto."

"I understand he had his own style of policing," said Michael.

Fern had never shared the details on why he left the police force. But Michael had heard the odd story about the risks to career and health Fern had taken while on The Job, from head-butting with the brass to getting stabbed, while off-duty, by a meth-head in a street fight. Some accounts came from Fern's former police colleagues, after a few drinks and a wink or a nudge that said *I shouldn't be telling you this, but...*

"I saw him downtown last week," said Rita.

"You were working in Toronto?"

"Downtown Burlington."

"Fern? A week ago? I usually can't drag him out here." Michael assumed his friend must have been working on another investigation.

"How does an ex-cop drive a new Jaguar?" asked Rita.

"He does okay. I can't see him crossing the line."

"Michael, that line got blurry for Da Silva so long ago he can't even see it."

"I trust Fern. Period."

Rita put out her cigarette on the railing and said, "You're probably right." She stepped forward and hugged him. "Take care of yourself, Michael."

He let out a loud burp.

She giggled and said, "I love you... buddy."

"Ditto."

As Rita was leaving, Michael opened the door to find Sophie fumbling for her keys on the front porch. She stepped inside and grabbed Rita by the forearms. "Rita, I *totally* forgot about tonight."

Sophie glanced from her father to Jessie. "Oh shit," she said. Jessie took a step toward Sophie with her hand extended. Sophie burst into tears and ran up the stairs.

They stood in silence for a few seconds before Rita said, "Good luck with that," and left.

"I'd better be going, too," said Jessie.

"I don't know what's got into Soph," said Michael. "She was really looking forward to meeting you."

"Michael, please don't worry about that. I sense her reaction wasn't directed at me, but who could blame her? Give her some time."

—

In the morning, Michael went into his office, opened up a spreadsheet on his PC, and summarized the notes from the whiteboard. He emailed the file to Fern, and wiped the board clean.

Barney Farrell hadn't returned his call, and Michael wondered if the terrific condo in Kingston had been scooped up by another buyer.

Michael stopped by Sophie's room when she had yet to make an appearance by ten fifteen. He tapped lightly on her door, which was slightly ajar. He waited for a few seconds, with no response, and noticed her en-suite door was closed, muffling the sound of the shower.

A scrap of paper was on the floor, just inside the door. He assumed it had fallen off the dresser that hugged the inside wall next to the doorway. He picked it up to put it back on the dresser, and saw it was a restaurant receipt, with a phone number scribbled on the back, and no name.

The older man?

CHAPTER 18

On Thursday morning, Michael and Jessie got off the first tee at Foster Glen as a twosome.

Jessie stickhandled her ball along the first hole. Michael generously gave her a seven on the scorecard.

"Was that all?" she asked. "It seemed like more."

"It always does," said Michael.

He helped her with some swing basics while waiting to hit on the second hole.

"Have you considered teaching others to play, perhaps like what Randy Goodman does?" asked Jessie. "I think he said one of his fellow instructors was leaving. You told me how you've missed teaching."

"You need to go to school for that, like anything else."

"You're still young."

"You never know," he said.

Michael had an unspoken desire to invest a chunk of his inheritance into creating a golf academy for kids. He planned to do it if life ever got the hell out of his way.

"Michael, I must say I am somewhat disquieted by your getting attacked at home the other morning," asked Jessie. He had told her about it just the night before.

"They're probably long gone," he said.

"I'm happy that Emily encouraged you to find someone else should something ever happen to her. I must say I admire her for that, my obvious bias aside."

"Well now, that came out of left field," he said. "But I do want my life to get back to normal, and look to the future."

Her tee shot on number two skipped into the woods. She winked at Michael, and asked him to help her find her ball.

—

Simone Vigorito, assistant librarian at the Burlington Public Library, did not fit the mould. She was more Goth than bookish, in black head-to-toe.

"Your wife didn't mention a specific painting, but did ask me to help her find the odd book on art," said Simone, typing at her computer as she spoke. "She seemed to spend a lot of time researching paintings from the U.K., specifically Scotland, of all places. Not that great paintings don't come from, well... all places."

"Was she alone?"

"Another woman was with her."

"Kinda mousy... plain?"

"Kinda."

"Why Scotland?"

"I got the feeling your wife had come across some artwork that she thought might be of significant value, but she didn't tell me its name. She asked me who I would talk to if I wanted to authenticate a piece of art, and I suggested she start with the source country."

"Scotland. With all due respect, Simone, why would she ask you?"

Simone stopped typing. "I majored in art history at university."

"Would this library have much material to help her with this kind of a search?" asked Michael.

"For its size, the library has decent art reference resources, but not much on works from Scotland." She swung around her computer monitor so they could both see it.

"I showed her this website dealing with Scottish art galleries," Simone clicked on the "Art Consultancy" tab, and pointed a black fingernail at the monitor. "Here's the guy. Duff McPhee. Your wife wrote his contact info down. He works at a gallery in Glasgow."

—

Danny's house was dark and the driveway empty. "I'll guess you'll have to meet him another day," said Michael.

Michael scribbled a brief note for Danny on a napkin he found in his glove compartment. Jessie ran around to the side entrance and stuck it inside the screen door.

"I peeked in," she said. "I'm sure the cleaning lady is due tomorrow."

Michael laughed, nodded.

"Looks like a gorgeous old kitchen table, maybe chestnut," she said. "But it is absolutely covered in papers, strewn haphazardly from one end to the other."

"Danny the writer."

"As in author?"

"He's trying. When his wife left him a couple of years ago, he sold a lucrative accounting practice and traded in his calculator for a word processor. He likes to tell people he morphed from miserably successful to happily starving, but I think the sale of the business left him in pretty good shape. And he's so friggin' cheap anyway."

"What's he write?"

"I think he's written short stories for the most part, but he said he's been working on a novel for quite a while now. I get the sense he spends most of his time on it when he's away from the golf course."

"Does he get published... his short stories?"

"Still trying."

Michael pulled into the last of a series of parking lots, at the end of a long winding road, near the beginning of a trail leading to the Spruce Lane Farmhouse in Bronte Creek Park. The massive park, with its natural scenery and seemingly endless trails, had been a favourite backdrop of Emily's for photography sessions.

Michael wished she'd brought her class here on the previous Thanksgiving weekend.

He stopped in the doorway of the old house, imagining Emily passing through that very spot, perhaps with Ruth Eisentraut.

The house had retained both the structure and furnishings of the late 1800s, with antique tools for cooking and sewing on the main floor, and short beds and paltry closet space in the upstairs sleeping quarters. Michael now recalled Emily telling him about visiting an old farmhouse. She said the house told her wonderful stories, and she felt as if the family that had lived there was right there with her. He'd heard other stories that said the place was haunted, so maybe they had been.

Michael bumped into a gangly young man with blue-rimmed glasses and an unruly tangle of yellow-dyed hair. He wore a name tag that identified him as Joel Pierce.

"*Pierce...* do your friends call you Hawkeye?" asked Michael.

Joel Pierce frowned and pushed up his glasses. "Um... no."

Pierce had worked there part-time since high school, and did recall the loan to the arts centre, and the fire that prevented the return of two borrowed paintings.

"The one with the golfer was, like, pretty cool," he said, "but I felt so bad for the lady who came to tell us about it. She was all 'I'm so sorry' and 'I feel just terrible.'"

"What'd she look like?"

"Emily? She was about—"

"Emily?"

"Yeah. I heard she died."

"She did, Joel. Emily was my wife."

"Um... sorry."

A harsh scraping sound from directly behind Michael made him flinch. Pierce sniggered, and moved to straighten a painting on the wall that had moved on its hanger and tilted to one side.

"Did Emily come here alone?" asked Michael.

"I only saw her here twice. The first time this other lady was with her, kind of a plain-Jane type. She had her hair up in one of those bun things. The other time Emily came alone."

"This other lady… do you remember anything else about her? Did she sound like she was from around here, or did she maybe have an accent?"

"Now that you mention it."

"An accent? What kind?"

"It was almost like she was from some other country."

Give me strength.

"But she didn't say a whole lot," said Pierce. "Emily was asking about getting some artwork for the centre, and the other lady just walked around, checking the place out."

"Do you know much about the painting with the golfer?"

"I know some lady from around here somewhere painted it. Some old lady, at least she was when she died. I liked the painting, mainly cuz I'm a golfer myself."

Michael did not peg Pierce as a golfer, but thought if he got those long arms extended…

"You might check with the admin office," said Pierce. "It's like a minute down the road from here. They have a few people working there who might know something about the paintings, but I wouldn't count on it. They're quite a bit older."

"Thanks," said Michael. He couldn't comprehend how the age of the administration staff could affect their ability to help him, but decided not to encourage the kid to share his pretzel logic on the subject. "That's a good idea. I believe I will."

"You aren't gonna go, like now, are you?"

"I was thinking of it. Should I not?"

"I wouldn't go now."

"Why not?"

"It's closed."

Michael sighed, and then smiled. "When would a good time be to go, Joel?"

"I'd go Monday morning, after 8:30. It'll be open then."

Michael thanked him, shook his hand, and wished him luck. He figured he would need it.

—

Danny stood outside the clubhouse, arguing with a young woman Michael recognized as a hostess from the lounge. As Michael approached them, she turned and retreated inside, shaking her head.

"Hey Mikey," said Danny. "Good timing. Let's go grab a beer."

Michael stopped to shoot the breeze with Randy Goodman for a minute, and then rejoined Danny.

The hostess stood inside the door to the lounge, twirling her hair while flirting with a young member. "We'd like a table by the window, sweetheart," said Danny. She gave him a dirty look and went back to her young man.

"What say we seat ourselves?" said Danny. They sat in the corner and ordered a beer.

"Word has it," said Danny, sliding forward, "that Little Jimmy Northcott was responsible for all the vandalizing that was going on here a few months back, when they first put Foster Glen on the market. You were off on your rehab vacation at the time. And this just as his old man was trying to buy the place. Apparently Northcott went into a rage when he found out, threatened to beat some sense into the kid.

"The kicker was that Northcott Senior found a way to blame it all on Artie Smitters, who had caught Jimmy rolling a golf cart into the pond on the fifteenth hole. Northcott pulled a few strings and got Smitters fired."

"The lousy prick," said Michael.

Danny leaned closer and said, "You should have heard that little cutie talking earlier."

"The hostess you were annoying?"

"She said there isn't a female who works here under the age of sixty who Northcott hasn't hit on. And this is a guy with a sick wife at home."

"I sense Randy hasn't got much time for him, but we know a lot of people do buy into that so-called charm," said Michael.

"I guess his new girlfriend watches him like a hawk," said Danny. Michael pictured a naked bombshell, mouth bloodied and looking for love.

Michael thought of the girl Northcott had allegedly forced himself on, back when he was really just a child himself. And what of Northcott's daughter? Paula would soon be old enough to work at the club, and probably would, now that her father owned the place. What would she hear about dear old Dad from her co-workers?

What did she already know about him?

Michael left a voice message for Dr. Gordon, asking if he could switch their Monday evening appointment to early Tuesday. He didn't know when the Foster Glen Classic might finish if the clouds opened up before they got eighteen in on Sunday. The tournament winner could remain undecided until well into Monday afternoon.

The phone rang in his hand as he set it in the cradle.

"You asked about this Ruth Eisentraut," said Fern. "I have a friend of a friend who caters from time to time for functions at the art centre. Apparently Ruthie is shy, straightlaced. One of those people where everyone remembers her but no one does. My friend heard Ruth left the country. Maybe Germany."

Germany. Ferguson Boone had heard the same thing.

"I'd like to track down this Ruth," said Michael. "I have a feeling about her."

"A feeling? Noted. What else?"

Michael told Fern about Jimmy Northcott vandalizing the golf club.

"Old news," said Fern, "The kid's more idiot than criminal."

"Anything on Eddie?"

"It's a dead end."

Michael wondered if Eddie was a little paranoid, looking for bogeymen that weren't there.

"What about this Alberts guy?" asked Michael.

"Because he's a friend of Northcott? I thought you let Northcott off the hook. Forget about Alberts, Mike. He's a solid cop with a good record. And forget Northcott, too, in case you haven't lost your hard-on for him."

Michael still had a bad feeling about them.

CHAPTER 19

Rain fell heavily on Sunday. Michael would have to wait until the following Sunday to tee it up at the 24th Annual Foster Glen Classic, as another tournament had already been scheduled for the Saturday.

Jessie invited Michael to come along while she volunteered at the food bank. He begged off. He had things to do. She understood. She always did.

Thinking a peaceful jaunt on the links would nicely complement Tuesday's therapy session, Michael booked a tee time for himself and Danny for later Tuesday morning.

After not hearing back from Duff McPhee, Michael called Simone Vigorito at the library to see if he could get additional contact info for the art consultant. He had left three messages on a general mailbox at the Glasgow gallery, and thought getting a cell phone number for McPhee might make Michael harder to ignore.

"Sorry, Mr. Flanigan. All I have is the gallery number from the website," she said.

He thanked her and asked for a call if she thought of anything else.

"Oh-oh-oh," she blurted. "Don't hang up."

"I'm still here."

"I thought of something after you left the other day. I don't know why I didn't think of it at the time."

"What's that, Simone?"

"Someone else was asking about Scottish paintings. It was months later, but I thought I'd tell you just in case it means something."

"Did you get a name?"

"The guy's name was Vincent. I remember cuz I called him

Vinnie, and he got all huffy about it."

"Do you remember his last name, what he looked like?"

"A big guy, kind of creepy."

"His name?" asked Michael.

"It was... not Fonda... maybe..."

"Fronda? Vincent Fronda?"

"That's it," said Simone. "Fronda. Now *he* asked about a specific painting."

One-eyed Vinnie Fronda.

"Do you recall the name of the painting, Simone?" asked Michael.

"Certainly. It's called *The Golfer*?"

He wanted to crawl down the phone line and kiss her.

Michael got through to a lady at the Glasgow gallery just as they were closing, still early afternoon in Ontario. Through the woman's barely intelligible Glaswegian patter, he discerned that Duff McPhee was backpacking through the Himalayas and unreachable. "Duffy" was due back within the week, and she'd have him contact Michael immediately. No one at the gallery had heard of Emily or a painting called *The Golfer*.

Emily. Fronda. Same painting. Same miserable fate.

He considered a call to the police, but decided he should have more to go on if he hoped to get more than a verbal reprimand for his troubles.

"Mr. Flanigan, good of you to stop in," said Boone, who formally introduced his assistant, Lisa. She smiled, and then looked back at Boone as if she was anything but an employee.

"I was just over on Brant Street getting some physio on my wrist," said Michael. "What's up?"

"Lisa was showing me some photographs she took at an event here at the centre last year," said Boone.

"They're not very good," said Lisa. "I'm not like a real photographer or anything."

Boone put his hand on her arm and said, "They're fine, my dear."

"Mr. Flanigan, I only met your daughter the one time," said Lisa. "I meet so many people here that—"

"My stepdaughter? Sophie?"

"Yes, your stepdaughter."

Boone put a photograph on the desk in front of Michael, and turned it to face him. "Is that not her?" Boone pointed to Sophie, standing next to her mother in the picture in a crowd of people.

"That's Soph. Why do you ask?" asked Michael, who thought they looked beautiful together.

"After you left here the last time you visited, I may have mentioned the gist of our conversation to Lisa, at a very high level of course. At any rate, Lisa approached me later to tell me about the last time she saw your wife. I don't know if it means anything, but since you showed such an interest in your wife's state of mind..."

"This girl, your stepdaughter," said Lisa, pointing to Sophie in the photograph. She put another photograph in front of him, and pointed to a man in the picture. "She was having an animated discussion with this man, before your wife interrupted them, all upset, and pulled your stepdaughter away." It wasn't a close-up, but there was no mistaking the smug self-importance of the ubiquitous J.P. Northcott.

Michael found Randy Goodman working late at the golf club.

"Any chance you know Northcott's cell number, or could get it for me?" asked Michael, hoping to exploit Goodman's distaste for his new boss.

Goodman didn't hesitate or ask why. "Are you kidding? The micromanager has me on speed-dial."

"Thanks, man. Can we keep this between us?"

"Got a pen ready?"

"Shoot."

Michael's hands were shaking by the time he finished jotting the number down. He knew he had seen it before—on the restaurant receipt that had fallen off Sophie's dresser.

Michael lifted his elbows onto his desk and buried his face in his hands. His mind raced in many directions, considering all possible reasons why his stepdaughter would have this vile man's phone number.

He didn't like any of them.

He slept on it.

During the drive downtown the next morning, Michael recalled sitting across from Dr. Gordon on her comfy old sofa in the comfy old parlour of her comfy old house. He soon came to enjoy the sessions, more so when he went alone as part of the counselling Dr. Gordon provided to Emily and him. Guarded at first, he soon bought in and invited the good doctor—as he and Emily referred to her—into places in him that even his late wife had never been. Michael could see how having an understanding, non-judgmental ear to dump your emotional garbage on could become a little addictive.

While all discussion sooner or later led to his union with Emily, much of it started elsewhere, at other times in his life, in other relationships. During his last visit, just after the patriarch Tommy Flanigan had died, Dr. Gordon suggested he write his dead father a letter, telling him the things he couldn't when he was alive. She said it could begin a healing process, to help him deal with the glut of issues between the two of them... and would help him deal with his other shit. He never wrote the letter. The wounds were healing, but the scabs too fresh to pick.

He parked on the street, directly in front of Dr. Gordon's Inglewood Drive home, the smallest house on a street lined with grand old homes. Those on the south side backed onto Lake

Ontario.

Taking a deep breath, Michael got out of his car and found himself bounding up the steps and through the front door, ready to go.

He leafed through an old *Life* magazine in the makeshift waiting area in the foyer. He glanced at his watch; just after seven. She was late. The tardiness was out of character, but she had agreed to start her day an hour early for him.

After waiting for a few more minutes, he wondered if she'd slept in. He walked to the bottom of the stairs, the old hardwood floor creaking beneath each step, and listened.

Nothing.

He thought she lived alone, and called out, twice.

Nothing.

He selected her number from the contact list on his BlackBerry, and in seconds heard the ring of an old phone, from a time when all phones sounded the same.

He followed the ringing down a short hallway, just past the shrink's office-parlour, to an open doorway, and peeked around the corner.

"What the—"

His BlackBerry fell from his hand and bounced off the hardwood. He jumped back, put his hands on his thighs, and threw up on the floor.

Michael grabbed some Kleenex from a table in the foyer waiting area, wiped his mouth, and stuck some extra tissues in his pocket. He reloaded with oxygen, and went back into the kitchen.

As he looked at the shiny handle protruding from between her legs, Michael wondered if she'd been sexually assaulted in the traditional way before being raped with the knife.

Her head was turned sideways, her face smeared with blood. The hair was straighter and shorter, but there was no question that the woman on the kitchen table was Dr. Brenda Gordon— and the good doctor was dead.

She had been bound at both wrists and ankles with duct tape. Lifeless eyes stared at him when he leaned forward. A familiar looking white, dimpled object forced her lips into a lazy snarl. The golf ball protruded from her mouth as if left on display. He leaned in to read the exposed label. It was a Callaway, with the Foster Glen logo.

Michael slipped on the splattered blood and banged into the corner of the table.

The golf ball shot from her mouth.

CLOMP.

"*Jeee*-sus."

Clomp-clomp-clomp...

The ball, picking up some of the doctor's blood on its journey across the kitchen floor, rolled to a stop against the opposite wall.

He wondered if her attacker was still in the house. He jerked his head around toward the kitchen doorway, then stopped and listened.

Nothing.

He continued on.

He grabbed an umbrella from a stand in the hallway and slowly wrapped his hand around the knob of the parlour door. He flung the door open.

Empty.

He assumed he was alone. If someone was still inside and had any thoughts of doing him harm, he'd had plenty of time to do so earlier while Michael flipped through magazines and waited for the good doctor who would never keep their appointment. He looked down at her, anger and grief washing over him. The doctor was out, and he wanted to return the favour, to beat on the monster who'd done this to her, to make him suffer.

What kind of animal could do this? Was it fun for him? Michael then thought of the common thread that continued to run through the recent trail of suburban horror: him. Part of him prayed it had been a drug-crazed addict looking for money, just some hideous act like you might see in places like Toronto and

Vancouver and Urban Decay, U. S. A. He spied a soft leather purse on the kitchen counter, bulging at the sides, with the corner of a wallet peeking out the top. The edge of a blue five-dollar bill all but covered the red fifty under it. So much for robbery.

He retrieved his phone and called 911 from the hallway, then noticed a filing cabinet resting against the wall inside the rear door of the house. The middle drawer wasn't flush with those above and below.

A moment after reporting the murder and location to the emergency operator, the phone dropped its connection. He didn't call back.

He moved quickly toward the filing cabinet. He opened the middle drawer, covering the handle with the tissues.

Patient files.

The middle cabinet started with the *M*s. A space between the *M*s and *N*s seemed to indicate someone had been pushing file folders aside in search of a specific file, unless that's where Dr. Gordon had last filed something.

During his solo counselling sessions, Michael had revealed all that troubled him at the time, including his relationship with Jacqueline Zetterfeldt. He had never referred to her by name during therapy, but it wouldn't take a seasoned detective long to jump to an incriminating conclusion from reading the doctor's notes.

What about doctor-patient privilege? Did it survive the death of the therapist? He sure as hell hoped it did, then realized once again that he focused on himself in the midst of another's tragedy.

He closed the middle drawer so the top one could be opened. Flipping through the *F*s, he couldn't find a file marked "Flanigan".

He went to the beginning of the row of files. After "Amo" and "Austin" came "Baggio, Emily" and, a dozen or so folders further along, "George, Sophie".

He knew Sophie had seen someone for counselling, and should have guessed she'd pick the therapist her mother had seen.

He imagined the riches of information that might lie in front of him. How much more could he learn about Emily, who'd had her own private sessions?

Michael pulled another tissue from his pocket and wrapped it around the edge of Emily's file. He stopped, frozen by an unsettling yet warm sensation—that his late wife was watching him. The feeling of her presence evaporated in seconds. He shook his head and removed the file.

He jumped at the sound of a screen door creaking open. He turned to see an elderly lady entering the foyer, carrying a tray of cookies. He slipped the file back in its place, gently pushed in the drawer, and stuffed the tissues in his pocket. The woman didn't appear to notice him. As he hurried toward her, she opened her mouth as if to scream but nothing came out. He twirled his finger to indicate she should turn around and get out of the house. He opened the door for her and said, "Trust me, ma'am. You need to step outside."

The police arrived as he was helping the old woman into a chair on the porch.

"I hear you made the call," said Speagle as he walked up the front steps.

Michael introduced Speagle to Mrs. Bellringer, the traumatized old woman who delivered the cookies she'd made for Dr. Gordon. The detective nodded to her, and led Michael over to the far end of the veranda.

"I gotta tell ya, Mr. Flanigan," said Speagle, removing his hat and scratching his head, "there sure are a lotta dead people following you around."

Michael went through it all for Speagle, from when he arrived before seven until he phoned for the cavalry.

"You touch the body?" asked Speagle.

"No."

"That's three dead in less than three weeks. We might get two or three homicides a year in all of Halton County.

"It's horrible," said Michael. "Unbelievable."

"And all victims had ties to you or your family."

He should have seen that coming.

"Well that's it—I must have killed them all," said Michael. "Wanna guess who my next victim's gonna be? I thought I'd poison my cleaning lady. I didn't like the way she did my toilets last week."

"You been a patient of the doc's for long?" asked Speagle.

"I've been before. Marriage counselling."

"And today?"

"I'm not sure that's any of your business," said Michael, thinking it a difficult question to answer anyway.

"I had a cousin who went to a psychiatrist," said Speagle. "I think he had some guilt issues."

"Cop?"

"Teacher."

"Oh yeah? Did he kill his shrink?"

Speagle grinned. "Can't say that he did."

CHAPTER 20

Jessie's home and cell phones both went to voice mail. Michael walked toward the sound of Artie welcoming someone at his front door, someone with an all-too-familiar voice.

"Forget something, Detective?" asked Michael of Leo Speagle, who stood twirling his fedora in front of him. They couldn't think he had anything to do with Dr. Gordon's murder.

"Mr. Flanigan, is there somewhere we can talk?"

Artie went back to the guest house and Michael led Speagle into the kitchen.

"I understand you've gotten quite friendly with a Jessie Hargreaves," said Speagle.

"I have," replied Michael, anxiety stabbing at his belly.

"Let me tell you from the outset that Ms. Hargreaves will be okay, but she was attacked at her home last night."

Michael dropped into a chair. Speagle grabbed a bottle of water from the fridge and handed it to him.

Michael put the water on the table. "Tell me."

"She was sexually assaulted, roughed up a bit," said Speagle. "She's down at Joseph Brant Hospital. She's got some bumps and bruises, but is doing well, considering, and will be just fine. She asked for you. I thought I should tell you in person."

Through his shock, Michael wondered if Speagle's act was one of kindness or just another police ploy, wanting to see his reaction to the news, wondering if he was somehow involved.

"Were similar things... *done* to Jessie as Dr. Gordon?" asked Michael, thinking of the river of blood that had poured from the doctor.

"He didn't kill her," said Speagle. "Be thankful for that. There are signs of trauma, but it appears that no weapons were used on Ms. Hargreaves."

Speagle told Michael an unknown assailant broke into Jessie's house, likely between nine thirty and ten. A neighbour rang Jessie's doorbell a few minutes after the hour, scaring the intruder out the back door, but not before he had raped and beaten her. He added that the neighbour may have saved her life.

"It was the same guy," said Michael, more to himself than the detective.

"It's an ongoing investigation."

Michael turned sideways in his chair. "Okay," he said softly. "I gotta get down there." He stood up and said, "Let me walk you out, Detective," and escorted Speagle to his car.

"I hear you're doing some sniffing around on your own," said Speagle.

"I'm not sure I—"

"Your wife's death."

Northcott. "I asked a couple of people some questions, if that's what you mean."

"Because you think someone killed her."

"I don't know what I think."

"These recent murders light a fire under you? Make you think there's a connection to your wife?"

"What do you think?"

"Mr. Flanigan, there's more to investigating than asking a few questions between golf games. Why don't you leave things to the professionals? We do know what we're doing, regardless of what you may think."

"I'm sure you do."

"It stops here," said Speagle. He got in his car and drove away.

A policeman sat outside Jessie's room at Joe Brant. The sight of him unnerved Michael. It struck him that if Jessie's attacker also killed Dr. Gordon, he may want to get rid of anyone who could point a finger.

Jessie had been moved from the emergency ward to a private

room. A floor nurse said she may still be under the effects of the sedative they'd given her.

He introduced himself to the watchdog, a Constable Stone, and showed some ID. Speagle had given the guard Michael's name.

When the door closed behind him, Michael said, "It's me, Jess."

Jessie lay on her side, her back to Michael. She didn't respond.

Michael pulled a chair close to the bed and rested his hand on her hip. She flinched, and he pulled it away.

Is this my fault?

She rolled gingerly onto her back and took his hand. Matted hair covered part of a huge bruise that ran from under her eye to the side of her face.

"Tell me something funny," she said, her weak attempt at smiling accentuating a cut on the corner of her mouth.

"Oh Jessie, I'm so—"

"Tell me something funny."

"Something funny."

He told her that his aunt, the former psychiatric nurse who probably thought she'd seen and heard it all, had listened in on their lovemaking in Jessie's kitchen.

After a meek attempt at a laugh, she grabbed at her side. "He punched me there, too."

"Jess, do you have any idea who could have done this to you?"

She cried softly, shook her head. "He blindfolded me, and didn't say a word while he was..."

She broke down. He grabbed some Kleenex from the side table.

"Michael, I think I need some time alone, to think about things. I'm so sorry, Michael, but I'm... afraid."

He wanted to object, but who could blame her. Like Speagle said, dead people followed him around.

"Maybe I should go and come back later," he said.

"I'll call you in a few days, Michael." She rolled back on her side, and closed her eyes.

"I love you, Jess."

"I know."

Michael was frustrated at not being able to stay by her side, to protect her, keep her safe—just as he failed to do for Emily. He was not exactly a lucky charm for the women in his life.

He'd forgotten about the golf game he had lined up with Danny, and decided to drop in at Foster Glen on the way home, to beg off in person. Where else would he go? Noon had not yet arrived on this horrible day, and he needed a friend.

Sitting with Danny in the corner of the clubhouse, Michael relayed the news of the assaults on Jessie and Dr. Gordon. Michael assured his friend that he was okay.

"How the hell could you be?" asked Danny.

"Were you here last night?"

"Played nine, and then edited four chapters sitting right in this chair."

"I don't suppose Northcott was here?"

"You don't think—"

"Was he here?"

"He was going on about this big presentation he's making at the dinner on Sunday."

"How long was he here?"

"He was holding court 'til after eleven, before taking off with his little nympho."

"How about Toner?"

"I did see the jerk-off, but he wasn't with Northcott all night."

"What time? What time did you see him?"

"I'm not sure exactly, but I did see him when I got here, early, and then saw him later, toward the end of the night. You think he..."

"No. I don't know. I have no reason to suspect the asshole, other than he's—"

"An asshole."

As Michael drove home, he wondered who could have carried out the brutal attacks... when Jessie might be ready to see him again... what to do about Sophie... what could possibly happen next. He just fucking wondered.

Barney Farrell called and apologized for not returning Michael's call sooner. He said his neighbours, the Lavallees, were game to show their home and listen to an offer if Michael could act fast.

It at first seemed absurd to Michael, in light of all that had happened, to take off for Kingston. But Jessie wanted nothing to do with him for the short term, and maybe longer.

Clint and Artie had plans to go to a drive-in movie in Oakville. *The Dark Knight* won out over a trip with Dad to Kingston. Artie would keep an eye on the boy until Michael returned.

Barney agreed not to say anything to Lucie about the condo, although Michael wondered if she had been in the room when Barney had called. Michael would pick her up at home and bring her over, to present his gift to her.

Michael parked in front of his house. He sat for a few minutes to think.

A photographer Emily hated is murdered.

The painting... Fronda and the painting... gotta talk to the Scottish dude.

The home invaders. Random? No, no way.

Where did Jacquie fit in?... please don't let that be my fault.

Doc Gordon... Jessie. Shit... Jessie.

Is Bobby George up to something?

Is Northcott sticking his filthy cock in my stepdaughter? He cringed at the thought.

I'm nowhere with this shit.

It's a fucking mess.

I'm nowhere.

He pulled off the 401 about halfway to Kingston, near the town of Colborne, to buy his aunt a pie at a roadside tourist stop called The Big Apple. He ended up buying one for his aunt and one for the old couple with the condo who were on their way to the American desert.

He wanted to call the hospital, but thought better of it. His best chance with Jessie was to heed her wishes, give her some space. He would wait for her call.

Would that call ever come?

Fern called just as Michael was exiting the parking lot.

"Sorry to hear about your lady, Mike."

"News travels fast." *In some circles.*

"A request was made for a DNA check, with a giddy-up on the order. Some patient files were taken from the shrink's place, as well as her computer. Any backup drives or backup disks she may have had were gone. He was obviously there for more than a little fun... sorry, Mike."

"Do they have any leads?" asked Michael, ignoring Fern's comment.

"I can't get that close to it."

"How could they tell some files were missing?" asked Michael.

"One lousy sheet of paper, if you can believe it."

"Huh?" Where did Fern get this stuff?

"They found a one-pager at the end of the file drawer that was a cross-reference to the patient files, like an index. Without that, with the computer gone, they woulda never known." Fern paused for a few seconds, before adding. "It seems your file is missing, Mike."

"You're kidding me," said Michael, not surprised, since he couldn't find the file either. "Who else?"

Michael could hear him flipping a page in his notebook.

"The other missing files were for Eugene Loni, Gary Murphy..."

I guess the sandbagger has guilt issues.

"... Mary Anne Naismith, Paula Northcott, Stanley Orr."

"Northcott's kid," said Michael. "Was Gordon the only therapist in town?"

"She was supposed to be pretty good."

"She was that," said Michael. "The missing files. They're alphabetical, bunched up, *L*s through *O*s, like he reached in and grabbed a handful."

"Very good, Sherlock."

"Were others left behind that would have fallen into that sequence, or were they consecutive files?"

"All in a row, but one."

"Mine."

"Yours."

"What do you think it means, Fern?"

"He may have grabbed more than he wanted, to throw us, I mean... the *police* off the trail."

"Once a cop?"

"I understand you and Barney golf at The Hill," said Michael on the trip to the new home that his aunt still knew nothing about.

"We do play a round once in a while," said Lucie, who laughed after hearing the ambiguity in her comment. "It's nice to go to the golf course without worrying about the loonies from the FCPH hanging around."

Michael chuckled at her irreverence toward the same patients she used to treat at the Frontenac County Psychiatric Hospital.

"Why would you be running into patients on the golf

course?" he asked.

"A couple of years back, I think it was, they had a program at the hospital for a while. I don't know how they ever got it approved. I didn't need to be thinking about that place while I'm on the golf course, where you *know* I'm trying to relax and forget about work. Some of the so-called low-risk patients got to golf for free once a week. Since the hospital is virtually across the street from the course, they could walk right over."

"Free golf and rentals. I guess it's good PR, helping people readjust to the community."

"So they said."

"They don't have this program going anymore?"

"So I hear. I still run into the odd person from the old nuthouse. I guess most of the inmates interested in golf aren't at the hospital anymore."

"Oh?"

"They *graduated*."

They arrived at Barney's condominium building. Michael had told Lucie that he wanted to take a look at Barney's new TaylorMade driver, as he considered picking up a similar model.

Michael stopped at an apartment three doors from Barney's and put his arm around Lucie. He opened the door before she could tell him he had the wrong place. His aunt cried in Michael's chest when she walked in the condo, found Barney inside waiting for them, and they let her in on the con. It was everything Barney had told Michael, with three bedrooms, a huge patio, and a view of the lake.

She walked over and put her arm around Barney, who looked down, blushing.

"Mr. Farrell here is taking me for a romantic few days in the States," said Lucie.

"Where you off to?" asked Michael.

"A charming little place, Barney tells me, called Cooperstown."

Michael smiled and looked at Barney, who winked at him.

"Aunt Lucie, I think a nice long weekend in upstate New York is just what the doctor ordered," said Michael. She had no idea that she was being whisked off for a romantic weekend at the home of the Baseball Hall of Fame.

"Oh, you've heard of the place?"

CHAPTER 21

A familiar vehicle followed Michael into his driveway.

What now?

Speagle parked next to him and got out. The two men leaned back on their cars, facing each other.

The detective flicked the lit end of his cigar on the driveway, patted the end of the stogie, and slipped it into his jacket pocket.

"Been away?" asked Speagle, eyeing the travel bag in Michael's hand.

"Kingston. Visiting family."

"When was the last time you saw Graham Zetterfeldt?"

"Not since I left the school. Why?"

Speagle pulled a ringing cell phone from his pocket, checked the display, and said, "I gotta run." He didn't answer the phone.

Michael ran and caught Speagle just as he was opening his car door.

"Detective, why did you put me in that jail cell?"

Speagle smiled. "Off the record?"

"Okay."

"That may have been a bit much."

Michael thought that was as close to an apology as he would get.

Speagle got into his car, lowered the window, and looked up at Michael. "Who'd you visit in Kingston?"

"My aunt, Lucie Donzelle." He spelled it for him. "The only one in the book." Michael leaned forward. "Detective, is Graham Zetterfeldt dead?"

"Very."

—

"So what's with you and J.P. Northcott?" asked Michael, as he drove Sophie to Ulrich Brothers Funeral Home in Hamilton on Wednesday afternoon. He glanced to his side, and caught her looking at him as if he'd grown a sand wedge out of his forehead.

"*Excuse* me?" she said.

"I know this might not be the best time for this, but I found something that kind of disturbed me. Just for the record, I was not snooping or invading your privacy, not in any way."

She just stared.

"I found a phone number I recognized on the floor outside your room," he said.

"What phone number?"

"J.P. Northcott's."

"You tried the number?"

"I *know* the number." And he did by then, so only a small white lie, he figured.

Less than a half hour from home, they drove west along the north side of Hamilton Mountain, just minutes from Dr. Gordon's viewing.

"I want to say it's not what you think," she said, "but I'm not sure what the hell you think."

"How well do you know him?"

"You think I'm fucking him or something?"

"Sophie, please. Someone mentioned to me that you and Northcott were in a heated conversation down at the arts centre."

"Yeah, I remember. He had too much to drink and made a smart remark. I called him on it. It was no big deal. I barely know the jerk. What are you accusing me of anyway?"

Michael sighed. "Can we just take a step back? Put yourself in my shoes. I think you know how I feel about this guy, but what you may not know is that he has a horrible reputation with women, how he treats them."

"Are you still pissed off at this guy because... what?... he stole your lunch money?" Sophie opened her mouth to add something, then turned and looked straight ahead. "There's nothing for you to worry about. Okay?"

"Then why the phone number?"

"Someone told me he had a photography gig coming up at the club, taking group shots at a tournament. It turned out to be nothing. Someone else got it."

"Sorry I brought it up."

But Michael still felt there was more to it than a job opening, if there even was one, and she never did say she wasn't sleeping with him.

A small receiving line greeted them at the crowded funeral home. Michael learned that Brenda Gordon was born in Gananoque, near Kingston. She grew up in Hamilton, a city Michael thought was like his old friend Danny, kind of rough around the edges, but with a lot to offer if you knew where to look. The good doctor graduated from McMaster University and landed a job at the Clarke Institute in Toronto, where she worked for eight years. She also spent some time in Kingston.

The wake, mercifully, was a closed-casket affair. Michael wondered if the police had shared the atrocities of her death with the Gordon family. The newspapers made no references to pools of red or duct tape or blood-smeared golf balls.

Sophie, the self-proclaimed agnostic, knelt before the casket, head down and crying softly, her hands locked together as if praying.

Michael followed Dr. Gordon's cousin, Lauren Taggart, to a spacious kitchen on the basement level. He poured her a coffee and they parked themselves at one of a half-dozen dinette tables.

Lauren was fortyish, petite, and "a lifelong confidante" of her late cousin. Michael told her of his Kingston connection, and asked the grief-stricken cousin about Dr. Gordon's time there.

"She had her own practice, and also worked at the psychiatric hospital for about a year, maybe less."

"The FCPH?" said Michael. "The Frontenac County Psychiatric Hospital?"

"She couldn't handle it there. They have some horrible people staying in those places."

"When did she work there?"

Lauren shrugged. "A couple of years ago I suppose."

He wondered if Dr. Gordon knew his Aunt Lucie, or if any of the doctor's former patients had paid her a visit in Burlington on Tuesday. The police, no doubt, would have had a similar curiosity.

"Were there specific patients who gave her trouble?" he asked.

"I don't know about that, but when I asked her about her job, she would act all funny and change the subject. After a while, I just gave up."

"Why did she tell you she moved?"

"Brenda said she moved to Burlington to be closer to home. She could drive to Aunt Millie's—her mom's—in a half hour."

Michael nodded. He did remember the doctor telling him and Emily that she had, in fact, moved to Burlington to be closer to home.

"But I think she really wanted to get away from that hospital," said Lauren.

Just when he thought the world could get no smaller, in walked a crying woman in a black dress that hugged her far too closely for the occasion. Lottie Denison sat down two tables away and seemed not to notice them. Her tears appeared genuine. The woman was grieving.

She turned toward them. Her eyes opened wider in recognition, and to Michael she said, "You hang out at the golf club."

"I play there," he said. She remembered him from Foster Glen, but retained either no shame for, or no memory of, the time he found her sprawling bare-assed in the basement office at the club. He would assume that drugs had been in play until someone told him different.

"You're a friend of J.P.'s," she said.

"I know him."

Her tears had dried. She crossed her legs, and Michael thought if her dress climbed another three inches she'd be winking at him.

Michael introduced Lauren Taggart. Lottie said she'd better get going, and came over to shake their hands. She hung on to Michael's for an extra heartbeat or two. "Will I see you at the tournament on the weekend, Michael? I'll be... what do they call it?... on J.P.'s bag."

Michael thought, *I bet you will*, but just smiled and nodded.

Armed with the password she had shared with him, Michael had checked Emily's personal emails soon after she died, looking for anything that might lend a clue to her death. He found nothing but innocuous communication related to work, family matters, bills, and online shopping orders.

When he got home from Dr. Gordon's wake, he scanned Emily's email folders again, thinking a clearer head could help him tap into something he may have missed the first time. Her Inbox contained nothing new, other than a handful of spam emails that had snuck past her junk mail filter.

Under her "Work" folder, he noticed a sub-folder she had named "Stuff". He hadn't seen it seven or eight months before, through his grieving, boozy haze. He opened the folder, which contained just a few emails, all dated within days of her death. One caught his attention—from Duff McPhee, the art consultant in Scotland, dated September 29, 2007.

It was a reply to an email from Emily:

"Dear Ms. Baggio. Received your letter. Thank you for photo. Painting could be authentic. Would need to examine closer to confirm. Nothing in photo suggests a copy or forgery, but would need to see in person. Could be quite a find if validated. Regards,

190

Duff McPhee."

Had Emily figured out that a certain painting should *not* have been attributed to the late Elaine Cavendish?

A second email from McPhee a week later, the day Emily died, was a short follow-up to his last note, asking if Emily planned to dig deeper into the identity of the painting. The art expert seemed intrigued at the possibilities.

A crowd milled around the dart boards in the back of the Judge & Jury. Michael found Freddy Charles at the bar, watching soccer on TV. The bartender replaced his empty mug and shot glass with a freshened pair.

"The boilermaker is on me," said Michael, dropping a twenty in front of the bartender. The bewildered look on the face of Northcott's manservant soon turned to one of recognition. "Well if it isn't my favourite dog lover," he said, more gregarious than the day he saved Michael from the Dobermans.

"Can we grab a table, Mr. Charles?" asked Michael. He dropped a couple of toonies on the bar.

Freddy looked at the four-dollar tip, and smiled at Michael. "It's Freddy."

They found a table on the patio. Freddy drank a third of his beer before he sat down. Michael ordered two more.

"Are you meeting anyone, Freddy?" asked Michael.

Freddy winked. "Same people I always meet."

Michael had no idea what that meant.

"You really do have a genuine hate on for your boss. Don't you, Freddy?" asked Michael.

"Him again?" asked Freddy. He gently rubbed a bruise next to his right eye and said, "I like his money alright."

Michael glanced at the bruise. He hadn't noticed it at Northcott's. "Is it worth the trouble?"

"At my age? What else could I do? Beats walking the mall, or holding a sign so some little brats can cross the bloody road."

The waitress set down the two beers, and got a gentle reprimand from Freddy when she moved her hand toward his not-quite-empty mug.

"Does Detective Alberts spend much time with Northcott?"

"He comes by the house."

Freddy downed the whiskey, slammed the shot glass on the table, and made a face. He chased the Dewar's with the remains of one mug and took a long guzzle of lager from the other.

"Are the detective's visits social calls?" asked Michael.

"He doesn't seem to enjoy them," said Freddy. "Not the friendliest sort."

"What do they talk about?"

"No idea, mate. They always go in the den and close the door. His nibs is a paranoid bugger. He seems to talk in riddles half the bloody time he's on the phone, and young Paula told me a while back that he got the place swept for bugs. Poor dear thought they were looking for roaches or something. I saw the blokes that came in, and they weren't looking for any bleedin' termites."

"Electronic bugs," said Michael. "Freddy, who were these blokes?"

"Never seen them, before or since. They didn't have a van, nothing with a company name on it."

Freddy observed Michael through bloodshot eyes. "I saw you arse over elbow at the feet of the great man," he said. "What's your interest here?"

"All I can tell you is I share your dislike for the man," said Michael, hoping he could play on their mutual disdain. "And I'm worried that he might be hurting someone I care a great deal about."

"Stop fannying around then. You're buying. Ask your questions."

As the booze flowed, Freddy's tongue loosened further. Frank Toner "looks like a nancy boy, but he's not right. I see it in his eyes, mate." Freddy made a "V" with his fingers and pointed to his own eyes. "In his eyes."

Lottie Denison seemed harmless enough, but was hard to predict. When not doting over Northcott, she badgered him over her suspicions that he was shagging someone else, a well-earned mistrust in Freddy's opinion.

"A scary union, those two," said Freddy.

"Ever see Northcott with especially young girls?" asked Michael.

Freddy grinned. "I'd say the freshest bit of stuff I've seen him with was maybe twenty-three, maybe twenty-five, maybe—"

"I get the picture. What about Northcott's wife?"

"Poor woman. She's got the MS, you know. Needs a wheelchair and a full-time driver to get her around when she's in an especially bad way. Stays in her own wing in that big old house. Northcott put a ramp in at the back entrance. Took a few pats on the back for that, he did, but I think he just wanted to get the wife to stay back there and out of his way. Makes it easier for Lottie to... *coexist*, you might say. The young lady stays back there, too. And now the poor dear with her troubles."

"Paula?"

"Well she's so sad, ain't she? And her old man doesn't help. I don't care how much he goes on about how he worries about her."

"How so?"

"For one, I heard the missus one day saying she was off to the psychiatrist with Paula, and the old man gave her a right bollocking about it, right in front of the girl. I think he just doesn't want the word getting around that his kid needs a shrink. All about him, don't ya see?"

"I get the feeling you and Paula get along alright."

"I treat her right, I do."

"Any other girlfriends of Northcott you know about?" asked Michael.

"I think he had a tidy piece on the go last year. He did get a real spring in his step, actin' like a schoolboy in love."

"A mistress?"

"Before Naughty Lottie came along. That's what I call her,"

said Freddy. "Naughty Lottie with the potty mouth. If there's a tradesman or someone workin' outside the house, you can bet Lottie will walk by a window, her bristols bobbing, on full display. Even flashed them at me one day, sunbathing in the altogether in the back garden."

"Was she young, the girlfriend?"

"Never laid eyes on her. Very discreet, he was, at least with this one. But word has it someone got her ear about his need for a little variety, including the odd working girl. She dropped him, and we all got the brunt. But before you know it, Naughty Lottie is on the scene and Bob's your uncle."

"What do you think is troubling Northcott's daughter?"

"Hard to say, mate. I haven't been here for long, but her mom said she was such a happy girl, but now..." Freddy took another drink.

Michael pulled a photograph out of his pocket and slid it in front of Freddy. "Freddy, have you ever seen this girl, maybe with Northcott?"

Freddy picked up the photo. "Cute kid, but I've never seen her before, with his nibs or otherwise. Someone special to you?"

"Maybe." He put the picture of Sophie back in his pocket.

Freddy stood up and said, "If there's nothing else then, I'm gonna go splash the boots."

After taking down Freddy's cell phone number, Michael reached into his pocket and pulled out a roll of bills that were wrapped with an elastic band. The nine inside bills matched the brown one on the outside of the roll—all hundreds. Michael placed it in Freddy's palm, rolling Freddy's fingers over it as he did.

"This is for your trouble," said Michael.

Freddy dropped into a chair at the next table. He licked his lips as he unfolded the roll. While Freddy counted his cash, Michael went inside to pay their tab.

Michael glanced up at the TV over the bar on the way out to the exit. The Blue Jays were beating up on the Yankees. Nothing in his world was normal these days.

CHAPTER 22

Michael braked suddenly when he saw her. Scalding black coffee splashed onto his bare thigh. He ignored the pain.

Jessie sat watching him from the shade of the swing on his front veranda.

She came down to meet him, pulled him close, and kissed him. As her tears trickled down his neck, she whispered into his ear, "I neglected to tell you something the other day at the hospital. I love you, Michael."

As she led him to the porch swing, she apologized for her fear, her doubts, and promised never to abandon him again.

"Abandon me? That's crazy, Jess," said Michael. "But I am worried about you being alone in that house, after…"

He felt her shiver beside him on the swing. She cupped her elbows in her hands and said, "I must confess that, even with my new security system, I am sleeping with the lights on, or at least trying to. I've never been an especially timid person. But now… every little bump in the night…"

They rocked slowly.

"What would you think about staying here with us?" he asked.

Her mouth hung open for a long few seconds, and she snapped it shut. "I can't tell if you're inviting me to come live in sin or offering me a room."

He took her hand. "I know it's kinda fast. But after what happened, I'm going nuts worrying about you."

She dropped her head. "I was worried you would look at me as so much damaged goods," she said. She looked a sad figure, with shoulders drooped and the purple-black souvenir from her attack still prominent on her cheek. The assault had taken its toll on her, and that crushed him.

"Jessie, don't ever think that. When I thought about what might have happened, the thought of losing you..."

"Look, we spend every second we can together anyway," he said. "And I think I've got to know you better in this short period of time than I have with anyone in... well, ever. These are crazy times we're living through, and I think moving in here is what's best for you right now. Think of it as an extended stay, see what happens. Keep your house for now if you like."

She bit at her lower lip, and tugged at her eyebrow.

"I'd like to raze that house," she said. "But I don't want a big step like this to be one we fall into out of fear."

"That's not it, Jess. I just want you here with me. Period."

She smiled up at him. He leaned over and ran the back of his hand over her bruised cheek, barely touching it. "Does that hurt?" he asked.

"It's getting better."

"So what do you think?"

"I squeeze my toothpaste in the middle. I think you need to find these things out now."

He hung his head.

"Darling, if that's a deal breaker, we may be in trouble," she said.

He lifted his chin. "With all that's been going on... I have to wonder if you're much safer here than you would be at home."

"Michael, I'll always feel safer when I'm with you, no matter where we are."

Jessie slept late. Artie drove her home to get a few things, enough to last her a few days. She could enjoy the luxury of not having to move in all at once, or worry about what to do with her house just yet.

Half an hour later, an email from Jessie popped into his Inbox, with the Subject line: "Cold feet?". He opened it and read her one-line note:

"Still want me to move in with you? I'm packing my bags."
Michael responded with:
"Only if you want to make me the happiest guy in the world."
Her reply came in seconds.
"Corny but cute. Now go fluff my pillow."

Clint was thrilled when Michael gave him the news about Jessie, and immediately called Artie into the kitchen to tell him. The three were soon high-fiving all around, and at that moment Michael felt a hope for the future that had been missing for so long.

Sophie wasn't home at the moment, but had stayed there more often since Michael got ambushed in his front hallway. She hadn't returned to the shores of Lake Muskoka, her "favourite place on earth", for days. He wondered if it had more to do with a falling-out with her older man than with a desire to bond with her family.

Michael had already laid the groundwork with his stepdaughter for a potential serious turn in his relationship with Jessie. But it had been nine short months since Sophie lost her mother, and he prepared himself for an emotional fallout when she heard his news.

Jessie and Artie returned within an hour, her quick reappearance giving Michael the image of Jessie racing through her home, grabbing what she needed, then getting out the door and leaving her house behind... her house of horrors. He cursed himself for not going with her.

Within minutes, she excused herself to take a nap. Sophie appeared unannounced, and noticed the bags inside the front door, which Jessie had yet to put away. She mustered a smile for Michael, hugged him tightly, and said, "I'm so happy for you," before retreating to her room.

—

A soft knocking was followed by Jessie's head peeking around the office door.

"You didn't nap long," said Michael, as he continued to make notes about his recent conversation with Freddy Charles.

Jessie walked over and stood beside him.

"Paula Northcott?" she asked, looking at his notepad.

"I had her in school," he said, flipping the page. "I still think about my kids, wonder how they're doing."

"And young Miss Northcott?"

"She played on my basketball team. A nice kid, nothing like her old man. One day, it was like her spirit disappeared. No spring left in her step, sullen, withdrawn. At first I thought it was me, but..."

"Any signs of abuse?"

Michael turned his chair to look at Jessie.

"Sexual abuse?"

While he had wondered what Paula may have seen within the walls of her home, or had heard about her father, Michael never considered the unthinkable.

Jessie sat on the edge of the desk.

"I'm certainly no expert," said Jessie. "But when I was a girl, a friend of mine... *changed*, much like you're describing with your young student. All at once she was always angry, cool to me, and others. I remember thinking at the time that she looked like she never got any sleep. Dark circles, moving slowly."

That described Paula to a tee. "Abuse," said Michael, tossing the notion around.

Was Northcott capable... his own daughter?

"When did you first notice her changing?" asked Jessie. "Is there a time and place you can think of where something might have set this off?"

Michael knew exactly when he had picked up the first signal that something was wrong. He'd asked Paula on a Monday morning, in the late spring of 2007, if she had enjoyed a weekend school trip to Ottawa. She cried and ran away. And he did nothing, forgot about it, writing it off to female hormones. The signals may have been there, but he had been caught up in his own shit.

Michael didn't make the school trip to the nation's capital, as that was the weekend he had spent with Jacquie Zetterfeldt. They rendezvoused in a dark corner of a cocktail bar in a downtown Toronto hotel. They sipped drinks, and after trading a few requisite transparent blurts of "I can't believe I'm here" and "I've never done anything like this" and "Maybe we should just go home", they ended up where they knew they would from the moment they sat down—in a room in the hotel, fucking each other's brains out.

He told Jessie of the trip. Jessie furrowed her brow.

"Did they do anything unusual on the trip?" she asked.

"The usual stuff, I think. The Parliament buildings, all that."

"You didn't make the trip?"

"No."

"How about Mr. Northcott?"

Michael phoned Derek Brennan, a math teacher at his former school and a good guy. Derek was on the school trip to Ottawa. They caught up for a few minutes before Michael asked Derek if any parents made the trip. None had. Only three teachers, the other two being women, travelled east that weekend—plus one other chaperone: the principal, Graham Zetterfeldt.

Of course Graham Zetterfeldt had been there. He had arranged the whole trip, and that's why Jacquie was oh-so-available.

"Derek, where did Zetterfeldt come from," asked Michael. "Where'd he teach before coming to T. J. Walsh?"

"It was a Catholic school, down east. On Cape Breton Island, I think. St. Peter's? St. Paul's? One of the damn apostles."

Michael flicked on his computer and opened his Web browser. He went to a website that a colleague had shown him, where students could praise or vilify their teachers online. Initially horrified by its very existence, he warmed to it a bit after searching his own name and seeing his ratings and comments were virtually all positive. But he still found such a website frivolous and irresponsible. He thought it fed on the cowardly instincts of kids—and parents—who liked to take anonymous shots at defenseless targets.

He found nothing noteworthy pertaining to Zetterfeldt's Burlington days, but Michael did come across an entry for "Zetterfeldt, G." in the teacher listing for St. Paul the Apostle in Sydney, on Cape Breton Island in Nova Scotia.

He clicked on Zetterfeldt's name. The reviews disparaged both his teaching skills—"dude needs another year in teacher's college"—and his personality. Regarding the latter, one comment stood out:

"let me speek 4 those who r afraid 2. this guy is a creep of the worst kind."

Wilf Gazelski was listed as principal at St. Paul the Apostle. Michael had tracked him down on the Yellow Pages website directory. He looked at his watch; still not late, even on the east coast.

"Zetterfeldt. He a friend of yours, is he?" asked Gazelski.

"I used to work with him," said Michael, thinking a mention of Zetterfeldt's murder could scare Gazelski into silence. And he could only hope that the homicide hadn't received much attention from the media down east. "He's a principal himself here now."

"I guess anything is possible."

"Why do you say that?"

"Let's just say I didn't care for the man, and leave it at that."

Michael wasn't about to let it go. "To tell you the truth," he said, "we received some anonymous notes that Mr. Zetterfeldt had been inappropriate with some of the children in your school. We're obviously concerned."

"Who's 'we'?"

"My former colleagues at the school and myself." The cause justified a white lie or two. "I was just calling to find out why he left the school, how he got along with the kids there."

"I suppose I should watch what I say," said Gazelski, "but at my age I guess I shouldn't give a holler."

Here we go.

"I don't know about *children*, and I hope to God there weren't more," said Gazelski, "but there was one girl in our school who had an incident."

"An incident?"

"There was a school trip down to Halifax, back in '03. I remember because I was watching them film some movie about the explosion that happened here in 1917, when I ran into Betty Cuthbertson. She taught at the school, until the cigs finally got her."

Another school trip.

"One of their stops was at Point Pleasant Park," said Gazelski, "where, the story goes, Zetterfeldt separated little Amy Lollar from the herd and took her into the woods. She came running out a few minutes later, crying, saying he touched her in a bad place. He said it was a big misunderstanding, said he could never hurt a child.

"Well, there are a lot of Lollars on the island, fourteen siblings in her father's family alone. Rumour has it a few of the Lollar men paid Zetterfeldt a visit one night. Before they left, they'd made it clear that Zetterfeldt should probably think real hard about a new career, and find a new place to start it."

"So what happened?" asked Michael.

"Zetterfeldt said the damage to his reputation had been done, in spite of his innocence, and had no choice but to move on. But it was the Lollars. He was afraid of them, and should have been."

"Was there no charge laid against him, no investigation?"

"They looked into it. His word against hers."

"How is the Lollar girl doing?"

"Seems fine. Queen of the Furrows last summer, down in P.E.I."

"That's great," said Michael, having no idea, but pleased to learn the girl had moved on.

What if Amy Lollar had not come out of the woods when she did? Would she be Queen of the Furrows today?

Was Paula Northcott not so lucky?

The phone interrupted Michael as he searched the Web for more info on Graham Zetterfeldt. A din of raised voices and clinked glasses identified the caller before he said a word.

"I don't know if this means anything *of value*," said Freddy Charles, "but I heard his nibs talking very hush-hush on the phone with someone, on about some big meeting on Friday. Something about the *out-of-town people* coming in."

"Who was he talking to?" asked Michael, who wondered how much of Freddy Charles's salary ended up in the pockets of the local pub owners.

"Sorry, mate. Haven't got that one."

"Is this meeting going to happen at Northcott's?"

"He said that would be too obvious, whatever that bleedin' means, and that these out-of-towners wanted to meet elsewhere. It'll be at the other place he keeps with that politician. He doesn't know I know about it, but I hear them talking."

"Politician?"

"I couldn't say it offhand. A Polish name I think. A bloody eye chart, it is."

"Wojciechowkski?"

"Ah, the one and the same."

Councilman Wojciechowkski was closer to Northcott than Michael realized, enough to share this place with him, and enough to blow Michael off with a lie when Michael went there looking for Northcott the previous fall.

Michael called Speagle, but had no luck prying anything from him on Zetterfeldt's murder. "Mr. Flanigan, we tend not to share the details of ongoing murder investigations with just any citizen who picks up the phone to ask," said Speagle. "I think it would be in the best interest of you and your family if you just got on with your lives. We're on the case."

"I was just curious about Zetterfeldt. What has that got—"

"It's pretty obvious that all of this starts and ends with your wife, rest her soul, and your obsession with finding some invisible killer who stalks nice ladies on photo shoots. It's not gonna bring her back, Flanigan. Do yourself a favour and move on. Now if there's nothing else..."

Michael had planned to tell Speagle about Zetterfeldt's sinister past but thought, *Fuck you, Speagle,* and said, "Not a thing, Detective."

Freddy Charles would have described the late Graham Zetterfeldt's landlord as drunker than a one-wheeled handcart.

Michael found Jerry Forbes's name online, in a newspaper article on his former tenant's murder, and hoped his condition could play to his advantage.

"Whadya say your name was, Detective?" asked Forbes.

"Briscoe," said Michael. "Has the place been cleaned up since the murder?"

"I tol' the other guy, I wan' some money for the blood on the floor. Won't come out, not all of it, leezways," said Forbes, who must have drowned any logic he may have possessed if he thought the police would pay to return a crime scene to its original state.

"I'll see what I can do," said Michael.

"What was your name again?"

Michael sat silent, until the landlord mumbled, "I shoulda wiped the mirror fore ya got here."

Michael took a chance. "Did all the words come off the mirror okay, Mr. Forbes?"

"There was only *one word*, fer crissakes."

"Of course. Sorry, I'm doing a follow-up and the investigating detective is on vacation, and I'm just getting up to speed."

"Fuckin' cops," said Forbes. "It said *ped-o-phile*, in big bloody letters—"

Revenge. A parent's revenge.

"—Thaz someone likes to fuck kids, or is that in your notes?" asked Forbes, who giggled at that and said, "Now about my money..."

Michael replayed the recording that Danny and Eddie had made, his third listen. He still couldn't recognize the voices, but his money was still on Whack Job and a party girl. He called Danny.

"Higgy, did you have to set up some kind of transmitter at Whack Job's office?"

"Who found it?" asked Danny, panic in his voice. "Please don't tell me—"

"Relax. That's not why I'm asking. Is there still a transmitter at Whack Job's office, maybe somewhere outside his window?"

"It's inside."

"Inside? Are you kidding? How the hell... never mind. And you didn't move it?"

"I forgot all about it. My friend with the management company probably took it out."

Shit. "The guy who put it there in the first place?"

"He stuck it under the desk in the front room. At least I thought he did. It didn't sound so clear when we had them pegged for being right there, at the desk."

"Did you ask him to follow up, to take it out?"

"Haven't talked to him since. Are you going to tell me what this is all about, or should I just sit here and worry about my future all fucking night?"

"I won't let this get back to you. Just don't mention this conversation to anyone."

"Who the fuck am I gonna tell?"

Michael cleared off a section on his desk and emptied out the box that Danny had left behind. After fifteen minutes of playing around with the audio surveillance equipment and accessories, Michael still had no idea how to use the high-tech gadgetry. There were no instructions in the box with the label that read "MegaEar" in big bold letters. It wasn't a name Michael would pick for the latest and greatest in state-of-the-art crime fighting tools. Danny must have picked it up second hand. The electronic gear showed signs of wear and tear, with scratches and what looked like a mustard stain. The botched surveillance of J.P. Northcott had not been the inaugural mission for the MegaEar.

Rita called. "Good time?" she asked.

"Just struggling with technology. Nothing new. I'm wrapped in cables as we speak."

"Don't know what you're messing around with, but I bet Artie could help."

Michael liked the idea. "What's up?" he asked.

"One of Eddie Kan's ex-customers is a client of the firm. We got to talking, one thing leads to another, and I find out the businesses that are taking the big bites out of your friend's client list are owned by... any guesses?"

"Don't freaking tell me. Why that worthless piece of—"

"Yup. J.P. Northcott. Northcott isn't hands-on with these outfits. They're numbered companies, owned by other companies. The former client I talked to—Al Heater's his name—came to Eddie from a referral. There was a string of them, a chain reaction, friends who kept referring the next friend to Eddie.

These clients, all *former* clients now, got calls from the same two companies. They undercut Eddie's rates big-time, and snuck in some nasty comments regarding his business practices."

"Eddie Kan? His smarts are surpassed only by his integrity." Michael fumed at the thought of anyone slandering his friend. And he wondered if Rita put herself at risk for sharing this information.

"You'll love this. One of Eddie's customers in this group of pals googled the two companies who approached him, and was able to trace these outfits back to Northcott. Apparently, that's one of the reasons the clients jumped ship in the end, the credibility from the association with Northcott."

"It has to be payback, for Eddie helping Tommy put together the *Oliver's Landing* deal. Who are the assholes making these calls?"

"Didn't get a name, but they're throwing around the word 'fraud', saying they heard Eddie was in the middle of some kind of forensic investigation."

"Bullshit."

"Funny, Heater said someone else called asking about Eddie, and he told him the same story."

"Did he say who?"

"Just said he was a private investigator."

CHAPTER 23

After spending an hour with Artie, Michael found Jessie in bed, lying on her beaten and bruised cheek, something that would have been too painful to attempt just two days before.

While dejected about having to delay her volunteer work at the shelter, Jessie felt that her facial wounds would make it difficult to convince the residents that a good life waited for them, once they put their abuse and abusers behind them.

As he undressed, Michael wondered what lay ahead. What might her attacker have robbed from her, from them?

She rolled over and caught him watching her. She smiled at him and said, "We'll be okay." He got into bed and was soon pressing his hardness against her, involuntarily. He didn't want to rush her. She reached down and whispered, "What do we have here?"

As he began to enter her, she pulled back, in obvious discomfort. Things were "still a little tender down there", but she assured him her resistance to making love was merely physical. She tapped her forehead and said, "Things are just fine here." He held her, and told her there was no hurry. He wasn't going anywhere. She was asleep in minutes.

Jessie rose early. Still distanced from her attack by mere days, she had filled her calendar for the upcoming week with as many bookings as she could manage, reasoning that keeping busy was the best medicine. "Some cowardly prat", as she referred to her rapist, wasn't about to keep her down. She had even lined up a couple of appointments to round out the day after her therapy session that morning.

Certain of the underlying denial in her admirable rebound,

Michael prepared himself for a hard crash from the bravado.

Michael couldn't come up with a good reason why Fern would not tell him about talking to Eddie's client, Al Heater. If Fern had, in fact, been the private eye who called Heater, Michael had to assume that Fern called Heater *after* Michael had last spoken to him—when Fern had reported that his probe into the exodus of Eddie's clients was a "dead end".

Michael called Rita to thank her for lining up Jessie with a psychologist friend. After some small talk, he said, "I should get going now. It's time to bring her home from the doc's."

"Bring her *home*?"

"Jessie's a great girl, Rita."

Rita paused. "She's lovely, Michael, but do you think you might be moving a little fast?"

"You said the same thing about Emily," he said.

"*And* Denise."

Michael sighed. "Rita, I'm sorry for not telling you sooner."

"No apology necessary."

The hour in therapy exhausted Jessie. She spoke little of it. Once he got her home, she cancelled her client appointments and he tucked her into their bed.

He would not go so far as to call her manic, but she did have blips, out-of-character highs and lows, and slept a lot.

He wondered what the therapist had in mind for making this wonderful lady feel whole again.

Artie had gone over the use of the surveillance equipment until Michael became as proficient as he was going to get in the short term. Michael had told him he wanted to record a conversation as part of a joke he was playing on a friend. Artie said not to worry about the frequency settings, saying that, "Once they're synced, they're synced." Michael just nodded, only concerned about whether the damn thing would work.

He knew it was a long shot that his little scheme would bear fruit, even if the transmitter was still in the office. Freddy didn't know who Northcott would be meeting or when they would arrive.

Michael drove past Northcott's estate on his way downtown. The house was dark and the driveway empty, except for Little Jimmy's MG.

Northcott had already left for his meeting.

After driving past the house, he checked his rear-view and saw a yellow Beetle pull into Northcott's. He pulled over, waited. Within a minute the Volkswagen's headlights came on and it tore out of the drive, tires squealing, and blew past him.

He recognized the driver, and wondered what reason his stepdaughter could have for visiting J.P. Northcott, or his halfwit son.

Just after dusk, Michael eased to a stop in front of the Locust Street low-rise where Northcott and the councilman shared the downtown office. Lights were on in two units on the second floor and one on the third. Michael's interest was in Unit 303.

Feeling somewhat conspicuous, he backed up under a broken street light in front of the office building next door. Based on the trial runs with Artie, he would still be within the MegaEar's range. He would soon know if the transmitter was still in place and functioning. If not, he'd be home for the eleven o'clock news.

He put in the earpiece, which was connected to a wireless receiver the size of a pocket novel.

Voices.

"Glad you could make it, John." *Northcott.* "Take it easy with the candy, Frankie boy."

"Sure you don't want a line, Johnny?" *Toner.*

The voices were distant, but discernible.

Someone was inhaling more than just air.

Cocaine.

"I told you, they test me."

Alberts!

"So take off your coat and make yourself a drink," said Northcott, his voice less clear now.

No silhouettes could be seen in any of the lit units. No one on the street seemed to take notice of him. He was just a guy listening to music, waiting to drive his wife home after her dinner out with the girls.

More snorting. The refusal from Alberts sounded bad-cop to Michael. *They test me.*

For the next few minutes, the three men made small talk, some of it unintelligible as the transmission quality fluctuated from high-pitched static to mediocre. When Michael could make out what was being said, Alberts said little. The other two men were animated, in a scattered and mindless conversation about golf and women and drugs. Northcott came across more buddy than boss with Toner. No doubt about it, both men were sampling the coke.

"I'm outta here," said Toner. "I'll be back with the star of our show. She's right around the corner."

"What's that supposed to mean?" A woman's voice, more distant but recognizable.

"Frank's bringing a friend by," said Northcott. "I'm sure you'll like her."

"I'll fucking bet," said Lottie Denison, just before a door slammed.

"Later," said Toner, and another door opened and closed.

He's coming out.

"Is she going to be a problem?" asked Alberts.

"She'll be fine," said Northcott. A desk drawer slid open.

Michael slid down in his seat, then wondered if Toner would recognize his car.

"Northcott, when the hell do I get to meet your friend?" asked Alberts.

A car started. Michael thought it came from the rear of the building. Toner must have parked out back.

"It was supposed to be tonight," said Northcott.

"I *know* it was," said Alberts, his simmering anger evident, even through the static.

"What can I say? He cancelled just before you walked in."

"What did I tell you about snorting the powder?"

"John, you know I need to do a bit to keep up appearances with my notorious associate... with Frank. Plus, the little lady in the back loves this shit, and is quite forthcoming after a little dusting of the white powder. Don't worry. Everything is under control."

"There will be no second chance if you fuck this up."

"Relax. The man is busy. Something came up. They want to set up another meeting for next week. Let's just look forward to the golf tournament, shall we?"

The man?

"Let's get through Sunday under the radar," said Alberts. "Keep the cheating and theatrics on the golf course to a minimum. Don't do anything to get under Flanigan's skin. Play the round, do your little presentation, and get the fuck out of there."

"So tense, John," said Northcott. "I resent the implication about cheating, and certainly don't need to with Flanigan, who can be counted on to choke when he's up against me. Besides, what does he have to do with any of this?"

"He seems to be watching you like a hawk," said Alberts. "We are too close to have him stirring things up. I need to take a leak."

Footsteps... a door opens, closes... another door opens... "For me?" from a woman, distant, had to be Lottie... more footsteps... a zipper?... Northcott, moaning... "I knew you'd like that trinket, Kitten."... *slurping?*... more moaning... a door opens... footsteps...

"What the hell... I was gone for two minutes," said Alberts.

"Want some of this, John?" asked Northcott.

"Give it up, Johnny," said Lottie, sounding slightly out of

breath. "Let's get that big black cock of yours out, get it workin'."

"I'm outta here," said Alberts.

"More for me," said Northcott.

In less than a minute, as the blowjob gurgled on, the door to the building opened and Alberts stepped out. He surveyed the street, up and down, taking in the Rover. He took a second look toward Michael's vehicle, this time more than a fleeting glance. Michael hoped it was just Alberts being a cop, a crooked one no less, taking a longer look at everyone and everything.

A black Mustang whipped into the parking spot directly in front of the building. Its headlights died, and Toner and an overdone blond got out.

Catching himself staring, relaxing his guard, Michael looked back to Toner—who seemed to be staring right at him.

Michael slid further back in his seat, and leaned to his right until they were out of sight. Hopefully, he was, too.

He braced himself for the appearance of Toner's ugly smile through the car window, maybe even waving a revolver.

Instead, he heard laughter.

Michael raised his eyes above the dashboard. The three were still in front of the building. The blond, a good six-feet-two of her, ran her hand along the detective's arm. His body language read embarrassed. He extracted himself and ambled down the street, in the opposite direction.

The hummer on the third floor continued, with mounting enthusiasm audible from both Northcott and Lottie.

Toner and his date entered the building. Michael listened in with the MegaEar, waited. A door opened on the third floor.

A woman who had to be the blond said, "Frank, is this what you meant when you talked about the good blow?" She let out a white-trash cackle.

"Who's this dork-snorkeler?" asked Lottie. "You hired a pro?"

"Watch it, honey," said the blond.

"You fucking piece of shit, J.P.," cried Lottie. Something heavy and hard bounced off a wall. Bare feet stomped along the hardwood floor.

Soon the golden-haired Amazon was servicing both Northcott and Toner. Michael wondered who was getting what done to whom.

He learned more than he ever could have hoped for. Northcott was a drug user, involved with Alberts, a crooked cop.

Toner was Toner, and Lottie Denison, with the mental stability of a yo-yo, didn't mind a ménage-a-whatever, as long as she was the belle of the ball.

Michael caught himself listening a little longer than he needed to, and decided he'd had enough of the amateur porn show. It was time to go home.

After a warm reception from Paulie and Silvio, Michael walked back to the kitchen, where Artie and Clint were caught up in a game of Scrabble. Clint said Jessie had been in bed for an hour.

"Buddy, sorry to break up the game, but could I have a few minutes with Artie?" asked Michael.

Artie followed Michael to his office.

"How'd things go tonight, Michael?" asked Artie. "Did the joke work?"

"Just fine. Artie, may I ask why you didn't put up more of a fight when Northcott railroaded you out of your job at Foster Glen? Everyone seems to know his kid did the things you were accused of."

"My kid needed braces," said Artie, dropping his chin.

Artie had been bought, and it would have humiliated him to take money from Northcott, to ignore the injustice done to him. Michael would never bring it up again.

"Listen, Artie," said Michael. "Do you think you could take something I taped and put it in some kind of a file that would run on a computer?"

Artie's tolerant smile appeared. "It's not a tape, Michael. It's a digital recording. And sure, I could create an MP3 file for you. You could play it on your iPod or your computer."

Sophie had taken dibs on Emily's iPod.

"I don't have an iPod," said Michael.

"But you have a computer."

Michael called Freddy on Saturday morning, too early to rouse a pub-crawler, but he was on Michael's payroll.

Freddy answered after five rings, just as Michael had decided to try him again a little later. "I'll be quick, Freddy. Did you ever see Northcott doing drugs?"

"I have seen his nibs with a little powder on his lip."

"Did he do it openly, in front of you?"

"Yes, sir, right in front of me." Freddy hacked a smoker's laugh. "When I looked through the crack in the door, and saw him doing it, he was right in front of me."

The fourth of July behind them, Michael hoped Lucie and Barney had decided to head back to Kingston before the weekend was over. He got lucky. They had just walked in the door when he called. Lucie had a new Avon customer, an old lady who lived alone on the outskirts of the city in Fort Henry Heights. Michael's aunt had taken a personal interest in the woman and had promised to take her to play bingo that night.

"I didn't pay all that much attention," said Lucie when Michael asked about the FCPH patients who made the golf outings to the Hill. "I guess there were two or three that I saw more than once."

"Any women? One named Lottie Denison maybe?"

"A mix. I didn't know their names. I never recognized any patients from my ward."

"Did any stand out? Maybe an attractive woman in her thirties, with a hitch in her swing, kind of like Jim Furyk's?"

As soon as the words left his mouth, Michael realized the chances were next to nil that Lucie would know of the elite American golfer. She turned from the phone and said, "Barn, who's that guy you said the girl from the hospital swung like? Was it Furis?"

Close enough, thought Michael.

"Close enough," said Barney in the background.

"Your message sounded urgent, Michael," said Rita. "What's up?"

Michael told her about his stakeout.

"*Mother of God*," said Rita. "You broke the law when you recorded that conversation. Don't tell a soul about this, and don't do a thing until you and I have sat down and I've had a chance to listen to it myself."

"Rita, I think I need to—"

"I'm tied up for the rest of the weekend, but march that tape into my office—my home office—on Monday afternoon."

"It's not a tape."

"What?"

"Never mind."

Michael sensed that learning of Lottie's stay at the same hospital where Dr. Gordon once worked didn't really give him much of anything. Lottie had been genuinely distraught at the funeral home. But with Lottie Denison, who knew what gem of a revelation waited around the next corner?

He had to find a way to get a CD into the hands of the right person, but couldn't shake his fear of going directly to the police to finger one of their own. And Artie could be up the creek for his role in this if Michael didn't play it out just right.

Why was he not worried about Artie's risk in this before he involved him?

A blend of fear and excitement scraped at the insides of his belly.

He had another plan.

He took a trip to *Best Buy*.

PART III — THE FINAL ROUND

"The most important shot in golf is the next one."

—Ben Hogan

CHAPTER 24

Michael woke early on Sunday, feeling rested. Clint sat by himself at the kitchen table, poking at his cereal with a spoon.

"Mornin', buddy," said Michael. "Ready to lug your old man's sticks at the Foster Glen Classic?"

"Dad, could you get someone else to caddy for you today?" asked Clint.

"I don't really need a caddy, Clint. I just thought it would give us a chance to hang out."

"I *was* looking forward to it."

"But?"

"It's that jerk Northcott. I heard that last year he fired Artie, for like no good reason."

Clint impressed Michael with his stand on principle. Michael himself would soon stop looking the other way, and hoped Clint would ultimately see a trace of nobility in his father's next trip to Foster Glen. Depending on how things went, it could be Michael's last visit to the club.

"It's okay, Clint," said Michael. "You're a loyal friend."

"Don't tell Artie, okay? He'd feel bad if he thought I wasn't going today because of him. We're going to a ballgame later. I just told him I like baseball better than golf."

"Not a word."

After Clint left with Artie, Jessie appeared at the foot of the stairs wearing only one of Michael's white cotton dress shirts and a burgundy ankle bracelet.

"Care to relax for a few minutes before heading out for your game?" she asked.

"Yeah... um... sure," he said, not entirely sure of her intent.

"Um sure?"

"I just thought, you know, you've been..."

She took his face in her hands and kissed him. "Will you relax, Michael? Just be the no-bullshit git I fell in love with, and stop trampling on the eggshells with which you've surrounded me."

She started back up the stairs, her curves in motion.

"Git? That's not good, is it?" he asked.

She glanced back at him over her shoulder. "Not as a rule," she said, and continued her slow climb.

"And who says 'with which' in normal conversation?"

She stopped and turned. She'd undone the shirt, down to the middle button. "People who speak the Queen's English, rather than MTV's." She ran a hand up her thigh. "Michael, I think we have a few things to... flesh out." She laughed her sexiest, throaty laugh.

Aroused, but also concerned she might be forcing the issue too early in her recovery, he followed her up the stairs to find out.

Despite playing the seductress just moments before, Jessie was tentative with her movements as Michael undressed her at the foot of the bed. He found her vulnerability alluring, like everything else about her. The hunger he had missed soon crept into her eyes, and they fell into a familiar sexual rhythm that he had feared may have been lost.

At first slow and gentle, his thrusts gathered momentum as her breathless cries grew louder, until an overpowering orgasm consumed them, assaulting his senses and completing their passionate dance. Jessie had come back to him, home at last.

As she lay there, her head on Michael's chest, tears ran down Jessie's cheek. Michael wiped away a teardrop with his thumb.

"Not to worry, darling," she said. "I feel fine. These are most definitely happy tears."

"Then cry some for me."

"Thank you for loving me, Michael."

"You're welcome."

She giggled. "How can I resist your charm? Aren't you supposed to be golfing?"

Michael rolled over top of her and onto the floor. He got to his knees, took her hand, and said, "I think I need a shower *before* I play today."

Michael grabbed a gym bag from the back seat of his car and spotted Eddie Kan on the Foster Glen practice green.

"Hey, Mike," said Eddie as Michael approached. "You ready to take on the field today?"

"Not sure if I'll scare anybody." Michael felt a familiar nervousness, the good kind, a feeling in his gut that told him he was ready to go.

He had radically adjusted his expectations, aware that his skills had peaked at a young age. He never really had a golf game he could have taken to the highest level of competition. And he didn't want to sound like one of those has-beens who talked of how great they were, or could have been, decades after any semblance of athletic triumph.

But on a day rife with distractions, Michael hoped to fight off the anxiety and kick Northcott's ass, on *his* golf course, in the Foster Glen Classic.

The summer's relentless foul weather, pushed aside for the moment by the blue skies above, had an impact on the schedule at Foster Glen. The remaining available days for golf would continue to dwindle as the weekends passed and the falling temperatures became more of a factor. The tournament, usually a three-day grind that would see the cream rise to the top, had been reduced to a one day, winner-take-all format.

While a shorter tournament left the door open for a lesser golfer to stand on his head for a single round and win the tournament, Michael was happy not to tax his wrist over a weekend-long marathon.

They would go off in groups of three. Northcott would play in the final group with John Alberts and a toady from Northcott's corporate office named Patrick Blais, a member Michael had yet to meet. Michael supposed Hizzoner the Mayor had other obligations.

Michael headed for the locker room and Eddie went to the first hole. Eddie's group would be well into their round before Michael's group teed off.

Michael scampered up the back stairs to the dining room. The room was empty except for a couple of youngsters setting tables. A heavy red curtain was pulled across the end of the room behind the podium. The kids paid him no attention, and when they stepped into the kitchen, he emptied the contents of his gym bag. He placed the Bose sound system on the floor behind the curtain, plugged it into a wall outlet, and inserted his new iPod into the unit. If Clint's similar system at home was any indication, the Bose would have no trouble penetrating the ornate old draping.

"I hope you're not in a hurry today, Mike," said Danny. He nodded toward the third member of their group, who was warming up on the driving range a few tee blocks away.

Having best friend Danny in Michael's group felt like a smoke screen, as it could never compensate for being matched up with the snail-like Everhart Lang. "He makes Ben Crane look like the fucking Roadrunner," said Danny, referring to the PGA player they call "Mr. Slow Play".

Michael would tee up in the second-to-last threesome, with Northcott up his ass in the final group, an arrangement tailor-made for the new dictator of Foster Glen. It was clear the groupings had not been determined by the usual random draw, Northcott's fingerprints were all over the player designations.

—

On the first tee, Lang introduced his caddy, Tony Pilkington, a fellow alumnus from both Appleby College, the private school in Oakville, and the University of Toronto law school.

"The shit should be flying today," said Danny to Michael as Lang teed up, not bothering to lower his voice.

Patrick Blais stepped forward to introduce himself, and Detective Alberts offered a friendly hello.

Northcott sauntered over as they waited for the group on the first fairway, which included the Murphy twins, to get out of range.

"I hope the marshals keep an eye on those two," said Northcott. Michael wanted to say something about calling the kettle a sandbagger.

The first balls hit by Lang and Michael landed a few feet apart, two hundred and sixty yards down the fairway, eliciting polite applause from a gallery of about fifteen. Danny found the first cut of rough just under two hundred yards from the tee.

The game was on.

Michael played an efficient first seven holes at even par. He felt comfortable over the ball and got out of trouble when he had to. Lang and Pilkington tended to have a meeting of the minds over every shot. As a result of Lang's deliberate approach, Northcott and his threesome breathed down their necks on every hole.

Danny chugged along, stickhandling to what would unavoidably turn into a triple-digit score, and compounding the distraction presented by Lang's plodding pace. Danny had recently added a prolonged waggling of his club to his pre-shot routine, à la Sergio Garcia, but it did nothing to improve his game.

Michael dwelled neither on the infrequent poor shot nor on

the issues that dogged him off the course. Quieting thoughts of his plans for later that day presented an entirely different challenge. But so far, he had coped.

The driver Michael had commanded early in the round deserted him for a couple of holes, fickle tool that it was, but he got it going again before making the turn.

He sank an eighteen-footer for a birdie on eight.

On the ninth fairway, Lang threw three handfuls of grass to check the wind, then hit his ball into the rear trap. Michael pushed a four-iron to the right, into the front bunker, but knew he'd made that up-and-down many times over the years.

"That's where they found her," said Pilkington, as Michael stepped into the bunker.

"Found who where?" asked Lang.

"The schoolteacher's wife. Jacquie somebody. In the bunker Flanigan's in."

The ninth, thought Michael. *How the hell could I have forgotten?*

Michael went to his cart, wiped down the grip on his sand wedge with a towel, and returned to his ball. Aware of his shaking hands as he readied to hit, he had the unnerving sensation that he was standing on what had been the temporary grave of Jacquie Zetterfeldt.

His ball rolled to a stop eighteen feet past the hole, but he managed to compose himself enough to two-putt for a bogey, and walked off the green at even par for the front nine.

Lang, who had played Michael stroke-for-stroke over the first eight holes, needed two attempts to exit the sand and then two-putted to make the turn at one over.

Michael scanned the area outside the clubhouse and realized he hadn't seen Frank Toner or Lottie Denison since arriving at the course. Perhaps her onit at Friday night's sex party had extended into the weekend.

The leaderboard showed that Nathan Rourke and Sam Killoran, a pair of twenty-year-olds, shot 69s and shared the lead in the clubhouse at one under. Michael didn't know either of the young men, and had a little work to do if he planned to beat the kids.

Northcott came up from behind Michael as he walked to the tee block on ten.

"Your playing partner thinks he's at the office," said Northcott, "billing by the hour."

"I hear that," said Michael.

"How'd you do, Flanigan?"

"Even. The lawyer's one over." Michael didn't know Danny's score, and guessed Danny didn't either.

"Well done. Sounds like you're on top of your game."

"And you?"

"Struggled to one under so far—"

Fuck off.

"—but fared better than my partners. Pat's getting there okay but he's not making anything. The yips are killing him—you know what that's like. He's at least a few strokes over. And I'm afraid Johnny left his game back at the station."

Michael stopped in his tracks en route to the tenth tee.

Jessie stood chatting with Danny. As people often did, she looked somewhat bemused as she listened to him. Michael could only imagine the gems pouring from his friend's mouth.

"Hey," said a voice from behind. "Okay if I tag along the back side?"

Michael turned to his grinning son. "What about the ballgame?"

"Artie figured out I was hanging back cuzza him, and he didn't like it. Jessie's last job finished early, and... well..." Clint shrugged. "Here we are."

Jessie winked at Michael and took Clint to the canteen for a drink.

"Jessie seems like a real classy lady, Mike," said Danny. "But with a little bit of zing." He grinned at Michael.

"More than a little," said Michael.

"I think you should buy her some flowers if you win this thing," said Danny.

"Why's that?"

"Your game has perked up more than your dick since you met that broad."

On the tenth hole, Michael hooked his drive into the woods and booted it around to a double-bogey.

After three-putting for bogey on the par-three eleventh, he parred the next two holes before dropping long putts for birdie on fourteen and fifteen—both soliciting raucous cheers from Jessie, Clint, and most of the couple of dozen spectators now following him—to scramble back to one over for the day. His driver had not come back to him entirely, but still showed signs of being open to reconciliation.

Everhart Lang stood at the sixteenth tee at three over. Barring a miraculous closing argument, the lawyer would lose this one.

Danny's game deteriorated further, but his mood didn't. He hummed and joked his way around the course. Maybe so much whistling past the graveyard, Michael thought, but he still envied Danny's ability to keep a lid on the frustrations of the humbling game.

Word came from a passing marshal that the one under posted by each of the two youngsters was still the score to beat.

Michael leaned on his bag on the sixteenth tee and assessed a burgeoning wind. He thought a low-flying "stinger" would help him control his ball on this short par four of three hundred and seventy yards. And while he had no intention of risking the club he could never master, Michael didn't see his two-iron when he looked at his bag.

He scanned his irons again. "What have I done with that stupid two?"

"You don't really want to use it?" asked Danny.

After some hesitation, Michael said, "No, but—"

"I took it outta your bag after nine."

"What?"

"It's in *my* bag. I could have a hundred clubs in there and no one would give a fuck."

"What the hell for?"

"What did you do recently when you demolished your wedge?"

"I replaced it."

"That all? Add anything else to your repertoire?"

"I bought a new sixty-degree lob wedge when I was at… shit."

"That's right, skippy. You've been luggin' fifteen clubs around for the whole fucking tournament. One over the limit."

"How the hell could I have—"

"You've had a lot on your mind."

"Good catch," said Michael, and then, "Huh."

"What?"

"By rights, to be fair, I should—"

"Turn yourself in? You do and you'll be wearing that two-iron out of your backside, and that would just look too funny," said Danny, his voice rising. "Do you think you've had any kind of advantage because you've had an extra stick in your bag that you never use?" The lawyers glanced over, and then went back to displaying the "anal" in their analysis of the next shot.

"That's not the point."

"Do you want to beat Northcott or not? Would you not like to wipe that smarmy, self-satisfied look off his face, stick it up *his* ass for once?"

For once. Had he never beaten him at anything?

A marshal chased the Murphys out of the woods alongside the fairway ahead. A spectator who had followed the final pairing for the previous few holes caught up to Michael's group. "Northcott is one under through fifteen," he said. "Blais and the big cop are blowing their brains out."

Michael put the thought of the extra club behind him. He chose a fairway wood for the stinger and executed the shot as well as he ever had, leaving himself a nine-iron from the middle of the short grass.

He hit his approach shot tight and made a tricky, downhill six-footer for birdie, looking for just a heartbeat like it would lip out before it dropped into the back of the hole.

He had two holes remaining, and was one behind the clubhouse leaders and the pompous proprietor of Foster Glen.

Michael hooked a four-iron on the long par-three seventeenth, and threw his club at his bag. It bounced twice and missed hitting Jessie by a foot.

"What the hell, Mike," said Danny.

Jessie gasped, and Michael's heart leapt into his mouth. The small crowd of followers went silent, including his son, who stood red-faced.

Michael walked over and took Jessie's hand. "Jess, I'm so sorry," intentionally loud enough for all surrounding the tee block to hear. "I promise you I will *never* throw another club again."

"Don't be silly, darling," she said. "I throw more clubs than you do. Now go hit your ball."

He hit a mediocre shot, but got a fortuitous bounce and drained a nine-footer for his par.

The eighteenth hole stretched out ominously in front of them. A long sloping green, guarded by a trio of yawning bunkers, sat four hundred and forty-eight yards from where Michael stood on the tee.

"The good Lord hates a coward," said Michael, pulling out his driver. He had little room for error on the tight fairway, the trees lining the left side less than thirty-five yards from those on the right.

With the wind at his back, Michael nailed the big stick, clearing three hundred and ten yards and landing in the first cut of rough. He could see most of the ball, a good sign that his lie might be kind.

As they walked along the fairway, Danny put his hand on Michael's shoulder and said, "I want this one for you, buddy."

The short rough cushioned his ball nicely, and Michael hit an eight-iron right at the hole, hitting the flag. The ball bounced fourteen feet past the hole. It could have been worse.

The leaderboard by eighteen confirmed that Michael remained one stroke behind the leaders.

On the green, as Michael read the line from back of his ball, Danny walked over and asked, "You got any muscle memory with this one?"

"Now that you mention it, I don't recall the last time I stood over this putt... not from here."

Michael circled the hole, inspecting all angles. He saw six inches right and slightly downhill. He took his customary two practice strokes, stood over the ball, and backed off. *Eight inches right.*

He needed the birdie putt to stay alive.

He repeated his pre-shot routine, and stroked the ball. *Too hard. Ten feet past if it misses.*

The ball pounded into the back lip, bounced straight up in the air... and dropped into the hole, to tie the leaders in the clubhouse. He heard a shout from Clint and a squeal from Jessie.

All stood and watched Northcott's threesome come up eighteen.

Northcott's approach shot stopped thirty-six feet from the flag. He had to get down in two to join Michael and the two others in a playoff or, if the golf gods had gone mad, make the putt to win the tournament.

Blais and Alberts finished up, setting the stage for a gripping finish, a drama starring The Great Man, as Freddy Charles had mockingly referred to Northcott.

Northcott surveyed the green surrounding his ball, then stood over his putt.

Danny crooked his mouth to the side and said, "If he makes this I'm gonna break another of your wedges, this one over his fucking skull."

Northcott put a lovely stroke on the ball. It seemed to have the line... was it hard enough?... had a chance... rolled close... and stopped, a rotation and a half from the cup. Michael realized he'd been holding his breath and emptied his lungs. He half-expected Northcott to wait for the wind to pick up with hopes it would nudge the ball into the hole, but he tapped it in, and tipped his visor to a smattering of applause.

A marshal announced that, in the sudden-death playoff format, the participants play one extra hole at a time, with those still tied for the lowest score moving on to the next hole until a winner has been determined. They would rotate through holes sixteen-seventeen-eighteen until one man was left standing.

Given their small stature, Michael assumed that each of the young men, Rourke and Killoran, had a short game to be reckoned with and would not be long off the tee. Rourke crushed his drive on the par-four sixteenth, long and straight, and Killoran did the same.

I should know better, thought Michael, as the slight-of-build Canadian star, Mike Weir, crossed his mind.

Michael and Northcott both found the fairway with three-woods, their shots falling short of the other two balls.

If Rourke or Killoran had a touch around the green, they didn't show it in the playoff. Both needed another two shots to get on, and both two-putted for bogey. Michael and Northcott made efficient pars, shook the hands of the other two, and went on to seventeen.

On the short walk to the par-three seventeenth, Michael looked over at Northcott, who seemed without a care, as if strolling to get his Sunday paper from the end of the front walk. Michael felt anything but relaxed. He wanted to win this thing.

And he hated that he craved it so badly, hated the hold that his hatred of Northcott had on him.

Michael hit first. He stood over his ball, calm and confident, the demons exorcised for the moment. *Tempo, tempo.* He drew his club back...

"*Aaah-chooo.*"

Michael tried to hold up on his swing, but could not. He shanked it, and his shot went skittering into the rough, less than a hundred yards from the tee. He turned toward the source of the sneezy outburst—toward Northcott—and tried to read him.

"Flanigan. My God, man. I'm sorry," said Northcott, wiping his nose with a silk handkerchief. "It's these gosh darn allergies. I've got no control over them. Please, tee it up again. If ever a mulligan was called for..."

"Can't do it," said a course marshal from a cart behind the small gallery.

"I beg your pardon," said Northcott. The Great Man looked stunned at being questioned by one of his subjects.

"Sorry, sir," said the young marshal. "A player cannot repeat a shot due to a distraction, without penalty, whether the distraction is from a spectator or a fellow competitor."

"You're sure about that?" asked Northcott.

"Yes, sir."

Northcott turned to Michael and shrugged.

Didn't take him long to cave.

Jessie stood with her hand on Clint's shoulder. They were watching Michael, waiting to see how he'd handle this.

"Not a problem, J.P.," said Michael, smiling. "These things happen. I'm happy to play it where it lies." *Would he stoop that low?*, thought Michael, but he knew the answer.

A glance back at the faces of Jessie and Clint told Michael that on this day, regardless of the tournament's outcome, he had won something there on the seventeenth tee.

Northcott hit the three-iron of his life, rolling it two feet from the hole. Michael could not deny being impressed by the clutch shot under pressure.

Michael had trouble getting out of the rough, and his second attempt went eleven feet past the hole.

Northcott tapped in his short putt and was the winner of the Foster Glen Classic.

Michael shook Northcott's hand, resisted an urge to pull him closer and knee him in the balls, and instead offered warm congratulations.

He had to move on from this battle to win the war.

"That sneeze sounded so totally fake, Dad," said Clint on the way to the parking lot. Jessie raised her eyebrows and nodded.

"Let's not worry about it, buddy," said Michael. "It's over. It's just another golf tournament, and I'm looking forward to having a nice dinner. It's too bad you guys couldn't join me."

Michael could later explain his little white lie about the limited seating at the post-tournament dinner. But he still felt bad about not being truthful with his loved ones.

The golfers did hog most of the seats at the dinner. Some members who didn't participate in the tournament, many of whom Michael guessed had little social life away from the club, came just for the meal and flowing alcohol. That would suit Northcott, who would want a full contingent for his inaugural Foster Glen tournament as Lord and Keeper.

"Could he not come up with something better than that?" asked Danny.

Michael suggested Danny forget about the sneeze if he were to have any hope that Northcott would help him find a publisher for his novel.

"Nine killed you," said Danny. "I've seen you hit that bunker shot tight a dozen times."

"Paying for my sins," said Michael, who again pictured Jacquie

Zetterfeldt, lifeless and lying in the bunker.

"What the hell does that mean?"

Michael didn't answer, but gave Danny a heads-up about his plan to bring down Northcott during the dinner. He didn't tell him how he planned to do it, but suggested he keep his distance from Michael lest he be found guilty by association in Northcott's eyes.

"You're planning to embarrass Northcott in front of the whole club?" asked Danny, like he wished the show could begin immediately. "Let's get the hell inside. I'm gonna make sure I have a ringside seat."

Northcott approached. Danny ignored Michael's advice. "Hey, J.P., weird your allergies sneaking up on you like that. But congrats on the big win, no matter how you got it."

"Thanks, Higgins. It was most unfortunate. My apologies again, Flanigan."

"Ancient history," said Michael.

"Funny thing, allergies," said Danny. "I have brutal allergies myself. But today I never felt better." Michael had never seen Danny with a Kleenex in his hand.

"They affect everyone differently. I forgot to take a pill," said Northcott, not biting. "Better grab a shower if you intend to, gentlemen. The playoff bumped into the dinner hour, and they'll be serving the grub before you know it." He continued on toward the clubhouse door.

"What kind of sportsman would pull a gutless trick like that?" said Danny to Michael.

Northcott walked back to Danny. "Say, Higgins. I forgot to give you the latest update on the publishing thing. It completely slipped my mind. I spoke to my pal, the publisher. Turns out he didn't care for your little story. Sorry it didn't pan out."

Northcott took a step away from them and turned back. "You know, Higgins, I hear self-publishing is all the rage," he said. "And my companies are always looking for competent accountants, if you want to flip me your resume."

Danny cursed him and marched inside.

Northcott turned to Michael. "I think I get your relationship with that sycophant now, Flanigan. He's someone you can always look good next to."

Michael smiled and said, "See you at dinner."

CHAPTER 25

Michael's table at dinner included Eddie, Sam Killoran, the two lawyers, and Lottie Denison. Danny's empty seat separated Michael from Northcott's concubine. She looked at him as if she'd like him to trade places with the cherry she had just slid into her mouth. He chugged half of the beer that someone at the table had ordered for him before he arrived.

The power she must have, thought Michael, this feral siren. He assumed her appearance at his table instead of Northcott's was a by-product of her contempt for sharing the floor, perhaps literally, with the hooker in the downtown office. Lottie's dress was more formal than golf-wear, and her tone more haughty than that of the nympho he'd stumbled upon in the club basement. A role for all occasions, he thought.

Michael looked around the crowded room. How would they react to his contribution to tonight's festivities? He kept his resolve. He would fight the good fight, and would deal with the consequences.

Northcott stood at the table next to his, holding court over a cluster of middle-aged members. He had changed into a tailored black sports jacket, with a white shirt open at the collar, cuffed taupe casual slacks, and black Italian shoes. He managed to appear cool and refreshed among a sweaty and haggard throng on the thick July day.

As a waitress emptied a tray of beer onto the middle of Michael's table, his insides began to bubble.

Damn. Not now.

Fucking colitis.

Michael checked his pocket for the Imodium and ibuprofen supply he'd stashed in a Ziploc bag for just such an emergency, and dashed for the men's room.

—

Michael returned after dinner had been served. Lottie chatted amiably with the captive audience at the table. While Danny had his most lecherous leer on display, a couple of drinks had Pilkington glassy-eyed with a locked-in, open-mouthed ogle. Michael thought that at any moment the lawyer just might leap across the table at Lottie.

Michael picked up sound bites from the surrounding tables... *did you hear... mother died Tuesday... so I pulled out my five-wood... who needs another?*

All conversation would soon be riveted to a single topic.

Michael's colitis symptoms had settled. He would try to stay calm to avoid another flare-up.

As the staff cleared the dinner plates, Northcott worked the room, slapping backs and shaking hands. He skipped Michael's table, either to avoid risking the contempt of Lottie Denison or a brush with Danny, who was well-oiled after a few cocktails.

Lottie glared at Northcott as he walked past them toward the front of the room. Two staff members wheeled a portable display screen front and centre. Speakers sat on chairs on either side of the screen. A laptop rested on a table off to the side.

Northcott cleared his throat, and spoke into a handheld microphone.

"I'd like to thank everyone for coming out today," he said. "I'd also like to apologize for being such a rude host by winning the darn tournament." Some polite laughter ensued, and he moved on.

"While you enjoy some dessert, I thought I'd say a few words to recap what I feel was a great year here at Foster Glen, and also to talk about some plans we have for the future. It's been my great honour to assume ownership of this fine old club. My pledge to the membership is to do everything in my power to continue to make the Foster Glen experience second to none for our members and their families."

The dinner crowd applauded. Michael sipped his beer and did not join in. Nor did Danny or Lottie.

Northcott walked to the laptop and said, "They tell me I just have to click on one button and we'll be off to the races."

Michael drank more beer. The impact of what was about to happen suddenly seemed more ominous.

Had he thought this through?

What have I missed?

Northcott continued. "Let me first thank some people..."

Sweat dripped from Michael's brow. His head got lighter. He looked at his half-full pint. He'd had less than two beers.

The screen filled with a slide of the hospice bearing Northcott's name.

Michael began to feel disoriented. He cursed himself for mixing alcohol with his medication, although it had never bothered him before.

"Let me now take us back to Ladies' Day," said Northcott, "one of our favourite tournaments of the year—"

"Are you listening, Detective Alberts?" asked Michael. The room was spinning now. He pulled the remote control from his pocket.

All heads turned.

He pressed the remote. Nothing.

"Flanigan, are you alright?" asked Northcott.

He pressed the remote again, a third time, and a fourth. Nothing.

I'm not alright, thought Michael as he attempted to balance his heavy head on his shoulders, feeling like a bobble-head doll as he did. *Whazgoing on... happening to me?*

Michael extended his arm, aiming the remote at the curtain, wildly punching the power button.

"You lithn up too Northcott," he slurred, just as the speakers came to life.

"*Yes, I have been unfaithful, but think of what I've been through.*"

The voice belonged to Northcott, on the edge of tears.

"*My poor wife, in a wheelchair, nothing I can do for her. My poor kid... all she's been through. That fucking monster. He got his.*"

The playback stopped.

The crowd gasped, a single shocked entity.

Michael dropped his head to his hands.

"Is this supposed to be funny, Flanigan?" asked Northcott. He turned to Danny. "Are you in on this, Higgins?"

Michael, fighting to maintain consciousness, blurted, "Supposa be different tape."

The crowd reacted.

"You're disgusting."

Can't stand up.

"Get some help, Flanigan!"

Am I dying?

"I hope you're proud of yourself."

Michael continued to weaken. Lucid thoughts were beyond him. He could barely hear his own words when he mumbled, "I heard 'em doin' drug... havin' seth."

Someone squeezed his shoulder... a hand on his face, lifting his head. "Are you okay, Mikey?" *Danny.* "Hig. Hep me, Hig."

Lottie giggled.

Michael caught a blurry view of the Murphy twins, shaking their heads. He managed to spit out, "He cheez at goff," before being launched through a door.

CHAPTER 26

Michael lay in the dark, face pressed against leather. He took in what he could of the room from his prone position. His hip ached. Locating the source of his discomfort, he yanked his pill supply from his pocket, and sat up.

As his eyes adjusted, he spotted a small fridge a few feet away. He hauled himself over to it, grabbed a bottle of water, and tried to assess his surroundings between gulps.

He opened the door to the room, slowly, and peered out to a dark, deserted hallway. He stood still for a few seconds, listened. Nothing. Dead quiet. He pulled the door shut and flicked a switch on the wall.

He knew the room, and the loveseat he'd just risen from.
I'm still at the club.

A vivid image popped into his head of the last time he'd seen the leather two-seater, when Lottie Denison lay naked across it, bleeding, inviting.

He instinctively checked the small couch for traces of old bodily fluids, and found none. He located his BlackBerry on the floor in the corner of the room. The time display read: "10:48PM". Dinner would have started before seven.

Photos covering the far wall took his mind off his grunge-mouth. Northcott was in most of them. He must have usurped Randy Goodman's office when he bought Foster Glen.

Northcott. The recording at the dinner... it wasn't mine. How the hell...

Michael sat down and closed his eyes, trying to find the hours he'd lost between the dinner table and the loveseat.

His BlackBerry vibrated; a message from Jessie. A tearful one, he soon learned. She'd heard about the "episode at the dinner", and pleaded with him to call her right away, to let her know he was okay. She couldn't locate the cabbie who taxied him from the club.

Cab? Had he left and come back?

Danny had left a similar message, minus the tears.

What the hell did happen?

Michael heard footsteps off in the distance, upstairs.

A call came in on his BlackBerry before he could listen to his other messages.

"Where the fuck are you?" asked Danny.

"I'm still at the club."

"At the club? How the... are you alright?"

"What happened to me at the dinner?"

"Man, you were zonked. Rahim said he put you in a cab."

"I don't remember a fucking cab."

"Easy, cowboy."

"Sorry, Hig." Michael filled him in on what little he could remember.

"Northcott ran out the back door of the dining room about ten seconds after Rahim and Alberts dragged you out the front," said Danny.

"Did you see me have more than a couple of beers?"

"Nope. But all of a sudden you were fucking blasted."

"Was Lottie still there?"

"She just sat there, calm as could be in the middle of all the chaos, canary feathers sticking out the corner of that great little mouth of hers. She did say, 'Maybe that'll teach the whoremaster a lesson.'"

"Northcott left right after me?" asked Michael. "Right. He was crying, on the recording." It was the last thing he remembered. Could Lottie have swapped in the other clip, or was she just enjoying the show?

"Northcott was all fucked up I guess, and took off," said Danny. "The shindig fizzled out in a hurry after that."

The footsteps got closer.

"Jessie called not too long ago, looking for you," said Danny.

"She was frantic, man, and said your boy was pretty upset, too."

Clint. Shit.

"How the hell did they find out?" asked Michael.

"Jessie's real estate friend was there. I guess she couldn't wait to call Jessie with the post-game summary. They aren't answering the phone at Foster Glen. I was just going to head back there to see if I could find anyone who could tell me what cab company they called."

Someone tapped on the door to the office.

"Gotta run," said Michael, and he stuck the BlackBerry in his pocket.

Rahim stepped inside. "You're still here, sir," he said.

"I guess I had too much to drink and someone put me in here to sleep it off," said Michael, aware that Rahim may have deposited him there.

"Quite alright, sir. Are you just about finished here for the evening? I was about to lock up."

"All set," said Michael.

Rahim walked with Michael to the parking lot, empty except for a few cars, probably belonging to golfers who cabbed it home after having a few drinks. A dark four-door was parked next to Michael's Rover.

"Rahim," said Michael, turning to face him. "Is that your—"

Rahim pointed a handgun at Michael.

"So sorry, sir," said Rahim, who grabbed Michael's arm with his free hand and led him to the sedan. Rahim pushed him into the car after cuffing his hands behind his back. "We aren't going to hurt you, sir," said Rahim, in the same calm, gentle voice he always used. Michael wanted to believe him, but wondered if Rahim said that to get him to drop his guard, just before emptying his gun into the back of his head.

Rahim got in the back seat next to Michael. A thick-necked goon with deep-set eyes sat behind the wheel. He put a disc in the CD player. Rahim slipped a hood over Michael's head.

"Northcott didn't have the balls to pick me up himself?"

yelled Michael over a blaring rapper who ranted about his motherfuckin' bitch. Michael was scared shitless, but would not let them see it. Would his name be in tomorrow's headlines?

"Where the hell are you—" Something hard, likely a gun barrel, poked into Michael's ribs, stifling his question.

"Turn that shit off," said Rahim, and the rapper went quiet. "Sir, this will be a more pleasant ride for all of us, especially for you, if you remain quiet."

Michael assumed the music had been cranked up to prevent him from recognizing any sounds that could help him retrace the route to the secret lair of his kidnappers. That gave him some hope that they didn't plan to kill him. Then the music died, and he wondered if he would too. He thought if the woollen hood continued to itch his face so severely, he might ask them to shoot him.

About a half hour later, they turned onto a gravel road. Hilly... potholes... branches scratching against the side of the car. After a few minutes on the back roads, the sedan slowed to a stop.

Rahim grabbed Michael's arm and led him away from the car, stopping after a dozen or so steps. After three knocks, a door opened. Nothing was said as they led him inside.

"Sit him down. There." He recognized the voice, and his hopes of walking out of the room under his own power took a sizeable downturn.

Someone standing behind Michael removed the handcuffs and pulled off his hood, but the relief was short-lived.

Detective John Alberts did not look happy to see him.

Neither did Fern Da Silva.

"I guess that explains the cuffs," said Michael to Alberts. He turned his stare to Fern. "I never thought you'd get in bed with the likes of him."

"Mike, shut the fuck up," said Fern, "before you say something you regret."

"A little late for that," said Alberts.

"I heard this guy in the middle of a coke-sniffing—"

"*Mike.*" Fern stopped Michael short.

They sat at a table covered with a vinyl tablecloth in the middle of a spacious old kitchen, not unlike Danny's. Alberts flipped open a notepad. An overhead chandelier provided the only light in the room.

"I can't seem to walk into a kitchen without you wanting to interrogate me, Detective," said Michael, referring to the morning his dogs found Vinnie Fronda.

"Why don't you lose the attitude, maybe even show a little appreciation?" asked Alberts.

"Come again?"

"And you can lose any notion you have about me being dirty."

"I should call home," said Michael.

"Soon enough," said Alberts. He looked to Rahim and the goon, standing off to the side. "Thanks, Rahim. And thanks a lot, Leonard."

Another Leo?

"What's with Rahim?" asked Michael.

"These men are police officers," said Alberts.

"Rahim? He's worked at the club for over a year. And since when can you just kidnap people off the street?"

"Would you rather we arrested you?"

"Arrest? For what?"

Fern pressed a finger to his lips and gave Michael one of his looks.

Alberts said he would tell Michael some things that he would not normally share with a civilian. Michael had his doubts.

Rahim, and a host of other officers from various departments and jurisdictions, had worked on a covert police operation for over a year. As part of the exercise, Alberts, while not technically undercover, got close to J.P. Northcott. Alberts gained his confidence and convinced Northcott that he could be had, for a price. During the course of the operation, Alberts persuaded Northcott to turn informant to help them catch a much bigger fish, in return for some "considerations" regarding his own "activities".

"Why'd you stick me in the basement at the club for three or four hours before dragging me here?" asked Michael.

"Too many folks around," said Alberts. "Easier to babysit you at Foster Glen until the place emptied."

"I talked to your sidekick Speagle. You knew I was poking around, that I visited Northcott."

Alberts nodded.

"Why didn't you pull the reins on me sooner?" asked Michael.

"We tried," said Alberts, "And then we thought you were really no more than a nuisance. We figured there was more risk to raising a flag by putting more pressure on you, until we learned that *Mister* Da Silva here was doing your *poking around*."

Mister. Alberts was reminding Fern that he was no longer a cop. These guys may be in bed together, but they didn't seem to like it.

"How did you find out?" asked Michael.

"Doesn't matter. Here's how this is going to play out. We will tell you only what we think you need to know to get us all on the same page here. Nothing more, nothing less. In return, you will do three things.

"You will answer all of our questions, no exceptions, holding back nothing. Secondly, you will stay away from J.P. Northcott. Lastly, you will repeat nothing we talk about today to anyone. If you do, I promise you that you will end up in prison, along with some of your friends."

"Prison? For what?"

"For starters, I understand that even before this latest fiasco you'd been illegally recording the conversations of private citizens."

Michael glared at Fern, who remained stone-faced.

"Is Speagle in on all of this?" asked Michael.

"Detective Speagle is up to speed. Tell us about the recording we heard at the club."

"I have no idea who was responsible for that one."

"That one?"

Michael told Alberts about the night he sat outside the unit on Locust Street. Alberts held up a palm soon after Michael had begun his account of the coke-snorting orgy. The cop had heard enough to confirm that Michael had been eavesdropping on their little party.

"So that's what you were going on about at the golf club," said Alberts.

Michael told them about his iPod setup, and the recording that never played.

"That explains the remote control," said Alberts, who then left the room for less than a minute, in all likelihood to call Rahim and tell him to look behind the curtain in the Foster Glen dining room.

"How did you get so wasted?" asked Alberts. "You weren't in there for more than a half-hour after you came off the golf course."

"I only remembering having a couple of drinks."

"Some tolerance."

"I'm on some drugs for my colitis. Maybe the mixing did me in. "

"What kind of drugs?"

"Over the counter stuff, for the pain."

Alberts turned to Fern. "Better get him checked out."

Fern nodded.

"How does a cop sit there and watch someone do cocaine?" asked Michael.

"I have no intention of explaining police procedures to you," said Alberts.

"I think I understand a little about how the police do things... like not telling the public about the message scrawled in blood on Zetterfeldt's mirror."

"You'd better have a good explanation of how someone would know that if they weren't at the scene."

"Relax, Detective. Do you really think I'd mention it if I'd been there? How'd you convince Northcott and Toner and whoever else is involved in this that you were, you know, *dirty*, so they'd trust you?"

"Not your concern."

"Is Bobby George involved in this?" asked Michael.

"Who?"

"Never mind. Lottie said something afterward about teaching Northcott a lesson. I don't think she likes sharing her man. Could she have set up the audio starring her blubbering boyfriend?"

"Huh," said Alberts, rubbing his chin. "I heard she was none too happy when that hooker walked in. And she is unstable, to say the least. But she's not a stupid woman. She seems to be able to play any role a situation calls for. But to pull that off..." Alberts mulled for a moment, then laughed. "She is a piece of work, isn't she?"

Alberts ran the tip of his pen over the notes he had taken. "Tell me the whole story," he said.

Michael gave his account without further implicating anyone. He wouldn't turn his back on the others who helped him get into this mess. He told Alberts that he bugged the office to get something he could use against Northcott, and had figured out how to use the surveillance equipment on his own.

"You told no one about this latest scheme?" asked Alberts. "Nobody helped you with any of it?"

"Not a soul," said Michael. "I swear."

"Your lawyer friend didn't know about this ill-advised piece of espionage?"

"Rita? She would have killed me if she'd known."

"How'd you get the transmitter into the office?"

"I uh... broke in," said Michael.

Alberts wrote on his notepad and said, "I'll probably want to talk to you about this again, but we can consider adding this to the waived charges if you don't impede our efforts to get to end of job."

Michael glanced at Fern. He hadn't told them about Danny's

arrangement with the building manager on Locust. He had let Michael decide how to play it.

"Thank you, Detective," said Michael, who did feel fortunate to have this deal. And he thought he'd better keep his temper and mouth in check before they took their offer off the table.

"How well do you know Rita Manale?" asked Alberts.

Rita again. "I'm guessing you already know the answer to that," said Michael, glancing at Fern.

"She doesn't seem too particular about who she represents," said Alberts.

"She's a *criminal* defense lawyer," said Michael. "Do you... are you referring to *me*?"

Alberts looked at his watch. "Remember, you don't breathe a word of this conversation, or get involved in any further criminal activity. If you do, you are on your way to jail, along with anyone else we find out is involved. You came that close," said Alberts, holding his index finger and thumb an inch apart, "to blowing an eighteen-month investigation."

"Seems I've had a lot of people telling me to keep my mouth shut."

"That tell you something?"

"I'm free to go?"

"You co-operated."

"And if I hadn't?"

"C'mon, Mike. I'll drive you," said Fern.

"What, no blindfold, Detective?" asked Michael. "So I won't be able to find your secret little hideout?"

"Oh, this is Leonard's summer place," said Alberts.

Michael stood to leave, and then fell back into his chair.

"What now?" asked Alberts.

"Rahim began working at the club over a year ago, last summer," said Michael. "Isn't that right?"

"Northcott spent a lot of time there. Why does that concern

you?"

Fern leaned over to whisper something to Alberts.

"Your wife?" asked Alberts.

Michael nodded.

"Here it is in a nutshell," said Alberts, who explained to Michael how they determined that J.P. Northcott did not kill Emily Baggio.

They were working on Northcott for months before Emily's death. When she died, Northcott had just flipped and began working with the police. Northcott was not alone the morning Emily went down the side of the Niagara Escarpment, as the police reported. Detective Alberts had been with Northcott at the time of the accident.

"He could have had someone do it," said Michael.

"It's highly unlikely," said Alberts. "We were monitoring his calls. We had to be careful after that, as his... *business associates* began instigating bug sweeps. But the point is, he spoke to no one about harming your wife. And no banking transactions were ever found that could be interpreted as a gun-for-hire situation. We felt that was a quite a leap anyway, but we had to pursue it, just in case. C'mon, Flanigan. Who's gonna take a hit out on a fine lady like your wife?"

"You guys really did look into it," said Michael.

"That's what we do," said Alberts. "So, unless Northcott sent his little girl or his English butler to murder your wife, we don't see how he could be involved."

"He's allowed to negotiate for that big Muskoka deal, and then to buy Foster Glen, with all of this going on?"

"Has to be business as usual for this to work."

"What about Toner?"

"We have no evidence that they even knew each other then."

Michael got up and walked toward the door. He stopped and said, "Detective, if you hadn't treated me like such shit, like such a criminal, I'd be tempted to apologize for being all wrong about you being a bad cop."

"What can I say? I take issue at drunks who publicly defame the badge. What you did, Mr. Flanigan, was deplorable, whether you were in mourning or not."

Michael hung his head, and nodded.

"I'm sorry," he said.

Michael thought he should throw Alberts a bone, in the spirit of mending fences.

He told him about Graham Zetterfeldt and Paula Northcott.

CHAPTER 27

"How long has Alberts had your ear?" asked Michael.

"He gave me no choice," said Fern.

"At least I know why you didn't tell me about Al Heater."

"Heater? Eddie Kan's client. Very good. We couldn't have you get even more pissed at Northcott."

"How much bullshit have you been feeding me?"

"It's all been good."

"Fern, you're supposed to be working for me. I'm paying you, for chrissakes."

"I was... am. It's just that lately my movements have been... limited."

"There's that word again."

"So you remember."

They drove in silence for a while.

"I got a reaction out of Alberts when I told him that Graham Zetterfeldt may have molested Paula Northcott," said Michael.

"I didn't see it," said Fern. "And he could have dug that up on his own."

Fern turned up a song by The Razorbacks on the radio. They listened for a minute until Michael turned it down and said, "This can't bode well for our old friend J.P."

"We might be talking witness protection," said Fern. He turned up the radio, not quite as loud as before.

Michael whistled. "Witness protection for J.P. Northcott. My oh my."

"It would happen overnight, literally," said Fern. "One day he'd be playing eighteen with the mayor, and the next day... we'd never hear from him again."

"What makes them think he won't just take off?"

"He's on a short leash. I think the people he's in bed with, the assholes the cops are after, present more of a concern to Northcott than the police. They'll have a sweet deal for him if he plays ball and sees this thing through. At this point, I don't see that he has a lot of options."

"Do you know what they have on him?"

"Alberts wouldn't say specifically. But reading between the lines, I'd say the drug trade."

Michael recalled Northcott telling Alberts he did the cocaine to "keep up appearances".

"Fern, wouldn't the deal be off if Alberts found out Northcott had committed a major crime since he's been working for the police?"

"Where you going with that?" asked Fern.

"Did you learn anything about how Zetterfeldt was killed?"

Fern's silence told Michael that he had.

"Did he have a golf ball in his mouth?" asked Michael.

Fern chuckled. "Not a golf ball."

"What then?"

"His mouth was stapled shut, and he was missing *an appendage.*" Fern looked sideways at Michael and raised his eyebrows. "Then they found a little surprise in his mouth."

"Ouch. Something tells me it wasn't an Italian sausage."

"I think he was Swedish."

"It makes sense. He molested Northcott's little girl."

"His history may suggest that Zetterfeldt was a pedophile," said Fern. "But from what you told Alberts, they found no proof that he messed around with Northcott's kid. And as far as I know, the cops have nothing else to suggest Northcott is good for this murder."

"The missing files from Dr. Gordon's. Find those, and I bet they learn that Paula Northcott was being molested."

"They'll talk to the kid's mother, if they haven't already. But the party line says it's one guy, a psycho who likes to play with knives. Run down the list. Fronda, the doctor, the Zetterfeldts. Did Northcott do all of them?"

"Northcott would have had a good reason to use the knife on Graham Zetterfeldt. Let the perv get a taste of his own dick. The perfect revenge. There's no reason to cling to the single killer theory."

"Is that so, Detective?"

"Fuck off." Michael sighed, took a second. "Sorry, man. I'm just—"

"Emily didn't get... she didn't die that way," said Fern. "Are you thinking her death might be unrelated to the others now?"

"The killer wanted that to look like an accident. Fern, Northcott killed Zetterfeldt, or had someone do it."

"Someone like who?"

"Toner would be a good bet."

"Nothing says Toner is a killer, but they would like to know where he is."

"So someone else then."

"Not your problem."

"Who the hell are the cops after anyway?"

"Gotta be big fish."

Michael shook his head. "Even with his ass on the line, up to his eyeballs in shit, this prick could land on his feet somewhere."

"If they *can* prove Northcott was involved with killing Zetterfeldt, they'll throw him in a cell next to the wise guys, once they get what they want from him."

"We can only hope."

"I know he's a low-life, Mike, but you've gotta smarten up about things. You did hear the little reference to prison from Alberts? You'll be dragging a lot of people down with you if you keep this up, not the least of whom will be yours truly. I get a pass so far for feeding you a few things, for now, but only if you do nothing to fuck up this operation for them."

Fern was right, and the additional risk of exposing unwitting accomplices like Danny and Artie was the tip of the iceberg. How would he explain to his family that dear old Dad was heading off to jail because he interfered with a plan to bring down a "big fish"?

He had to get home, explain things to Jessie, and to Clint. But how?

Would his performance at the club get back to the prospective buyers of *Oliver's Landing*? His Uncle Don sounded more nervous with each email to Michael, the last one mentioning threats by the investors to pull out because of the media attention from the protesters.

"Maybe Northcott killed Jacquie for revenge," said Michael.

"Made Zetterfeldt suffer for a while in this world before sending him off to the next?"

"Works for me."

"Beats the alternative," said Fern. He looked over to Michael, who did prefer the Northcott-as-killer scenario versus one where Zetterfeldt butchered his wife because of an adulterous tryst with a certain former gym teacher.

Michael wondered if Fern had told Alberts about *The Golfer*.

"What was Alberts going on about... about Rita?" asked Michael.

"If they were looking at her for something, I doubt they'd be telling you about it. By the way, she is kind of hot, in her way. Is she seeing anyone?"

While Fern flipped through a year-old *Sports Illustrated*, Michael scanned the three-quarters full waiting room in the Joseph Brant emergency ward. A transvestite in a red dress, with a two-day beard and a black eye, sat in a corner chair next to a uniformed cop. Fern didn't know the cop and showed no interest in impromptu bonding with someone from The Job.

In the seat next to the man with the shiner, a woman with close-cropped hair and an extra hundred pounds rested a badly swollen wrist on a roll of her girth. She took every breath like it might be her last. A nervous little man with a nicotine-stained beard patted her good hand and told her repeatedly that "it shouldn't be too much longer".

Two chairs up the adjacent wall, a tall balding man of about forty, wearing a tux and a pained expression, sat with his forearms crossed over his groin.

Tuxedo threw a dirty look at Black Eye, who blew back a kiss. Without looking up from his magazine, the cop said, "You two stay the hell away from each other."

"You might not have the best story to tell in the room," said Fern, who threw the magazine on a table.

"I don't need to be here," said Michael. "I feel okay."

"Give it a rest, Mike."

"You said the cops would like to know where Toner is?"

"You didn't see him at the club. Am I right?"

Michael strained for a memory that wasn't there. "I don't remember seeing him, but..."

"I heard Alberts talking on his cell," said Fern. "He seemed concerned that the person on the end of the line didn't know where Toner was at."

"Like they were tailing him, and lost him?"

"No fucking idea," said Fern, in less of a whisper than was appropriate, drawing raised eyebrows from a young woman in the seat across from him. He returned an exaggerated expression of contrition. She blushed and smiled, and lowered her head.

A woman in her thirties grabbed a folder from the slot on the examining room door. She closed the door behind her as she read the file, and introduced herself as Dr. Baweja. Michael had anticipated an accent, probably Indian. She had none. He told her about the events at the club.

"You mentioned having problems with your balance, some recollection of being confused, not able to focus," said the doctor. "Then a headache afterward, pronounced memory loss."

"Right."

"Have you experienced this before?"

"I have lost consciousness before," said Michael. "And I had a headache and some memory loss when I came to. But the circumstances were different."

"Tell me about it."

Michael told her about getting mugged at home, and waking up on the kitchen floor. "I was clubbed on the head, and wasn't taking any meds." He rubbed his scalp. "I can still feel a little lump there."

"This all happened to you in the past couple of weeks?" she asked.

"I lead a charmed existence."

She examined his head, checked his vision, took his blood pressure, and had him close his eyes and stand on one leg. She steadied him when he had trouble with the latter, and wrote something in the file.

"Mr. Flanigan, while you shouldn't be mixing alcohol with over-the-counter drugs like ibuprofen, it's highly unlikely the combination would cause the symptoms you described."

"What about the Imodium?"

She shook her head. "Did you go to the hospital when you were hit on the head?"

"In Oakville."

"And?"

"It was a crazy night there, an overflow crowd in emergency. They checked me over. You know, for concussion, blood pressure... everything. Said I was good to go."

"We'd better take a look."

"How long have you had this red mark on your buttock?" asked the doctor. Michael was face down on the examining table, bare ass skyward. "Or are you even aware of it?"

"Yeah, I noticed it a while ago," he said. "It was a little tender for a while, itched a bit. I figured it was a pimple or something."

"Have you had any shots lately in this area? Any needles?"

"No."

She pulled down his gown. "I think maybe you have."

"Someone stuck a needle in me?" asked Michael.

"Not tonight, but it does appear you've had a mild reaction of some sort to an injection you received recently. You said you noticed it a while ago?"

"Right," he said, and thought about it some. "I'd say about two weeks ago."

"Around the time you were assaulted in your home."

"I suppose. Are you telling me... but I was bopped on the head. I don't remember feeling anything else."

"Let's run some tests and see what they tell us."

"So I could have been given a needle to knock me out, like that serial killer does on TV? He gives his victims some sort of horse tranquilizer before he slices them up."

"How charming," said the doctor. "If someone did stick a needle into you, I doubt it was etorphine. It would be too risky, even with naloxone. Maybe dihydroetorphine, but my guess would be something like midazolam. Ninety-eight percent of a drug like midazolam is out of the system within fifteen hours, but we can take a look, for that and a few others."

"What about my passing out at the golf club?"

"The tests will tell us more, but your symptoms are consistent with a drug like flunitrazepan, commonly known as Rohypnol."

"Isn't that one of those date rape drugs?"

"One of the more popular ones, I'm afraid."

"Well at least I know I wasn't raped."

"It doesn't look like it," she said.

"You checked?"

She smiled. "It did present like a cut dosage of flunitrazepan, in that it affected you so mildly. Not to make light of this, Mr. Flanigan, but it could be much worse, especially when mixed with alcohol. At the very least, victims of this drug are usually out for four to six hours or longer."

"Are you telling me I may have been drugged twice in the past couple of weeks?"

"We'll let you know. And we will have to report our findings to the police."

"Of course," he said. "I'm with an ex-cop friend of mine now. He brought me here. I'll be telling him all about this." Why was he being defensive, when he was the one who kept getting violated?

"Are we done here?" he said. "I need a shower in a bad way."

"I would have to agree with that diagnosis."

Michael listened to a voice mail that his Aunt Lucie had left while he was at the hospital. He listened to it three times. The connection was brutal, and the message startling.

After a call from Michael, Lucie had checked with an old colleague from the psychiatric hospital.

Dr. Gordon left her job at the FCPH in early 2007, under unexplained circumstances. Rumour had it, said Michael's aunt, that the hospital brass—specifically a friend of the guy who ran the place—learned of an affair between the good doctor and one of her outpatients. The friend kept her mouth shut and Dr. Gordon resigned.

The doctor told colleagues she wanted to move closer to her hometown of Hamilton. She moved to neighbouring Burlington and set up the practice she ran until her murder.

The outpatient who had the fling with Brenda Gordon was Lottie Denison.

"Drugs like Rohypnol knock you on your ass for several hours," said Fern.

"She said it was a light dose from the looks of it."

"Someone wanted you to look drunker than you were."

Michael told Fern about Lottie and Dr. Gordon. Michael proposed the possibility that Northcott learned of Lottie's affair with the doctor, resulting in the latter's murder. Fern discarded the logic at once. Michael soon followed suit. He'd heard Northcott and Lottie in action. Northcott had to be aware of his paramour's wide array of sexual propensities. A penchant for switch-hitting would be more welcome than threatening to whatever relationship Northcott thought existed between him and Lottie Denison.

CHAPTER 28

Jessie stood on the front porch of their home, arms folded. It was close to three a.m. Her posture suggested a shiver, despite the blanket of hot air that smothered the night.

Michael hadn't called home. He got out of his car and leaned back against it. How much more would she take?

She ran to him, and buried her head in his chest. "Please don't scare me like this again."

He started to explain, but she put her hand on his mouth. "Just come to bed," she said, and led him inside.

Clint stood expressionless at the foot of the stairs. What had the busybody realtor conveyed to Jessie about his performance at Foster Glen?

"I'm sorry, buddy," said Michael. "I didn't mean to upset you guys... to embarrass you."

Clint just stared at his shoes.

He thinks I was hammered.

"I don't want you guys to worry," said Michael, "but I stopped at the hospital. I'm okay now, but they think someone may have put something in my drink."

Clint lifted his head.

"Yeah, it looks like I coulda been drugged," said Michael. "But I'm okay."

"Oh, Michael," said Jessie, and she slipped her arm around him.

Clint stepped closer and said, "Can we go golfing sometime soon?"

Michael showered and joined Jessie on the bed. She wanted to know what in God's name was going on in his life. He begged off, tired, asked if they could discuss it in the morning.

Jessie was gone when Michael got up, leaving a note to say she had sessions scattered over her Monday calendar, and hoped to find time to get her car tuned up somewhere in between. Nothing was going to derail her quest for normalcy, to put her nightmare behind her. He wished the same for himself.

Clint went off to Wonderland before ten, ushered away to the amusement park in a gaudy rust-coloured SUV driven by the father of a friend who lived down the road.

Michael got two Cokes from Danny's fridge. On the way back outside, he noticed close to twenty letters on Danny's kitchen table. He skimmed over a few. All were rejection letters from various magazines and publishers.

He stepped outside, handed Danny his Coke, and sat down on the step in front of him.

"How could someone have known about the setup with my recording, and then neutralize it so quickly?"

"The recording of Northcott was run from a laptop, the one he used for the presentation. Someone probably embedded it into his PowerPoint file."

Michael chewed on that for a moment. Could Lottie have pulled that off?

"What about my iPod? And the sound system?" he asked.

"It could still be there for all we know," said Danny.

Michael knew better, having told Alberts about the setup. "What exactly did Northcott say on the audio clip?" he asked.

"He said he was unfaithful... wife in a wheelchair whimpering... his poor little girl, and something about a monster... 'he got his' or some fucking thing."

"A monster did something to his daughter?"

"That's what I got from it."

And he got his.

"I didn't notice it myself," said Danny, "but Eddie said Northcott was in the middle of a crowd of members, soaking up their sympathy, when he pulled an envelope out of his pocket. Eddie said Northcott looked surprised to find it there. J.P. pulls away from the crowd, takes a piece of paper out of the envelope, reads it, then looks over right at Lottie Denison, Eddie thought, with this sick-like look on his face. Then he ran the fuck outta there."

"Sick-like?" asked Michael. He thought of the note Emily pulled from her pocket on the escarpment, and her "annoyed" look. Or was it *sick-like*?

Did Lottie know that Graham Zetterfeldt had molested Northcott's daughter? Perhaps the sabotage of Northcott's presentation wasn't meant to merely embarrass J.P., but to show that he had motive for killing Zetterfeldt. With Alberts looking on from his front-row seat at Northcott's table, Northcott could have sensed the offer of witness protection going out the window.

"I wasn't snooping, Higgy," said Michael, "but I couldn't help but see the pile of letters on the table inside."

"Snoop away," said Danny. "They're rejection letters. The majority of successful writers get rejected by tons of places before getting published in any meaningful way. It's all part of the process. Those letters will be on the bulletin board over my workstation by the end of the day. I see them as motivation."

"So you're okay with that?"

"Mike, this is what I do, who I am. From now on."

Michael thought of the old axiom that says a man should find what he loves to do, and then find someone to pay him to do it. At that moment he envied Danny, because he was halfway there.

Fifteen minutes north of his home, Michael parked behind the Lowville Bistro, where he envisioned the rack of lamb and sweet potato fries. Rita had other plans, buying them each a two-scoop cone at the ice cream parlour next to the restaurant, and leading him into Lowville Park, another of Emily's favourite haunts.

They stopped at a bench. Rita lit up a cigarette, and moved to Michael's opposite side after a gust of wind dropped a cloud of smoke on him. She puffed and exhaled upward, staring at him through the smoke.

"Okay, Michael," she said. "Spill it."

Michael looked at the ground. "The recording I told you about. I set it up to play during Northcott's little speech at Foster Glen."

"Good God in heaven," she said.

He recounted the details around the dinner at the club and the trip to the hospital, skipping the stopover at Leonard the Cop's cabin in the woods. It seemed a little less horrible after saying it out loud, but not much.

She butted out her smoke in the bottom of her ice cream cone, and said, "What aren't you telling me?"

He played dumb, but soon caved. "I ran into Alberts. He alluded to the fact that you had some clients that weren't the nicest of people."

"Fancy that, a criminal defense lawyer defending people who might be criminals. And what the hell is John Alberts doing, offering up these little observations to you?"

"I thought it was kind of an odd thing for him to say," said Michael.

She crossed her legs, her top foot jiggling fast, and shook her head.

"Fuzzy Mavis's youngest boy, Teddy," she said.

"Whoa. Fuzzy Mavis? Isn't he a big-time hood, killed a bunch of people? He's in prison, isn't he?"

"For now. I'm trying to see that his son doesn't join him."

"Good luck with that."

"Just for the record, Michael, and you should already know this... I would defend Teddy's father in a heartbeat if he needed a defense. Otherwise, I should have chosen another profession."

"I was just curious," said Michael, feeling a little guilty for bringing it up. "I find your work interesting, Rita. I wasn't questioning you."

"Yeah, you were."

Jessie texted Michael to say she'd picked up another job during the course of her day, and later had a date for coffee with Mrs. O'Brien from her gym. She'd be home by ten thirty, and Clint had said he'd roll in around ten. Still edgy and not wanting to wander a big empty house, Michael dropped off Rita and stopped to hit a bucket of balls.

Dr. Baweja called from Joe Brant, and asked him to come to the hospital.

He waited for over an hour in the waiting room. Dr. Baweja appeared, offering no apology. She confirmed that he had, in fact, been drugged, probably twice in recent weeks, as she had suspected during her preliminary analysis. Rohypnol had been present, as well as traces of what "could have been midazolam". The tests for the latter were inconclusive, but it would help explain the episode with the home invasion.

The news threw Michael, even with the heads-up that it might be coming.

"I suppose I should let the police know," he said.

"Done," said the doctor.

Michael called his home number around ten, and then Artie's cell, getting no answer at either. He waited for ten minutes and tried both numbers again. Jessie wasn't due home for a while yet, and it wasn't unusual for Clint to be a little late. But Artie was always reachable, usually picking up on the first ring since Michael bought him a new phone.

Unease set in.

Michael chastised himself for worrying about nothing, and headed home.

CHAPTER 29

Michael's BlackBerry rang as he yanked it from his pocket to call 911. The display read "Unknown Number".

"Hang in there, Artie," he pleaded to his friend, who lay unconscious at the foot of the guest house steps. Michael called out again for Clinton, and again got no response.

He took the call. "*Yes?*"

"Could I please speak to Mr. Michael Flanigan?" asked a man in a soft voice.

"I can't talk now," snapped Michael.

"It's Frank Toner, Mike. How's it going, buddy?"

Toner laughed and... groaned?

"What are you assholes up to?" asked Michael. "Were you here, at my home?"

"I may have popped by," said Toner, and then, away from the phone, "Hold on for a second there, hot lips."

"What the hell is going on, Toner?" Michael bent over and shook Artie, but couldn't stir him. He had to get him help.

"Flanigan, do not phone the police, under any circumstances. Not if you want to see your punk kid again."

"My kid?" Michael steadied himself on the railing of the guest house steps. He heard a whimper over the phone, in the background, followed by what he thought was a slap.

"Call the cops, and your boy is dead. It's that simple. And I promise you, I'll have loads of fun with him first."

Clint. "I swear, Toner, I will—"

"The big ape behind the house will be fine. I just gave him a little something to help him sleep. So no 911. Understand?"

A car pulled up out front. Michael ran toward it while yelling, "If you hurt my son, Toner..."

Jessie got out of her car, alone. She frowned.

He put the phone to his chest. "Jess, do you know where Clint is?"

She shook her head slowly, as her eyes widened and filled with terror.

Michael put the phone back to his ear. "Toner, is my son there with you? *Where the fuck is my son?*"

"Your boy? I don't think you'll find him at home," said Toner, laughing. "But by all means have a good look."

Michael was already through the front door of the house. "What have you done with him?"

"He'll be okay, Flanigan. So long as you do what I tell you, to the letter."

"Are you insane?" said Michael, shaking. He ran from room to room on the main floor, and motioned for Jessie to check the lower level. The dogs greeted her when she opened the door to the basement, but Clint wasn't with them.

"Now, now," said Toner. With his mouth way from the phone again, he said, "Why don't you give your mouth a rest, sweetheart? I've gotta talk to Daddy. Not a fucking peep or the next thing I stick in your mouth will be the barrel of this gun." Someone coughed in the background, gagged. A female?

"Toner, who's with you?" His insides ached. He knew the answer.

"I'm sorry I missed your little woman back at the ranch, Mikey. I was looking forward to getting to know her, but I've got one hell of a consolation prize here with me now."

He's got both of my kids.

"Listen to me, Flanigan," said Toner, all humour gone from his voice. "This is going to end very soon and in one of two ways. *How* it ends is entirely up to you, rich boy. My new girlfriend—*Sophie* I think her name is—Sophie and me have been havin' a grand ol' time."

Michael scaled the stairs to the second floor, two at a time, but he knew he wouldn't find his son.

"Aside from a little gag reflex, Sophie's doin' just fine," said

Toner. "And she's keeping her chompers pulled back after taking a coupla smacks. Oh, and Flanigan, if the cops want some of my DNA, you can just pump her stomach."

Sweet Jesus. What have I done to my children?

Michael ran down the stairs and arrived in the kitchen to find Jessie sitting there, crying, trembling. She shook her head.

"Where's Clinton?" yelled Michael into the phone.

"Oh, he's around here somewhere," said Toner, and he cackled.

"What do you want?"

"Why, money of course. You have lots of it, and you're going to share some with me. See how it works?"

"How can you do this? These are innocent children."

"Ol' Soph here isn't looking all that innocent at the moment. Doesn't she have the softest flesh? Oh, maybe you wouldn't know that. I guess yer just gonna have to take my word for it."

"I swear, Toner... where's Northcott?"

"Don't call the cops and she'll be good as new in no time. Otherwise, she and her boyfriend..." Sophie screamed, and then cried, "No. Please. Please don't."

The phone went dead.

Michael stared at the phone.

Boyfriend?

Had he been too fast to disregard Northcott as her "older man"? Michael couldn't even remember why he had ruled him out... too much to process... he wasn't keeping up. He stared at the phone.

It rang.

"*Toner?*"

"That was just to get your attention. Now shut up and listen."

"You got it."

Toner wanted a quarter million in cash. Michael did keep a lot of cash in his safe at home, but he had only shared that with Rita and Sophie, and they would never betray the confidence. But why would anyone, even someone as off-balance as Toner, think that Michael could get his hands on a quarter million—unless he knew he already had it?

Michael was to get in his car and get on Highway 407 eastbound. Toner would call him on the road with further instructions.

"And don't forget that I have nothing to lose," said Toner. "I can have all the sex I want in prison, and I hear the food ain't that bad. And no cops, or everyone dies."

"How do I know you won't kill us all anyway?"

"It's a no-brainer, Flanigan. You'll never miss the money. Do what I say and in a few hours you'll all have your lives back."

"Tell me what to do."

"Be on the road in ten minutes. Take a shit and give your bitch a goodbye kiss, but I'm gonna call you in ten minutes, and you better goddam well be in your car."

Michael quickly filled Jessie in.

"You have that much money?" she asked. "Here, in the house?"

"I'll explain later."

"You aren't going to phone the police?"

"My gut tells me that's a bad idea," said Michael. "This crazy piece of shit would start shooting if he even smelled a cop. I think he just wants to take the money and disappear."

He scribbled Danny's numbers while telling Jessie to have him come by, help with Artie, and keep his mouth shut. Michael had to assume that Artie had been injected with the same drug that he was given during the home invasion. If so, he should be okay.

He got the biggest travel bag he could find and filled it with two hundred and fifty thousand dollars, almost emptying the safe in his office.

"Let me get you something," said Jessie.

She ran upstairs, aware of Toner's ten-minute deadline, and reappeared in less than a minute with a gun in her hand.

"Please take this," she said. "I would feel so much better."

The gun was smaller that any Michael had seen up close, although his exposure to firearms was limited to a couple of trips to a firing range with his father. He dreaded the notion of even carrying a handgun, but the thought of having it when confronting Toner offered some comfort.

"Is it loaded?" he asked.

She nodded, and her tears returned. "I got it some time ago, to feel safer. I've not fired it, but I imagine it works." She held him tight and said, "Come home, Michael."

"I love you too, Jess."

Toner called shortly after Michael set out. "Have you got the money?" he asked.

"Two hundred and fifty thousand, in cash."

"Get off at the 400, and head north," said Toner. "I'll call you back."

The 400. He met Toner for the first time at Weber's burger joint. Did he have a place in Muskoka?

He tried to free his mind of what his children might be going through. He needed to calm himself, to think.

He couldn't make any sense of this undisciplined move to grab his kids, which made him wonder if Toner had acted on his own. Was Northcott there, with Toner's gun trained on him as well?

Or had both men attacked Sophie?

He questioned his decision to not contact the police, and walked through the logic again that convinced him taking on Toner by himself was his best bet for getting his kids back alive.

Sophie was strong. He prayed she'd be strong enough.

What's he done with Clint?

Toner called back.

"Get on number eleven, until you get to Gravenhurst."

"Grave... Toner, are you at *my* cottage?"

Insane laughter shot down the line. "Better hurry, Flanigan.

I'm not horny anymore, but I'm getting kind of restless." Toner hung up.

Michael assumed Toner had to be coked up. It occurred to him that his immediate neighbours on the lake were all away. Did Toner know that?

Could Sophie be in on this?

No fucking way.

He thought Lottie Denison could be along for the ride, all of the deviants in on it together.

But not Sophie.

Was thinking for a moment that his stepdaughter had a bad drug problem more palatable than the truth that lie ahead?

What am I missing?

CHAPTER 30

A short distance from the cottage, a burst of lightning lit up a column of wooden signs nailed to a huge maple tree, each sign narrowed to a point at one end. The top one flashed "THE WYNNES" before going black again. Michael had meant to replace their old sign with one bearing his name. He hoped he'd get the chance to do that one day.

He turned onto the final dirt artery leading to the cottage, swerving to avoid an oncoming car while reaching for his BlackBerry. He cursed as he answered the phone.

"Fuck what?" asked Toner.

"I just dropped the phone."

"You better not be fucking with me."

"Why the hell would I? I have your money, and now I want my kids back."

"Are you alone?"

"Of course."

"Did you call the cops?"

"No."

"Anyone else?"

"No. Not a soul. I swear."

"You *swear*?" Toner laughed. "Pull into the second parking spot and get out of the car. Leave the keys in it. Hold the bag with the money in front of you, *with both hands*. Walk toward the cottage. The door will be opened for you. Don't say a word. Anybody makes a move, or even says a fucking word unless I tell 'em to, you all die."

"You said you wouldn't—"

"Starting *now*."

As he slowed to descend the steep driveway, his headlight caught the front bumper of a car hidden in the trees on the other side of the driveway. He assumed it belonged to Toner, or whoever the hell was in there with him.

Was this how it would all end for his family?

He eased down the drive. He had a thought that Danny might have himself a bestseller if he wrote the tale of Michael Flanigan. But the ending wasn't right. He should be confronting J.P. Northcott in a tension-packed, mano-a-mano climax. Instead he was trying not to shit his pants as he prepared to face a depraved loser, while praying he could save his family. Maybe he'd do better this time—better than he had for Emily.

Thunder roared. At least that fit the script.

Michael parked the car as directed. A shadow spilled onto the walkway. Someone stood a few feet back on the other side of the screen door.

He got out and held the bag in front of him as he approached the cottage. The door opened—

Toner or Northcott?

—and out stepped Eamonn Flanigan.

Michael took a step back and said, "Why you worthless little —" Michael's younger brother shook his head vigorously, but Michael went on. "I shoulda known, if drugs were involved..."

"Bring him in," said Toner from inside the cottage.

Toner stood in front of the sofa wearing a crazy-haggard sneer. Snorting coke and being hunted didn't agree with him. Sophie was curled up in the corner chair next to the couch, looking quite small and near catatonic. Her shorts were unbuttoned and a shoulder strap on her top was ripped off at one end. Her only reaction to his arrival was to open her eyes for a second and then close them again. Small patches of blood were smeared across her chin and under her nose, but she had no visible wounds.

A fury brewed in Michael, inflaming the back corner of his skull. He wanted to fly across the room and hurt Toner in every way his imagination could muster. He took a deep breath. He had to think.

He glanced around; no Northcott, and no Clinton.

"She's been like that a while," said Toner, holding a revolver by his side. "A *love* hangover, I guess."

A sandwich bag of white powder and a half-empty bottle of Remy Martin sat on the table. Toner had located the liquor cabinet, and Michael hoped the addling effect of the cocaine-booze mix might work to his advantage—or it could make their captor so out of control that he just might start shooting for no damn reason. A large knife with serrated edges lay next to the cognac bottle.

"Where's my son?" asked Michael.

"Put the bag down and shut up," said Toner. Michael obeyed, and Toner looked to Eamonn and said, "Count it." Toner whistled while Eamonn counted the money.

"I got two hundred and fifty-five grand," said Eamonn.

"Close enough," said Toner, who put the oversized barrel of a handgun to Sophie's temple, getting no reaction from her. "Get over here, Flanigan."

Michael walked over, sunflower seed shells crunching under his feet, until Toner put up a hand to stop him.

"One false move, any move, and you'll finally learn what it's like to get inside her head," said Toner, who snorted at his own pathetic joke, the gun barrel tapping on Sophie's head as he did.

"Flanigan," he said, "you should really take a shot at this great little piece of ass sometime."

Toner put out a hand to frisk Michael, up and down, front and back. He found the BlackBerry and threw it off the wall. Eamonn jumped. Sophie didn't budge. Michael prayed Toner wouldn't check his crotch.

"You're not blood," said Toner. "So what's the problem? She's kinda tired me out."

Michael considered jumping Toner while his hand was running up Michael's calf, but decided the risk-reward balance was not in his favour.

Toner grinned, his eyes lifeless. "Maybe I should sit back and watch some father-daughter action... have myself a little drinkey-poo."

Michael looked to Eamonn, who stood leaning against the fireplace, head in hand. How could his own brother...

Toner's face went dark.

"In fact, that's exactly what we're going to do," he said. "Let's see what you got, pencil dick."

He put his hand on Michael's crotch, and blurted, "What the —"

Toner smiled up at Michael. The barrel of Toner's gun slid off Sophie's forehead. He pointed the weapon at Michael, glanced back at Sophie, and reached inside Michael's pants. Toner pulled out the 22-calibre, snickered at the sight of it.

"You fucking bitch," he said.

Toner put the undersized handgun in his pocket, and said, "Oh, I'm going to have to make a mess now."

The madman slammed his own gun against the side of Michael's head, stunning him, knocking him to his knees.

Toner reached for his own zipper, and said, "Just for that, *Mikey*, the last thing you're going to see in this life will be your darling little douchebag chokin' on a mouthful of Frankie. She's been rehearsing for the show, so you should enjoy it."

I will not let it end this way, thought Michael. His head throbbed, and he felt wobbly.

"You're about to live the last hour of your life. And it's going to be a long one," said Toner. "And when we're done here, I think I'll pay that girlfriend of yours a visit."

As he leaned on one knee, Michael caught a look from Sophie, eyes open... lucid? She closed them again. Her hand was jammed between the sofa cushions.

Toner undid his pants, exposing a huge penis, which he began to fondle. "This is what your little girl's been playin' with while she waited for you to show up, Dad."

Michael glanced to Eamonn, leaning against the mantle that rimmed the fireplace, feet still cemented to the floor. But the fear in his face had transformed into a look of rage. For the first time, Michael noticed a cut lip and slightly swollen jaw on his brother. He had never been able to guess what Eamonn was thinking, but Michael prayed his younger sibling would stand up and do the right thing if he got the chance.

Michael needed to get Toner's twisted mind onto something else. "Where is Northcott?" he asked.

Toner cackled, and continued to stroke himself. "Don't worry about that rat. If he hadn't gone after Zetterfuck for doin' that little cunt of his..."

Northcott did *kill Zetterfeldt, or had him killed.*

"Rat?" said Michael. "Did Northcott give you up for something?"

"I thought I told you to shut the fuck *up*," said Toner, spittle flying. He grabbed Sophie by the hair and said, "It's time for you to take over, darlin.'"

Toner pulled Sophie's head toward him. Her near-limp body offered no resistance.

"Once your little whore gives me an angry old woody, I think I'll fuck your ass with your nice little family watching," said Toner, stopping to tilt his head back and howl. "And you better hope I don't cum too fast, Mikey Boy, cuz when I do I'm gonna blow the back of your fucking head off."

Sophie half-opened her eyes, just a slit.

Toner yanked her head closer.

Her eyes shot open. She drove something into Toner's scrotum.

Toner wailed, hunched over, staggered backward, and cried, "You fucking... little... *bitch*."

Michael lunged at Toner, but was pushed aside by Eamonn, who was on Toner in a flash. Sophie darted for the door to the dining room on their right, bloody weapon in hand. *Scissors?* Toner got an elbow under Eamonn's chin and knocked him against the huge window that looked out onto the elevated deck. Eamonn bounced off the glass and back toward Toner. Toner shot him and Eamonn flew back against the window.

Michael heard the screen door in the dining room slide open. Sophie was making her escape onto the deck. The deck lights were on, the thunder now directly overhead. A staccato crackle in the electric sky cast a glow on the lake below.

Michael got to his feet. Toner swung around and fired, somehow missing him. Toner completed his pirouette without stopping, and fired through the window at Sophie, the glass exploding, as she scrambled over the back railing of the deck.

Michael couldn't tell if Sophie had been hit. The fifteen-foot drop from the deck could do enough damage, without the help of a psychopath's bullet.

Michael made a run for the side door at the rear of the opposite wall. As he cleared the doorway, Toner fired again, and missed again. The gunfire was ear-splitting.

Toner followed him out the door. Michael leapt from the side shadows and punched Toner with everything he had. In doing so, Michael slipped on the wet wooden landing, but caught enough of the side of Toner's head to knock him down.

Michael's follow-through catapulted him down the stairway that stretched down toward the lake. His feet flung out from under him and his ass slammed onto the edge of a step, and then another, coming to a stop near the bottom of the stairs. He cursed, tried to ignore the pain.

Back on his feet and running into the night, Michael jumped sideways as a bullet ricocheted off a nearby rock. Michael wondered how many bullets Toner's gun held, and prayed it was one too few to bring him down.

He needed to find an edge on Toner. As he ran back along the outside of the cottage, he heard Toner bouncing down the steps at a greater clip than he would have thought possible for a man running through a storm with bleeding nuts. Putting his trust in the darkness and the storm, and his familiarity with the surroundings, he began to move away from the cottage, hoping to draw Toner further away from Sophie.

The sound of Toner's sloshing feet grew louder as Michael made the turn at the top of the driveway. His unhinged pursuer was making up ground.

Michael ran past the car hidden under the maples. He heard a thump, out of tune with the thunder. Could Northcott be in the car, hiding, waiting for Toner to do his dirty work?

Michael strained to will some purpose into his gait as he neared the jogging path he'd zigzagged along so many times before. But his hipbone ached from the spill on the outdoor stairway and, even in this death chase, he could only move about three-quarter speed. Factor in the weather conditions and *advantage madman*. Unless...

Toner's raging got louder, closer. "*Dead man. I'm chasing a dead man.*"

Michael entered a thickly-treed stretch just before the Sutton property. Toner fired another stray bullet and called Michael a "dead motherfucker".

Michael had to guess. He slid down the side of the embankment beneath the path. He grasped for and found what he was looking for: the huge jutting root that he had failed to grab onto when an angry German shepherd had startled him down to the feet of Tina Sutton.

The soggy night hindered both his footing and his hold on the slippery old root. He perched on the natural shelf beneath it, and felt he could hold on until Toner had passed.

The rain hammered down.

"I'm gonna cut your balls off, Flanigan." Toner's voice had taken on a wounded whine.

He brought his knife with him.

Michael hoped that Toner's own testicles were leaking blood. With his head against the embankment, Michael struggled to hear him.

Hugging the earth, Michael turned his head toward the Sutton place, in darkness except for a dim boathouse light.

Another lightning flash illuminated the lake, leaving Michael feeling exposed.

But it also spotlighted a painting hanging inside the Sutton cottage. A second lightning strike put the artwork on display once more.

He'd never seen the painting before, but felt he knew it well.

And it had allegedly perished in a fire.

"Well what have we got here?" said a voice from above. Michael pulled his head away from the embankment. Toner, a vague form in the dark, pointed his gun down at Michael, and said, "You can join that punk kid of yours in hell."

Clinton.

"What did you do to him, you worthless coward?!" screamed Michael.

Toner pulled the trigger, but the gun didn't fire.

A wild yell from above was followed by two large forms flying past him and onto the ground, grazing him on the way down and knocking him from the ledge. He tumbled down the rest of the way, his plunge partially cushioned by... could it be?

Michael would never have imagined that he could be so happy to see Bobby George.

Michael and Bobby got to their feet. Toner, dripping and grinning in the glow of the moon, pointed the pocket-sized 22-calibre pistol at Michael's head. Toner's small cannon had run out of ammunition, but he had a backup, courtesy of Michael Flanigan.

Toner twirled the knife in his other hand.

The rain let up, the skies quieted.

"Who wants it first?" asked Toner, waving the gun between the two men. From Michael... to Bobby... to Michael. "Who wants to be the first eunuch?"

He cocked the gun.

Michael and Bobby took a step back.

Toner giggled and said, "Bobby boy, why don't you yank down your asshole friend's trousers, like you used to do for—"

Thwop.

Toner went down.

A screech of "*Motherfucker!*" penetrated the storm from the rear. Michael turned to see Sophie standing on their deck, holding something by her side.

He walked to Toner, who lay motionless.

"You taught her well, Bobby," he said, his eyes fixed on the arrow embedded in the late Frank Toner's throat.

CHAPTER 31

The rain stopped.

"You saved my life, Bobby," said Michael. He looked back to Sophie, now sitting on the deck and slumped against the cottage.

"I think I heard a noise from inside the trunk of that car at the top of the drive," said Bobby.

Michael bolted for the cottage. His hip had loosened up and movement came easier.

Eamonn was conscious, sitting up and leaning back on the fireplace, and had Michael's BlackBerry in his hand.

Eamonn pulled back a red-stained towel to reveal a bloodied bicep, and said, "I think it just nicked me. It's not really bleeding all that much." He grimaced. "The battery came out of your phone when that piece of shit threw it against the wall, but I snapped it back in and got it working. The scumbag took our phones. I just called 911."

"So now he's a piece of shit?" said Michael, relieved his little brother was still among the living. "At least you stepped up at the end and did the right thing."

"It's not what you—"

"I've got no time for this, Eamonn. Is that Toner's car parked up top?"

"I guess."

"No one was with him?"

Eamonn shook his head.

"Where are the keys? Have you seen Clint? Where are the damn keys?"

"No... I don't know... *Clint?*"

Michael grabbed a flashlight from the mantle over the fireplace and darted back toward the door.

Toner's body lay in moonlight. Michael searched the corpse

until he found the keys. The largest key had a rubber "Toyota" cover on the end.

Michael wiped Toner's blood from his hands on a patch of grass. He ran up the hill to the car, a Toyota Camry. Before checking the trunk, he crept up the left side of the car to confirm there was no one waiting in prey.

J.P. Northcott was in the passenger seat, with a hole under his ear the size of a golf ball. Michael half expected a Foster Glen Callaway to pop out and bounce along the dash. The wavy, salt-and-pepper hair and the scar on his chin confirmed his identity, even in the dark... even under all the blood.

He's dead. Maybe it ends here.

Michael moved to the back of the car. He heard some movement as the key found the lock.

He popped the trunk open.

Clint's grateful eyes looked up at his father.

"*Clint!*" cried Michael. "Thank God." He swung Clint's legs out, slid his arms under his son, and lifted him out. Clint pulled his arms free once Michael had loosened the rope on his wrists. Clint ripped the tape from his mouth, cursed, and bent over as he sat on the edge of the trunk, gasping for air.

"I heard you, Dad, from inside the trunk," said Clint, breathing heavily. "I knew I'd be okay."

"Buddy, I am so sorry," said Michael. He sat beside his son, his arm around him and his head resting on Clint's. Had his son witnessed the carnage in the front seat?

Clint put his hand on his father's. "For what, Dad?" he asked.

"Let's get you inside, son," said Michael.

Clint got to his feet, wobbled. Michael put his arm around him and the two limped down the driveway to the cottage.

Michael fell next to Sophie on the couch. Bobby released his bear hug on her to let Michael give her one. He squeezed his stepdaughter. Both cried, saying nothing.

Michael sat back and scanned her body.

"No hits," said Bobby. "He missed her. But she won't be

dancing for a while." Her left ankle was purple and swollen.

"I can't dance anyway," said Sophie.

"Let's get some ice for that," said Michael, grateful that Toner had been such a dreadful shot. He kissed her forehead and said, "That was some shooting, Soph."

He had looked right at it, without seeing it.

He had to pay Northcott one last visit before the cavalry arrived.

There it was, sticking out of Northcott's jacket pocket. He recoiled at the closer view of the massive wound on Northcott's head.

Michael slid the envelope from Northcott's jacket pocket. He grabbed a Kleenex from his own pocket and removed a piece of paper from the envelope, unfolded it, and read the text printed across the middle of the page:

THE ANSWER TO MY QUESTION IS... YOU!!

Lottie?

Michael slipped the paper back in the envelope and put the envelope back in Northcott's jacket pocket.

Northcott was dead. Michael did not feel good about it, but he didn't feel bad. He closed the car door, and went to tend to his family.

He stepped into the bathroom inside the cottage door. While he scrubbed Toner's blood from his hands, he recalled how he shook in horror while rinsing away the blood of Vinnie Fronda. But now, as he removed the blood of an animal, he felt nothing.

Clint had pulled up a chair in front of Eamonn, who sat next to Bobby. Sirens sounded in the distance. Bobby pointed to the kitchen. Michael followed him, and gave Bobby a quick version of what had happened since he arrived home and found Artie, and got the phone call from Toner. Without getting into the details, he told Bobby that Toner had probably assaulted Sophie. Bobby sagged. Michael clutched his arm.

Earlier in the evening, Sophie had called Bobby on the cottage land line and they were immediately disconnected. Bobby said he got no answer when he called back, and had no luck with her cell. He assumed she was fine, but wanted to be sure. Bobby George was a better father, and man, than Michael had given him credit for.

The two men left the kitchen, and froze. Clint sat grinning into a magazine, showing no signs of the trauma he'd just experienced, other than the dark circles under his eyes.

Eamonn had moved to the couch. Sophie's head was buried in the crook of his neck, while Eamonn slowly dragged his fingers through her wet matted hair.

Michael's younger brother was the older man.

"Something you guys want to tell me?" asked Michael. Clint put down his magazine, clearly eager for an update himself.

"You saved our lives, Mike," said Eamonn, who then shook Bobby's hand and introduced himself. "And you too, sir."

"Eamonn, you were here with Sophie the whole time?" asked Michael.

Eamonn nodded.

Bobby crouched down, took Sophie's hand from the ice pack on her ankle so he could hold it for her, and asked, "Sophie did he... did he—"

"Did he rape me?" She shook her head, lowered it, and said, "He hit me a couple of times, pulled my hair, and made me, you know... do other things. He pointed his gun at Eamonn almost the whole time." She broke down, pressing her face to Eamonn again.

"He was waiting for us when we came back from a swim," said Eamonn. "He tied us up at first. He went outside. We heard a shot. Mike, if you hadn't shown up when you did..."

"Sophie, you okay?" asked Michael.

She pulled her head up and stared blankly over Eamonn's shoulder. "I will be," she said.

Michael pulled up a chair close to the sofa. Bobby crouched next to him.

"One hell of a way to bring you two together," said Sophie.

"So... you two," said Michael. "I'm trying to figure out what the hell—"

"Sophie, your stepfather is trying to ask you what's going on between you and his brother," said Bobby.

The sirens were closer.

"We're pregnant," said Eamonn.

Michael glared at his brother. "*We're what?*"

"Got a problem with that?" asked Sophie.

"Do I have a problem... are you sure it's his?"

"Dad, c'mon," said Clint. "Please don't. Not now."

"Don't you dare judge us, Michael," said Sophie. "Keep it up and I'm going to forget that you just saved our asses."

"You saved ours, sweetheart," said Bobby, who looked at Michael and said, "Back in the kitchen."

Bobby grabbed two beers out of the fridge and handed one to Michael. "You think they need your approval at this point?" he asked.

"We're talking about my stepdaughter—*your daughter*—and my kid brother."

"I understand the implications here," said Bobby. "But I'm not sure you do."

"Doesn't it seem a little... *perverse* to you?"

"If anyone should have a problem with this, it's me. She's my baby girl and always will be. But she's an adult. There's no blood, and really no prior relationship betrayed. And there's what, seven or eight years between them? They've always been peers, really, never spending much time together back when the age difference would have mattered. They were strangers, really."

"You're saying he's never really been her uncle."

"Succinctly put, Michael."

"It doesn't feel right. And with his history of drug problems…"

"To be honest, that's my only concern here. But what are we gonna do? Take it from someone who knows. If you don't want to lose them, you'd better get on board. And hey, then you can keep an eye on them. Otherwise…"

Michael thought he had lost Eamonn years ago. Could this help bring them all together? His family was alive. That's all that mattered, wasn't it?

What would Tommy think?

The sirens grew louder, then quickly whirred to a stop.

The police questioned everyone and then got them out the door for the hospital. They would have more questions. The medics let Sophie and Eamonn ride together in the ambulance.

Clint sat in the front of Bobby's Ford Escape for the drive to the hospital in Bracebridge. Michael, relieved Clint was well enough after his ordeal to forego a trip in an ambulance himself, sat in the back trying to piece things together.

"These are your CDs, Mr. George?" asked Clint.

"Indeed they are, Clinton, and call me 'Bobby'. You don't care for my collection?"

"You've got some awesome tunes. I just remember my Dad saying you preferred songs from movies. You know, musicals."

Michael groaned.

"Is that a fact?" said Bobby, glancing at Michael through the rear-view. "Did you blame your drinking on being Irish?"

"Touché," said Michael. "Fresh start?"

"You got it."

Michael, Sophie, Clint, and Eamonn were all examined and treated at South Muskoka Memorial Hospital.

Michael reached Jessie on her cell phone. After she confirmed that Artie would be okay, Michael filled her in on the night's terrible events. Horrified, she still cried with relief to learn they all had survived the ordeal.

The bullet from Toner's gun tore through flesh but did not settle in Eamonn's arm. Clint bruised a rib and aggravated a Little League knee injury, but was otherwise fine. Michael had a badly bruised hip.

Sophie had scrapes, bruises, and mild sprains in her wrist and ankle, but no concussion. While waiting their turn in the hospital emergency room, she answered the questions that until now Michael had no opportunity to ask.

She had gone to Northcott's home to warn him to stay away from Eamonn, on whose Victoria, B.C. doorstep she had landed the previous fall when escaping the reality of her mother's death. Their relationship changed dramatically soon after she arrived on the west coast.

An anonymous caller had told her that someone working for Northcott was selling cocaine to her boyfriend. Eamonn had admitted a recent relapse, and Sophie told him the next time she would not only leave him but turn him in to the police. And she would have.

She had tried some drugs when she was younger, but hadn't touched any in years. She said she preferred life at its own speed, and would not have drugs around her new baby. As for the day Elliott Kennedy saw her wasted at the ball game, "I got hammered at a freaking baseball game," she said. "What else am I gonna do? The Jays were getting waxed by the Tigers. I didn't learn about the baby until the day I screwed up that dinner, when I invited Rita and then didn't show up."

"When's the baby coming?" asked Michael.

"Six months," said Sophie. "You'll be a step-grampa."

"And an uncle," said Michael. Maybe the kid would just call him Mike. He considered the notion, and liked it alright.

"Soph, you commented a while back on money coming

between family," he said. "How did you know that money, in addition to the drugs, was at the root of the issues between Eamonn and me?"

"Mom told me that Tommy's will said you could decide when Eamonn could have his inheritance, and it was based on him staying clean, off drugs."

"For two years. Seemed fair."

"Did it seem fair that your father all but blamed Eamonn for Oliver's death?"

"The old man had a blind spot when it came to Oliver, his fair-haired boy. I told Tommy that Eamonn didn't give Oliver the booze or the drugs, and there was little he could have done to keep him from getting behind the wheel that night. But the old man had made up his mind, and pinned it on Eamonn."

Alberts showed up at the hospital just after four a.m., looking as bad as Michael felt. Michael gave him a rundown of the evening, and Alberts showed genuine concern. He didn't have much to say about Northcott, but Michael assumed the detective had to be devastated. His link to whichever criminals he'd had in his crosshairs had taken a bullet in the head, and would snitch no more.

Alberts said he'd have to ask Rita if someone could have learned from her that Michael kept a sum of money in his safe, but Michael doubted that could go anywhere. She was the most trustworthy person he knew.

Michael offered to show Alberts the video from his home security cameras, to see how much it had captured of Toner's attack on Clinton and Artie. He told the detective he did not care to watch his son being abducted, but Alberts was free to take the video away, and blow it up if he needed. Alberts told Michael he'd seen too many cop shows, saying that the vast majority of home security videos were not of a quality that supported any material enlargement, or improvement on resolution. He would send someone by Michael's and take a look at what his cameras had picked up.

A nurse woke Michael. He didn't know how long he'd been dozing. His watch must have fallen off back at the cottage. The sun shone through the hospital entrance, and the emergency waiting room was almost empty.

His family was standing in front of him, waiting to go home. Sophie was crying into Eamonn's good shoulder.

They would all need counselling.

Bobby, Sophie, and Eamonn went on ahead to Burlington, while Michael and Clint hitched a ride in a police cruiser back to the cottage. Two police cars remained at the top of the driveway. While Clint waited in the Rover, Michael told a cop standing just inside the cottage door that he was going to run down to a neighbour's for a few minutes.

Michael retraced his route when fleeing Toner the night before.

Toner's body had been removed from the murder scene, but a slick maroon puddle marked the spot where Sophie had taken him down. He examined the area where Sophie would have landed when she fell off the deck, and thought it a miracle that she hadn't broken any bones, or worse. Michael had put off clearing away the brush that must have cushioned her fall. He would never again reprimand himself for procrastinating.

A red Mazda Miata that wasn't there earlier was parked behind the Sutton cottage. The blinds were drawn on the window he'd looked through while clinging to the side of the embankment and wondering if he would live to see the sunrise.

He knocked once, twice. Waited. The door finally opened. Tina Sutton, wearing nothing but an oversized T-shirt that said "Property of Boston Red Sox", asked him to "come on in". He walked into an open area that strung together kitchen, dining room, and TV room.

On the wall hung the reason for his visit.

"Sorry to bother you Mrs. Sutton."

"Tina. What can I do for you, Michael?"

"I just have a minute. My kid is waiting in the car." Kevin and Tracy had told him that Dr. Sutton had suffered a fatal stroke while out on the lake in his boat, and Michael had no time for Tina's seductive overtures. "Tina, I was very sorry to hear about your hus—"

Movement from behind Tina shut Michael up.

Dave Douthwright walked out of a room at the back. Their neighbour from up the bay wore only a pair of red boxers on his immense frame. They had a Red Sox "B" stitched on the front of a pant leg and were a match for Tina's shirt.

"Nice to see you, Michael," said Douthwright, offering his hand. "What's going on over at your place? The cops asked us if we saw anything unusual, but we just rolled in a while ago."

Michael gave them an understated recap, not mentioning the nature of Sophie's assault.

"Damn," said Dave, who saw himself as the guardian of the lake. "If only I could have been here."

"Don't let your head go there, Dave," said Michael.

He looked over to the wall, at the painting of a lone golfer on the tee block, Scottish heather in the background. "Do you mind if I ask you where you got that painting?" he asked.

"*The Golfer*?" asked Dave. "Don't you recognize it? Your wife gave it to me. She asked if I could hang onto it, but she didn't say when she'd want it back. She said you guys were getting some new artwork or something."

The shock in Michael's face must have been obvious.

"You can have it back," said Dave, looking to Tina, who said, "Sure. I hate golf."

"May I?" said Michael, moving forward. They stepped aside to allow him a closer look.

"Things are obviously kinda crazy at the moment, Dave," he said, starting up at the painting, at the man with the golf club in his hand. "Why don't you hang onto it for a while, if you don't mind?" He thought this might be the safest place for it in the short term. He took a step closer to *The Golfer*. "How did it end up here?"

"I told Emily I really didn't have any room for it, but she asked if I could take it anyway. Tina was over recently, and I just had it kind of leaning against the wall off to the side..." Dave was stammering now, embarrassed that he'd given it away.

"A nice gesture, Dave," said Michael, letting him off the hook. *Could she have stolen the painting?* "When did Emily give you the painting?"

Dave lowered his head, and said, "Just before, before she..."

Michael put up his hand. "It's okay, Dave. I thought so."

Michael felt certain the painting in front of him was the original, and that an imitation had been in the fire at the arts centre. "What can you tell me, Golfer?" he asked aloud.

Emily agitated... quarrelling with Ruth Eisentraut... Fronda?... over this thing?

He didn't think the painting was even that good. But what did he know?

At times Michael felt like the people in his life were living in an alternate dimension, beyond the reality that he knew, beyond what he could grasp.

Could Emily have been involved in something dishonest, for the love of a painting? He didn't think so, but what did it matter now? He wondered if Vincent Fronda had learned about the existence of a second painting, and if that got him killed. But at that moment he didn't give a damn about Ruth or Fronda or whether the painting was worth ten dollars or ten million. His wife had been a good woman, and she was gone. If Northcott or Toner had anything to do with her death, they had received their final justice.

It struck him then just how much he had, and how much he'd almost lost.

More than counselling, the family needed each other.

It was time to let it go.

CHAPTER 32

"I have a big favour to ask of you," said Bobby, resting his coffee on a *Hockey News* that was sitting on the corner of the desk in Michael's office. "I can shed just a little bit of light on what's happened to you over the past few weeks."

"And the favour?" asked Michael.

"This goes no further."

"Sounds ominous."

"I know who broke into your house that morning."

Michael said nothing, waited.

"It was Frank Toner and me," said Bobby.

Bobby made no excuses. He found himself under Toner's control, but knew what he was doing was wrong, and did it anyway. Toner had told him that he learned Michael stashed a lot of cash at home, and wanted Bobby along for his knowledge of the house layout.

"You've been to my house?" asked Michael. "Before, I mean."

"Sophie gave me a tour when I was going through town last year."

"How did you and Toner get in?"

"I'm not sure exactly."

"How's that?"

"I'd asked Toner how he planned to get into your place, when he first talked about doing it. He said, 'Don't worry about it. I'll get in.' When we got to your house, he pulled out a little cloth bag, told me to turn around and keep an eye out, and in a second he's in."

"You don't know what was in the bag?"

Bobby shrugged. "Tools of the trade, I suppose."

"My God, Bobby. I know you probably hated me, but... *my God*."

"I did hate you, Michael. You stole my daughter from me, or at least that's how I saw it. And Toner said he heard you had been more than a stepfather to Sophie, if you know what I mean, and that was why she had stayed away from you after Emily died."

"Why would you believe that low-life?"

"I guess I wanted to. He made it sound convincing, said Northcott had told him. Plus I'd grown afraid of him. He made me go to your house that night. I know he just wanted me there as an accomplice. I wouldn't be inclined to blow the whistle on him if I was in the house with him. He could control me."

"Did Toner know my alarm wasn't on, or did he just get lucky?"

"I don't remember discussing it."

Bobby said that, the day after the break-in, Toner told him it was time to go their separate ways. Bobby was to never contact Toner again, and Toner threatened to hurt Sophie in the worst way if Bobby said a word to anyone about their uninvited visit to Michael's house.

"So Toner was bisexual?"

"I'm not so sure you could put such a label on someone so warped. He was getting what he wanted from me. I swear I could have been a cocker spaniel."

"Did you get the feeling it was just the cash he was looking for?"

"He didn't tell me much. But he seemed to spend a lot of time checking out the prints you had hanging around the house. I asked him why he was wasting time and I got a smack in the mouth."

Michael thought Toner could have known that the authentic painting of *The Golfer* still existed. Toner would have checked out Michael's walls, on the slim chance that Emily had hung it at home.

"I know you're a good stepfather, Michael," said Bobby. "You're good to Sophie. I gotta admit it got me jealous, how close the two of you got, considering she wouldn't give me the time of day for the longest time. She thinks a lot of you."

"I'm not so sure about that at the moment."

"What, because you aren't doing cartwheels over her and your kid brother? Relax. So dramatic. Are you sure you aren't gay? Things blow over. She knows you'll be there for her, once the two of you finish this little dance of yours."

When did Bobby George get so smart?, thought Michael, but he just nodded.

"We're okay then?" asked Bobby.

"We're good."

The two men stood up. Michael said, "How did you guys knock me out that day?"

"Frank stuck a needle in your ass. He said he'd done it before, said there was no risk. He also gave you the bop on the head, hoping you'd think that kayoed you."

"What was in the needle?"

"I think it started with an *M*. Mizza..."

"Midazolam?"

"Could have been."

Michael had just researched the drug on the Internet. "The bastard could have killed me if he screwed it up."

"He knew what he was doing."

"How do you know?"

"He used to be a nurse."

Toner, the ex-nurse, had injected both Michael and Artie. Could he have practiced his trade at the same Kingston psychiatric hospital where both Lottie Denison and Brenda Gordon had spent time?

Artie returned from an overnight stay in the hospital. He had, in fact, been injected with midazolam, and had a broken ankle. Michael apologized, again, for the shit he rained on yet another life and, like the others, Artie put no blame on him.

A uniformed officer came by the house to pick up the footage taken by Michael's security cameras on the night Toner abducted Clint and bushwhacked Artie.

Michael and Jessie stood at the foot of the bed, frantically ripping at clothing. Their lovemaking was freeing, a rebirth. Michael felt the cloud of madness lifting from his poisoned life. He sensed a real joy, a shared consciousness, and a future of endless possibilities.

After, they sat cross-legged and naked on the bed, holding hands.

"Do we have our lives back, Michael?" asked Jessie.

"What do you say you let me make an honest woman out of you?" he asked.

She gasped, and put a hand over her mouth. "Michael, I love you, but, I mean... we just..."

His shoulders sagged, and suddenly he felt as naked as he was.

"Of course, Jess," he said. "I understand. Any sane person would have doubts."

"I have none," she said firmly.

"Well then?"

"I need you to be sure, Michael. You have a family that would be affected by all of this. I have only me."

He grabbed her forearms and gently pulled her closer. "I've never been more sure of anything."

She blushed, glowed. "Are you sure it's not just the great sex asking?" she replied.

He smiled. "I'm hoping the great sex will make you say 'Yes'".

She covered her face with her hands, trembling, then stared at him for several long moments, and said, "Yes."

Michael announced their wedding plans over a late dinner in the rarely used dining room. Sophie smiled throughout the meal, but he perceived a sadness beneath the surface. Michael knew she was quite fond of Jessie. He hoped the demon Toner had not taken part of his stepdaughter's smile to his grave.

Sophie got up to hug Jessie, and was joined by Clint.

Both kids had showed signs of recovering from their ordeal, their healing gaining momentum every day. And now they all could focus on welcoming Jessie Hargreaves into their family, for good.

They talked of a June wedding, tossed around New Year's Eve, and then decided they couldn't wait.

They planned to marry in a month.

Michael called Rita to tell her about his pending marriage and the nightmare with Toner on Lake Muskoka. He knew he'd given his old friend a lot to process in a single phone call. Rita adored Michael's kids, and was still crying when he hung up.

He would have guessed that his skin would have thickened somewhat by now, with regard to the media and its intrusion on his life. He was on the front page again, in papers across the country, and once again had news vans appearing along the road in front of his house. At times he felt trapped in his own home.

Sophie agreed to stick around for a few more days, and she and Jessie grew closer each day. Jessie seemed to know just when and how to pick Sophie up when a dark cloud would hover. Sophie never spoke to Michael about the atrocities she endured at the hands of Frank Toner. He could only guess at the memories that haunted her.

Eamonn had left the west coast and its temptations behind, but as Rita once said to Michael, "Wherever you run to, there you are." Artie had offered to put Eamonn up in the small second bedroom in the back of the guest house, an arrangement that meant Michael didn't have to deal with the idea of his brother and stepdaughter sleeping together under his roof, not just yet.

—

On Wednesday, Michael found Eamonn and Sophie stretched out on the sofa in front of the television in the rec room, watching a familiar rerun from one of the ubiquitous *Law & Order* series. Jessie sat on the floor with her back to the couch.

"Oh, please," Jessie mumbled to herself—at the same moment that Sophie said, "Here we go."

Michael turned to the source of their scorn on the big TV. Detective Benson perched in front of a computer in the squad room, taking a request to execute an online search for a certain type of killer, with similar previous arrests in a specified date range in such and such a geographical area. She logged in and, within seconds, said, "Here he is."

"I love that, too," said Michael. "I guess when they only have an hour to do the show, we have to buy into the fact that the average cop is a lightning-fast typist and a world-class Web surfer, running the best software on the most powerful computers that money can buy."

Sophie looked at him like he'd just asked her to wash his dirty socks.

"I'll shut up," said Michael, smiling, and he backed out of the room.

CHAPTER 33

Clint's mother returned from Europe alone, reporting that her boyfriend turned out to be quite the cad. After hearing of Clint's ordeal with the late Frank Toner, she insisted her son return to Kingston. Michael hated to see him go, but understood that Denise needed to see her son, to see that he was safe, and to not be alone after her latest breakup.

As Clint was boarding his train for Kingston at Toronto's Union Station, he turned back to his father. "Dad, I was checking out some of Sophie's photos earlier today."

"Not bad, eh?"

"I'd like to go to Pickett's Farm," said Clint, just before the train doors slid shut.

Michael shook off Clint's casual comment about wanting to take a field trip to the scene of Emily's death. He was sixteen years old and could not always be expected to tap into the sensibilities of others.

Speagle and Alberts were waiting when Michael returned home.

The security footage from Michael's cameras showed Toner outside the guest house, bodychecking Artie and then injecting him. But there were no shots of Toner's abduction of Clint, who was taken as he walked home from the house of the friend he'd accompanied to Wonderland that day.

DNA samples from the rape kits done on both Dr. Gordon and Jessie had been matched to that of a recently deceased individual.

"Frank Toner, I presume," said Michael.

"Graham Zetterfeldt," said Speagle.

Zetterfeldt. "That worthless prick. I'd like to dig him up and kill him again."

"He got his and then some," said Speagle. "We now believe that Paula Northcott was assaulted by Zetterfeldt. Her father likely found out, and sent Toner to take care of Zetterfeldt. Toner left behind a calling card of sorts. Looks like he wanted a little insurance in case Northcott turned on him."

The note on the mirror: PEDOPHILE.

"And you think Zetterfeldt killed Paula's shrink and took her file on the kid," said Michael.

"He had to think the file could incriminate him if the Northcott girl spilled her guts to the doc," said Speagle.

"That's kind of drastic, considering Paula's mother could have known everything."

"If she did, she never told anyone," said Alberts.

"But why Jessie?" asked Michael, hoping they had something beyond the Michael Flanigan connection.

"We know he didn't care for you much," said Alberts.

"Thanks for the reminder," said Michael, but he sensed Alberts regretted the comment the moment it left his mouth.

"Don't beat yourself up, Flanigan," said Speagle, who threw a look at Alberts. "Concluding that this could be revenge over your little feud with Zetterfeldt would be a bit of a stretch. There's really no predicting what a psycho like this guy will do, or why."

Michael wondered if Jacquie had confessed her infidelity to her husband, maybe even rubbed it in his face.

"The guy killed behind my house. Fronda. Is he connected?" he asked. "Or are you still trying to figure that one out?"

"We've learned that Fronda and Zetterfeldt had similar... interests," said Speagle.

"Was Fronda a pedophile?"

"We found some things in his home," said Speagle.

"They knew each other," said Alberts, who had a strained look while he said it, like he was telling Michael more that he should but felt he owed it to him. "They may have had a falling-out. We're looking into it."

"Doesn't Northcott's murder screw up that thing you've been working on for so long?"

"We're good," said Alberts. He didn't elaborate further. They must have got what they wanted before Northcott was shot.

"Why do you think Toner killed him?" asked Michael. "He did kill him, didn't he?"

"Our guess is Toner learned Northcott was helping the good guys, and likely ratting him out, too," said Speagle.

Michael's mind raced at a hypomanic pace.

Zetterfeldt killed Fronda? Fronda and Emily, Ruth and Toner... all interested in The Golfer. Northcott ran from the club... he looked at Lottie. The note. Art... golf... art. Where the hell is Lottie Denison?

"We haven't located Lottie Denison," said Alberts.

Did I say that out loud?

"Are you alright, Flanigan?" asked Speagle.

"Yeah. Fine."

"Lottie Denison. Have you seen her?"

"No, not since that night at the golf club. I barely knew her."

"Knew?"

"Huh... I did say that."

Speagle spread his arms wide, and said, "Well, you can forget about all this nonsense now. Either way, Zetterfeldt, Toner and Northcott are history. Enjoy life with that nice family of yours. How are the kids doing anyway?"

"They're coming along," said Michael, but the two cops were already walking away.

Michael wouldn't tell the detectives about the painting. If Emily was murdered, the man who killed her was dead, whoever that might have been. He had to focus on his family, help them heal. He would not tell Sophie, as she tried to become whole again, that her mother may have been an art thief.

But why would Emily steal a painting? She didn't need the money.

Once again, Michael felt like he never really knew her.

Michael found Jessie sitting up on their bed with the dogs.

"Will the police ever stop these unexpected visits?" she said.

"It's over," he said.

He cleared his throat.

"Graham Zetterfeldt is the one who assaulted you," he said. "The man who was killed himself recently."

"Your old principal," she said, and lay down on her side, facing away from Michael.

Michael fell into his office chair.

We'll be okay.

What else could he think?

On Friday morning, as Michael stood waiting for his toast to pop, Danny called to say he'd won the runner-up prize for a short story he submitted to a contest held by a publishing firm in Dublin, Ireland. Danny downplayed it, but Michael could hear the pride in his voice.

His second-place award included a deal with a literary agent, based in Galloway. While Danny had the attention of the publishing house, he sent them his novel. They told him they loved it, saying that murder mysteries set in foreign lands were hot now, and they wanted a face-to-face meeting.

"I know it's probably bad timing," said Danny, "but I wanted to make the offer anyway."

"Offer?"

"They got me a great rate for a four-day stay for two in Dublin at a nice hotel. I have some flexibility on when I can go, and if you wanted to join me..."

Michael said he'd love to play some Irish courses, but didn't feel he could leave Jessie alone, not so soon. He begged off, and while Danny said he understood, Michael could hear the disappointment in his voice.

"Well aren't I the most fragile little thing?" said Jessie, about a minute after Michael hung up the phone. He turned from the kitchen table to find her leaning against the doorway.

"You heard," he said.

"Darling, you are going to be a fabulous husband, but I want you, I *need* you, to live your life. That way, you won't resent me, and will love and adore and spoil me for the rest of my life. See how it works?"

"I would never resent—"

"Michael Flanigan, I don't want you to be one of those guys who go on about needing to get a pass from the old ball-and-chain, so you can go golfing or watch hockey matches with the boys or whatever it is you guys do."

She grabbed a Kleenex from a box on the counter and wiped some peanut butter from his chin. "Part of being a good husband is listening to your wife. Now get on the bleeding plane with your little buddy Mr. Higgins. I don't plan to spend the rest of my life licking my wounds, eating bonbons, and watching the telly. I am going to continue my work therapy, and will be a busy little bee while you're chasing a little ball around some golf course in Ireland."

Michael and Danny took separate cars to Pearson International Airport in Toronto, as Danny had a meeting with a book cover artist in downtown Toronto a few hours before their flight.

Michael took a call on the way to the airport.

"Mr. Flanigan, this is Julie Chisholm calling," said the soft-spoken woman. "I'm Teresa Amodeo's niece."

Michael offered his condolences on the passing of the other member of Emily's photography outing who didn't survive that Thanksgiving weekend.

Julie Chisholm explained that she tracked down Agnes Pickett through a chance encounter on Facebook with Markie Forster, who was in the group at Pickett's Farm on that fateful October day.

"I've been away studying in Paris, and when I got back home to Sudbury, I learned that my aunt died. I didn't really even know her, but my parents are both dead and, by default it would seem, my aunt left me a bit of an inheritance. I don't know that my aunt had many friends, but with so little family left, I wanted to find someone who knew her, who could tell me about her."

"How can I help you?" asked Michael.

"Markie Forster said you had contacted her and the other people from the outing to Pickett's Farm. She had a feeling you weren't convinced that your wife's death was accidental?"

"Julie, I don't know what I think about my wife's death at this point. I have no evidence that it was anything but an accident. It was just a bad day for our families. By all accounts, the other folks who were with your aunt at Agnes Pickett's dropped everything to take care of her."

"Like I said, I felt I had to call."

"I spoke to some of them afterward," said Michael, "including a woman named Huntley, a vet. She comforted your aunt when she fell ill up on that hill, said she seemed very nice. What part of Italy was she from?"

"Italy? My aunt?"

"The vet mentioned her charming accent."

"That's strange. Amodeo was my aunt's married name. She was a Chisholm, fourth-generation Canadian, and definitely not Italian."

—

Michael thought he must have misunderstood Jenine Huntley's account of the fateful day on the hill. Perhaps she thought she had detected an accent in Mrs. Amodeo, and Michael assumed it had been Italian because of her surname.

While he waited for Danny at the airport, he called the veterinarian, who remained adamant that the accent was Italian, "and thick". She didn't recall if she'd mentioned the accent to the police when they questioned her the morning Emily died.

"Mike, I talked to Alberts today," said Fern without a hello, just seconds after Jenine Huntley had hung up. "He told me about Zetterfeldt."

"Yeah, they were unusually forthcoming with the details on how they figured things out."

"Maybe they were still looking for more from you, maybe were impressed by your work. You know, the investigative work you'd been doing lately."

"You really think so?"

"Course not."

"Very funny."

"Speagle has always been a bit of a rogue. He's retiring soon, and probably wanted to show off a bit, show you how crimes really got solved, probably told you things they did that you never would have thought of doing."

"To show me how incompetent I was," said Michael.

"In a nutshell."

"Well, now that you've cleared that up, I guess you can go back to working for your more legitimate clients."

"Negative to that. They canned me."

"What?"

"They found out about some of the work I was doing for you

off the books," said Fern. "They said it could hurt their relationship with the various police units, and blah-blah-fuckety-blah."

"I don't know what to say, Fern," said Michael. "Looks like I hurt everyone who helped me with this shit, in one way or another."

"Hey man, turn down the drama a notch. I'm good, glad they forced my hand. I was thinking about moving on to something else."

"Like what?"

"Still thinking about it."

"Alberts have anything else to say?"

"Northcott was holding out on Alberts. He documented some of the juicier stuff, stuff he wasn't sharing with the cops. A file was to be sent to the cops should Northcott meet an untimely demise. He did and Alberts got a courier a few days later."

"What was in the file?"

"They should have enough on Fuzzy Mavis to *keep* him locked up for the rest of his miserable life."

"Mavis. The gangster. *He* was the guy that Alberts was after?"

The existence of the file explained why Alberts wasn't upset that Northcott—his informant and gateway to Mavis—hadn't survived long enough to sing to a jury.

"I guess Mavis Sr. will need a good lawyer now," said Michael.

"He's got one," said Fern. "Your good friend, Rita Manale."

"No shit."

"She got the kid off, and now it's Dad's turn. So much for cleaning up the streets."

Michael didn't respond.

"It turns out Northcott was also keeping a certain local councilman in powder, too," said Fern.

"Whack Job? Cocaine? Where does it end?" asked Michael. "Did they ever find Lottie Denison?"

"Don't think so, and I have a feeling they may not."

"You mean she disappeared, or maybe someone made her

disappear?"

"Take your pick."

Michael told Fern about Teresa Amodeo's niece, but Fern said he'd heard it a hundred times. He put little stock in an accent "someone *thought* they heard nine or ten months ago".

Jenine Huntley had convinced Michael, but he let it go for the time being.

"I was thinking of hiring you for one last little job," he said.

"Mike, c'mon. This thing is over. Who gives a shit about a painting or whatever else it is you've got in mind? I've got news for you. When a murder case is solved, there are often questions that are left unanswered. But once we get the answers to the right questions, the ones that tell us who did the crime, we move on."

"You're out of work, aren't you?"

"That's not the point and you know it. Besides, I'm comfortable enough. I don't need to steal your money to chase one of your whims."

"What about the divorce?"

"I'll be okay."

"I'm moving on, Fern, and will soon be on a plane to Ireland. I just want you to dig a little further into something that's gnawing at me."

"Let me guess... the ghost named Ruth Eisentraut?"

Michael paused, impressed again by the instincts of his investigator pal. "I need to find her, Fern," he said. "If Emily's death hadn't been ruled an accident, the cops would be beating the bushes for this anti-social waif, who just happened to disappear into thin air just hours after Em died."

"What is it you think we're gonna learn about our gal Ruth?" asked Fern.

Michael paused. "I don't know. I guess we'll find out when you locate her. This'll be your last job, Fern. Just find Ruth."

Fern sighed and muttered, "Fuck me."

"I'll give you ten grand," said Michael.

"I guess you can never be too comfortable."

Michael felt anything but comfortable. Was he full of shit, continuing the chase, while telling one and all, including himself, that he was moving on for the good of everyone?

He might even think that investigating crime was in his blood, if only he were better at it.

Who the hell is Ruth Eisentraut?

CHAPTER 34

The passing thunderstorm that delayed their flight didn't dampen Danny's spirits. He was jazzed, and spent much of the trip talking about his writing. Michael found the creative process interesting. He had never appreciated the effort Danny had made to complete his novel. Danny told Michael he would rather see his name on a book, sitting on the shelf of the local Chapters, than win the lottery. After a couple of drinks, he told him again.

The talk turned to women, and Danny told Michael how lucky he was to find two great women in one lifetime, adding "no offense to the former Denise Flanigan". Michael asked Danny how things were progressing with Ronnie Donovan.

"They're not," said Danny.

"You don't seem too upset about it."

"She had no sense of humour."

"Your sense of humour can be an acquired taste."

"She didn't acquire it."

"Gimme a fer instance."

"Okay. The last night I was at her place, there was a ballgame on, and she starts getting a little, you know... frisky. I tell her it's the last inning, a tie game, whatever it was. She says that sometimes she thinks I'd rather watch the game than have sex with her."

"And you said?"

"I said, 'Hey, I don't know how *the game* is gonna turn out.'" Danny looked at Michael as if to say "Go figure", and said, "So that's one example. Another time—"

"I think I get it, Hig. No sense of humour." Michael had to laugh, but it reminded him again why he would never set up Danny with a friend. Maybe Danny would meet a nice, tolerant Irish girl to bring back to Canada, to help him enjoy his pending success as a published author, and just maybe help him grow up.

Danny agreed to extend their stay to more than a long weekend, and to let Michael pick up any expenses not covered by the contest prizes. Michael didn't have to make that offer twice.

Neither of them had managed more than an hour of sleep on the plane. A baby in the seat directly behind Michael cried for most of the flight, and the woman to his left threw up during a turbulent descent into Dublin.

Michael buried his head in a map on the trip into the city. Their cabbie negotiated endless construction before arriving at the downtown hotel where the publisher had booked their rooms.

Things got worse.

The staff at the hotel, more of an inn really, a glorified bed & breakfast, had never heard of the publishing house. Nor did they have rooms booked for an up-and-coming literary talent from Canada by the name of Daniel Higgins. Danny had them re-check their bookings a second and a third time.

Danny stormed out of the small lobby and headed toward the book publisher's office, just a few blocks away according to the directions they got from the elderly front desk clerk. The old man didn't recognize the name of the street they were looking for, but directed them to the nearest intersection on the makeshift map that had come with the publisher's letter.

The look in Danny's eye told Michael they feared the same thing.

Danny ran up and down the street, looking for an address they both now sensed did not exist: 2424 Etihsbog Lane, the alleged site of the "one-hundred-and-twenty-eight-year-old building that housed Moran and McGonagall Press".

Two beat cops turned the nearest corner. Danny ran toward them. Michael came up behind as the tall redheaded cop, puffy and pink, said, "You'll not find that street around here, sir. It doesn't exist."

The second patrolman, in a slightly heavier brogue, said,

"May I see that, sir?" He took the letter and map, and then bit his lip. "Sorry, sir."

"What is it?" asked Danny, a vein sticking out on his neck. "What the fuck is so fucking funny?"

Michael put his hand on Danny's shoulder and said, "Easy, Hig," and then to the Irish cops, "You'll have to forgive my friend. We've travelled all the way from Canada, and it seems Mr. Higgins here may have been lied to by someone who was to meet him at this address."

Michael stood beside the second cop and looked at the letter. "What is it you noticed in this?" The first cop stuck his chin over Michael's shoulder, also curious to hear his partner's answer.

"The street name," he said. "If you spell it backwards, it spells 'Gobshite'."

The first cop snickered.

"What?" asked Danny.

"Gobshite, sir," said the second cop. "It's an Irish term, for someone who is..."

"Who is what?"

"A fool. Sir."

The cops asked Danny if he'd lost any money to the so-called publishing house. Danny didn't answer, just hung his head and walked away. Michael dragged him into a nearby watering hole. Two rounds of Irish boilermakers, as Michael referred to the Jameson's Whiskeys with Guinness chasers, did little to numb Danny's heartache.

"What's the fucking use?" asked Danny, who threw some euros on the bar and stumbled out of the pub. Michael followed him out and convinced him to check in for the night at the inn they'd stopped at earlier. The jet lag was catching up with them.

The inn had one vacancy, with twin beds. Michael took that as a blessing, not wanting to let Danny out of his sight in his present state of mind.

Danny unpacked a few things and stretched out on his bed. Despite his disappointment, he was snoring within minutes.

A stack of bound paper rested on top of Danny's suitcase. A cover page read "Mayhem in Suburbia by Daniel Higgins".

He planned to leaf through Danny's novel until he nodded off. More than a hundred pages later, he was still awake and reading, captivated. He'd read his share of fiction, mostly mainstream stuff off the bestseller lists: John Sandford, Stephen King, Grisham. He was no critic, but thought he could tell a good book when he read one, and he was reading one now.

As Michael became absorbed by the chapter where the protagonist Martin Fletcher fought with his lawyer friend Dani Gonzalez over her drug use, he heard Danny stir from the opposite bed.

"I put so much into that thing," said Danny, lying on his side and facing Michael.

"You gave the scam artists some money?"

"Couple grand... to subsidize production costs, or so they said. They called themselves that, a *subsidy* publisher. They made it seem so... real."

Danny had seen just what he wanted to see, his dream coming true. Michael checked his watch, which he'd set to Irish time on the plane, and saw it was well into the dinner hour. "I think they serve food downstairs," he said. "I'm gonna see if they have a computer I can get on. I'll meet you downstairs in ten."

They sat at the bar where the front desk clerk now functioned as bartender. They learned he was the father of the inn's owner, and lived on the premises. The old man joined them in a Guinness. In his limited experience, Michael observed that Irish pub owners were none too worried about a drinking man working the cash register.

After staring blankly for a few minutes at a soccer game on the tiny TV over the bar, Danny finally asked the question

Michael knew his friend had been dying to ask.

"So how much of it did you read?" asked Danny, dispassionate, not taking his eyes off the Liverpool-Chelsea friendly from England.

"I got pretty well into it," replied Michael, matching Danny's indifferent tone.

They sat silent for a minute, then a second minute.

Danny turned to Michael, and said, "*Well...* what the fuck?"

Michael wiped foam from his Guinness from his upper lip, and said, "I'm only about halfway through the book, but I think it's a great read." The corners of Danny's mouth crept upward, and Michael continued. "Really. I'm being totally objective. It's damn good. If the rest of the book is as good as the first half..."

Danny swigged his beer and turned back to the TV. "It's better," he said.

"Martin Fletcher, eh?" said Michael. "Interesting initials. And a druggie lawyer to boot."

"I swear I did not consciously—"

"Hig, my life is like being in a bad novel. Your story is good."

"There are some similarities with your life, with *our* lives really, especially in the latter part of the story. But it is fiction. The lawyer doing the drugs... she is not a knock-off of your friend Rita. Besides, Rita's off the stuff, isn't she?"

"For a long time now. I think it's a great book."

They drank.

"How would I get involved with pushing a book like this?" asked Michael.

"Pushing?"

"You know, backing it. Putting some dough behind it."

"It's a nice thought, Mike, but you aren't a publisher."

"What about that self-publishing thing?"

"Then you're on the hook to print and promote it, all out of your own pocket."

"So let's do that."

"I'm a little torn. I see that as more of a last resort."

"How so?" asked Michael.

"I always kinda thought you self-published if no one else wanted anything to do with your book, kinda like taking your cousin to the prom."

"I thought it was about getting people to buy your book."

"It is, but..." Danny shrugged.

"I just went online and googled 'self-publishing,'" said Michael. "I figured some people must be getting their books out there on their own, or why would anyone do it? I mucked around, looking for people who had done it, and found a list as long as your arm: Margaret Atwood, Zane Grey, even Hemingway. And a bunch of others I'd heard of."

"No shit?"

"If you don't find another publisher, let's do something ourselves. At least consider it." Michael took a drink. "I would love to make this happen for you, Danny, get you over the hump. And think of how much fun we'd have doing this together."

Danny grinned, ordered two more Guinness and said, "I did have a cousin who was kinda hot." The enthusiasm he'd shown on the plane had bubbled back to the surface.

"Don't be mistaken, I'd want my cut from the sales," said Michael. He clinked Danny's glass and said, "To my new favourite author."

Danny turned away and looked into his beer. Michael watched a tear penetrate the head of his friend's Guinness. For the effect it had on Michael, it was Niagara Falls.

"I haven't forgotten how to do my old job, you know," said Danny, running a finger under one eye. "I will do your entire family's taxes, and any accounting work you ever need."

"No you won't," said Michael. "You're an author."

Both men passed out soon after returning to their room. They woke up early, their internal clocks not yet adjusted to the time change. Michael read more of Danny's book while the author showered. "You're right," said Michael when Danny reappeared. "This book does get better. That Valerie what's-her-name is an insatiable nymphomaniac, and a psychopath to boot."

"Yeah, I kind of fell in love with her character when I was writing it."

"Your sex scenes are great, very creative. Who knew you had it in you?"

"It helps to be horny as hell when you're writing them."

"No kidding."

Danny raised his hand and did a jerking motion.

As they set out from Dublin into the rich green countryside, Michael soon understood why they called it the "Emerald Isle". Through Tommy's old contacts, passed on to Michael from his uncle, they got tee times on three of Ireland's prime golf courses. His father had once told Michael if a man went on a "walkabout" through Ireland, he would leave knowing what he should do with his life. Michael could see the potential of such an introspective journey across this beautiful country. But rather than do a walkabout, he wanted to come back someday with Jessie, maybe to see the country by bicycle.

Danny hugged hedges of the narrow Irish roads in their compact rental sedan. He turned a blind corner outside Galway and swerved to miss a small herd of sheep ambling across the road.

A ferry ride across the Shannon River took them to The Old Course at Ballybunion, where Michael felt some disappointment about the benign conditions that greeted them. He'd heard of the wind ripping off the ocean, challenging the best of ball-strikers. But the holes that ran along the Atlantic did offer jaw-dropping views. The highlight of the round was a wayward tee shot by Danny on the first hole, which came to rest in the cemetery that ran alongside the fairway, bouncing off the headstone of someone named Leonard Kelly.

A few wrong turns in County Clare proved fortuitous, as it afforded them the opportunity to unearth the quaintest of pubs in places like Killaloe, Ennis, and Lisdoonvarna, where the annual Matchmaking Festival was just weeks away. One of the town's legendary matchmakers told Danny that he and a thirty-something barmaid, who had served them a round of Guinness, were doomed from the beginning were they to embark on an affair.

By the time they reached Lahinch, a course deemed "as precious as yeast to Guinness", they had concocted a plan for getting *Mayhem in Suburbia* on the shelves of bookstores across Canada. Their strategy scaled from local book-signings to full-sized ads on *GO Transit* trains and buses, where commuters could be induced to pick up a copy of an edgy new novel, set in their own backyard, to pass the time during the trip to and from downtown Toronto.

From Lahinch they headed for Connemara in the remote town of Ballyconneely. Connemara, another majestic links course, was in great contrast to the marketing machine that was Ballybunion. It wasn't open yet when they arrived at dawn, but they were able to tee off within the hour. While cheaper and less crowded than the previous stops on their tour, Connemara matched the beauty of the other courses. And it was long, the longest in Ireland they were told.

Michael launched a rocket down the middle of the first fairway, energizing him until he found the ball in hillside fescue. It required an almost baseball-like swing to knock the elevated sphere out of unforgiving hay and onto friendlier terrain.

They struggled and scored horribly and had the best of a time. The beer and insults flowed, and Michael saw a spring in Danny's step he had not witnessed in years. This could be Danny's walkabout.

Clouds hovered on fourteen, and while neither man's game flourished, they refused to surrender to the elements.

"I'm finishing this round if we have to swim to the eighteenth green," said Danny.

"Look at you with the golfer's heart," said Michael.

The weather held off until seventeen, where a gusting wind made a steady rain seem heavier than it was. They both parred the second-last hole, a first for the twosome on the day.

They stood on the eighteenth, taking in the panoramic backdrop of the par five stretching out ahead.

"You could reach this in two, Mikey."

"I'm looking at potential trouble that is trying to convince me otherwise," said Michael.

Two menacing bunkers guarding the front slope of the elevated eighteenth green looked back at them like deep-set, evil eyes.

"Those traps will look even bigger up close," said Michael.

Danny stood over his ball, hesitated, and backed off.

"I hope the future is half as bright as we've been talking it up to be," he said, before driving the ball down the middle and onto the short grass.

Michael's second shot found the greenside bunker on the right, and Danny's third plunked into the one on the left.

The skies opened up.

As they stepped into the cavernous bunkers, each having a formidable lip to clear to get up onto the green, Danny said, "If one of us gets up and down, then the days ahead will be rosy."

"Spoken like a true lefty," said Michael. "Very flaky." He dug in, hoping he could get his ball over the lip and sit it down within ten feet of the flag.

Michael, not aware that Danny was hitting, struck his ball a millisecond before him.

"Sorry, Hig," said Michael. He watched his own ball clear the lip and take a funny bounce on the hill in front of the green. It rolled back down and into the trap, resting in virtually the same spot from which he'd struck it.

Danny's ball cleared as well, hit the hill, and followed the same reverse path as Michael's had. As he watched it, Danny's body language took him backward, in step with the ball as it came back toward the bunker. It cost him his footing, and he landed on his butt just as the ball found its way back into the sand trap.

Michael laughed until his sides hurt. Danny lay back in the sand and howled. Michael looked back to the empty fairway behind them, said, "Don't move," and ran to his bag. He sat in the trap beside Danny when he returned, and handed him a Guinness. After seventeen holes of rattling around inside Michael's golf bag, the beer cans spewed like mini-volcanoes when they popped the tabs. They sat and drank in the bunker, smiling, saying nothing, as the rain beat down and the wind swirled.

"I never really cared much for golf," said Danny, breaking the silence.

"You've sure played it a hell of a lot for someone who doesn't like it," said Michael.

"I played it because you did, Mike. It was something we could do together."

They checked in at Boyle's Bed & Breakfast, whose accommodations were a couple of rooms in a residential home, down the hall from the owners' master bedroom. Michael hooked up an adapter Jessie had given him to recharge his BlackBerry. When he couldn't get a signal, the Boyles let Michael use their land line to make a call home. Michael had slipped the husband twenty euros and promised to be less than two minutes on the phone. Declan Boyle palmed the euros, winked at Michael and said, "Take five if you like."

Jessie reported that everyone in the Flanigan household was doing just fine.

Danny spread out a map and some brochures over a corner table at the local pub. They had almost two days before their return flight left Dublin, with nothing else scheduled on their itinerary.

Danny read from a brochure that he picked up at the inn in Dublin. "Leopardstown Racecourse was completed in 1888 and was built by Captain George Quinn, having been modelled on Sandown Park Racecourse in England."

"You got the racing bug?"

"Not so much, but it looks like a fun day out. I wouldn't mind going if we're gonna be flying out of Dublin anyway." Danny pushed away from the bar and said, "Give it some thought. I'm off to the loo."

Michael's BlackBerry vibrated in his pocket.

"How are the Irish lasses looking, Mike?" asked Fern, the connection from Canada surprisingly clear.

"I only have eyes for an English girl these days," said Michael.

"Yeah, yeah. Anyway, speaking of England, I got something for you on Ruth Eisentraut."

"She's British? Not German?"

"Oh, she's German alright. Born in Munich in 1975. But she went to school in London in the nineties. Some artsy private academy in Fulham, an area in west London. I guess this school churns out some decent artists."

"Painters?"

"Painters, sculptors, like that I guess."

"Where's she living now?"

"The latest address they have for her is in Cologne."

"Do you know if she's there? Did you actually speak to her?"

"Haven't reached her yet. Anything you'd like me to ask her?"

"Just talk to her. Confirm she was in Burlington, for starters. I actually had a funny feeling that the woman who worked at the arts centre with Emily may not have been who she claimed to be."

"You thought maybe someone was running around Burlington, Ontario *pretending* to be someone named Ruth Eisentraut?"

"I know I'm all over the place with this, Fern. But I can't lose the image of this mousy little nobody, who wouldn't say shit with a mouthful, shouting and dropping f-bombs at Emily up in Milton. It's not consistent. And then she disappears into thin air."

"And you think that whoever the hell she is, she could be connected to your wife's death, her *murder*?"

"Go find her, Fern. Please."

After another long pause, Fern said, "You got anything else?"

Danny returned to the table, carrying two pints.

"Has anyone found the Denison woman?" asked Michael, then mouthed "Fern" to Danny, who had lowered the pint glass he'd begun to hoist.

"Not that I've heard, but here's something for you," said Fern. "It seems that at one time the shitbag Toner was a nurse at the laughing academy in Kingston. They knew him as *Calvin* Toner. And no criminal record, believe it or not."

"The psychiatric hospital? Was he there at the same time as Brenda Gordon?"

"And Lottie Denison. All three were there at the same time."

"Holy shit. Toner was there."

"Close to three years ago, Lottie landed from England and moved into the Kingston home of a terminally ill aunt, her mother's sister, allegedly to care for the old woman. Lottie immediately became friendly with a neighbour. Dr. Brenda Gordon. The aunt dies, and a few months later Lottie is an outpatient at the hospital. Who knows if she started seeing the doctor professionally, and then a relationship developed, or if it was the other way around?"

"I'd bet the relationship happened first. It seems more likely than Lottie landing in Canada and deciding to see a shrink right away."

"She is fucked up, Mike."

"She is, but I'd go with the sex first."

"So maybe the appointments with the doc weren't all that... professional."

"Yeah. It fits."

"I bet the doctor had a couch in her office."

Michael again thought of Lottie the first time he met her, spread-eagled on the love seat and bleeding from the mouth. He pictured the doc roughing up the nympho Lottie, maybe drawing some blood. The image didn't resonate, but he didn't discount the possibility.

"She follows the good doctor to Burlington," said Michael, attempting to reconstruct the path Lottie Denison may have taken to Northcott's doorstep. "She runs into Northcott and notices the bulge in his back pocket. Maybe after doing some research on the potential marks in town with the most dough."

"And then she introduces Northcott to Toner," said Fern, "who she had to know from the hospital."

"How easy is it to do that, to change your name?" asked Michael.

"Easier than you might think," said Fern.

"Why wouldn't anyone have known that before he did all this?"

"Alberts may have known. It's not always so easy to trace, but he could have."

"What about Dr. Gordon?" asked Michael. "If they were at the same hospital, and somehow she found out about Toner's new identity, maybe from Lottie. Who knows what Lottie might have been up to? And if Toner found out he'd been exposed..."

"Yep," said Fern. "Toner probably did the doctor."

"But I thought they found Zetterfeldt's DNA on Dr. Gordon."

"Alberts found that a bit too convenient. They looked a little closer. Turns out the pubic hairs they found on the doc and your lady friend had decomposed."

"Pubic hairs?"

"They were too old to have just recently fallen from the perpetrator."

"Where would Toner get Zetterfeldt's pubic hairs, or do I want to know?"

"They belonged to the same fitness club. He waits for

Zetterfeldt to change, and when he's off working out..."

"It wasn't Zetterfeldt," said Michael to himself.

"Nurse Nutjob is how it looks," said Fern.

"And Toner also assaulted Jessie. The crazy prick should have been in his own rubber room, not treating patients."

"Zetterfeldt even had an alibi, post-mortem. It came out of the woodwork, but I understand it's rock solid."

"What do the police think of the notion that Northcott killed Jacquie Zetterfeldt to avenge his kid being abused by Jacquie's husband?"

"That's what they're going with."

"But why attack Jessie?" asked Michael, feeling a measure of relief that Graham Zetterfeldt hadn't attacked her to settle a score with him.

"Maybe thought another victim would complicate things even more, throw a bigger smokescreen over Northcott's revenge killing," said Fern. While that made little sense to Michael, he thought the cokeheads Northcott and Toner would enjoy hurting someone Michael loved.

"Alberts is clearly no dummy," said Michael.

"And a cop, too," said Fern. "Go figure."

"I deserved that."

"I'll be out of touch for a day or so. You flying back soon?"

"I'll be a couple of days. I have a stop to make on the way home."

"I was afraid of that."

"No lecture?" asked Michael.

"I'm not your mother," said Fern, and he hung up.

"Please tell me that stop is Dublin," said Danny.

"London," said Michael. "Fulham, actually."

"London? I assume this has got something to do with the phone call from Da Silva."

"Just some personal business I have to take care of."

"Personal business. What's all this about the Denison broad, and the lunatic asylum... changing names? I thought you were done with all that."

So did I.

Michael filled in Danny on the salient details from Fern's end of their conversation.

"Look, this Ruth person knew Emily, had some shit going on with her," said Michael. "It's the last door I have to close. And now it looks like Toner had been at the hospital in Kingston when Dr. Gordon was there."

"So what?" asked Danny. "They solved the murders back home, didn't they? It just makes more sense now, doesn't it, with Toner maybe killing the shrink for something that happened at the loony bin."

"I have to go there, while we're over here anyway."

"You still gotta get on a fucking plane, Mike. Whaddya need to know? Can't you just phone the fucking school or wherever it is you're going?"

Michael had no interest in arguing the point further. "I'm going to see if I can get a flight from Shannon," he said.

"If it's all the same to you, I think I'll check out the nags in Dublin."

Michael waited to get back to the Boyles' B&B to make his flight arrangements, where Mr. Boyle happily accepted another ten euros for the use of his desktop computer to allow Michael to book his flight.

Danny had not said a word on the walk back from the pub to the B&B, and stared blankly at the floor while Michael firmed up his reservations online in a small study on the main floor. Michael also forwarded Ferguson Boone a link to a photo gallery on the Foster Glen website, which included a picture of Northcott and Denison sitting together after the recent rainout of the charity tournament.

After Michael turned in, Danny went for walk. Michael didn't hear him come in, didn't see him again until his travel alarm woke him at 5:45 a.m. Danny was on the edge of his bed with his back to the window, the moonlight creating a rumpled and bloated Higgins silhouette. His bags were packed and sitting next to him.

Michael flicked on the light and squinted. "Wha..."

"Fulham. It's part of London, you said?" asked Danny. "I think they have a soccer team."

CHAPTER 35

Their Aer Lingus flight arrived on time at Heathrow Airport at 9:45 a.m.

As they shot along the London Underground, Danny said, "There are probably some nubile young art students running around this academy, and you know what they say about artists."

"No. What?"

"I was hoping you'd know."

They took a cab to the Fulham Academy of the Arts, a tired-looking brick building, more than three hundred years old according to Headmaster Rowan Alanson.

"Like Mr. Bean," said Danny during the introductions.

"That would be 'Atkinson', sir," said the headmaster, upper lip unyielding. Alanson had two wisps of white hair branching off in opposite directions from a nearly bald pate.

"Mike, I think I'll just sit down and keep my mouth shut," said Danny. He settled into a soft chair in the corner of the office.

They learned that Alanson had been at the school for twenty-six years, the past fourteen as headmaster. He remembered Ruth Eisentraut. Michael had called ahead and told Alanson he'd heard great things about the school from a friend of the Eisentrauts. He told Alanson that he was thinking of recommending that his daughter attend the academy, and wanted to learn of Ruth's experience there. Michael added that he planned to make a generous donation to whichever school his daughter attended. The headmaster agreed to give Michael thirty minutes of his time, with a tone that suggested he was granting Michael an audience with the Queen.

"A quiet young lady," said Alanson. "A good student, a fairly gifted sculptor as I recall."

"Ruth was a sculptor?" asked Michael. "Not a painter? I

suppose she could be both."

"Some students dabble, some even excel, in a variety of areas. But I believe Miss Eisentraut stuck to her sculpting."

"What else do you remember about her?"

"Not to be uncharitable, sir," said Alanson, "but I would say she was memorable only for her utter lack of any memorable traits. A true wallflower, engulfed by such a shyness that it brought attention to herself."

"Have you seen her since she left, talked to her?"

"I have not."

"Anyone around here ever mention seeing her?"

"No, sir."

"Did she have an accent? A German accent?"

Alanson thought about it for a moment and said, "A moderate accent, I suppose."

"Do you have any pictures of her? Perhaps in a yearbook or something?"

"I thought you were here to evaluate our academy for your daughter... and perhaps..."

"The donation," said Michael. He handed Alanson three twenty-pound notes, saying, "Would you please accept this initial gift? I don't need a receipt."

Alanson accepted the bills without hesitation, and slid the money into the top drawer of his expensive-looking mahogany desk, making Michael wonder how donations to the academy were distributed.

"I got the referral second-hand from her parents," said Michael. "But I think I may have met this Eisentraut kid somewhere. And for the life of me, I just can't remember where or when. It's been bugging me. You know the feeling, don't you?"

Alanson paused, then nodded. "As a matter of fact," he said, turning to a bookcase behind his desk, "when you called to say you were coming..."

Alanson opened up a dusty brown book with "1995" on the cover. It looked like a thinner version of the yearbooks at T. J.

Walsh Public School. "I was just looking for... ah, here we go." He opened to a page he had bookmarked and pointed to a photograph. Three rows of casually-dressed young women smiled into the camera, their bohemian attire in contrast with the headmaster's pickle-up-his-ass deportment.

"You will notice that Ruth was absent from the photo," said Alanson.

"Are there any other pictures of this class," asked Michael. "School clubs maybe? Sports teams? Anything Ruth Eisentraut might have belonged to?"

"The academy exists mainly from the generosity of others, sir. We accept gifted arts students, based solely on merit, not on financial wherewithal. Some can pay, some cannot."

Michael wasn't sure where Alanson was headed with this little sidebar, but assumed the man lived in constant pitch mode for donations. Michael frowned in response, and Alanson added, "We don't have traditional yearbooks per se, Mr. Flanigan. You'll note the austere binding. At the end of the year we take a photograph, *one* photograph, of each graduating class. We offer a copy to each student, and bind the photos for that year in the fashion you see here."

"So nothing of Ruth anywhere in here?" asked Michael.

"Oh my, what was I thinking?" said Alanson. "I doubt very much that we will locate any photographs of young Miss Eisentraut."

"Why not?"

"I just now recalled that she had a dreadful skin problem, more pronounced than just a bad case of spots."

Michael recalled that Ruth wasn't in the staff picture at the arts centre. "Spots," he said. "You mean pimples. Acne."

"Quite. And to top things off, Ruth couldn't wear makeup. She had an allergy, a severe one. It was noted on her profile when she enrolled. So the poor girl didn't really have a chance, did she?"

"How severe was it?"

"No tolerance at all. She'd get conjunctivitis, dermatitis. I recall the latter being quite disfiguring at its peak."

"You've seen one of these reactions?"

"One of the students brought in a variety of cosmetics that were ostensibly hypoallergenic. I understand she told Ruth that it was the best on the market, the answer to her dreams."

"But it wasn't."

"We encouraged her fellow students to avoid staring, poking fun. The girls were quite good about it. The incident soon became a distant memory."

Michael looked back to the picture of Ruth's classmates and asked, "Did Ruth have any friends in the class, someone she was particularly tight with?"

Alanson donned the glasses that were hanging around his neck and studied the picture, running his finger along the rows of fledgling artists. "It was a long time ago," he said. "And, as I have already stated, she mainly kept to herself." He studied it a while longer. "I'm sorry. It *was* a long time ago."

"How tall was Ruth?" asked Michael.

"Let's see. I'm about six foot. I'd say she was perhaps five-seven, five-eight perhaps. Maybe taller. She tended to slouch. I don't know... it was—"

"A long time ago."

Michael flipped through the pages of the yearbook. A collage of sorts made up the inside cover and front page, candid shots of students in various parts of the school: outside having a smoke; hanging out in what looked like a cafeteria; mugging for the camera.

"*Jesus, Mary, and Joseph,*" said Michael.

"What, Mike? What?" asked Danny, rising from his chair.

She was younger in the photo, and mugging for the camera. And she looked... *different*, beyond the contorted grin on her face. But it was her.

"This one here," said Michael, pointing at the girl. "I'd swear I know her from somewhere. Who is she?"

"Ah, Miss Jeffrey," said Alanson. "Now she would be hard to

forget. Quite dramatic indeed."

"Would she have been in any of Ruth's classes?"

"No, sir. Miss Jeffrey was a bit younger, came here a couple of years after Miss Eisentraut arrived."

Jeffrey. Where did Michael know that name from?

Alanson did recall that Charlotte Jeffrey had lived in nearby Barnes in southwest London, with a Canadian mother whom he thought had married a Brit. Charlotte's mother, Natalie, had worked part-time in the academy's office before her daughter attended the school, and before Alanson had become headmaster. Alanson remembered little about Natalie Jeffrey, other than her name and Canadian roots.

"Would you know if Natalie Jeffrey remarried before she died?"

"I didn't really know her."

"Does the name Denison ring a bell?"

"No, sir."

"Did Charlotte always go by the name Jeffrey? She reminds me of a kid I knew as Denison. And since you said the mom was a Canadian, I thought maybe..."

Alanson shrugged, shook his head. "Why don't I have my assistant check our records for any details we have on the family?"

"Can she do it now?" asked Michael. "I'm so darn curious."

"She's off today. Leave me your email address. I'll forward any information we have to share."

Michael smiled. "That'd be great," he said. He'd pushed it far enough, considering he'd allegedly set up the meeting to assess the academy.

He let Alanson deliver his closing sales pitch on the merits of attending the school, gave him his contact info, and thanked him for his time. As he opened the door to leave, Michael turned back to the headmaster.

"Did Charlotte have a nickname?" he asked, sensing he'd overlooked the obvious answer to his question.

"I referred to Miss Jeffrey as Charlotte."

"How about the other kids? Did they refer to her by another name?"

Alanson frowned. "I don't know. *Charlie* perhaps?"

"How about Lottie?"

"Now that you mention it."

"Lottie and Ruth, working together on... what? I didn't see that coming," said Michael, as their black cab headed for Chelsea. "Wait a minute. What did he say?" Michael stopped, looked away.

"You gonna make me guess?" said Danny.

"Jeffrey?"

"I guess you are."

"Oh my God. It wasn't Jenkins," said Michael. "Hig, my aunt said the girl Northcott assaulted behind the school when we were kids was named Jenkins. But Lucie's memory is crap these days. It *wasn't* Jenkins."

"Shit, you're right. It was Natalie Jeffrey."

Michael called Fern from their Chelsea hotel. He left a brief message to inform his P.I. that Lottie Denison and Ruth Eisentraut had attended school together at the Fulham Academy of the Arts.

Michael thought if Lottie had taken her mother's maiden name, Natalie Jeffrey may have never married. Denison could be Lottie's married name. If she did have a current or former husband somewhere, Michael imagined the man would have some stories to tell.

Or Lottie's father could have been Mr. Denison, whom Natalie may have divorced before reverting back to her family name. Lottie may have elected to go by Denison once she was old enough to make the decision for herself.

The more options he considered, the more confused he got.

They settled for dinner in the hotel restaurant, neither man having the energy to search out any of the places Jessie had suggested.

"Are you ready to let the cops figure things out from here?" asked Danny.

"I guess that confirms that *was* Ruth Eisentraut at the arts centre back home."

"You thought it was some impostor of homely broads? You didn't answer my question."

Michael jumped to his feet. "Or maybe it wasn't."

"Michael Flanigan. What the fuck?"

"I have to call the arts centre in Burlington."

The following day, Michael and Danny huddled in the corner of a lounge at Heathrow Airport.

"Are you sitting down?" said Michael into his phone.

"I'm lying down, Sherlock," said Fern. "It's still six in the goddam morning here."

"Shit. Sorry, I was excited and forgot about the time difference."

"Don't sweat it," said Fern. "This isn't the first call this morning."

"I know who Ruth Eisentraut was."

"Who she was? I picked up your message. Ruth Eisentraut and Lottie Denison went to the same school in Fulham. You said you figured they were maybe up to no good together in Burlington. "

"Right, that's what I said."

"But that's *all* you said, other than asking me to find out if Denison had a husband, which I haven't had time to check on. You didn't say what the hell you figured the two broads were working on."

"I don't think that now, that they were up to something together," said Michael. "Not since last night, when I spoke to Ferguson Boone, the director at the arts centre."

Fern sighed. "Okay, let's have it."

"It's my belief that Ruth Eisentraut, at least the Ruth that Emily knew, was actually Lottie Denison."

"She was *what*?" asked Fern and Danny in stereo.

"I know, I know. It sounds nuts. But the more I think about it the less crazy it seems."

"So get me thinking about it," said Fern.

"Okay, hear me out," said Michael. "Boone told me that on the day Emily died he found Ruth at the arts centre, sobbing violently. He said she looked awful, with dark lines under her eyes. At the time I thought he meant her face had lines from all the crying, being run down, distraught. But it didn't occur to me that he had been talking about *makeup*."

"Makeup," said Fern.

"Makeup. The dark lines were from the mascara she was wearing, running down her face from all the crying. The guy at the school in Fulham said Ruth Eisentraut had violent allergic reactions to cosmetics of any kind. He implied she would *never* go near them again."

"Makeup."

"Yep. Makeup."

"Wouldn't Lottie Denison know about this allergy? They were classmates."

"Not classmates," said Michael. "Schoolmates. The last time Ruth had this allergic reaction was two years before Lottie got to the school. And Lottie may have decided to put *some* makeup on her unblemished face, to give the appearance that she was covering up *Ruth's* bad skin, to really be in character. To really *be* Ruth. Otherwise, Lottie would have needed to take the opposite approach to pull off the charade."

"You're saying that if Lottie *didn't* wear some kind of cover-up makeup, but really wanted to nail the disguise, she would've had to make herself up to appear to *have* the horrible acne that Ruth had." Fern paused, and said, "You're givin' me a headache, Mike. You got anything else to support this wild theory of yours?"

"Boone confirmed that *his Ruth* in Burlington was about five-seven, give or take, the same height as the Ruth in London. I noticed at Foster Glen that Lottie Denison was about the same height as Eddie Kan. And Eddie is five-seven."

"Well, if the two Ruths were the same damn height, then one of them *must be* Lottie Denison. What the hell, Mike? Are you still trying to shake a bad case of jet lag? Maybe got into some bad Yorkshire pudding over there?"

"I'm not saying the height match does anything more than support the fact Lottie could have posed as Ruth."

"Ah Christ, Mike," said Fern. "I haven't had my first coffee yet."

"Think about it, Fern. Old Ruthie seems to be utterly forgettable to everyone, but the volunteer known as Ruth Eisentraut at the arts centre matches the demeanour of the girl who went to school in Fulham. Who besides Lottie Denison would know that?"

"It could be that *she is* Ruth Eisentraut."

"But what about—"

"I know. The makeup. Why would Lottie Denison go to all that trouble to impersonate her old schoolmate?"

"She *revels* in it. Lottie is constantly changing her act," said Michael. "She lost her British accent somewhere over the Atlantic, and never looks or sounds the same way twice. Nympho, jock, society girl. Whatever fits the occasion. That's gotta be why she didn't show up for the staff picture. She knew it might incriminate her later. But she had to *become* Ruth as best she could to cover her tracks after the fact. If I'm wrong about this, where is Ruth Eisentraut? Where the hell is she?"

"Quite a stretch, Mike, even for you," said Fern. "I still haven't heard a good reason why Lottie Denison would do this."

"Does anyone have more than an address on Ruth Eisentraut?" asked Michael, ducking the topic of motive. He felt strongly that an elusive painting was a prominent piece in the puzzle, but wanted to keep that to himself for at least the time being.

"Still haven't tracked her down."

"I'd bet a dollar Lottie also played the role of Teresa Amodeo up on the Niagara Escarpment one day in October."

Fern laughed. "Another disguise. This just keeps getting better. What happened to Ruth then? Did Lottie whack her so nobody could track her down, so she could *be her* without risk of having someone find the real Ruth before things played out for her?"

"That'd be my guess," said Michael. "Ruth allegedly left town after Emily died, and people kept getting killed. I'm thinking whoever that volunteer was, who called herself Ruth Eisentraut, is still here in Burlington."

"I get it... I think. Because you're convinced Emily's death was no accident, and that her death is also tied to the other murders, you've come up with this unbelievable theory that allows for this... logic. Lottie dresses up as the decoy, Teresa Amodeo, while an accomplice pushes Emily over the side of the Niagara Escarpment. So it would be no sweat for Lottie to knock off someone else, someone like Ruth Eisentraut."

"It makes sense, does it not?"

"Why would she kill your wife, Mike? Did she get in Lottie's way, too?"

"Lottie Denison might be the one I was looking for all along. She's like a damn chameleon."

"Was."

"Was what?"

"Was a chameleon. I got a call a half hour ago. They found Lottie Denison's shoe on the strip of beach down the road from Spencer Smith Park."

"Are they sure it's hers?"

"Pretty sure. The leg that's attached to the shoe, cut off at the knee, likely with a power saw, has the same tattoo of a black widow on the right ankle that Miss Denison had."

"Lottie Denison is dead?"

"As dead as she's ever gonna get," said Fern.

"Any other dead bodies I should know about?" asked Michael, a little pissed off at Fern for playing games with him.

"None that I can think of," said Fern.

"Huh. Maybe that does close it off."

"It does if your theory on Ruth being Lottie is correct."

"Do you buy into that?"

"I got nothing better at the moment, and definitely won't if you don't let me get some caffeine into me."

"So who do you think killed Lottie?" asked Michael.

"I hear the smart money is on Fuzzy Mavis finding out about Denison's relationship with Northcott," said Fern.

"The mob guy? Maybe she knew too much?"

"That's how I see it," said Fern, who segued to inquire about the golf courses in Ireland. Danny got up to "go to the loo".

"I sure get my money's worth from my P.I.," said Michael. "Huh. I would have never..." Something clicked in his head.

"Never what?" asked Fern.

"Did you tell me last year that an old girlfriend of yours... Lana... Lara... she got a transfer to the regional police headquarters, some kind of office job with a major crime unit? Maybe in Homicide?"

Fern hesitated. "Lara Peterson."

"It's her, isn't it?" asked Michael. "The *associates* you referred to?"

"What did I tell you about this?"

"Fern, the woman could be in serious shit if she's feeding you the information you've been giving me."

"I can't worry about that and do this job. Did I not tell you people would be at risk? Did you think this stuff was falling from a tree?"

"Please just let me know if you find Ruth."

"The meter's still running."

"Can we forget that painting ever existed?" asked Michael.

"What painting?" asked Fern.

Michael thanked Fern and hung up, more certain than ever that whoever was responsible for Emily's death had been purged from this world, and that her good name would not be tarnished from any involvement she'd had with *The Golfer*.

Golfers. She never had much luck with them.

CHAPTER 36

Walking into Jessie's arms at his front door, Michael was reminded again where his focus, and his heart, should be.

They made love, starting in the foyer, moved up to the bedroom, and finished in the shower.

The next morning, Michael wandered down the hall from his office to find Clint and Sophie waiting for him at the kitchen table. Sophie hugged her stepdad and proudly announced that Eamonn was out on a job interview.

Clint's mother had consented to let him come stay as long as he liked, agreeing that the danger was over.

"Agreed with who?" asked Michael. He stood behind Clint and massaged his shoulders. "Did you pester her, boy?"

The kids looked to Jessie.

"You?" asked Michael.

"She's really quite a reasonable woman," said Jessie.

Michael had his doubts about that, but knew Jessie was speaking for Clint's benefit now, and he loved her more for it. He kissed the top of Jessie's head and joined them at the table.

"There were break-ins up by the cottage," said Sophie. "A few places got hit."

"Where'd ya hear that?" asked Michael.

"I went up there."

"You what?"

"I had to, Michael," she said. Jessie put her arm around her, and Sophie added, "I can't let him win."

"Him?" asked Michael. "Oh." *Toner*. "And our place?" he asked.

"They left our cottage alone," replied Sophie. "For once we got a break."

"Who got broken into?" asked Clint.

"Not sure how many exactly," said Sophie. "The Sutton place, Dave Douthwright."

Michael's heart rate jumped.

"What'd they take?" asked Clint.

"Dave said they took some paintings, and some other stuff," said Sophie.

Fuck me.

"Would anyone keep paintings of any worth at their cottage?" asked Jessie.

"No kidding," said Sophie, sitting next to her. "And *Dave Douthwright*?"

Michael felt he knew one piece of art that was no longer hanging on Tina Sutton's wall. "Maybe they were cheapies," he said.

Plus there was the painting that Emily may have stolen and given to good ol' neighbour Dave who kindly passed it on to the widow Sutton whom he'd been comforting in other ways.

Did Toner, on the last night of his life, see *The Golfer* hanging in the Sutton cottage? He could have made a phone call before Sophie sent him off to answer to his Maker.

Is it not over?

Ferguson Boone finally replied to the email Michael had sent him from Ireland, the one containing the link to the online picture of Lottie Denison at the golf club. Boone's email read, "It could be her – hard to tell – not a great picture".

Boone's response perplexed Michael. The scanned picture he had sent Boone was of high quality. If Lottie had roamed the arts centre as Ruth Eisentraut, her disguise must have been clever indeed.

Michael called Dave Douthwright at his cottage and confirmed that *The Golfer* had been taken in the burglary at Tina Sutton's. Michael tried to appease his lakeside neighbour, who felt terrible about the stolen painting, but had limited success.

Tina hadn't mentioned the connection to Emily to the police.

Michael spent the rest of the day glued to Jessie's side. Sophie joined them for the first part of their stroll along Lakeshore Boulevard in downtown Burlington, where she gave Jessie a few introductory photography instructions, mainly showing her what buttons to push.

Sophie's fire was returning, as well as her smile. Maybe Toner hadn't taken a piece of her to his grave, and only the devil's hands were in there with him, pulling him toward his eternal home.

Michael and Jessie had a late lunch at Sakai on Fairview Street, and worked off their sushi with a prolonged tilt in the bedroom that took them past the dinner hour.

Life was getting damn good for Michael Flanigan. He figured it was about time.

Michael was in his office when Fern called. Jessie was downstairs on the treadmill, getting in a quick workout before a late morning appointment.

"They've decided to exhume Teresa Amodeo's body," said Fern.

"You're kidding me." The cops actually listened to him. "All because of the accent."

"Seems it got the ball rolling," said Fern.

"Do they think she may not have had a stroke, or a heart attack? Or if she did…"

"Someone may have helped it along."

"They agreed with my theory about Lottie masquerading as Ruth, as well as Teresa Amodeo?"

Fern hung up.

Later in the day, Michael and Jessie lounged in their room, reading, doing crossword puzzles, mainly just enjoying their time together. The bright, blue sky of the future was shining through.

The heavy weight of a life that almost drowned in violence had begun to drift away.

Jessie fell asleep.

Michael sat up in bed.

What had Alberts said to him?

He grabbed his robe and went down to the basement. He found the remote and paged through the list of recorded TV shows. He hoped the one that interested him had not been deleted.

He found it.

After Rowan Alanson's elderly-sounding secretary redirected Michael's call, the headmaster immediately jumped into an explanation of why he and his assistant were at work on a Saturday. They were developing a brochure for an AIDS fundraiser that the Fulham Academy of the Arts was putting on in conjunction with a school in Putney. Michael knew Alanson did not mention the AIDS appeal without motive. That was alright, Michael thought. He'd opened that door himself.

"It's a worthy cause," said Michael. "Send me a soft copy once the brochure is finalized."

"I will indeed, sir."

"You got my note, Mr. Alanson?"

"I received your email, Mr. Flanigan. I spoke to my executive assistant, Miss Ansell. She retrieved any documentation we had on the Jeffrey girl."

Michael guessed that Alanson had worked with his secretary for years and didn't know her first name.

"My assistant had recently spoken to a former colleague who knew the girl's mother," said Alanson.

"Natalie," said Michael. "She *knew* her?"

"Natalie Jeffrey apparently died of a brain aneurysm a few years ago."

"Would your records tell you if Jeffrey was Lottie's...

Charlotte's mother's maiden name?"

Michael heard drawers open and shut, papers being shuffled. He waited, until Alanson said, "Yes, that would be her mother's original surname, sir. Natalie Jeffrey. I don't think Charlotte's father was in the picture for long."

"Do you have her father's surname?"

"The gentleman on her account profile is listed as her stepfather."

"And?"

"His name is Denison, which I believe is the name you mentioned on your visit. Kenneth 'Kep' Denison. Lottie's legal name is Charlotte Jeffrey Denison."

Lottie Denison. Lottie had managed to ditch her British accent and used her legal surname, her stepfather's name, when she left to invade Canada.

"Did Charlotte always go by the name Jeffrey as far as you know, never using the stepfather's name?" asked Michael.

"She referred to herself as Charlotte Jeffrey. That's how we knew her."

Alanson slurped on a drink. Michael pictured a dainty teacup and a pinky dangling free, in contrast to the headmaster's audible lack of phone manners. "Miss Jeffrey had a half-sister, I believe a couple of years younger, from her mother's first marriage. I met her once or twice."

"Did she go to the academy?" he asked.

"No, but she came by periodically to gather Miss Jeffrey after school," said Alanson. "A most inquisitive sort, as I recall. We got to know her a bit around here."

"What was her name?"

More shuffling of papers. "Here it is. Her half-sister was called Mary Anne Naismith, from her mother's first marriage."

"Natalie Jeffrey's first husband."

"Apparently Mr. Naismith had problems with both alcohol and maintaining gainful employment."

"He was a lazy drunk." Michael assumed Miss Ansell had

provided Alanson with more information than was in Lottie's school file.

"That would be him," said Alanson.

"Mary Anne was a *half*-sister from Natalie Jeffrey's *first* marriage, but she was a bit younger than Lottie?"

"Correct."

"The drunk, Naismith, was Natalie's first husband, and not Lottie's father. And you said this Denison guy, hubby number two, was Lottie's stepfather," said Michael. "Then who was Lottie's father?"

"I believe Charlotte's father and mother were never married," said Alanson. "Someone she left behind in Canada, before emigrating."

Lottie's father was a Canadian. It was all coming together for Michael. And it repulsed him.

"Tell me a little bit about the half-sister," he said.

"Mary Anne was attractive enough," said Alanson. "Not much resemblance to Charlotte..."

Naismith. Mary Anne Naismith.

"... there was an attack at the family home. The poor Naismith girl was assaulted, quite viciously I understand, but she survived..."

Mary Anne Naismith. Dr. Gordon's list. One of the stolen files.

"... thank goodness Charlotte wasn't at home, but her stepfather wasn't so lucky."

But the doctor had no file on Lottie Denison.

"... at any rate, Mr. Flanigan, when your email arrived, I must say..."

Jessie had entered the room, wrapped in a towel, wet curls hanging over her shoulders.

"... Mr. Flanigan?" said Alanson.

"I'm listening," said Michael, refocusing.

"Miss Naismith had an interest in the arts herself. She would pop into my office when she stopped by, not able to resist any opportunity to show off her knowledge of photography, art history, you name it. She did makeup for a local theatre troupe, and even tinkered with our computer network after a cock-up by one of our staff."

Michael assumed Mary Anne Naismith had honed her makeup skills on her half-sister.

Jessie walked over and sniffed the top of Michael's head, then kissed it. She sat opposite him, where he noticed she was doing the *Saturday Stumper,* her favourite crossword puzzle. She smiled at him, then frowned.

He turned his own frown into a smile and whispered, "It's okay."

She smiled and went back to her puzzle.

"Frankly," said Alanson, "I was a tad perturbed at how poor my memory has been getting, not recalling Miss Naismith. But then she... came back to me."

"It has been a few years," said Michael.

"Granted, but she would be hard to forget. Quite a vivacious, beautiful young lady."

So much for "attractive enough".

"Miss Naismith went to an arts school in Kensington, and claimed to have stimulated Miss Jeffrey's interest in the arts," said Alanson. "I called an old classmate of mine who teaches at Kensington to inquire. Apparently Miss Naismith was quite a gifted painter, skilled in many of the arts. Quite brilliant, actually. What you Yanks might call an off-the-charts IQ."

"Impressive," said Michael, letting the Yank reference go.

"Indeed. Also spoke a few languages if memory serves, but with an ego and... *attitude* that matched her intellect."

Michael smiled as Jessie tugged away at her eyebrow as she did her crossword.

"Funny, now I can picture Mary Anne... Miss Naismith... like it was yesterday," said Alanson.

"Oh yeah."

"... an elbow resting on her hand... her piercing, intelligent eyes..."

He's gettin' all worked up. Calm down, old fella.

Michael smiled over at Jessie again, head still buried in her crossword, eyebrow still getting a workout.

"... pulling at the corner of her eyebrow," said Alanson.

"Listen, thanks again, Mister... I beg your pardon?"

"She took the pictures for our yearbook, the pictures you saw. I'd forgotten when we spoke last, but when I saw your email... with the photograph of the girl sitting at a table, and the other standing behind her by the bar."

A whiny gasp escaped from Michael. Jessie looked up, concerned. He could only stare, struggled for breath, sucked some air in.

"What is it, sweetheart?" she asked.

"I'm good," he said.

"Mr. Flanigan, are you there," asked Alanson.

"My email?" asked Michael. Lots of people pick at their eyebrows. Don't they?

"Well you can just imagine my surprise at seeing the two girls in the photograph."

"Two?"

"Miss Jeffrey and her half-sister."

Michael's couldn't process what he was hearing. He felt dizzy, thought he might pass out.

"That has to be Miss Jeffrey sitting at the table," said Alanson.

"Right," said Michael. He took a long drink of water.

"And leaning against the bar in the back of the photograph... it's been more than a few years, and she looks like she may have had some work done. I'd say both of them may have. But I'd bet ten pounds I'm looking at Miss Naismith."

Jessie.

Jessie's standing at the bar in that picture.

Dear God.

Jessie took her hand from her eyebrow, and put down her pen. "Is everything alright?" she asked.

"The colitis," he blurted.

"I beg your pardon, sir," asked the headmaster.

"I have to run," said Michael. He hung up, banged the phone into its cradle, and ran from the room.

"Are you okay?" called Jessie, as he ran down the hall.

"Just the usual stuff," he yelled back.

He grabbed his BlackBerry from the desk in his office and ran to the bathroom in the far corner of the main floor.

Surprised his colitis hadn't flared up, he sat on the toilet with the lid down. He shook, and watched his sweat drop from his forehead to the mat below. He fought a bubbling nausea.

There had to be a good explanation.

And he was afraid he already knew it.

Michael sat in his office, trying to figure out the relationship of the Toner-Denison-Naismith troika.

Did they murder Emily, and kill the others, too? Did Lottie introduce Toner to her half-sister Mary Anne?

Bobby George had said that Toner had been interested in the artwork hanging in Michael's house. Did Mary Anne Naismith, and not J.P. Northcott, dispatch Toner to invade the Flanigan home?

Mary Anne Naismith was arrogant and brash, some kind of hotshot photographer.

Jessie Hargreaves was sweet and kind, and prior to her recent tutorial with Sophie, did not know which end of the camera was up.

Or did she?

This woman loved him, wanted the two of them to spend their lives together.

But for how long would that be?

He backtracked. Things said and done by the woman he knew as Jessie Hargreaves, the woman of his dreams, rattled around in his head.

After leaving a message for his aunt, he called Sophie, who

sounded like she was in bed, and not alone. Still getting past his discomfort with the relationship between his stepdaughter and younger brother, he got right to the point.

"Sophie, you and Jessie had a good laugh over one of the *Law & Order* shows recently, when you found a scene quite implausible."

"Yup. I remember."

"What was so funny about it?"

"The cops blew up a security tape from a hole-in-the-wall bodega in a bad neighbourhood, and used the larger view to nail the bad guy."

"I remember that," said Michael, who had watched that part of the program for first time when he rewound the recorded episode the night before.

"It's so phony," she said. "The odds that a little shit-hole of a store would have a security camera that could produce that sort of enlargement of a shot, taken from that distance, are slim and none."

"Right, the security camera," said Michael. The ladies weren't mocking the detective's uncanny data retrieval skills on the computer. It was about the damn camera.

Alberts did tell Michael he'd seen too many cop shows.

"I guess only a photographer, someone who knew their stuff, would know something like that," said Michael.

"I guess," said Sophie. "Someone who knew about cameras. But then again, Jessie picked up on it, too."

Exactly.

Michael's heart sank a little further. The case against his fiancée consisted of what *Law & Order* D.A. Jack McCoy might call circumstantial evidence, but it was building.

She is Mary Anne Naismith.

"I love you, Sophie," he said, perhaps trying to jump-start the aching organ in his chest.

"Ditto, Step Diddy. You chill, okay?"

He might not chill again.

The rose-coloured glasses had slipped off.

The gaps lined up at the door to his memory.

Why hadn't *Jessie* mentioned the mark on his ass from the needle Toner had stuck in him? Could she have missed it? It had begun to look like anything but polite reticence. She knew about the invasion of his home, and the injection.

But she was attacked, and *raped*. Did she fake that? The doctor did say she was very lucky. Her post-rape exam showed few of the usual signs of forced penetration.

He felt like the more that he knew, the less he knew. Was she in on all of it?

Michael thought of a painting hanging in the farmhouse in Bronte Creek Park—not *The Golfer*, but the one that had tilted sideways on the wall behind him as he talked to Joel Pierce, making Michael jump. The watercolour of two dueling men had a woman sitting off in the background. She was clearly the focal point of the painting.

He called Ferguson Boone.

"Mr. Boone, you had trouble deciding if the woman in the photo I showed you could be Ruth Eisentraut," said Michael when the arts centre director answered the phone. "But you weren't talking about the woman at the table in the centre of the picture, were you?"

"I was referring to the long-legged lady in the background, standing at the bar. Her dress and demeanour, the way she carries herself, certainly aren't Ruth. But her facial structure... I tend to notice that in a woman. Anyway, it could be her, but I only say that since you asked. I wouldn't look at this picture and definitively say 'Ruth.'"

"Did Ruth have any quirks, habits, anything at all that stood out?"

"None that I recall," said Boone, who hesitated for a moment and said, "Oh... wait. Do you mean that thing with her eyebrows?"

Michael's chest tightened, but Boone had just confirmed

what Michael already knew. He thanked Boone and hung up.

Lottie wasn't Ruth. Michael's fiancée, who turned out to be Mary Anne Naismith, had played that role as well. As Ruth, she befriended Emily, fought with her over *The Golfer*, and then played Emily's husband for the most gullible of all fools.

He called Fern.

"We can forget about Germany," said Michael.

"I already have. The police found the real Ruth Eisentraut," said Fern, "stuffed into a plastic bag in the trunk of a car, in a dump down by Sarnia."

"She was here in Canada the whole time."

"They also found a room that Lottie Denison rented in some fleabag motel in Toronto. Interesting stuff they found... German language tapes, other books on Germany, and some pretty drab clothing they figure was worn by whoever said she was Ruth Eisentraut. And cosmetics. A ton of makeup was found in the room."

"How convenient," said Michael, knowing the stash had to belong to Lottie's half-sister. "I bet if they looked they wouldn't find any makeup on Ruth." He grunted.

"What's with the tone?" asked Fern. "It looks like you were dead on with this one, buddy. Lottie Denison was masquerading as Ruth Eisentraut."

"I'd better not quit my day job."

"You don't have a job."

"Mike, I don't like the way those dots connect," said Fern. He set his coffee on the hassock by his chair in Rita's sunroom.

"Mother of God," said Rita, sitting next to Michael on the sofa. "Your old pal J.P. was... with his own kid."

"And he probably didn't even know it," said Michael.

"I hope to hell that neither of them did," said Rita.

Michael considered the unholy alternative, that one or both had been a willing participant.

"That's *it*," he said.

"What's it?" asked Rita.

"At the club, the night I was drugged. Eddie said Northcott read a note that someone had stuck in his pocket. He said he looked at it like he didn't know it was there. He looked at the note and then looked *in horror*, Eddie said, at Lottie Denison.

"*The answer to my question is you.*" Michael repeated the message on the note he'd found in Northcott's pocket. He now thought he knew the question.

That was the moment J.P. Northcott learned that Lottie Denison was his daughter.

"You've read this note?" said Rita.

Fern stared at Michael, who thought he might soon have to explain why he knew the contents of a note the police found in Northcott's pocket the night he was murdered. Instead, Fern just grinned and said, "Someone told Papa who he was diddlin.'"

"But who?" asked Rita. "Don't tell me Lottie wrote the note, that she knew he was her father all along and was doing him as part of some bigger plot to... what? Get at his money?"

"The oldest reason in the book for doing something naughty," said Fern.

"Naughty doesn't begin to describe this," said Michael. "Unless..." He got up and walked to the window.

"Unless?" asked Rita.

Michael turned to face them. "What if Lottie really didn't know she was sharing her father's bed?" He knew that would mean someone other than Lottie would have planted the note, after that same person had posed the question to Northcott that was answered in the note.

"Naismith was a patient of Brenda Gordon," said Rita, repeating what Michael had told her minutes before. "Now that's interesting."

"We gotta tell the cops," said Fern.

"We do, but not just yet," said Michael.

"Michael, it is *over*," said Rita. "Am I the only one who thinks the betting money is on this Naismith gal offing her own sister, then setting Lottie up as being the Ruth impersonator to deflect suspicion from herself?"

"Do ya think?" said Fern with a smirk.

"I know how we might be able to force her hand, to bring her out." Michael looked at Fern. "I got the idea from something you once told me."

He explained his plan.

"That might just work," said Fern after Michael had laid it out. "It'd be nice to hand this to the cops on a silver platter."

"I'm not hearing any of this," said Rita.

CHAPTER 37

Michael's colitis provided an excuse to forego any meaningful physical contact with the woman he knew as Jessie Hargreaves, who acted rather frisky when he walked in his front door... *their* front door. He tried not to stare, but caught himself doing it anyway, looking for the psychopath hiding behind the softest, kindest eyes he'd ever seen.

Maybe there was an angle he hadn't considered, one that would explain away everything.

She frowned at his penetrating gaze, and he said, "I can't get over how much I love you." In a way, it still sounded right to Michael. Letting go is hard.

Fern's email was waiting when he sat down in front of the computer. Michael printed a hard copy, along with a number of unrelated and innocuous emails. He stacked them on his desk, with Fern's piece of creative writing on top.

The Woman Known As Jessie walked in a few minutes later with a rye and ginger and set it on the desk next to Michael. He had strategically placed the email pile facing out where she couldn't miss it, with the hooks he wanted her to nibble on underlined in boldface.

He swivelled his chair to the bookcase on the wall behind him, saying, "Excuse me, honey. I'm looking for some old photographs of the kids. I'm sure they're in one of these boxes." He went through the motions of scouring the boxes on the shelf behind his desk, allowing enough time for Jessie to read the printed email five times if she cared to. If she was indeed Mary Anne Naismith, she would read it.

He turned back to face her. Nothing in her eyes suggested that she had just read the news that her half-sister died a rich woman. If she was a fake, she was good. Hell, if she wasn't the

Jessie Hargreaves he knew, she was a mad fucking genius.

She kissed his forehead, and said, "I hope you feel better soon, dear. Just call if you need anything." She turned and left the room.

She had been sleeping when Michael got home from Rita's earlier in the day, no doubt still recovering from the horrific rape and beating, the poor dear. He had found the invoice for the tune-up on her Mercedes under a pile of bills on the kitchen counter. The invoice was dated July 6, the day before the nightmare on Lake Muskoka with Frank Toner.

The odometer reading, as noted on the invoice, was 48,988 kilometres. When Michael had first ridden in the car with her a few weeks before, he glanced at the kilometre reading to help him gauge the age of the vehicle. He was certain it had just over 45,000 kilometres on it. It'd take a lot of trips, in a city that's twenty-five minutes end-to-end, to eat up close to 4,000 clicks.

He'd slipped outside while she napped, and cupped his hands over the driver's window on the Mercedes. The sunlight worked in his favour, and he could see that her odometer now read 49,638. Since her tune-up, she'd travelled another six hundred and fifty kilometres.

Had she taken a late-night drive to Lake Muskoka to follow him to his confrontation with Toner?... and maybe a few trips before then, to fine-tune her plan?

He seethed at the thought she may have known the fate awaiting his children at the hands of Frank Toner.

Of course. It hit him, and hard. If she had faked her own sexual assault the night of Dr. Gordon's murder, someone had to have been inside her; a little rough, but not too rough. And the cops now liked Frank Toner for Dr. Gordon's murder.

She would have fucked Toner.

She'd been sleeping with the monster who terrorized his family.

Now that the inheritance scam had been played on Naismith, Michael knew he couldn't keep Fern from going to the police for much longer. But he needed to know how she had played him, and wanted a piece of her for himself.

Michael recalled Alanson saying something about a "cock-up" with his school's computers.

Miss Ansell put Michael through to Alanson immediately. The headmaster couldn't expand on the computer troubleshooting efforts provided to the academy by Mary Anne Naismith, other than to say, "Something about a virus. She said we wouldn't have to worry about it again."

Michael waded through scads of old emails, looking for anything that could help a sultry but psychotic hacker looking to mess with his life.

He found an email with the subject line, "You're a good man, Charlie Brown, but...", sent to him from Rita almost a year ago, commending him for keeping "enough money to nourish a small country" in his office safe, to hand out to anyone he thought might need it more than he did. She'd also said it was a bad idea.

Maybe he hadn't needed to print a hard copy of the email from Fern. Naismith, fixer of cock-ups, may have already read it.

As Michael started for the guest house, he remembered Artie had taken his daughter to a water park in Niagara Falls. He could call him, but didn't want to interrupt the precious little time the two of them had together, just to pick Artie's brain about computer security.

Michael parked his car in a lot on Elizabeth Street and walked three blocks to Brant and Lakeshore, at the foot of downtown Burlington.

The new residence of the former owners of Michael's home fell short of expectations. From the tiny foyer he could see that the entire home was about half the size of Artie's guest house quarters. It looked to have maybe two bedrooms and a bathroom, and a small galley kitchen that opened to a cramped living room.

Boyd Manahan didn't seem to mind that Michael showed up

at his door unannounced. Michael sensed that the old guy didn't get much company. Manahan said he'd read about Emily's passing, and offered belated condolences.

Manahan must have caught something in Michael's eye when he scanned the condo. "We were pretty heavily mortgaged in the country home," he said, neither upset nor embarrassed, just an old man who had accepted what life had thrown at him. Michael decided he liked the man.

"And then we got Ponzi'd," added Manahan. "Investment banking was incredibly good to me, but now... we're lucky to have this."

"Not the mess with that crook in Toronto?"

"May he rot in hell."

"I'm sure he will," said Michael, recalling how some of the most well-heeled folks in the area, many of them older couples, had lost everything they owned in the investment fraud scheme. "I had no idea."

"We didn't tell the real estate agent when we listed the house. My name hadn't hit the papers yet, and I didn't want to get people low-bidding because they smelled blood." Manahan smiled the smile of a man with no regrets, and said, "It's a great house, isn't it?"

That explained why the agent who found the house, Emily's old friend Rachel Takahara, didn't mention the dire financial situation of Boyd and Christine Manahan.

Christine Manahan blew into the room. She looked overdressed and too made-up for the time and place, particularly standing next to her husband, who sported a black nylon track suit and well-worn sneakers.

She put the brakes on, surprised to see she had company. But she turned a quick smile and offered Michael her hand. "Mister..."

"Flanigan. Michael Flanigan." She didn't remember him from the one time they met, when the sale of the house had closed. "Good to see you, Mrs. Manahan."

She smiled. "It's Christine," she said, and left the room.

It hadn't registered when Michael first met them, but she looked at least twenty years her husband's junior. Money could buy an attractive younger bride, but Michael wondered how long a Ponzi'd old man could hang onto this one.

Michael asked Manahan about the computer setup at his old house, recounting that Rachel had said it was "fully secured".

"Is there a problem?" asked Manahan.

"No, I just thought I'd like to do an upgrade soon," said Michael, "and thought it would be best if the same people worked on it."

Manahan laughed when Michael asked if he configured his computer setup himself. "I love to use the new technology, but I'm afraid I need help when it comes to getting it up and running."

He fished through a kitchen drawer and pulled out a stack of business cards wrapped in an elastic. "We had just switched over to a wireless connection before we had to sell the place. You know, so I could roam the house with my laptop, get on the Internet."

Like Sophie does at home.

Manahan flipped through a few cards and said, "Here it is." He handed it to Michael and said, "Keep it. We won't need it again." For the first time, a tangible sadness permeated his speech.

Michael took the card. He knew the company name, Geek Patrol, from the gaudy ads he'd seen on purple PT Cruisers around town.

He also recognized the name of the Geek on the card—Joel Pierce, the obtuse tour guide from Spruce Lane Farmhouse in Bronte Creek Provincial Park.

"This Joel Pierce secured the computer setup at the house?" asked Michael.

"He did our wireless setup, Michael. You'd need to get your own router and hook it up." Manahan chuckled. "I figured your wife looked after such things in your house."

"Why is that?"

"She called not long after you bought the place, asking who set up our computers for us."

"She did?" *She did look after such things.*

"Did someone recommend these guys to you?" asked Michael.

Manahan shrugged. "Who remembers?"

"Did you give Pierce's number to Emily?"

"Didn't have to. He had already called her, asked if she needed his services. She didn't think he sounded too bright, so she called us. I told her he did a good job. I think she was going to ring him back."

Joel Fucking Pierce?

"Did you meet this kid... Pierce?" asked Michael.

"Just long enough to say hello and point him toward the basement. How did you know he was a kid?"

"Aren't they all?"

Michael called Ferguson Boone from the street. Boone confirmed that Emily credited Ruth Eisentraut with the idea of soliciting paintings from Spruce Lane Farmhouse for their exhibit.

He drove to Bronte Creek Park, wanting to see the Pierce kid's reaction when he asked him... hell, he didn't yet know what he would ask him. He tried to piece things together. Pierce worked alongside the controversial painting and set up the computers, including the security, in Michael's house. How did a lame-brained teen-man, the former guardian of *The Golfer*, fit into the middle of this mess?

"Mr. Monahan called me, asking if I could check out their computers," said Pierce, leaning against the exterior red brick of the farmhouse.

Michael hadn't phoned ahead, but got lucky and found Pierce

working at his part-time job that afternoon, preparing for the farmhouse's participation in a local "Haunted House Tour".

"Manahan," said Michael. "The name is Manahan." He couldn't imagine a kid this thick could be in the thick of *this*.

"What-*ever*," said Pierce.

When Michael had first arrived, Pierce excused himself for a moment to straighten the same painting that had inexplicably moved off-kilter during Michael's last visit; the painting of the woman with a subtle, self-satisfied smile sitting on a tree stump, seemingly ignoring two swarthy men preparing to duel. The name of the painting was in Italian. The backdrop made him think Tuscany. Michael typically found art too abstract to appreciate, but he got the theme behind this one.

Pierce informed Michael he had fifteen minutes.

"Joel, did someone refer you to the Manahans?" asked Michael. "You know... recommend you?"

"Most of our business is word-to-mouth," said Pierce, fumbling a phrase he'd obviously heard from someone else. "Plus we have our cars all over town."

"How long have you worked at Geek Patrol?"

"Coupla years." Pierce put a cigarette to his mouth, cradled by two nicotine-stained fingers that Michael hadn't noticed before.

"And here?"

"How long have I worked here?"

Michael sighed, gritted his teeth. "Yes, Joel, how long have you worked *here*?"

"Since last summer. I actually started Labour Day weekend, so probably more like the fall."

Christ. "How'd you get the job here?"

Pierce finished blowing a chain of smoke rings and said, "Ad in the paper."

"And with Geek Patrol?"

"My dad got it for me. Somebody he knew or something."

"You must be pretty good with computers, Joel," said Michael. "Not just anyone could get a job like that."

Pierce pulled his frame away from the building and grinned. "My dad says I'm a regular savant."

"You said my wife stopped in here a couple of times."

"Yup."

"You didn't tell me you'd been to our house."

Pierce jerked his head toward Michael, then turned away. He flicked his butt at the wall and began to walk away.

Michael grabbed Pierce by the arm and pulled him back, not stopping until they had turned the corner around to the far side of the house.

Pierce whined like a little girl. "Hey, you can't—"

Michael squeezed the back of Pierce's neck between his thumb and forefinger to stifle his plaint, and with his other hand pushed the young man back against the brick. Pierce whimpered and slid to the ground. He sat up, knees bent, and buried his face in his arms.

While Michael waited for him to calm down, a passing couple stopped a few feet away while their Bernese Mountain Dog did his business.

"Everything okay, here?" asked the man, unraveling a balled-up plastic bag.

"It will be," said Michael. "I'm his probation officer."

The couple scooped and scurried, and Pierce quieted. Michael crouched in front of him and tousled Pierce's hair.

"Look, son," said Michael. "I don't mean to frighten you, or hurt you. But I have had enough. All I want is the truth."

Michael pulled a pack of cigarettes from Pierce's shirt pocket and removed one from the pack. Pierce stood, lit up, and continued.

"This hot older lady comes by, says she noticed me here before. I'd never seen her before. I woulda for sure remembered."

"Okay. She noticed you. Then what?"

"It was a weekday. I was here alone. She asked me for a tour, and when we got upstairs... in the bedroom..."

"She did you in one of the antique beds? Are you serious,

kid?"

"I couldn't believe it was happening."

"What was her name, Joel?"

Pierce raised his head, looked off as if in a mini-daze, and said, "Jessie."

It was the name Michael had expected to hear, but it still stabbed him in the heart, which had acquired too damn many puncture marks.

"Do you think Jessie already knew you worked for the Geeks before she... you know... *upstairs*?" Michael gestured upward with his head.

"I bring the Geek Patrol car to work here sometimes. My boss there lets me take it overnight when I'm going back in the next day. The first time I saw her here she asked me where the car was."

It soon became obvious that she owned Pierce from that point on. She also knew the Flanigans had just moved into their new house, and had Pierce call Emily to set up their wireless connection.

"Did she know the Manahans?" asked Michael.

"I think she helped the old guy with his exercises."

Boyd Manahan had a personal trainer.

Pierce went on to talk about back-door access and spyware and encryption.

Michael interrupted him. "Look, kid... in my language. I just want to know if Jessie would be able to get at my emails, files, whatever... because of what you did when you when you were at my house fucking around with the computer setup."

Pierce dropped his head. "I gave her the passwords. If she knew what she was doing..."

"Did she say what she wanted to get at on the computers, specifically?"

Pierce shrugged.

"I'm sure you know you could be fired for that, Joel," said Michael, "not to mention charged by the police and put in jail."

"That's what *she* said."

357

Michael could imagine Jessie at her sexiest, with the accent working for her, the hypnotizing sway, teasing this poor kid into a horny frenzy. At that moment he felt a weird kinship with Joel Pierce. The kid wouldn't have stood a chance.

"If you have anything else to tell me, Joel, you'd better do it now," said Michael.

"A couple of days later, she called me, said she wanted me to help her get one of the paintings from the farmhouse here."

"Get it? You mean steal it?"

"She said she had one just like it to put in its place. She said if I helped her she would help make sure nobody found out about me showing her the passwords and stuff."

One just like it.

Michael knew the answer to his next question, but asked it anyway. "Which painting did she want?"

"I never did find out. She hung up without telling me, and the next time I talked to her, she told me to forget all about it. She said she thought it over, and she cared for me too much to make me do anything where I could get into trouble."

Cared for him too much. Right. She fucked him, used him, and then scared him shitless.

Michael assumed that Naismith didn't need Pierce after convincing Emily that the Halton County Arts Centre should borrow a couple of paintings from the Spruce Lane Farmhouse for an exhibit. Instead of substituting a forgery for *The Golfer*, she decided the fake would die a fiery death at the arts centre.

"How often have you heard from her since then?" asked Michael.

"Every few months or so. She phoned me once, and another time she stopped by my booth when I was just sitting in McDonald's having a burger."

"What did she say?"

"Nothing much. Just asked if, you know, it was still our little secret. She said she'd been busy, but was looking forward to spending some time with me again."

Michael wondered what her real plans had been for the poor sap, since he could potentially put her behind bars.

He called Rachel Takahara, whose picture adorned "For Sale" signs on some of the grandest front lawns in Halton County.

"I didn't approach Emily about the Manahan property," said the real estate agent when Michael asked what had led them to their new home. "Forgive me, but I knew you'd come into quite a comfortable sum, and I did ask Emily if I could keep my eyes open for her. But I didn't push. And she waved it off, saying she was very happy in your old place on Hadfield Court. I never brought it up again.

"A couple of weeks later, she calls to say she saw one of my listings and thought you would die for it. I followed up with an email, sent her some extra pictures I had that weren't on my website, and you know the rest of the story."

He did. Emily told him over a late breakfast at The Sunset Grill that she wanted to take him to see their future home. They made an offer before the day was over.

Had Emily known "Ruth" then? His timelines were out of whack.

Did his current fiancée tell his late wife about the beautiful house in the country, the one that Michael and Mary Anne Naismith now called home?

"Rachel, did you know I was engaged?" he asked.

"No, I didn't. Emily would be happy for you, Michael," said Rachel. "Do I know her?"

"Jessie Hargreaves is her name. She's a personal trainer. I think she may even know the Manahans."

"I don't know the name, but she's a lucky girl."

Her luck just ran out.

CHAPTER 38

Michael's chest pounded as he negotiated his Rover through a blinding sun. He knew he had enough to hand it all over to the cops and watch them crucify Mary Anne Naismith.

But he wanted her for himself.

A note tied with an elastic band to the door handle of his fridge informed Michael that The Woman Known As had prepared a salad. If he had some of it for a snack, he was to save enough for dinner. The note closed with, "Running a few errands, will get fish to go w/ salad. Back 7:30-8. Luv u. Jess."

Remnants of sliced tomatoes and chopped green onions sat on a cutting board by the sink, next to empty packaging for the chicken substitute he usually ate. He opened the fridge. A large bowl of salad covered in cellophane took up half the middle shelf.

The pending encounter made him restless, uneasy. He grabbed a beer, hesitated, and put it back. He would need to be on top of his game over the next few hours.

He wasn't sure how it all pieced together, but had assembled enough of a database in his logical mind to believe that he'd been planning to spend the rest of his life with a diabolical... *genius?*

Mary Anne Naismith had disguised herself to live separate lives, as both the German Ruth Eisentraut, shy wallflower and arts centre volunteer, and Jessie Hargreaves, vivacious and charismatic personal trainer with apparently no real interest or talent in the arts.

Rowan Alanson had described her IQ as "off the charts". She had to be quite brilliant. Or was her plan just so daring and crazy that no one would suspect such... craziness?

Whatever Emily had shared with Ruth, she had really shared

with Naismith.

Michael was relieved that he had booked Sophie and Eamonn for a week up at the Rocky Crest Resort on Lake Joseph. Clint had returned to Kingston to spend more time with his mom, who was still trying to rebound from her own personal setback.

Michael's BlackBerry vibrated.

"Mike, we need to talk, and soon," said Fern. "I'm just pulling into Foster Glen. Meet me on the range and we'll split a bucket."

Michael looked at his watch. Jessie would get home in about three hours, if her note was accurate. "I haven't got a lot of time, Fern. What's on your mind?"

"My cousin Gil... he's been working with me... Gil followed your beloved this morning to a little roadside market near Puslinch, in the middle of nowhere. The place was packed, a big corn sale or something going on. She had an intriguing shopping list: tomatoes, dill, green onions... and chicken. Real chicken. Gil confirmed it."

Michael felt a chill. There'd be only one reason she would buy chicken. "Anything else?" he asked.

"That stuff could kill you, right?" asked Fern.

"It could."

"See you in fifteen."

Michael took the bowl of salad from the fridge and set it on the counter. He pulled back the cellophane and picked out a chunk of what was either chicken substitute or the real thing. The pieces had been cut small. He couldn't distinguish harmless from lethal from a visual inspection.

A sniff confirmed nothing, and he wondered if he could afford a lick, or even a small bite. From experience, he knew he should easily survive minimal exposure without inducing symptoms that would require a trip to the emergency ward. But past bouts taught him that the severity of one's allergic reaction could vary from one flare-up to the next. Even the more benign incidents were quite unpleasant. Acute attacks were frightening, if not fatal.

As he weighed his options, he pulled open the middle drawer where he kept his EpiPen. If used soon after consumption, the device could be counted on to reverse any symptoms that poultry ingestion brought on.

He pushed aside the playing cards and spare car keys and other miscellaneous junk in the drawer. He did the same with the drawers above and below.

The EpiPen was gone.

He walked to his office to make sure his backup EpiPen was still safely tucked away in his desk. He placed it in the loose lower pocket of his cargo pants. He put a cell phone that he rarely used into the pocket on the opposite leg.

Michael went out to the garage and rummaged through the garbage and recycling. He found no Styrofoam trays with revealing traces of chicken blood in any of the three green bags that had accumulated in the past week. Holding his breath, he went through the bags in the compost bin. In the bottom bag of four, Michael found evidence that tipped off Mary Anne Naismith's next murder weapon of choice.

Chicken bones. And she even thought to compost them.

An idea came to him, and he almost discarded it out of hand. But he had nothing better, and decided to get his feet moving before he... chickened out.

He found Artie in the guest house playing cards with his daughter Janey. The two men stepped outside, and Artie reminded him that he and Janey would be leaving a little later for the baseball game in Toronto, for which Michael had given them tickets.

"No worries, Artie," Michael said. "I just need you to pick up some groceries for me before you take off, and prepare a little snack. But it has to be made a certain way."

Michael jogged toward Fern at the driving range, and said,

"Fern, I know she's our girl—"

Fern held up his hand, just enough to tell Michael to shut up. A hand slapped Michael on the back.

"I hear someone's getting married," said Randy Goodman, who took Michael's hand and gave it a prolonged shake. "She had you lined up right from the beginning, Mike. All the best. You deserve it."

After Goodman left, Fern hit a half-assed three-iron and stepped behind the driving block toward Michael.

"I called because I wanted to get you out of the house," said Fern.

"And you did."

Fern stepped closer. "At the age of nineteen, Mary Anne Naismith was raped at her home in Barnes, a suburb of London, England. She was home alone with her stepfather, Kenneth Denison—Kep they called him—who was killed by Miss Naismith's rapist. Miss Naismith had relatively little trauma to her genital area, and was otherwise unscathed apart from some scrapes and bruises."

"Where have I heard that before?"

"Barnes is an upscale, trendy area. A few local celebrities live there. But Mary Anne and her family lived in what they call council housing, meaning they got assistance from the government."

"They stick welfare homes in the middle of the cushy 'hoods?"

"More or less. Their assailant, a two-time felon by the name of Reginald Munday, was found murdered two days later. Naismith later identified him, plus it seems old Reggie left behind enough of himself to close the case."

"DNA?"

Fern nodded

"How the hell did they solve anything before DNA?"

"We struggled by."

"Was it pubic hair?" asked Michael.

"Dunno. Years later, Mary Anne Naismith ends up in New Brunswick, where she marries a doctor. They divorce. She makes allegations of abuse, which is never proven, but she walks away with a very huge chunk of the doctor's money."

"She must have run out. And I was elected to be the next sucker."

"She travelled around after that. Australia. Some time in Hawaii. A little over two and a half years ago, a guy in the U.K. accuses Mary Anne of ripping *him* off for a considerable sum."

"Didn't you say Lottie Denison left England for Kingston just under three years ago?"

Fern nodded.

"And Dr. Gordon moved from Kingston to Burlington around two years ago." Michael took a practice ball from Fern's bucket and tossed it from hand to hand. "Was Lottie involved in the scam?" he asked.

"The English guy only named Mary Anne. But he said he knew Lottie."

"But Lottie left town before the guy pointed the finger at Mary Anne."

Michael grabbed an iron out of Fern's bag and took a few swings while he digested what Fern had just told him.

"Was Naismith ever a patient at the FCPH?" he asked.

"The Kingston hospital? Negative," said Fern.

"What kind of doctor was he, the ex-husband?"

"A plastic surgeon. Dr. Peter Selby. The happy couple belonged to the same golf club in Moncton."

"She was a golfer?"

Fern shrugged and said, "She was a member."

"Was he a Brit, Selby?"

"American. From Des Moines."

Alanson had said the half-sisters looked like they had some cosmetic work done. Michael thought of Lottie's attempted seduction of him in the basement office at Foster Glen, and the well-formed breasts that seemed immune to gravity. If the two women had had a nip and tuck, Michael presumed the former hubby of Michael's batshit crazy betrothed would have done the work.

He thought back to a quickie he had with Naismith at Foster Glen, after she hit a stray shot into the woods. She had dropped to her knees and said, "This is why they invented golf towels" before sending him over the top.

Was she good enough to put that ball in the woods on purpose?

Why hadn't he made the connection before? He had once told Emily about such a golf course fantasy, but they had played little together, and had no opportunity to act it out. He'd assumed she wouldn't have been up for it anyway. Did she tell her friend *Ruth* about it? How close were they?

He sensed his mind deep-diving into things that didn't matter anymore. Michael told Fern about the attempts of Boone and Alanson to identify the women, and of his chats with Boyd Manahan and Joel Pierce.

"You don't store passwords on your computer, do you? You know, for accessing your bank accounts online, or any other sensitive information?"

"Emily and I both did. We kept lists... in Word documents."

Fern gave him a look.

"I know, I know," said Michael. "It's just too hard to remember them all. But I haven't noticed any money missing. Nothing funny at all, not in any of my accounts."

"Okay. I'm going to go see our buddy Alberts, Mike. It's over. I'm planning on hanging up my own shingle, and this should give me some goodwill with the locals. It'll make my job a lot easier when my next case rolls in."

Michael frowned, tensed up.

"You're with me on this. Right, Mike?" asked Fern. "We need to let the police take it from here. And they'll want a word with you, my friend."

Michael nodded. "Once this warped skank is put away, I can

feel safe for my family, get on with things."

"I'm sorry how this worked out, Mike."

Michael just waved it off.

"Where is she, right now?" asked Fern.

"Running errands or something, said she won't be back until later tonight." Michael still wanted to have a chat with the woman who may be responsible for both his wife's murder and the unspeakable attacks on his children. "You could have gone right to the cops, Fern."

"She's your fiancée, buddy."

It surprised Michael that Fern had given him so much latitude, especially with Fern's brownie points with the cops on the line. But he wasn't about to question it. His friend was stepping up when he needed him.

"When are you heading in?" asked Michael.

"I called. They said Alberts was incommunicado. I left him a message to call me ASA-fucking-P."

"You could give it to someone else."

"Nah, Alberts deserves it. But if I don't hear from him soon, I'll have to dish it off. Just stay the hell away from your house until then. She is dangerous. Your kids are away?"

"They're good. I'm gonna drop in on Hig. Haven't seen him for a while."

"Does he know about this shit?"

"I haven't told anyone."

"Just as well you keep it that way."

Michael didn't know how talking about it could affect anything now, but doubted he'd be talking to Danny Higgins or anyone else before he saw Naismith one last time.

"Meet me at the Halton HQ before eight," said Fern. "I'm gonna grab a bite and then head on over."

She wasn't due home until seven thirty, if not later.

Fern went off to the men's room.

Michael jogged to his car and headed for home. Halfway there, he called Eddie Kan, caught him at home, and asked for a favour.

CHAPTER 39

Michael walked through his front door a little after six thirty.

A candle burned on a ledge just inside the kitchen.

He dropped the box from under his arm onto the table. He inspected the fridge and checked the phone on the counter.

No dial tone.

He nodded, thinking of the Bell Canada guy he'd noticed earlier just down the road, his hair tucked under his helmet as he opened the green Bell box. He didn't recall seeing a company truck in the vicinity.

The balls on that broad. Doesn't miss a trick.

He sat at the table and opened the box.

The stage would soon be set.

The Woman Known As arrived twenty minutes later, showing not a care in the world. Michael was ready for her, and her unexpected early appearance took some of the pressure off. He would have an hour or more before Fern would come looking for him.

She coated her gaze at Michael with a passion that would melt any unsuspecting man's heart.

She kissed him softly and said, "Why don't I change and get the salmon on? Open us that bottle of Aykroyd red, would you, love?" She turned on the oven and went upstairs.

Michael's insides turned a bit. But despite the familiar dread in times of stress that his colitis might rumble into play, he looked forward to the evening ahead.

He opened the wine.

She reappeared in a black exercise outfit, the fetching cat burglar.

Naismith broiled the salmon. She chit-chatted about nothing, and a few minutes later the oven beeper went off like the opening bell of a prizefight.

His prey had yet to bite on Fern's email, which told a story that mirrored a case Fern had worked on years before. He'd shared the details of that case with Michael over a beer one night.

Michael had to assume that Naismith didn't suspect he was on to her.

She hugged him and kneaded his back with her palms, the way she did. The evil he held in his arms revolted him. The scent of her hair, once intoxicating, had become rancid to him.

He sat down and sipped his wine, then hid behind the sports pages.

She arranged place settings on opposite sides of the table.

Naismith removed the salad from the fridge and set it on the table next to the fish.

"Thanks for making dinner, sweetheart," he said, setting aside the newspaper. His own voice sounded calm to him, loving, convincing.

"One of my better efforts, I think," she said, sugar sweet.

He glanced at the plant on the side table by the back window, on a diagonal to his right. Emily had picked up the table on sale at IKEA, a week after they'd inherited millions. He made a mental note not to look in that direction again. The tiny audio recorder that Eddie had loaned him earlier was well-hidden, and Michael was confident his dinner companion wouldn't spot it.

Eddie had suggested that Michael slip the recorder into his shirt pocket, but Michael thought that too risky. Eddie walked through three sample recordings to let Michael hear the device in action. Michael did a few more test runs when he got home, until he felt he had it down cold.

According to Eddie, the gadget had enough space to record a conversation "from dinner to midnight". Michael planned to get what he wanted much sooner.

Naismith set down his plate and took her seat. Michael lifted a forkful of tomato and cucumber.

She watched.

He lowered the fork before it reached his mouth.

She stabbed at her lettuce.

He emptied his fork.

"Everything okay, Jess?" he said, his mouth half-full of salad.

"Couldn't be better, love."

He speared some lettuce and cheese. "I didn't realize how famished I was." He had some wine. "Oh, I ran into the Manahans today," he said. "They were the people I bought the house from."

"Boyd and... Christine. How are they?"

"You know them?"

"Small world. Boyd is a client of mine, or at least he was. Where'd you see them?"

"Downtown, running errands. You know the wife, too?"

"Just a bit. I found her a bit *aristocratic*. How's the salad?"

"It's great," said Michael. "She was a little full of herself?"

"A tad privileged."

"Had you been here before, in this house?"

"In this house? I would have remembered, silly. Boyd came to my home studio. Didn't stay with it, though. A lovely man, but personal training just wasn't his thing."

Michael dug into his salad, taking a bit of everything this time. "I'm getting used to this fake chicken. It's really starting to taste like the real thing."

She just smiled.

Artie hit the mark in mimicking the portions for the ingredients. And the scented candle was a deft touch. Aided by the air purifier in the corner of the room, the candle masked any lingering cooking odors.

They ate in silence for a short while, until Michael set down his fork again. He closed his eyes and massaged them, and then blinked several times. She ignored it. He rubbed his eyes again, and she asked about it.

"I'm sure it's nothing," he said.

—

The conversation on their first date, when Michael told Naismith the story behind his condition, had laid the groundwork for tonight. His allergy to poultry had been recognized at an early age, but deemed run-of-the-mill. He didn't show a sign of anaphylaxis until an episode in his early twenties. Even then, he had written it off as a nasty but relatively benign reaction to a couple of bites from a chicken leg. His symptoms that night had all but disappeared in less than an hour, as had his concern.

The next occurrence was a decade later. He'd eaten chicken-laden spring rolls, advertised as vegetarian, on a golf junket out west. The finger food almost killed him—and would have if an ambulance hadn't shown up within minutes to give him an injection of epinephrine.

The emergency doctor had cautioned that a future flare-up could either be milder or more severe. She couldn't predict, but advised him to prepare for the worst. "Never be far from an EpiPen," she'd said. If his symptoms grew serious, they could take him down in a hurry.

He had some time to work on Naismith and still reveal the allergic reactions at a resonating pace.

"Oh my," said Naismith. "The horse."

"What horse?" said Michael.

"I was down the road at Howard Fowler's today for an appointment. His neighbour, the farmer... what's-his-name... Hogan. He came by on his horse, and I was petting it, and..."

"And when you hugged me just now..."

"I'm so sorry, sweetheart. I forgot about you and horses. Let me go take a shower."

You'd like that. Come back down to find me dead.

"No, no, honey," said Michael. "I'm enjoying relaxing here

with you too much. You're at a pretty safe distance now."

He went to the sink and splashed some water in his eyes. As he dried off with paper towel, his BlackBerry vibrated on the counter. He picked up the phone and read Fern's name on the display. The clock on the wall said he still had at least half an hour before Fern should expect him at the police station.

"Hey," he said. "We're just having a bite."

"Are you at Higgins' place?" asked Fern.

"Yep."

"Have you heard from your little crumpet?"

"Not a thing," said Michael, praying that Naismith would keep quiet.

"Alberts walked into the station a few minutes ago," said Fern. "He's in with his boss. I'm gonna grab him when he comes out, so get your ass down here." He hung up.

For effect, Michael threw a little more water on his eyes before returning to the table.

Naismith sat glassy-eyed. Tears fell down her cheeks. Michael tried to read the play, couldn't. He set down the phone.

"Michael, I've lied to you." She sniffled, wiped her nose with her napkin. "I'm not really who I said I was. What I mean is, I'm still the person you know, but..."

"Who you said you were? What's going on, honey?"

His phone vibrated again. He glanced down at the caller ID; Fern again.

Michael debated not answering, but picked up the phone.

"You were a little quiet on the phone a minute ago," said Fern.

"How so?"

"You still over with Higgins?"

Michael hesitated, and said, "Not a good time."

"I bet. I just called Higgins."

"I'll call you later," said Michael. He hung up and put the BlackBerry back on the table.

Naismith reached over and grabbed it.

"Enough of this then," she said, and walked into the adjacent dining room.

He slid his hand into the cargo pocket on his pant leg and touched the backup cell phone for reassurance. In the next room he heard a drawer slide open and shut. *The bottom drawer on the hutch*, he thought, the only drawer with a lock.

When she reappeared, he pushed aside his plate and dragged a knuckle along the corner of his eye.

"Sorry about the phone calls, sweetheart," he said. "You were saying?"

"Michael, Lottie Denison, the girl that was murdered, is... was..." She wiped her eyes with a tissue. "Charlotte was my half-sister."

She bit. She read the email and she bit.

"My God, Jess," he said. "I'm so very sorry, sweetheart. Why didn't you tell me about her?

"I followed her here, to Burlington, to keep an eye on her. It was our mother's dying wish that I look after her." She lowered her head. "Some job I did," she said, and covered her face with her hands.

This revelation from her could only be a response to Fern's bogus email, which said Fern had executed a bank-sweep on Northcott, finding assets hidden in offshore accounts. That was all true, but the section of the email that said Northcott had bequeathed just under three million dollars to his companion Lottie Denison was fiction worthy of a Daniel Higgins novel.

Naismith had her sights on an inheritance that didn't exist.

Her face remained buried in her hands, but the crying had wilted to a whimper.

Michael leaned forward and said, "I'm afraid there won't be anything coming your way from your half-sister's estate."

CHAPTER 40

Lottie Denison's half-sister lifted her head, separated her fingers, and peeked through at him. Naismith dropped her hands and said, "Michael, Charlotte had no money."

Michael smiled and said, "I know."

The blubbering started up again. "Then what are you talking about, Michael?" She threw her arms on the table to cushion her forehead.

"There were more obvious things that happened, stuff that should have jumped out at me. But it was the little things that finally... got me thinking."

The sobs grew faint.

"You knew things only Emily could know," said Michael. "The golf course fantasy on its own was nothing, easily a coincidence. And understanding her moods, reflected in her works of art? I could write that off to the sensitivity of another woman. But you talked about how Emily said she wanted me to move on if something ever happened to her."

Her shoulders tensed, not much, but he caught it.

"It finally hit me. I didn't discuss that with anyone except my wife. I know it. And who was Emily spending a lot of time with when things were rough between us?"

Naismith's head twitched.

She knows she fucked up. Michael let her chew on it for a moment, then said, "That would be you, would it not, *Ruth*?"

She raised her head enough to reveal the tops of soulless, angry eyes.

"*Cocksucker!*" she cried, and bounced her fork off the side of his head.

He flinched. "You crazy..." He dabbed his fingertips at the point of contact and found no blood.

"I thought you might be on to me," she said, then laughed like a demented ghoul.

Sweet Jesus. I was gonna marry this lunatic.

The laughing died, cut short like someone had changed the channel. Her chin fell to her chest. Seconds later, it shot up.

He barely recognized the woman across the table, mildly contorted and timid looking. But he thought he knew who he was looking at.

"Why is it that you ask about me?" she asked in a German accent.

Ruth had joined the conversation.

He stared in wonder at the most talented and cunning person he'd ever met. But she belonged in the penthouse suite at the giggling academy. And she scared him. When the time was right, he'd relish the sound of patrol cars screeching up the driveway.

He had to move things along. After the last call from Fern, Michael knew the police could show up anytime.

He scratched his jaw.

"When I finally woke up and figured out who you were, *Mary Anne*," he said. "one question led to another, and they all led right to you." He opened his mouth wide, as if trying to feel his lips. "Like how would Frank Toner—known to some as *Calvin*—expect me to come up with a boatload of cash, late at night, on the spur of the moment?"

"You know my name, and the former moniker of my dead associate." She clapped her hands. "Brilliant. It's good to know the name of your future bride." She stuffed in a mouthful of salad and said, "Sorry, love. I haven't eaten all day."

"Talk about only seeing what I wanted to," said Michael.

"Darling, you saw only what I wanted you to see."

"Where is the real Ruth?" he asked. "What did you do with her?"

"Your wife, my *BFF*, was so unhappy," she said. "Did I tell you how tragically unsatisfied my dear friend Emily had been with her life? A sad story hers."

"Tell me about it."

She began to softly sing "Be-Bop-A-Lula", the old Gene Vincent song. The German accent was gone.

He wanted her to talk about Emily, and Naismith knew it.

"You were patient. I'll give you that," he said.

"I wanted to give you time to mourn, darling."

"You like to write notes. The one in Northcott's pocket stirred things up."

"Darling, if you want to get a rise out of someone, stick a note in their pocket. The better the note, the bigger the reaction."

"Like the note you stuck in my wife's pocket, *you crazy bitch*? Northcott wasn't lying after all. He had no clue about Emily. What was in that note?"

"Now that's beyond rude," she said.

"Did Emily know it was you, her friend *Ruth*, disguised as Teresa Amodeo with the bad heart?"

She shrugged. "Who can say?"

"Teresa Amodeo didn't want the vet to touch her," he said. "*You* didn't want her to see that your soft skin was nothing like that of a badly scarred older woman."

"You should know, lover."

"I always assumed Lottie was the master of disguise, not you," he said.

She spat out her wine. "Are you joking? My late half-sister only went for different variations on the come-shag-me look."

"Why the Italian accent on Mrs. Amodeo?" asked Michael. "That was just... careless."

"I didn't learn until later that the old tart had a nurse stop in once in a while, an *Italian*. She must have set up her answering machine for her." Naismith looked off, smiled, shrugged again. "Or it could have been some other dago she knew. I should have let her get a few words in before I, well... you know."

"They're exhuming Teresa Amodeo's body," said Michael.

The fire returned to her eyes again, then left just as quickly, leaving her expression vacant.

"Let... them... dig," she said.

"We'll know soon enough how you killed her."

"Will *we* now, Detective Flanigan?" Naismith laughed while shaking her head.

"Why did Vincent Fronda have to die?" he asked. "And what was that all about, cutting out his eye?"

"Frank said it would send a signal to others. For the life of me, I don't know what others he was talking about. I think he just enjoyed doing it."

Michael thought of the arrow jutting from Toner's throat. *Vinnie Fronda is smiling somewhere.*

"Why are you afraid to tell me what was in that damn note in my wife's pocket?"

"I think I've said enough about that. It's much more fun watching you agonize over it."

Michael detected a sense of pride in her smile, impressed with her own mastery of disguise. He felt certain not only that Naismith had masqueraded as Teresa Amodeo, but that she'd been responsible for the murder of his wife.

He rubbed his eyes and then his nose.

"Such a cliché you are," said Michael. But he hoped there weren't two like her. "Just another two-bit gold-digger with a cockamamie scam."

"My plan was *brilliant*," she said, leaning over the table and baring her gums like the mad dog she was.

The con had been remarkable. He thought he might visit her in prison to ask her all about it.

But he sniffed and shrugged, afflicted and unimpressed. He wanted Naismith to let it all out, to boast of her imaginative but misguided scheme, giving each cunning ploy its well-earned tribute. And he felt certain she would if she anticipated he would slide to the floor before the salmon got cold.

She'd *need* to tell him about how she had worked Emily, and why his wife had to die.

He patted his lips, feigning the tingling and numbness he'd

experienced during his genuine life-threatening confrontation with anaphylactic shock. He then recoiled, aping the pain that had accompanied those symptoms.

His earlier dress rehearsal in front of the bathroom mirror helped him nail the scene.

"Okay," said Michael. "Let me see if I can guess how this thing got started."

Naismith sat back in her chair. As did Michael. She wanted to talk about it.

"If I may hazard an educated guess," he said, "you learned within the past few years that J.P. Northcott had assaulted your mother back when they were teenagers. If you'd known about it earlier, you would have been over here sooner." He glared at her. "And I'd be having dinner with my wife tonight."

He waited for her response. He softened his expression, not wanting to antagonize her into silence.

"And instead, you're dining with your fiancée," she said.

"You, and probably your half-sister, were up to no good in England," he said. "Ripping off some poor schmuck like me, with more money than sense. The guy gets wise to you. Lottie comes to Canada. This is three years ago. You stick around the U.K. for a few more months, then join her. I'm not sure why you waited to come over, but I assume the plot to go after Northcott had already been mapped out."

"Charlotte had a place to stay until I could join her," she said.

"At a relative's in Kingston," he said.

"Very impressive, darling. I was still working the old fart in London, and decided to cut my losses and come across the pond when he started to make accusations. The silly old prick."

"*Your* losses?"

"I invested almost as much time on that wanker as the one sitting in front of me."

"Why did Lottie go by her mother's name, Jeffrey, when she was at school?"

"Our stepfather was a pig. Rejecting his name was Charlotte's way of shutting him out of her world when she left the house in the morning. He'd adopted her and given her a new surname that she didn't want."

"You must have thought her somewhat capable, that she could charm her way into Northcott's life. You probably encouraged her to lose the British accent as well. Am I right?"

"It had to go before she got off the plane in Canada, to minimize the similarities between us. Charlotte was born in Canada. She just had to get her old voice back."

"Did Lottie know that Northcott was her father?"

"I may have forgotten to tell her that. I didn't know myself until Mummy announced it on her deathbed. The old girl said she didn't want a nickel of *that bastard's money*. That's where she and I differed."

"And you enlisted your unwitting sister to do your dirty work."

"I like to manage people, oversee projects like these."

"You mean let others take the chances."

She frowned and sat back, and he realized he had to pull back again with the attitude.

"I'm sorry, Mary Anne," he said. "I'm being rude again."

She ate some salad.

"So Lottie had no idea who Northcott was?" he asked.

She drank some wine.

"I wanted my dear half-sister to get close to the asshole and his riches," she said. "She may not have wanted to suck his cock if she'd known he was her daddy. But then again," she said. "A willy's a willy."

I've been sleeping with the devil.

"Did I offend you, darling?" She pushed back her hair, sat up straight with hands folded on her lap. "Not tonight dear, I'm still a little tender," she said with exaggerated propriety, mimicking the performance she had given while *recovering* from her *assault*. "Sound familiar? If nothing else, it kept you from waving that dodgy little dick of yours in my face every time I turned around."

She sipped her wine, and said, "*Frankie* on the other hand..."

He winced.

"That's right," she said. "What can I say? Frank had the big smile, big hair, big *everything*."

"I assume he's the one who *raped* you."

"A little rough fun to support the cause."

Michael rubbed his eyes with the heels of his hands, as he gathered himself, and considered where to go next with his questions.

"I gotta think that Lottie running into Dr. Gordon wasn't part of the plan," he said.

"That distraction was the first of two unforeseen risks I faced. But I welcomed kismet into the equation and turned a challenge into an opportunity."

"Kismet?"

"The shrink decided to move to Burlington... where Charlotte's daddy lives. *Perfect!*" Naismith laughed and drank more wine.

"Toner raped Dr. Gordon, killed her. For what?"

"Who helped you arrive at these amateurish conclusions? Perhaps your little cunt auntie from the hospital in Kingston?" Her head jerked, like a light went on. "Or was it that lawyer who's head over her pointy fucking stiletto heels in love with you?"

"You mean Rita." He snickered.

She read his reaction. "You don't even know. How pathetic. Who do you call first when you're in trouble, when you need something... which is quite often, you needy little man?"

Rita?

"Was it just to get your hands on the doctor's files?" he asked.

"Oh please."

"I would love to see what's in your file," he said.

"Oh yes, the file," she said. "I couldn't believe the drivel in that stupid thing. I didn't see the quack on a professional basis."

"You weren't a patient? Why else would Dr. Gordon have a file on you?"

"Me? A patient? Please, darling."

"Perhaps you paid Dr. Gordon a visit after learning that the fling with Lottie was still alive, maybe trying to leverage it to your advantage... maybe tried a little blackmail?" He paused. "After what happened with the two of them at the hospital in Kingston, that would be frowned upon by whoever frowns on such things. It would explain why she had a file on you, and no file of Lottie's had been listed on Dr. Gordon's patient index. Lottie had never received any *conventional* therapy from her."

"The controlling doctor bitch didn't approve of Charlotte and her beau, Mr. Northcott. Didn't think it was *healthy*." Naismith grinned. "I couldn't have her filling Charlotte's head with such nonsense, now could I?"

"Lottie even went on golf outings while a so-called outpatient at the FCPH," said Michael. "Fucking incredible."

"We both love the sport."

"I heard you and your ex, the cosmetic surgeon, liked to play," he said. He looked her face up and down. "He does okay work."

"*You* couldn't get enough," she said.

He couldn't argue the point.

"And Toner? I presume Lottie introduced you?" he asked.

"I did Frank a few times," she said. "I recognized a... *disposition* that could be useful for addressing some of the more challenging jobs."

"You mean to brutally murder innocent people."

"Innocence is in the eye of the beholder," she said. "You of all people should know that, Michael." She assumed a demure posture and a doe-eyed, virtuous expression.

"And you had your sister introduce Toner to Northcott."

"Frank was there to keep an eye on her, and she him for that matter. As for Northcott, he let his little baldheaded yogurt-slinger make all his decisions for him, just like the rest of you."

"You mentioned two risks, Mary Anne," he said.

"Well you can just *imagine* the look on my face when I ran into baby sister's sad little school chum Ruthie at a bleeding Starbucks in Burlington fucking Ontario. What *are* the fucking odds?"

He shuddered. The coincidence named Ruth Eisentraut had eventually led to Emily's murder.

"I can't believe you were able to pull off the disguise after Ruth had already been at the arts centre... despite your talents," he said. "You had to have met her before she was able to start the volunteer gig."

"Spare me the horseshit flattery," she said. "I obviously had to dispose of her quickly lest she ruin the rouse. Ruthie told me about her plans to volunteer, the noble little lass that she was. I'd already googled Northcott, to learn he was a patron of the arts and a regular visitor to that god-awful gallery. Little did I know that I would become confidante to a miserable woman whose hubby had inherited millions."

And my fucking money got Emily killed.

Michael scratched and cursed the itch and pushed on.

"And you eventually killed your own sister," he said.

"It seems the poor misguided urchin sent a letter to a certain Mr. Mavis which, among other things, foolishly informed him that she knew some rather shocking details about his criminal enterprise."

"Fuzzy Mavis. The mobster. My God, you set her up. You sent the letter. Not exactly what yer old mum had in mind."

"She hasn't complained."

"How about the Zetterfeldts? That was just plain sloppy."

"I never had the pleasure of meeting the Zetterfeldts," said Naismith. "Shame about your girlfriend. Not quite what Frankie's employer had in mind."

Girlfriend. She knew of his relationship with Jacquie. Maybe he had mentioned her by name during therapy, or Naismith just figured it out from the doctor's notes in his stolen file.

"So Northcott did call that one," said Michael, nodding. "Jacquie was payback for Paula."

"Frankie got a little carried away," she said. "Northcott's directive was to stop at *enthusiastic defilement*. C'est la vie."

"Unbelievable. Toner was also doing Northcott's bidding. As you saw fit, of course."

He expected to hear the cops pull up at any minute. He drew his fingernails along both jaw lines, and picked up the pace.

"I got to observe that sick fuck Toner before he died," said Michael.

"Before your dead wife's only daughter put an arrow through his throat."

"Yeah, she's a great kid. But I can't fathom why a demented bastard like Frank Toner would pass up the chance to rape a defenseless woman like Jacquie."

"As I alluded to just moments ago, Frank could get lost in his work."

"And... what? What happened?"

"He killed the bitch before he could do her."

"Good God," said Michael. "I'm surprised that even stopped him."

"That's what *I* said," said Naismith, and she shot up her hand for a high-five.

"You put the idea in my head that Paula Northcott had been abused," he said, ignoring her gesture. "You knew it would lead me to Zetterfeldt. Shit, I was just another pawn."

"But you were such a willing pawn, dearest."

More pieces fell into place, and he realized the plot was more complex than he'd imagined. "Lottie told you about Paula getting abused, and you knew from Toner what Northcott had planned for my old principal. You get Graham Zetterfeldt's short-and-curlies from the gym, and pin both the doctor's murder and your staged attack on him. You know he'll be dead before he can deny a thing."

He ran his fingernails hard along his neck, hoping to draw some blood to really sell his predicament.

"Got an itch I can help you with?" she asked with a leer.

"You had Paula's file anyway, just in case the police hadn't nailed down her father's motive for killing Graham Zetterfeldt," he said. "You had to tell Toner to steal the file, because that's what Zetterfeldt would do. But you had it in your back pocket if you needed it."

He continued to claw at his eyes, now actually sore and itching.

"You haven't finished your dinner, my love," she said.

"But that ridiculous ploy of stealing my Leafs cap and leaving it near Jacquie's body..."

"Agreed, darling. Two birds with one stone, Frankie said. I didn't have him around for his intellect, and the drugs were fucking him up. He started doing things on his own, stupid things. And Michael dear, no one crosses me and gets away with it. So I told him we were adjusting our plans."

"Was it his cute idea to leave a golf ball in the mouths of his victims?"

Naismith just giggled.

"You told him about the cash in the safe," said Michael, "after reading my emails, after messing up that kid from Geek Patrol. Did you get at my bank accounts? Some credit card info you thought you could use?"

"Shit-eating" didn't do justice to the grin on her face.

"That became a relatively pedestrian option," she said, "once I'd set my sights on the bigger prize." She lifted her hand and examined her engagement ring.

"I thought Toner was calling *me* a bitch when he found the gun on me," said Michael. "But I bet he recognized that it was *your* gun, and figured you must have given it to me to... what?... to set up a gunfight by the lake?"

"I did think it would increase the odds that things would... take care of themselves."

"So Toner became expendable."

"He was becoming too much of a liability. Surely you can see that?"

"Well it almost worked," said Michael, recalling the tiny weapon that Toner had aimed at his head.

"Can we lighten up this conversation and enjoy our meal?" she asked.

"I saw the extra mileage on your car," he said. "I think I can explain some of it now. You followed me up to Muskoka, didn't you? You were right by the cottage that night, probably ready to take out Toner if he shot me first. Lucky for you he didn't, sweetheart. You'd get no inheritance from a dead fiancée."

"If things had gone the other way, any attorney worth his salt could have persuaded a magistrate to give me a substantial portion of your estate, as a dependant."

"You're self-sufficient. You've never depended on me for anything."

"None of my income is on the books," she said. "Besides, my loving stepchildren wouldn't want their new mummy tossed out on the street."

"How did you expect to marry me under an alias?" asked Michael, and he knew the answer before she opened her mouth.

"So naïve," she said. "I need two pieces of documentation. I have four."

She ate salad. "Yummy."

"The substituted recording at the Foster Glen dinner. You heard me at home, testing the playback of my recording on the iPod. You figured it out. Did sis pull off that little switch for you? I bet Lottie has a drawer full of recordings starring Northcott."

No reaction.

"You insisted we try the restaurant in Chelsea," he said, "after the headmaster had recommended the White Hart Pub on the Thames. The White Hart is in Barnes, just down the road from where you walked away from a homicidal deed in your previous life. You didn't want me running into any locals who knew you then, and maybe heard some rumours."

"You enjoyed yourself, didn't you? I hope you tried the prime rib in Chelsea. It's to die for."

"Never made it."

He nodded toward the fingers that tugged at the corner of

her eyebrow.

"That's what gave you away," he said, his voice now hoarse. "I may have never put the rest of it together."

She jerked her hand away, stuck it in the salad, and threw a handful at him.

"You are pathetic. Spending so much of your precious time focused on your old nemesis," she said, "thinking J.P. Northcott could possibly be behind it all. He was so... small-time."

He picked a piece of lettuce off his face, not taking his eyes off her.

"And that *gook spook* you think is so fucking smart... the little half-breed, Eddie what's-his-fuck."

He cringed at her offhand racism, and was surprised that anything she said could still shock him.

"Why do you waste your time with these... *people*? They aren't even your own kind."

She snorted, then looked over Michael's shoulder with a blank stare. When she came back, she was Jessie again.

"Thank you for making me feel so good about myself, old chap, sexually and all that."

Naismith giggled. She drooled down her front, and didn't seem to notice.

Michael tried to tune out the gibberish, to separate the mad ramble from her version of the truth.

"... and that mug Higgins..."

He bent over and coughed.

She ranted.

"... Artie Fartie, the fucking retard..."

She examined her fingernails and belched, causing her to chortle yet again.

"How are you feeling, by the way?" she said. "How's your *chicken*, darling?"

Michael picked a piece of "chicken" from his salad and sniffed it. He licked it, frowned, then looked at the smiling sociopath.

"You didn't," he said. "Is this..."

She pointed a finger at him and said, "Gotcha."

"Oh my God."

With the most desperate body language he could muster, he staggered to the counter. He scoured through the column of four drawers, from top to bottom and back.

The next warning signs, when he brought them to life, would indicate that the anaphylaxis had gained momentum. It could be too late for an EpiPen, and the pain would soon be over.

He turned to face her. "Where is it?"

"Are you referring to that little injector thingy?" she asked, remaining serene, no doubt anticipating that her latest quarry would soon fall.

"Mary Anne, I need my epinephrine. If it gets any worse..."

She smiled and shrugged.

He lifted the counter phone from the handset; still nothing, as he expected.

"It's dead," he said.

"Who in the world are you planning to ring?" she asked.

"Oh my God. You're actually... you're planning to kill me," said Michael. "Here, in my own kitchen."

"You aren't presenting any of the more serious indicators of anaphylaxis. *I think* you should be okay without an epinephrine injection until the more frightful symptoms take hold of you. But then again, these things are *so* unpredictable."

She had done her homework, and he was glad she did.

He fell into the chair next to Naismith.

"I don't get it," he said, wheezing. "What about all the charity work, the women's shelter... the little girl in the wheelchair?"

"Building a body of work, completing the character. Oh, I didn't follow through on the shelter. Turns out they get a little personal with their background checks. My unfortunate violation by the intruder in my home provided reason enough to forego that particular act of altruism."

She stroked her ring with her thumb, leaned forward and whispered, "You love me."

He sucked at the air like it was trying to elude him.

She didn't react.

The breathing problem should have told her the finish line was in sight.

"You must know... you'll never get my money now," he said.

"Sad but true. Those glorious riches won't be mine, at least not the substantial sum I'd worked so hard for."

She grinned.

He frowned. "What else could you..."

Fuck me.

Her grin grew wider.

The safe.

"You didn't," he said.

"That's right, my sweet," she said. "How fortunate for me that you are so foolishly and undyingly contrary. The police suggest you don't keep so much money in the house after the little incident at your cozy lakeside sanctuary, and what do you do? You put it right back in the safe."

"Fuck," he said, no louder than a whisper. But he didn't give a damn about the money. He planned to see that she'd never get to spend it.

"Don't feel too badly," she said. "You felt any threat to you or your family had been eliminated."

"How did you—"

"How did I steal a quarter of a million dollars from right under your nose?"

He waited.

"Since you asked," she said. "I was put onto—and became rather friendly with—a splendidly talented young chap who makes quite a nice living by pilfering debit card numbers. He puts a little skimming device of some sort into an ATM machine and, like magic, he has the card numbers of many of our fine fellow citizens."

Michael closed his eyes. "Ah shit."

"All he needs to do then is set up a—"

"A pinhole camera, in the ceiling or somewhere, to get the PIN numbers for the cards." Michael had recently seen a news feature on card data theft. "So you found another sucker."

She grinned. "For a few... favours, this energetic young man showed me the tricks of his trade."

"Classy to the end."

"Well darling, at least for this job I didn't have to lick the dick of a pimple-pussed halfwit."

"Glad to hear the skimmer had a better complexion than your boy Joel Pierce," said Michael. "I suppose I'll find one of these cameras in my office, which you used to catch me entering the combination to my safe."

"*Yes*. Very good indeed. I hope you don't mind that I used the same duffle bag, the one you used the evening you went up to visit Frank and the kiddies. I already knew all of that money of yours would fit inside the bag."

He clutched his throat, tried to swallow. *So difficult to breathe,* he thought, the dying man immersed in his role.

She smiled, sat up. She recognized a symptom that told her they'd hit the homestretch.

"Dizzy... the other EpiPen," he said, his head teetering. "I'm begging you. If you wait any longer... name your price."

"My price, darling? You're paying it as we chat."

"Was it all necessary, this misery you've inflicted?"

"People serve a purpose, and then... I like to have a lot of irons in the fire. It makes it more difficult to find the underlying clarity in apparently random events. It's basic chaos theory. Don't you see, darling?"

"You killed my wife," said Michael, his hoarse voice no longer an act. "What happened on the escarpment that morning?"

"Ah, back to the minutiae surrounding your little wifey's demise, the incidentals you are so desperate to learn."

"How did my wife die? It had to be Toner. Who did the cowardly act for you... *you filthy slut*?"

"I think that closes off our discussion on that topic, Michael."

She ate salad.

"I think Vincent Fronda did see something," he said. "Did he find out about the painting? *The Golfer*? And did you or your cronies sneak some kiddy porn or something into his house, setting him up to look like a pedophile, to link him to Zetterfeldt?"

"I'm struggling to follow your rather suspect logic, darling."

He took another quick look at the clock, exasperated by the impatience of the racing big hand.

"Irons in the fire? How about paintings, *paintings* in the fire?" he asked. "*The Golfer*?"

Naismith smiled. "Art is not what you see, but what you make others see. Edgar Degas."

"Tell me something, Mary Anne. Did you set fire to the Zetterfeldt's house *and* the arts centre? Did your psycho pal the nurse help you? How did that work exactly?"

"You really should conserve your strength, love."

Collapsing slowly onto the table, he rasped, "Please help me. I'll give you anything."

Naismith stood up, but Michael was around the table and on her in a second. He squeezed her collarbone and pressed her back into her chair.

"That *hurts*," she cried, and looked up at him. "What? How are you—"

"Shut the fuck up," he said. "I want to show you something."

CHAPTER 41

Michael went to the cupboards on the side of the kitchen.

Naismith jumped up and watched him from the opposite counter. "What are you doing?"

He hopped up on the chair beside the counter. He reached over the top of the cupboards, found what he was looking for, and got down off the chair.

"More salad?" he asked, holding the bowl he'd found in the fridge a few hours earlier.

She stared at the bowl containing the salad she'd prepared.

He held it out for her. "Go ahead. Try some."

Her eyes opened wide. She raised her head and smiled.

He returned the smile. "Gotcha."

"Very *good*," said Naismith.

She reached behind her and pulled a small handgun from her waistband. It looked like a sister of the miniature pistol she'd given him for the clash with Toner.

"How many guns do you own?" asked Michael.

"Poor Michael. Always a step behind."

He hadn't prepared for this, and cursed himself for it. She had a backup plan to the murder-by-appetizer plot. He hated guns, but wished he had one as he stared at the business end of her Plan B.

"What is wrong with you, Michael? I know you aren't the bravest of souls, but no matter what harm was put in the way of all that meant anything to you... your kids, your own safety, *me*. No matter what was at risk, you wouldn't back off. Can you be that daft, so utterly stupid?"

"I guess I always sensed my enemies were cowards who could be brought down."

"Sticks and stones, Michael." She pointed the gun at the salad bowl in his hand. "Take off the wrap."

"There isn't a chance in—"

Crack! A bullet hit the cupboards, how far from him he couldn't tell.

Where are those damn cops?

He removed the wrap. He stared down at the salad with the real chicken and fought off a small wave of nausea, brought on by the memory of allergic reactions past. He knew he could survive two or three bites of the deadly poultry, but probably not for long.

She raised the gun. "Eat it. And I don't mean the fucking tomatoes."

He heard a beep to his left. It caught her attention. A few seconds later, another beep.

The recorder. Shit.

She glared at him, and pointed the weapon at his head.

The pistol veered right. Naismith fired at the plant that held the hidden the recorder. She missed, blowing the corner off the side table. She fired again. The pot shattered and the recorder hit the floor. The next bullet hit the little gadget square. It hurtled into the wall, rebounding back to the feet of Naismith.

The next bullet's for me, he thought, already shaken by the gunfire.

She picked up the gravely wounded recorder and examined it. She flew into a spasm of laughter, but not the maniacal outbursts he'd been witnessing. She was *laughing,* from her gut.

"The batteries," she said, struggling to calm herself long enough to speak. The recorder fell from her hand. "The batteries were low. You... you let *batteries* foil your little dodge."

Now.

Michael hurled the salad bowl and knocked the gun from her hand. The gun slid across the floor. As she lunged for it, the small pistol rattled down the narrow gap between the stove and counter. Thank God for skinny little girlie guns.

He moved in behind her and reached for her throat. Naismith reacted quickly. She grabbed the closest thing to her, whirled around, and drove the coffee pot into the side of his head. He hit the floor hard, pain shooting through him.

He sprang to his feet and leaned on the counter to steady himself. He realized at that moment that he had chosen the wrong side of the kitchen to hide the salad bowl.

On the opposite side of the room, a couple of feet to her left, sat the knife rack.

She followed his eyes. She reached back and pulled out the biggest knife from the end of the rack.

He moved fast. He grabbed her wrist. He squeezed hard, twisted. The knife hit the floor, but her confident smile remained.

Naismith spun her right hand around and jabbed a smaller knife into his side.

"Cunt!" He grabbed her by the collar and threw her onto the kitchen tiles. He stomped on her wrist, freeing the much smaller knife. She wailed, and rolled onto her side, legs splayed.

Michael lifted his shirt. He bled from the stab wound below his ribcage, but thought it was superficial.

Michael thought of Emily, the kids, Dr. Gordon. He felt a burning hate, which only heightened the pain in his head. Her shapely ass was raised just enough...

He kicked her hard between the legs, then kicked her again.

She screamed after the first, could only whimper after the second.

"I'd say you've been disabled," he said calmly.

But he couldn't enjoy the moment.

Not now.

His insides were about to explode.

He doubted Naismith could even crawl across the kitchen, but removed his belt and tied her hands together. He grabbed both her car keys and his own from the corner table, and flew down the hall to the bathroom.

She cursed at him after he pulled the bathroom door almost shut. She soon went silent.

Rain pattered against the window behind him.

He ripped off his shirt. He found a heavy-duty bandage in the cupboard and slapped it over the wound.

Where the hell were the police? Fern should have managed to at least get a patrol car there by now.

He heard something. *The screen door.* She wouldn't get far on foot.

My spare keys.

He ran to the kitchen. The spare keys were missing from the hook on the back door. Outside, a car engine came to life. He scanned the kitchen floor. Naismith had grabbed the recorder on the way out, he assumed to ensure the shot-up device could not be resuscitated.

Michael ran out the back door and turned the corner of the house. He caught his foot on something and fell.

"What the..." He picked himself up and looked to his rear.

Danny Higgins sat on the ground, holding his head and with blood on his hands.

"I'll explain in the car," said Michael, helping his friend to his feet.

CHAPTER 42

"*Jessie?* Are you *kidding* me?" said a disbelieving Danny, whose car keys had been lifted from his pocket by Naismith.

"What did she hit you with?" asked Michael.

"No idea."

"I can't see much blood from under that mop of yours."

"All I know is my head is throbbing," said Danny. "It looks like she tagged you one, too."

Michael gently ran his hand over the lump on his head, courtesy of a coffee pot that he had failed to duck.

He punched the button for the GPS control centre on the dashboard of Naismith's Mercedes. He had darted upstairs for her spare keys after Naismith had fled in his Range Rover.

"I can't believe it," said Michael. "I hoofed her where it counts, twice, and hard."

Danny held his palm against the side of his head, just above his left ear. "Doesn't count as much with girls, Mike. They have no balls as I recall, unless you count the ones they've ripped off us."

OnStar, the GPS provider, answered his call.

"Hello, it's Michael Flanigan," he said. "This is an emergency. My Range Rover has been stolen. I'm following it right now in my... fiancée's car." As he rhymed off his birthday and pass code to oblige the security formalities, he saw one lone vehicle in the distance, but couldn't tell if it was his Range Rover.

A steady rain and prematurely blackened skies provided minimal visibility.

"One moment, sir," said the dispatcher, who identified herself as Abby.

"The crazy bitch really stabbed you?" asked Danny.

"Didn't go deep," said Michael, lifting the black T-shirt that he'd grabbed from a pile of dirty laundry before leaving his house.

"The bleeding seems under control for now."

Michael regretted that he hadn't managed to nudge Naismith to elaborate more about her relationship with Emily and the controversial painting. But he then thought that, even if he had, he shouldn't believe a word out of her mouth.

"The unit is moving west on Number One Side Road," said Abby the dispatcher. "It's just east of Cedar Springs Road."

"The golf course," said Michael, pulling back onto the road. "She's near the entrance to Foster Glen."

"What's she doing at the fucking golf course?" asked Danny.

Michael raised his hand to shut Danny up, and asked Abby for an update.

"She's still at the same position," said Abby.

"She hasn't moved?" asked Michael.

I'm almost there.

Just as Michael pondered the notion that Naismith may have abandoned the car, Abby said, "The vehicle has mobilized, heading west along Number One Side Road."

"She's making a run for it," yelled Danny, who seemed to be enjoying the chase despite his headache.

"I see her, Hig," said Michael. "We've got her, buddy."

"Mr. Flanigan, the police are being notified," said Abby. "Please do not try to apprehend the individual on your own. And please stay on the line until—"

"Don't worry, Abby," said Michael. "I've got a friend with me."

He disconnected the call.

The tail lights ahead were less than a hundred yards away. The vehicle made a sharp right.

"I think she turned in to the golf course," said Michael.

"She won't get nine holes in, not in this weather," said Danny, both hands on the dashboard.

Michael made the turn into Foster Glen, just in time to see a dark blur moving away from the Range Rover. Its front tires had lodged in a bunker near the practice green.

"She shoulda spent more time practicing her chipping," said

Danny, as they passed the vehicle stuck in the sand. "She woulda known where that sand trap was."

The rain fell harder.

"By the pro shop," yelled Danny, pointing.

"I see her," said Michael.

Only three cars remained in the parking lot. He skidded to a halt by the outside stairs leading to the upper level of the main building, which was mostly dark.

"I lost her," hollered Michael.

"She must have gone inside," cried Danny. "The place looks deserted."

"No. Look," said Michael. He grabbed Danny by the shirt and turned him around to face the eighteenth fairway. "She's in a golf cart."

"Where's she think she's gonna get to?" asked Danny.

"She's heading onto the damn golf course."

Danny ran to a nearby garbage can, yanked something out, and ran to the row of carts.

"Not one of yours, is it?" said Danny, brandishing a bent three-iron, likely discarded by a short-tempered duffer. "I never hit a good three into this green."

Michael pounded their cart down the hill from the eighteenth, the vehicle ahead in sight, but still a good seven-iron away.

She spun her wheels for a moment, and Danny said, "We got the crazy bitch," but she found some traction and continued on, just as they had closed within a hundred yards.

She reached the seventeenth hole, turned sharply, and ripped across the second fairway.

"I think she's got a faster cart," yelled Michael.

"She's heading into the woods, Mike," said Danny. "*Your* woods."

She entered the woods at precisely the same spot that

Michael had a few weeks prior, when she fulfilled his little sex-in-the-woods fantasy.

Did she plan this?

"You can only drive in so far," said Michael.

"So you told me, lover."

"Why do I tell you anything?"

Through the wet, dark night, Michael could just make out the clearing ahead where he had parked that day with Naismith.

He reached the clearing sooner than he expected. He failed to brake in time, and the cart spun out and caught the side of a tree. Michael braced himself, but the fender bender caught Danny unawares. He flew off the cart. Within seconds, he climbed up and leaned on his seat, splattered with mud. "Let's get her, Mike."

"Wait a second," said Michael, scanning the woods around them. "Where the hell is she? I don't know of any other paths in here that a cart would fit through."

He jumped off the cart, and cupped his hands over his eyes in a futile attempt to block the rain. He looked around, circling twice. No path was in sight, nor was her cart.

Danny ran back to the fairway, reappearing in a few seconds. When he returned, he just shook his head and said, "Nothing."

Michael turned to the roar of sirens. "Okay, let's not give up."

Danny grabbed the broken three-iron from the cart. "She'd better hope *you* find her," he said.

Michael ran on a forty-five degree angle into the woods on the left. Danny followed him in and took another route through the dense trees.

Less than a minute later, scratched from unseen branches and bleeding from his knife wound, Michael exited onto the fairway on the other side of the woods.

He heard a noise from behind, and turned just in time to see the golf cart roaring alongside the trees.

She was ten yards away and headed in his direction.

Danny lunged from the woods and cracked her on the skull with the club, knocking her from the vehicle. Her cart veered to

Michael's left. He dove to his right, getting clipped on the foot by the cart as he tumbled to the ground, just feet from the homicidal cart operator who'd tried to run him down.

She crawled closer to Michael. She got up on one knee and raised her hand over her head, her fist wrapped around a knife handle.

Danny hit her in the face with the broken iron, and twice more when she hit the ground.

Fresh pain shot through Michael's foot as he got to his feet. He held his hand over the knife wound he'd received less than an hour earlier in his kitchen, and leaned on Danny's shoulder.

She didn't move, not a muscle.

"Oh my God," said Danny.

A long, narrow boning knife lay on the ground next to her.

A siren blared, stopped, blared, stopped, not far away.

Michael knelt on the ground, turned the fallen enemy onto her back, and brushed back her wet hair.

Gazing up at him, with one open dead eye, was a bashed and bloodied Christine Manahan.

CHAPTER 43

Michael sat on a dock on Howe Island, sipping an iced tea and congratulating himself for his decision to buy the property on which he sat. He had been renting the place from a former schoolmate named Brian Shipman, who had moved back into Kingston proper. The cottage had been winterized just a few years before, and offered all the warmth and protection he would need, even from the coldest winter nights the St. Lawrence River had to offer.

He hadn't closed the deal yet. The cottage hadn't been listed, and he sensed the sale price he was quoted by his childhood chum was a bit low. He hadn't told Shipman of his financial means, and didn't want a hometown discount from his old friend.

Michael went inside to email Rachel Takahara from his new laptop. He sent her the property details, asked what she thought it was worth, then went outside to his new favourite chair on the river-facing deck.

If Muskoka held the designation of God's Country, Howe Island was knocking on heaven's door. The kids would love it year-round. Clint could fish or play shinny on the river, and Sophie loved to ski, both water and cross-country. Michael thought he might even bury the past for his son's sake. Clint could bring his mother along for the twenty-five minute trip from Kingston, maybe for a barbecue or a ride in the boat he planned to buy.

As he looked out to the river, his thoughts returned to the usual place.

She was still out there somewhere. If she played it smart, she would distance herself from Ontario and the prison cell with her name on it. But he couldn't trust that the amoral and unpredictable psychopath, with whom he'd had the bone-chilling battle just two short weeks ago, was inclined to run and hide for long.

She might patiently wait, and seek cold revenge. She could bide her time with his quarter of a million dollars.

But he believed she would return to visit him one day.

He still had no idea how or why Christine Manahan got involved with Naismith. The police would not discuss the matter with him, and ordered him to stay away from Boyd Manahan, and the investigation in general.

A familiar pang of guilt jabbed at Michael as he sat enjoying the refreshing mist blowing off the St. Lawrence. The Halton and Burlington police forces had done a remarkable job. He would talk to both Alberts and Speagle, write a letter to their boss.

Michael thought of those who had passed. He agreed with the official stance of the police that either one or both of Naismith and Toner had a hand in the deaths of Emily Baggio, Vincent Fronda, J.P. Northcott, Dr. Brenda Gordon, Teresa Amodeo, Lottie Denison, Ruth Eisentraut, and the Zetterfeldts.

Northcott likely did choreograph, if not carry out, the murder of Graham Zetterfeldt, but the cops had no real proof, and didn't seem to care. The loop was closed. All were dead.

And from everything he'd learned, it all started with a damn painting.

To swing his focus to the positive, he decided to plan a time when his closest circle could come together for a weekend. He went inside to get his phone.

"Just pick a weekend and I'll be there," said Rita.

He told her about the ever-tilting painting in the farmhouse at Bronte Creek Park, with the dueling Italians and the woman in the background, and his feeling that it tried to speak to him, that *Emily* spoke to him. It gave him the idea to focus on the woman in the *rear* of the photograph that he'd been circulating, the woman he now knew to be Mary Anne Naismith.

"At first glance the painting is all about two guys looking like they were about to get into it," he said. "But it's really about her, the woman in the back of the photo."

Rita did not respond, or ask why he had been in the farmhouse.

"I guess it does sound kind of silly," he said. "Normally I don't believe in such things."

"I believe in those things, Michael. They do say the Spruce Lane Farmhouse is haunted. And very accommodating to spirits of all shapes and sizes."

"You've been there?" he asked.

"I know the painting you mean. *Amicizia*."

"I don't remember the name, but that sounds about right. Do you know the translation? 'The Duel' perhaps? Or how about 'Rivals'?

"It means 'Friendship.'"

Michael woke up in the deck chair with Danny's manuscript on his chest. He looked at his watch. He still had plenty of time before he had to meet the budding author for their golf game.

While Michael told Danny that money wasn't an issue, Danny still booked a 3:15 p.m. tee time at Awahilidihi, to take advantage of The Hill's late-afternoon discount rather than of Michael's generosity.

The skies fluctuated from partly sunny to threatening as Michael relaxed on the dock.

It seemed they hadn't had a dry weekend all summer. He felt like he stirred up the weather gods whenever he reached for his clubs. Staying right where he sat appealed to him more than driving to the other side of Kingston to have their golf game washed out by yet another storm.

But Danny saved Michael's life that horrible night on the golf course, and Michael planned to make his old friend more of a priority from that day onward. He thanked God that the police had determined Danny had acted in self-defense—more so in defense of Michael—in subduing the knife-brandishing Christine

Manahan.

Michael flipped through the pages of *Mayhem in Suburbia*, stopping at his favourite passages, usually the ones where the fiction had clearly been stolen from fact.

"Oh God," he said aloud, as he read the chapter where Martin Fletcher had run into the beautiful Darlene Terrence on the putting green.

A darkness came over him, in step with a menacing gang of clouds that pushed aside the afternoon sun.

He lurched up, and whispered to the river, "Fuck off, Flanigan."

Don't go there.

He had a quick shower before looking up Randy Goodman's number. He found the golf pro winding down a lesson.

Ignoring Goodman's attempt at small talk, Michael said, "Randy, the last time I saw you, you said Jessie Hargreaves had me lined up right from the start, something like that."

Michael's BlackBerry beeped in his ear. He checked the display and let the incoming call from Rita go to voice mail.

"She bugged me for that time," said Goodman. "I had no openings that day. She showed up, asked for a quick lesson, slipped me a twenty up front. She was hard to resist."

"Just when I planned to be there."

"Yep. Otherwise, she would never have been there."

"*Amicizia,*" he said to himself, thinking of the painting that would lean askew during his visits to the Spruce Lane Farmhouse.

Maybe Emily had tried to send him a message.

"What's that, Mike?" asked Goodman.

"Thanks for the info, Randy," said Michael, and he hung up.

Friendship.

As Michael was about to shut down his laptop, an email came in from Rachel Takahara. She said Brian Shipman could have asked more for the island property, but the price seemed fair, not especially low. She suggested he check with a local real estate agent who knew the area better if he wanted to pursue it further.

But her reply was not what grabbed his interest from Rachel's email. She had added her response to an earlier email thread containing an exchange with Emily, which included the pictures of what would be their future home.

She had sent it to both of Emily's email addresses, including an old Hotmail address, which Michael had forgotten about.

Emily had used more than one email address for years, but had carried out virtually all electronic communication for the longest time leading up to her death—at least as far as he knew—using the email address provided by the local cable company.

She had set up her email account for "emilybaggio@cogeco.ca" to store her emails on her computer, so she wouldn't have to go to the Cogeco website to retrieve them.

But her "ebaggio27@hotmail.com" emails remained on a remote server. She had to visit the Hotmail website to read those messages.

Fortunately for Michael, Emily's Cogeco password, which she had shared with him, was the same one she used for her Hotmail account.

He didn't feel so lucky once he logged in to the account.

All but two emails, other than spam, had been deleted.

Either one would have knocked the wind out of him.

PART IV— EXTRA HOLES

"To find a man's true character,

play golf with him."

—P.G. Wodehouse

CHAPTER 44

Driving through Kingston on the way to the golf course, Michael pulled into City Park, parked near a statue of some guy long dead, and cried.

While he sat on the Howe Island Ferry less than a half hour earlier, a call from Duff McPhee, the Scottish art expert, and a return call to Rita told Michael all he needed to know.

The chance meeting that followed, while he removed his clubs from his trunk in the Awahilidihi parking lot, had put an exclamation mark on it.

They waited behind the twelfth tee at The Hill, as the foursome two groups ahead knocked their putts back and forth across the green ahead.

"Where are the damn marshals these days?" asked Michael to no one in particular. Danny and Michael lagged back from the group waiting to hit next.

The late afternoon weather forecast kept most golfers in the clubhouse bar. The day remained dry, but looming blackness overhead suggested that might soon change. The group ahead talked about getting their asses off the course before the skies opened up.

"The Hill is still my favourite course," said Danny.

"Gotta love The Hill," said Michael.

"Hey, what's happening with *Oliver's Landing*?"

"International Oil bought it. Sometimes you just get lucky."

"An oil company?"

"Uncle Don called me last night. It'll hit the papers tomorrow. They needed some good PR after that big spill in the Atlantic earlier this year. They paid a good price, and will preserve the heritage land that was gonna be used for the back nine on the second eighteen."

"The tree-huggers must've had a circle jerk," said Danny.

"They're a happy bunch."

When they were finally able to hit on the pretty par three, Danny waggled his six-iron before stroking his ball from the elevated tee. It hit eighteen feet past the hole, almost clearing the green, and then rolled back to within a foot and a half of the flag. Danny raised his fist in the air, then turned and said, "I wish I could do that on purpose."

A loud crack preceded a cloudburst.

Danny yelled, "I'll take the ladies," and ran from the tee. Michael grabbed the umbrella from his bag, then clued in to Danny's plan. He headed for the portable men's latrine twenty yards away, while Danny took cover in the women's john next to it.

The combination of the stench and oppressive humidity of the plastic outhouse was a marginally lesser evil to the weather outside.

"The summer of fucking rain," said Danny.

"How long you willing to wait?" yelled Michael, not knowing how well his friend could hear him in the adjoining can.

"Got nowhere else to go," replied Danny. "And turn the volume down, will ya?"

"Did I tell you they found the owner of that three-iron you used to save my life?" asked Michael. "It was one of the Murphy twins... Gary."

"You'll never curse him again."

"He said he snapped after taking a snowman on eighteen."

"If he said eight, he had at least a ten."

"Minimum."

"Have the cops located the psycho bitch yet?" asked Danny.

"I don't think they have any idea where she is," he said, as Danny steered the conversation in a direction in which Michael would have soon headed. "She could be anywhere."

"With your money," said Danny.

"She actually did okay on her own. Turns out her personal training services were rendered while horizontal. And in any other number of positions, I suppose."

"She was a hooker, too?"

"And a high-priced one I understand," said Michael.

"The papers still aren't saying much about Christine Manahan," said Danny, "besides the fact that she got killed. That was quite a switch she pulled off with Naismith by Foster Glen."

"They're still trying to figure out the connection between the two," said Michael.

"And Naismith is still on the loose."

The rain let up.

"Did you tell me you'd never met Naismith when she was masquerading as Ruth Eisentraut?" asked Michael before exiting the toilet, opening his umbrella as he did.

Danny didn't answer. He didn't step out until a minute later.

"I eventually had to use the facilities," he said. "Never used the ladies' before. Maybe I should start hitting from the squatty tees."

"Emily's fake friend, Ruth Eisentraut. Did you know her?" asked Michael.

"I don't recall running into Naismith as the German broad. I thought I told you that."

"Yeah, I think you may have, come to think of it. It's just that I know you spent a bit of time down there, at the arts centre, with Emily. I thought you would have probably run into her pal Ruth."

The downpour had chased the golfers around them from the course, but it still looked playable.

"Care to finish the hole, maybe slosh through a few more?" asked Michael.

Danny's ball had blown to the edge of the green. "What do the rules say about *that*?" he asked. "Fuck it. I'll hit another and play the best ball. I love hitting this tee shot."

Michael placed his ball on the tee, then stepped back and

said, "I ran into Lanny Paulson in the parking lot."

"He's got a gig down our way in a couple of weeks," said Danny. "We should hit him up for tickets, maybe get backstage after the show."

"He asked about your book, said he might be interested in a piece of the action.

"Get out."

"He said something else I found interesting. He saw you recently, at the casino east of town."

"Did he?"

"He said it was the last time we were in Kingston. It woulda been the night I took my aunt out for dinner."

"If you say so. Are you going to hit?" asked Danny, taking agitated, jerky practice swings at the rear of the tee block.

"You drove by the restaurant, Woodenheads, on your way to your date with Ronnie Donovan."

"You're losing me."

"Paulson saw you feeding the slots that night like there was no tomorrow."

Danny hesitated, then laughed and said, "Ronnie likes her games of chance. I humoured her, and believe me, it was worth it."

"Good to hear."

Without a practice swing, Michael hit an eight-iron to the open, unguarded side of the green, twenty-five feet from the hole.

"Playing it safe, Alice?" asked Danny.

"It's about time I took the safe approach with something."

Michael stepped back and leaned on his iron. Danny saw something he didn't like on his ball and walked back to his golf bag for another.

"Rita called me on the way here," said Michael. "You know Fuzzy Mavis, the mobster she was defending in that big case?"

Danny stopped in his stride for just a moment, then continued on to his bag.

"Sure," he said. "He's been in all the papers."

"Mavis pled out when things looked bleak for him," said Michael. "The prosecution had an interesting piece of evidence that never came out in the media when they didn't go ahead with the trial."

"Oh yeah?" Danny approached the tee.

"A list of gambling debts, some big ones, people who owed Mavis."

"I think I'll go with a seven," said Danny, marching back to his golf bag, red-faced.

"Lanny Paulson didn't see Ronnie at the casino."

Danny yanked the club out of his bag. "Okay," he said. "For crissakes, things didn't work out with Ronnie and me, right from the get-go. I was too embarrassed to say anything, after talking so much about her. I went to the casino to kill time. Are you happy now?"

"Northcott's name was on the Mavis list."

Danny walked to the tee. "I guess I shouldn't be surprised."

"Your name was on the list, Danny."

Danny hit and found the trap guarding the pin.

"Looks like you'll be playing your first ball," said Michael.

Danny slammed the heel of his wedge into the ground. "Your lawyer friend could be disbarred for telling you that."

"I don't see that happening," said Michael.

Danny paced around the tee block, slammed his club again, paced some more, then stopped. "I'm sick, Mikey."

"Sick?"

"There's some bad people out there who'd like to kill me."

"What did you do to me, Hig?"

"Mike, what the fuck does that have to do with you?"

"What happened, Danny?"

"I'm an addict."

"An addict?"

"Gambling."

Michael mouth fell open and he stared long and hard at Danny. Could all of this have happened because his best friend liked to gamble?

"She went to your side door to leave you a note, the day we stopped by," said Michael. "How would she know you always use the side door, and not the front?"

"I beg your fuck?"

"She could have made a lucky guess, but she'd been there before. I know it's not much, but if you add it all up."

"She. Who she?"

"Just like with her... Naismith," he said. "The little things got bigger, started to add up."

"Always with the riddles."

"And just like with her, I didn't want to see them."

"You've lost your mind. I really believe that."

"You know, it was a scene in your book that got me thinking," he said. "It's like you wanted me to find out."

"My book? Find out what?"

"The Terrence chick, stalking Martin Fletcher at the golf course."

"You're starting to get on my nerves. I just spilled my guts to you about some pretty serious fucking trouble I'm in, and all you can do is give me these mind games."

Michael turned his head to face his friend. "You always say the best defense is a good offense," he said.

"I think I say go big or stay home," said Danny. "Why not go for the green if you have a shot?"

"Yeah, for the *green*. No pun intended, right? Do you remember a while back, you looked after Paulie and Sylvio when I went out of town for a couple of days?"

"Yeah, so?"

"I'd forgotten that I gave you a house key, and never got it back. Tell me, Danny, did Toner give it back to you after he used it to get into my house that night, the night he clobbered me and stuck a needle in my ass?"

Danny said nothing.

"Bobby George said it only took Toner a second to get the

door open... suggested maybe he had some kind of burglary tool," said Michael. "But I don't think that's what the filthy prick used. There was no sign the lock had been tampered with. None.

"On top of that, he'd have to know that my security alarm was disabled. How the hell would he know that? Got any ideas on that, Danny Boy?"

"So you're buddies with Bobby the arse-puncher now?"

Michael walked to within two feet of him. In a soft, measured tone, he said, "Look at me, Hig... don't look away. Jessie Hargreaves, as *I* knew her, knew I was going to hit a bucket of balls at three o'clock the day I first met her." Michael leaned closer. "*She fucking knew it!*" he bellowed, making Danny jump.

Quieter, Michael said, "And you, my friend, were the only person I told about it. I racked my brain... only you. How did she know? How did that psychotic twat know that she could walk into my life at that moment, and kick off her plan to fuck with everything that's dear to me?"

"Look, Mike, I don't know where you got the idea—"

Smack. Michael punched Danny in the jaw. He hit the ground hard. "Only you knew I was going to the driving range that day," said Michael, standing over him. "And then a day later you're encouraging me to get back in the saddle, to ask someone out on a date."

Michael paced a full circle. "My kids, Danny," he said. "*My fucking kids!*"

"You loosened my tooth," said Danny, whimpering. "And I think you cracked my tailbone." He moved slightly, winced. "That's what this is about? A goddam golf lesson?" He got up on one knee.

"Don't get up," said Michael, pushing Danny down. "The crazy cunt didn't mention you the night I confronted her at my house, after she knew I was on to her. Why wouldn't she taunt me with it, that my best friend was in on it with her, helping her come after me? I'll tell you why. Because you were still working with her on getting at my money. You conveniently showed up, as always, right on cue."

"She hit me. You were there."

"Yeah, yeah. You were hit. She was raped."

Danny dabbed at his bloodied lip with his shirt tail, and wiped mud from his cheek. He fell back, crying. A minute or so later, he said, "I didn't know what she had in mind. She called me, said things were fucked up and she needed a distraction. I thought she was planning to take off, to disappear."

"Without my money?"

"She said she didn't need you anymore. I thought she'd fuck off, get out of your life—out of our lives—and we could all go back to the way things were."

That came as no surprise to Michael. Earlier, while Michael sat on the ferry, Duff McPhee told him about a painting he'd researched for Emily called *Golfer at Dawn*, a piece of art that had been missing for years—and was worth millions. A quarter million of Michael's cash would tide her over until she hocked the masterpiece.

"You knew about the painting, Hig. *The Golfer*."

"Not at first," said Danny, now sitting up.

Michael lightly tapped the handle of his eight-iron against his own forehead. He lowered the club and said, "Of course. You called her, Danny, the night before we flew to London. You called to report in, to tell Naismith my suspicions about Lottie Denison. You didn't change your mind about going to Dublin to play the horses. She changed it for you. She told you to tag along to the academy in Fulham to see what I got up to, see what I found out."

"I had to, Mike. What if she found out, maybe from you, that you mentioned it to me and I didn't say anything? I woulda been fucked. That was basically my role in the whole thing. Call her if I heard or thought of anything that might help her."

"She set up her own half-sister to be murdered because of your call."

Danny looked away, and said, "You, throwing bags of money at any fucking stranger who had half a sob story. But did you toss any my way?"

"I thought you were flush from selling your practice. I just never thought..."

"Exactly. You never thought. My ex took half of it, and the slots the rest."

"How much did you owe Mavis?"

"Close to three hundred."

"*Thousand?*"

"I told you. I have a serious problem."

"For how long?"

"I went to Vegas on a junket after I sold my practice."

"I remember."

"I'd never played the slots, never had any inclination to. And then when I got home, I couldn't stop."

"Slot machines," said Michael, shaking his head in disbelief. "The whole wad? Is that where it went?"

"Most of it. I bet on some games, the nags, but it's not the same."

"How so?"

"Not the same... rush."

"Pushing coins into a machine? That's what gives you a rush so big it was worth throwing your life away, not to mention mine... or Emily's?"

"You'd never understand. Only another addict would."

"When did it all start, with Naismith I mean?"

"I was blindsided myself, but didn't know it. I dropped in on Emily at the arts centre one day. When they went to get her, I get a call on my cell from some arm-breaker. I'd started to fall behind with Mavis, and he wanted his money. I'm pleading with this clown for some extra time, and I turn to see this weird-lookin' chick hovering nearby. I think nothing of it, just blow past her. I figured out later it was the broad they knew as Ruth what's her-fuck, but had no idea then that it was actually Naismith, and she'd been listening to the call.

"The next time I meet her—although I have no idea at the

time that it's the same girl—she's Jessie Hargreaves. *Jessie* seduces me, then before long convinces me... she said I could have it all. My money problems would be gone, and in the long run you would be fine, would still have lots of money. And I would live, Mike. Don't you see?"

Michael sat down on the bench.

"You were there when Fronda got it, on the fairway behind my house," he said. "And then you conveniently show up when I get mugged and drugged by Toner. How well did you know him, by the way?"

"Cut me some slack here, will ya? I'm your best friend. Check that. I forgot, to me you were *my* best friend. It's always been that way. One-sided."

"You're turning this back on me, *friend*?"

"I was a dead man if I didn't come up with the money. And she tricked me," said Danny. "That first night, with Fronda... I had no idea what they had planned for him. But then after it happened, after they kill him, she said I was an accomplice. I *was there.*"

"You pushed the tequila on me," said Michael. "I would have never touched that stuff again."

"I remembered you blacking out, back in the day. Naismith wanted me to look for Emily's notebook. She saw her writing stuff that could be useful, if not harmful, so Naismith said. She didn't seem to really know what could be in it." Danny's voice softened. "I don't know, Mike. I just... did it."

"What happened with Fronda?"

"I had no idea they were gonna... Toner just butchered him. Fuck, Mike, he seemed to enjoy it." Danny was trembling now. "I thought I was going to be next. Toner could tell what I was thinking. He just smirked at me and said, 'Don't worry, asshole. We have plans for you.'"

"And then she had you by the balls."

"I tried to pull back, but the further in I got in..."

"Why, Danny?"

"Jessie is so clever, in her twisted way. She can be so... motivating. "

"Of course," said Michael, throwing his hands in the air. "Her favourite weapon. You were screwing her, too."

"I never had any idea that she had anything to do with Emily's death. I swear. That would have been it for me."

"How noble."

"Hey, Mike, no matter what I've done, I loved Emily."

"I'm sure she would have been proud of how you looked out for her daughter."

"I would have walked in front of a bullet to stop that. I had no idea."

Michael glared at Danny. "My God, the whole Ireland thing. The writing contest. That was all a setup?"

"She wanted you away from everything, in case you still wanted to play detective... so you'd forget about things, move on. She knew you always wanted to go to Ireland. I took you across the ocean and led you right to the truth."

"To the school in Fulham."

"I considered staying right in Ireland, to get ready to fuck off somewhere when the shit hit. I was sure I was fucked, that I'd be found out, even then."

"She sure played you."

"She was always preaching, little sayings about gaining people's trust... to keep them off balance, create smokescreens, feed on the fear and self-interest of others. Christ, it didn't hit me at the time that she was doing it to me."

Chaos.

"Wait a minute," said Michael. "You made that first recording downtown, trying to get something on Northcott, for *me*."

"She wanted to keep you going off in that direction, your mindless obsession with Northcott. And if I appeared to be helping you..."

"You once said my swing had improved since I met her."

"It had."

"You must have told Naismith that I was asking about the transmitter, maybe suspect I might go back down to Whack Job's office?"

Danny said nothing.

"Of course you told her," said Michael. "Then Lottie must have known the transmitter was still in the office, that I might be listening. It sounded like she was planning to pull a train when the pro showed up."

"Sure Lottie knew. She put the fucking transmitter there in the first place. Your listening in wouldn't have slowed her down. Naismith said it would make her cum harder. Naismith found your recording and listened to it before the tournament. She didn't give a shit about Alberts and Northcott talking drugs and hookers. She decided to let Lottie rig her own recording, the one that really fucked up Northcott... for the Zetterfeldt murder."

"I suppose exposing Northcott as an incestuous murderer had more of an appeal than listening to the clip I made, and would be more *chaotic*. I bet you were fine-tuning your strategy when you and Naismith were chatting at the tournament, after we made the turn on nine. You already knew what I was up to before I told you."

Michael paced, chipped a few twigs off the tee block, trying to recall other times he had been oblivious to the motives behind Danny's behaviour.

"She was quite brilliant, Mike," said Danny. "I mean over-the-fucking-top. And for the record, we weren't joined at the hip. She got her hooks into me, made sure she had something on me, and then called me when she needed me. I usually didn't know what the hell she was up to."

"Did you know that she knew the Manahan woman?" asked Michael.

Danny shook his head, slowly, as if sensing where the line of questioning was headed.

"You gave Christine Manahan an extra whack or two with the golf club. That's why you seemed so eager to hunt her down that night at Foster Glen. You thought it was Naismith, the one person who could tie you to all of this. You hoped to get to her first. Did she turn on you, and you decided to shut her up, for good?"

"Toner was already dead, and Naismith was the only other person who could put me at the Fronda murder scene. I started to believe she planned to do just that, to keep all the money for herself. I decided I'd rather take my chances with Mavis than get fucked up the ass in a prison shower for the rest of my days."

"Did you put Rohypnol in my drink at the Foster Glen? Did Toner give it to you?"

Danny stared at the ground. "I never really knew the guy, never saw him much after the Fronda thing. I got it from Jessie... Naismith... the fucking bitch."

"You knew him well enough to tell him I'd be at the cottage, the night after Fronda got it. If I hadn't decided to come home early, I might have avoided a needle in the ass."

They sat there for minutes, saying nothing, Michael on the bench, Danny on the wet ground. The skies blackened.

"Now what?" said Danny. "Can I make this right? If you can help me out, with the Mavis people, I'll do anything for you, Mike. Anything."

Michael peered into Danny's eyes, looking for his old friend, trying feel some empathy, wanting to understand what an addiction like this could do to a man.

He sighed and said, "Let me think about it. We can talk on the way in." But he knew there was nothing left to talk about.

Thunder rumbled in the distance. The two men moved toward their cart. Lightning snapped, and the heavens rained on them again.

"I'm gonna grab my jacket," said Danny. He walked behind the cart and unzipped a pocket of his golf bag.

Michael did the same. He put on his windbreaker and went to jump behind the wheel.

Danny was already in the passenger seat.

And he was holding a gun.

CHAPTER 45

"Everybody's got a goddam gun," said Michael. "Are you kidding me? What are you going to do, shoot me right here?"

"Now that'd be kinda stupid, now wouldn't it?" The revolver shook in Danny's hand.

"Where would you get a gun?"

"Did you really think I believed you would consider letting me off the hook, you self-righteous prick?"

"You can say that after—"

"Shut the fuck up. Get in and drive, towards fourteen."

The fourteenth. The farthest hole from the clubhouse.

"Where did this come from... this hate?" asked Michael.

"I knew you wouldn't have a clue. And you talking about how fucking conscious you want to be, be *more aware* of what's really important to you. Well it was pretty fucking obvious that didn't include me."

It was like Michael had never met the man pointing the gun at him.

It was raining hard again, and Michael couldn't see a soul in any direction. Smart golfers head for the clubhouse with the first sign of lightning. He prayed to find some players as foolish as them.

"Where'd it come from, Mike? Part of it's from you spending your whole fucking life treating me like a second fiddle."

Michael veered hard right.

"Where the fuck are you going?" yelled Danny, and jammed the gun hard into Michael's ribs, hurting him. But he was grateful it was the side without a stab wound.

Michael pointed the cart back toward the fourteenth hole.

"You know what washed away the guilt over what I was doing, at least most of it?" asked Danny. "It's the way you treated Emily."

Michael slowed down and looked over at Danny, who said, "Yeah, that's right. I loved her, too, you blind bastard. But she loved you, even after you fucked around on her."

"Naismith told you about Jacquie Zetterfeldt," said Michael.

"Shut up and drive."

Michael drove on. "Now what?" he said.

Danny waved the gun in the direction of a patch of woods on fifteen. "Pull in there."

"Into the woods?"

"Don't be counting on a blow job this time."

"What should I be counting on?"

"I woulda shot you back there if I was planning to. It's still me, Michael. What do you think I am?"

They scaled the perimeter of the mini-forest that hugged the edge of the fairway to their left. Danny pointed the barrel of the gun away from Michael, again using it to give directions. "Over there," said Danny.

Michael jerked the steering wheel hard to the left.

Danny toppled off the cart and yelled, "You fucker, Mike."

He plowed the vehicle through a stretch of newly planted maples that fronted the older and larger growth, getting the cart stuck in the process. The pain in his side sharpened, expanded. *Is this what a broken rib feels like?* He could only hope Danny's fall from the cart had slowed him down.

Crack!

Michael slid off the cart, face first into the mud. *Shot?* His left shoulder burned. *Did he really shoot me?* Maybe grazed. The pain was tolerable.

He raised himself up onto his knees, checked his shoulder. He'd just been nicked. The bleeding wasn't bad.

Danny poked the end of the warm gun barrel firmly into Michael's neck.

"Who's second fiddle now, hot shot?!" screamed Danny, inches from his ear.

"You wanna shoot me, Hig?" said Michael, still on all fours

and facing the ground.

"I think I already did, you stupid fuck," said Danny, pushing Michael down and kneeling on his back. "I think this is where I tell you to say your prayers."

"After all we've been through, Higgy? C'mon, man. You'll never get away with it."

"Spare me the *old friend* bullshit. I have no choice. And why wouldn't people believe me? I'm getting good at this stuff. I learned at the feet of the master... your fiancée." Danny added emphasis to the word by pushing the gun a little harder into the side of Michael's neck. Michael tried to turn his body to push Danny off, but couldn't budge him, and got pistol-whipped for his efforts.

Michael lay face down, spitting mud. He turned his head sideways and said, "You're not like her."

"And I'm not like you, Mike."

"So much for being grateful for helping you get your book published."

"Oh sure," said Danny. "'I'll get it done for you, Danny. I'll make it happen, Danny.' That was mostly about you, Mike. Something to amuse the rich boy and feed his ego."

"You expect them to think someone else shot me?"

"Why the fuck not?!" barked Danny. "Why would anyone think I would shoot my best friend? My car is parked in my uncle's driveway, a short walk from the fourteenth green. He's playing here today, dropped me off in fact. The skies opened up. We said our goodbyes. You headed back in on the cart. I went to my car."

"You planned this."

"I wish I could say I had, but it's like my backspin on twelve. Sometimes things just work out."

"Thinking on your feet. Naismith taught you well," said Michael. "By the way, Rita knows about more than your gambling debts. She knows about Naismith and you... she knows about everything."

"Bullshit."

"I swear, man. She knows you're up to your eyeballs. You'll spend the rest of your life behind bars."

"I'll be dead before I see a jail cell," said Danny.

Michael's disbelief matched his fear. Was this lifelong friend going to murder him right there on the golf course? A feeling alit, like one he'd had recently, but it felt more real now: *It all ends here.*

His terror grew in the following seconds, taking root in his chest, moving through his gut and down to his balls.

God, please take care of my kids.

Danny tumbled over him. The gun scraped Michael's neck and fired. *My ear... fucking loud... not hit.*

Jackson Corey, the ex-hockey player, was on the ground by the cart. Michael thought he must have bowled Danny over and fallen down with his follow-through.

Danny fired toward Corey and missed. Corey scrambled around the cart, taking cover.

Danny hollered, "You're a dead man, hockey boy." He moved in on Corey.

Corey darted toward the woods.

Michael got to his feet.

Corey slipped, fell.

Danny moved slowly.

He must be hurt.

Michael rushed to his bag and yanked out a broken wedge, the one that Clint made him keep after Michael broke it during an angry outburst after a poor shot.

Danny raised his weapon and took aim at Corey.

He's gonna shoot him in the back.

Michael lunged and bodychecked Danny onto the ground.

With two hands on the half-club, Michael drove the broken shaft into Danny's backside. He rammed it in further, and stepped back as Danny howled in agony. The wedge rose from his ass like a flag.

Danny wailed and swung the gun around.

Shit.

Michael pushed down on the wedge as he coiled inward and away.

Corey approached from Danny's rear.

Danny, crying from the pain, pointed the gun at Michael's head.

Danny's head snapped sideways, the arm with the gun falling limp. Corey kicked him again. He stood on Danny's wrist, removed the weapon from his hand, and said, "That's a major and misconduct, little man."

CHAPTER 46

Michael sat on the back of a cart that a policewoman had driven to the scene of his fatal skirmish with Danny Higgins. A purplish splotch soaked the left side of his T-shirt. A paramedic provided fresh dressing for both his reopened stab wound and the shoulder grazed by the bullet from Danny's gun. The EMT also gave Michael an ice pack for the bump on his head where Danny's pistol had struck him.

Corey leaned against the cart, sipping on a beer. Thank goodness the former defenseman liked to play in the rain. Michael had tried to thank him, but Corey said, "I was driving by anyway" and walked away.

Danny had died before the paramedics or police showed up. Tracks from their vehicles stretched across the course, reminding Michael of the night that he and his old friend, now lying thirty yards away with a broken wedge sprouting from his rectum, had chased Christine Manahan to her death.

The spate of murders had kept a lot of groundskeepers busy, and Michael had seen enough police tape to wallpaper his kitchen. He looked over at Danny's now-covered body and wondered if the pitching wedge or Corey's golf shoe delivered the killing strike.

Another golf cart, this one driven by a young policeman, pulled up next to them. A burly, older man with an open raincoat stepped down from the other side of the cart.

"J.J., it's been a while," said the man to Corey. "Enjoying a cocktail, I see."

"Ace," said Corey, who gulped down the rest of his beer, crumpled the can, and tossed it on the back of the cart.

The cop introduced himself as Detective Ace Gobeil. After a quick examination of Danny's corpse and a debriefing from the policewoman who had been first on the scene, Gobeil questioned Corey and then Michael. The detective came across as quick-minded and professional, but his questions had an underlying accusatory tone. Michael thought of Alberts and Speagle, and wondered if all good detectives took that approach.

Before leaving, Gobeil revisited Danny's body. As he got back in his cart, he said, "That's some wedgie."

I guess someone had to say it.

CHAPTER 47

A week after the funeral of Danny Higgins, Michael reread a hard copy of one of the two emails he'd found the day he played golf with Danny for the last time.

He read it again, sipped his scotch, and called his stepdaughter into the kitchen.

"What's up?" said Sophie.

"Soph, this is from an email your mother wrote last year: 'James, I understand you saw Sophie again. She's right about this. It has to stop. It's over.'"

Sophie's mouth fell open.

"It was sent to jpnorthcott@cogeco.ca last September," he said.

"So you know."

"I thought you said there was nothing going on," he said. "Was it before Eamonn? Were drugs involved?"

Sophie sighed.

"I'm not going to judge," said Michael. "What was your mom trying to stop... between you and Northcott?"

"Let me see that." Sophie took the email from him and read it. She closed her eyes. "Shit." She slid the email in front of Michael, got up, and started to leave the room.

"Soph, you can't just—"

"Michael, wake up," she said, turning back to face him. "Me and this old guy? C'mon."

"An older man."

"Older, as in Eamonn, not ancient."

He read the email again.

"I'll be back," she said.

She was back in her seat at the kitchen table within a minute. "I never wanted you to know this," she said. "But you've got me backed into a corner."

"I understand."

"No, Michael, you obviously don't," she said. Sophie pulled a piece of paper from her pocket, uncrumpled it, and handed it to him. It was the restaurant receipt he had found on the floor of Sophie's room. He read the handwritten note again.

"Did you really take a good look at this?" asked Sophie.

Michael shrugged. "It says 'cell phone' followed by a phone number... Northcott's cell phone number."

"Recognize the handwriting? Only a couple of words—printed, mind you, and it's mostly numbers—but you should know it."

Shit.

"Yeah," she said.

"It's your mother's writing."

"Look at the date on the receipt."

Michael flipped it over. "I never thought... it's last year."

He looked up at Sophie.

"Yep," she said with a sigh.

"Emily was calling and emailing Northcott. So what does—"

"Read it," she said. "Read the email to me, out loud."

"James, I understand you—"

"Stop there. Anything seem a little curious to you about that?"

James. Not J.P. or Mr. Northcott. *James.* He had paid little attention to Emily's use of his proper name. He assumed she didn't know Northcott well enough to use the initials most knew him by.

Sophie had a tear in her eye. "I barely knew the guy. That's not what Mom and I fought about, not what Northcott and I fought about. It wasn't Mom trying to keep Northcott from seeing *me...*"

No. Don't say it.

"... I was trying to keep him away from Mom."

The air left Michael's lungs. "Sophie, are you trying to tell me..."

"It was right after you had your little fling."

"Emily? Emily and..."

"She wanted to hurt you, Michael. I know you don't want to hear this, but he was often quite charming when we saw him, when Mom did, when he attended events at the arts centre, showed up at fundraisers. Then I found out what was going on. Mom said he treated her very well. I think they were only together a few times."

Together.

Michael emptied his scotch glass and poured himself another.

He thought of Northcott at Emily's wake, the knowing look. That's what Northcott meant when he said Michael might "learn more than he bargained for".

Emily was the mistress who, according to Freddy Charles, had Northcott acting like an infatuated schoolboy.

"Why did you have this?" he asked, holding up the receipt.

"I found it in a shoebox I kept of Mom's old stuff. I wanted to talk to him, when I thought he was selling drugs to Eamonn."

"The big fight with your mother," said Michael. "You said she was judging you."

"I came home drunk the night before. I'd been driving. I knew it was stupid, but I didn't want to hear it from Mom."

Michael shrank further into his chair. Could Emily have really done this, even in the darkest period of their marriage?

Of course she could. I did.

Michael finally realized what didn't ring true in something Northcott had said when he had confronted him at his home. He had referred to her as Emily, not "your wife". He talked like he knew her.

Sophie dropped her head and cried. It was the last thing she had discussed with her mother. Michael watched his stepdaughter relive the agony across the table from him.

Sophie wiped her tears with her shirtsleeve.

"They hooked up in Savannah, Georgia, of all places," she said.

Sophie had snapped at Michael on the escarpment when she mentioned her mother's trip to Savannah. He thought at the time Sophie had been pissed at him for forgetting where Emily had gone on her trip.

"That's why Mom was quitting her job. Northcott was starting to hang around the arts centre a lot, and she wanted to avoid ever seeing him again."

When Sophie had argued with Northcott at the arts centre, she was telling him to stay away from her mother.

"You okay, Michael?" asked Sophie.

"I will be."

Michael dozed off on the deck. He awoke in a sweat, with a headache from the scotch.

He'd never know why Northcott had kept quiet about his affair with Emily, how he could have passed up the opportunity to cripple Michael with that most unthinkable of betrayals. He wondered if his dead foe truly cared for Emily and had chosen not to sully her reputation posthumously. But Michael had to believe that Northcott had just protected his own worthless ass, not wanting the revelation of their illicit relationship to raise any suspicion of him in her death.

He felt more shocked than hurt at the revelation about Northcott, and that personal insight surprised him even more. Maybe the mourning of his late wife was winding down for good.

Michael hadn't shared the contents of the second Hotmail message with Sophie. He read it once more.

"Hi Ruth.

I can't be party to this. The piece is somewhere safe now, but it can never be yours. It just wouldn't be right. If you are the person I think you are, I know you will understand.

FYI - the Scotsman has been inquiring about our find.

I hope we can be friends again one day.

Love,

Emily"

Naismith did find the piece, at the Sutton cottage, and for now it was hers.

He deleted both emails and shut down his computer.

CHAPTER 48

The stone skipped seven times along the St. Lawrence River before it sank. "Beat that," said Sophie, punching the air.

"Now there's something you'll be able to teach my nephew," said Clint from the Howe Island shoreline, "unless it's a girl, of course."

"I couldn't teach my daughter how to skip stones?" asked Sophie, eyebrow raised.

"No," said Clint. "What I meant was—"

"Don't sweat it, Clint," said Eamonn. "You were right the first time."

"You know?"

"Found out yesterday. It's a nephew."

"*Yes*," said Clint, now his turn to fist-pump.

Michael watched from the deck, then looked off over the river. He put his hand under his shirt and felt the remnant of his knife wound. While aware of the almost peaceful state of mind he'd achieved during the three weeks of shutdown time since Danny's funeral, he felt a familiar chill that hit him sporadically, one that might never go away. And maybe it shouldn't.

He'd risked the lives of everyone he loved, and for what? Truth? Love? Vengeance? All of the above, he supposed.

"Where's your head at the moment?" asked Rita. "As if I didn't know."

Michael hadn't heard her come out.

"All settled in?" he asked.

"I threw my bag in the corner bedroom." Rita took a chair across from him. "What a beautiful island."

"Do you remember a warmer September?"

"I hope the demons aren't resurfacing," she said. "It's too nice a day."

"I'm usually pretty good these days."

"Still beating yourself up?"

She could always tell what he was thinking.

That's love, he thought.

Where did that come from?

"Can I get you a drink?" he asked.

"I'm good for now. I want to say a couple of things."

"Sounds heavy."

"You be the judge," she said. "First... Naismith. She was beautiful, sexy, intelligent, took any crap you threw her way, and treated you like a god. Any man with a pulse would have reacted the same way."

"What's the other thing?"

"Danny. Michael, we haven't had much of a chance to talk about him. I've known addicts of all shapes and sizes. They can only love their addiction, and are powerless against it while in the throes. There are some great support groups for loved ones of gambling addicts, just like there are for alcoholics or drug addicts."

"Loved ones? I don't think—"

Rita put up a hand. "I just wanted to tell you that it might help you to show up at a meeting. It doesn't have to be tomorrow, or next month. Just promise me you'll think about it."

"What's the point? He's dead."

"It might help you understand the behaviour, if you feel you want to get some closure."

He hesitated, then nodded.

They heard a car pull in on the other side of the cottage.

"Sit, Michael," said Rita, springing to her feet. "I'll take a look and get some snacks while I'm up."

Clint came up the steps from the other direction with an empty glass in hand.

"Not more Coke?" asked Michael.

"Just one more, Dad. Half a glass."

Clint opened the screen door to go inside, then shut it and

walked back to take the seat Rita had just vacated.

"Rita's nice," he said.

Michael smiled. "She is."

"I think she really likes you, Dad."

Clint jumped up and ran into the house.

Michael hollered after him. "Thanks, Detective."

"Artie and his kid are here," said Rita, as she reappeared with two cold Molson Canadians and a bowl of potato chips. She sat down, looked at her watch and said, "Happy hour star-r-r-ts... *now*." She took a swig from her beer and grabbed a handful of chips. "Who's the detective?"

"Clint. Pretty amazing stuff really."

Michael told her that, during their visit to Pickett's Farm, he didn't realize Sophie had taken photographs of the inside of the shed up on the escarpment. Clint had flipped through the photos recently. Something caught his eye in one, and he got Michael to take him to the escarpment.

"And?"

"Sunflower seed shells."

"Sunflower seed shells?"

"Toner always had a bag of seeds on the go."

"And he left some in the shed? No one noticed them back then?"

"You saw the floor of the shed. It was a mess. Mrs. Pickett never bothered to clean it, said the animals always got in there anyway. She kept it locked just out of habit.

"Clint got Sophie to blow up one of the photographs. He admitted afterward that it was a shot in the dark, and we didn't know for sure until we went back, but there they were. Sunflower seed shells, mixed in with raccoon crap and dirt and who knows what else. There were half-gnawed apples, from squirrels or whatever. The police could have figured the shells were left by animals, if they even took note of them. They had no reason to think otherwise. They didn't have foul play on their radar."

"You cutting Halton's finest some slack now?" asked Rita.

"Long overdue."

"Can they match the shells to Toner... after all this time?"

"They apparently decompose slowly, and Alberts said he'd check it out. I never heard back from him."

"So they may not be able to prove Toner was in that shed."

"I don't care. Either way, Toner's dead. And I found out that Little Jimmy Northcott had a key to the shed, which Toner could've easily got his hands on. I'm convinced."

"That Emily was murdered, murdered by Toner," said Rita. "How do you feel about that?"

"Funny, I'm not feeling the vindication I expected. I couldn't get Naismith to tell me what she wrote in the note that drew Emily away from the group that morning... but it doesn't really matter now. I did find it hard to believe that Emily didn't see through her disguise. But Teresa Amodeo always covered herself with a scarf, to hide scars left over from a car accident. Naismith must have found that out and did the same... and with the dark, the fog..."

"Maybe Emily did know it was her," said Rita. "The note could have been as simple as 'It's me. I need to talk to you. Meet me by the shed in two minutes.'"

Michael tossed that around. "Whatever the damn note said, I feel like I finally did right by Em. I could even enjoy rubbing the cops' noses in it, if I hadn't been such an asshole with them."

The top half of a head of curly blond locks sped along the edge of the deck. Janey Smitters turned and waved. She ran to the shoreline to join the others, who were standing in the water tossing a Frisbee.

"Where's Artie?" asked Michael.

"He noticed the corner of your fence needs mending," said Rita.

"He's supposed to be getting away from it all, like the rest of us." Michael stood up. "I'll have to talk to him."

"Sit down, Michael. It makes him happy," said Rita. "I expected to see your aunt here."

"Lucie's dropping off an Avon order on the way out, in Fort Henry Heights, and then taking the lady out for a couple of hours to play bingo. My aunt said the old gal has become her surrogate Mom. She doesn't plan to stay overnight here, and we're a bed short anyway. I'm soon gonna replace that ratty old couch in the front room with a sofa bed."

A long dark tress blew across Rita's face. The sun brought out a hint of copper in her hair. She cleaned up well in her lawyerly attire, but Michael thought she looked even better in blue jeans and a T-shirt.

She caught him staring, and blushed. She looked away, smiling. He didn't see that girlishness in her often. Maybe he just hadn't noticed. He liked it, liked noticing.

"Where is Mr. Da Silva?" she asked.

"Fern got on a plane headed south last week, with an out-of-work office administrator from police headquarters."

"Lucky girl," said Rita, the sarcasm evident.

"Let it go."

"I had a drink with Detective Alberts the other night," she said.

"What was the occasion?"

"We compared notes."

"He shared?"

"I am your legal counsel. Besides, even though we are usually on opposite sides of a fight, there is a feeling of being in the trenches together."

"Could you get in any hot water for telling me about that list, the people who owed money to Fuzzy Mavis?"

"I'm not concerned. I'm not sure I want to do this lawyering thing much longer anyway."

Michael set down his beer. "Serious?"

She nodded. "I kind of envy you, sitting back, wondering what to do next." She licked salt off a potato chip, which absorbed him for the moment. "I've tucked a bit away," she said. "I have options."

"Rubbing elbows with the likes of Mavis and his ilk finally getting to you?" he asked.

"It takes its toll, but it's not that. It just might be time to do something else. The fact that I'm even thinking about it..."

"I think you'd make a great psychologist... or psychiatrist," said Michael. He didn't really know the difference. "Or any kind of head doctor."

"So you have been paying attention."

It wasn't a good time to tell her that Sophie had informed him of Rita's career aspirations.

"Would my free therapy be over?" he asked.

He looked out over the river again.

"She's long gone, Michael," said Rita.

"Naismith left me a message about a week ago," said Michael. "She said when I roughed her up at the house, that I killed... our son. She laughed, and hung up."

"Oh Michael. I wouldn't put much credence—"

"Don't worry, Rita. I didn't believe her, and even if it was true..." He wouldn't want to father a child with Mary Anne Naismith.

He picked at the label on his beer bottle. "She could be somewhere making her plans." He slammed the beer down on the arm of his chair. "Piss on her," he said. "So tell me... your talk with Alberts."

"Believe it or not," she said, "much of the violence Naismith had a hand in seemed to be rooted in a quest for a painting."

"A painting?" asked Michael, not letting on.

"As you know, Naismith was a personal trainer with benefits, one of the beneficiaries being Boyd Manahan, the gentleman from whom you bought your house. It seems his wife started to piece things together, and threatened to expose the woman she knew as Jessie Hargreaves. But Mrs Manahan never followed through on her threat."

"But she did try to run me down in a damn golf cart."

"They think Naismith, as Jessie Hargreaves, struck a deal with

Christine Manahan, perhaps offering her a chunk of the proceeds from whatever she got for the painting. Christine had likely become too accustomed to her high-end lifestyle, and was facing a future she couldn't stomach."

"Being holed up in a tiny apartment with an elderly, penniless husband," said Michael.

And Emily stopped them.

"No wonder Christine Manahan looked so surprised to see me show up on her doorstep," said Michael. "It probably explains why Naismith expedited her efforts at bringing about my demise. Our girl Christine must have dropped a dime to tell Naismith I was getting closer."

"A uniform told Alberts that Mr. Manahan didn't seem too upset when they made the visit to tell him his wife was dead."

They sipped their beer. Michael had to tell her.

"I knew about the painting," he said, and told her about Emily and Naismith-as-Ruth researching the painting, Fronda expressing an interest of his own, the disappearance of the work they knew as *The Golfer*, and the newsflash from Scotland that the painting could be worth a lot of money. "They thought the so-called masterpiece, *Golfer at Dawn*, had been destroyed years ago. The experts still need to see the painting in the flesh, so to speak, but I bet it's the real deal."

Rita sat back and grinned. "Duff McPhee flew in from Scotland a few days ago," she said. "They tested the painting that was destroyed in the fire, at least what was left of it. It had been done with acrylic paints."

"So?"

"The original was painted in the early part of the *nineteenth century,* by Muirhead Inglis."

"And acrylics weren't available then?"

"You got it."

"The painting destroyed at the arts centre wasn't signed."

"Inglis hadn't got around to signing this one. It was his last painting before he died."

"She actually painted a duplicate of the original, and set fire to it?" asked Michael. He thought about it. "Why wouldn't she just burn it beyond recognition?"

"I assume she thought that would have raised more suspicion," said Rita. "She probably never dreamed anyone would test it to the degree that they eventually did. Or who the hell knows? Emily and Naismith, as Ruth, reportedly put out the fire. Maybe Emily doused the flames a little sooner than Naismith wanted."

"And it let the mastermind show off her talents," he said. "In the end her ego did her in, just like it did with her overdone portrayal of the *Italian* woman, Teresa Amodeo."

"Alberts doesn't think the original ever left the gallery while she worked on the forgery. A safety deposit box rented to Jessie Hargreaves contained photographs of *Golfer at Dawn*. High quality, too. They were taken when the work was still hanging in the farmhouse, maybe before she'd met Joel Pierce. She'd have needed some time to paint the forgery, and could have used the photographs."

"Where did she paint the fake, the one that burned in the fire? Right at home?"

"The police didn't find any specific evidence of that," said Rita. "But she could have. They found another painting she'd done with similar acrylics. It's Mr. McPhee's opinion that the same person did both paintings."

"I wonder who she's pretending to be now," said Michael.

Rita took a drink and said, "They found an injection hole under a fold of skin on Teresa Amodeo's neck."

Michael had all but forgotten about the autopsy.

"Best guess is someone shot an air bubble into her," said Rita, "causing a cardiac arrest, and with her pre-existing heart condition—"

"Teresa Amodeo didn't have a chance. The crazy bitch as much as told me that she killed Mrs. Amodeo *before* taking her spot in Emily's class."

Michael assumed Toner taught Naismith how to perform the lethal injection. Michael knew she'd be a quick study.

"Throughout all of this, couldn't they have traced an incriminating phone call or text message, or something along the way? A lousy email, maybe?" he asked. "Toner was calling me on a cell phone from the cottage. He must have made other calls to Naismith. Or maybe a fingerprint left somewhere?"

And how did she put all those clicks on the Mercedes?

"She was obviously very careful," said Rita. "Alberts is a good cop, and a good guy. He was quite generous, even humble. Nice-looking, too. If he wasn't so darn serious all the time..."

"Should I be worried about him?"

Why did I say that? Shit.

Rita tilted her head, grinned.

Michael coughed, cleared his throat. "No, I didn't mean... what I really meant to say..." He stammered a bit longer. *What am I doing?* "Anyway, you were saying?"

She was across the deck in a flash. She pressed her lips on his. When the shock passed, he settled into a long, warm kiss.

She pulled back, smiling, her eyes glued to his. The audience on the shoreline began to applaud. Rita ignored the kids and said, "I'm only here for the weekend, Michael, and I didn't care to listen to you tripping over your tongue until Sunday afternoon."

"Wow," he said. "I like your technique."

"I don't have a technique, Michael. This is... how I feel."

"You know, I'm not afraid of this," he said. "It feels right."

"Not afraid. How romantic, Mr. Flanigan."

"I just mean... you know, risking our friendship and—"

Rita put her hand over his mouth. "You can tell Auntie there's an extra room at the inn," she said, before disappearing into the cottage.

As Michael and Rita lay enjoying the breeze from the bedroom window, the phone rang in the front hallway.

Halfway down the stairs, Michael heard Eamonn answer the phone. "Some lady for you, bro," said Eamonn. He handed Michael the phone and joined the others outside.

"Miss me, love?" asked the familiar voice.

He dropped onto the closest chair. He took a deep breath and said, "Where are you, Mary Anne?"

"Did you get my recent message, darling?"

"You can't push my buttons anymore."

She laughed. "Is that a fact?"

"Any specific reason for your call?" asked Michael.

"I suppose not. I'm lounging in my lovely little home, admiring my enchanting painting... as well as the exquisite photo on my mantel of my dear deceased friend and her fetching daughter. It's a shame I'll have to move on again soon."

"The photograph you took from Emily's desk at the arts centre. Did you call me just to gloat over your bounty, Mary Anne?"

"I'm also trying on some makeup I took delivery of this afternoon."

Michael rose from his chair.

"Where did you get the makeup, Mary Anne?"

"I'm pretty good with this stuff. You simply wouldn't recognize me."

The extra mileage on her car.

Burlington to Fort Henry?

Michael fell back into the chair, the phone shaking in his hand.

The old bingo player.

"Mary Anne, where did you get the damn makeup?" he asked.

"Where else, darling?" she asked. "From my Avon lady."

.

CPSIA information can be obtained at www.ICGtesting.com
Printed in the USA
LVOW061800240613

339991LV00007B/824/P